PIER 33

PIER 33

A NOVEL BY

NICK JANICKI

To Allie: for supporting me from day one, sacrificing countless hours together so I could chase down a dream. Love you.

To my family & friends: for standing behind my creative itch, coming along for the ride on every last one of my ideas – good, bad or ugly.

To Rewired Cafe: for fueling my body with gallons of espresso for nearly two and a half years.

FLOWERS IN YOUR HAIR

My hands fall from my ears. The thunderous roars fade into infinity while my eyes remain shut. One sense at a time. The rest of my body shakes on a cold, damp floor.

Several moments of tranquility ease my mind. Just breathe. Remember the meditation. I peer out of one eye. It is still dark as night, only this time the single beam of light fighting its way through the doorway has vanished. Complete blackness. Was there a power outage? Did a storm cloud brew from above? The mind races to find any logical conclusion to cling to in moments like this.

Minutes feel like hours. As my eyes adjust to the darkness, one sense refuses to resume: sound. Silence swallows the building, letting out a quietness more painful than the loud claps that have subsided. Nothing adds up. Screams of terror should echo for miles after the bizarre phenomenon.

Touch—feeling—guides me through the room. I rub the new bump on the side of my head. Is this all a distant dream? My feet ache as I inch toward where the opening was once located. It was there—I am certain of that much.

A single thud bounces off the four walls as my body slams into a metal surface. The contact shakes the silence with an all-encompassing echo. The chilled wall is an endless surface of icy steel. It scales floor to ceiling where an open space once stood. Finally, a protrusion. Hinges. This is not a wall—it is a door. A locked door.

My heart buries itself in the deep confines of my chest. My fists pound against the door. Bang. Bang. Each collision leaves my hands stinging in pain. Terror wrestles discomfort and comes out on top.

I disturb the lingering silence. "Hello? Anyone there? I'm locked behind this damn door!"

No response. I am alone; dazed and trapped and—for the first time in as long as I can remember—alive.

The mind can only ignore the body's cries for help for so long. I am soon left kneeling in front of the metal blockade begging the inanimate object to obey my commands. The solution rests in my mind, a place Doctor Polk sends me when other therapeutic methods fail. It is nothing more than a distraction; however, it is a better alternative to broken knuckles.

Meditation sends me to a vault of memories from the last few days. Does this stem back to the life-altering choices implemented to break free of a meaningless life?

I commend the sun-worshipper that suggested the idea of time zones. The concept of a world where everyone wakes to a bright, glorified sunrise only to finish the day with the slow fading of a sunset.

The world revolves around the sun, doing so from an astronomical perspective as we simultaneously craft our bleak lives around this massive fireball. Humanity perishes without it. With it, we remain slaves to its rise to glory each day and descension into nothingness each evening.

A dependency on the Sun God requires sun-worshippers to rely on routine. Routine is survival. Wake up; go to work; go home; go to bed. Wake up again. My routine mirrored anyone else's, except most of the time I carried alone the burden of realizing how trapped we are in this endless loop.

I await the day we take our last breath as it is our gift back to the Sun God. We greet each sunrise and sunset until we are no longer around to witness its glorious cycle. And yet the sun continues its endless journey, oblivious to our presence. It is careless about the life that remains to worship it.

These thoughts pass through a mind traveling above the rest of civilization. This is the closest opportunity sun-worshippers get to be near the Flaming Divinity. The Almighty. Still, it is not quite close enough to be at its dreamed-of level.

The curious aspect of cross-country air travel is that it presents the opportunity to experience the power of time zones. A flight takes off at eight in the morning on Eastern Time and lands at eleven in the afternoon Pacific Time. While it takes the plane six hours to travel, it misses three hours of the day. In some cases—take a flight from Indianapolis to Chicago for instance—the aircraft arrives before it departed. More time in the day is the last thing I need, so I will pass on that particular scenario. Still, it is curious.

West Coast to East Coast travel is much more appealing to a slave like me. This is a chance to skip three hours so the Almighty sets a little sooner than the location of departure. The winged wonder can bend both space and time all while providing its captors with bags of peanuts and non-alcoholic beverages at no additional charge.

These thoughts also pass through a mind suffering from what psychiatrists label a major depressive disorder. Whatever that means. I thrive on these mental deficiencies, as Doctor Polk calls them. I cannot see the benefit of being like the sun-worshippers. This is my primary excuse as to why those magical pills now treat the inside of a toilet. 'Take once daily,' the label reads. Another inescapable routine to a life already cluttered with order.

What gives another sun-worshipper the right to tell someone what is wrong with them? They slap four- or five-word diagnoses on a patient's forehead and collect an enormous paycheck. These are lessons and procedures passed down from generation to generation, originating from another flawed human's subjective findings. We are a society reliant on the history of itself for sustained life. We do not grow like the trees around us; we do not evolve anymore.

I am as guilty as any of conformity. I went to school, studied and stumbled on a desk job. I have blended in with society for over three decades—a slave to the Sun God despite my constant denial. Of course, I am an accountant. I do not pretend to know the ins and outs of the human psyche like Doctor Polk. Fuck Doctor Polk. And his pills. As a bonus, this profession requires minimal human interaction. That, and I remain objective in my work. Numbers are not open to interpretation. These factors led to my almost ten years at the company. Nearly a decade withering away in a cubicle.

"Excuse me sir. You'll need t'put your tray in the upright n' locked position as we prepare for landing," the stewardess whines. She mimics the caring tone all mothers use when waking their child each morning. She thrusts me from my mind and tosses me back on earth. Five hours later and our cloud quest has ended. Time for reintegration.

She continues her landing routine as she moves throughout the cabin, restoring the plane's seats to their original positions. She ensures every tray table is locked. These are the keys to a safe and successful landing. These are her priorities in life, the procedures that make her feel important.

A loud yawn wakes my fellow passengers from their slumbers as I tend to tired eyes. I have been awake the entire flight. These idiots do not deserve to sleep if I am not able to rest. We suffer together.

Blobs of color outside the window sharpen. My built-in lens focuses. San Francisco. San Fran. S.F. The Golden City. Or my personal favorite, Fog City, due to the city's hot air rising and the frigid ocean air rushing to replace it. This phenomenon causes the fog devouring the city each day. This is where the Sun God drags me today.

The plane continues to descend. The notion of giving up life to this metal machine amuses me. The little guy with the special hat qualifying him to hold the much-respected title of captain plays God for a few hours. If the bird chooses to go down, its passengers go down with it. There is nothing they can do about it. We are in it as one, taking our last breath as a collective group. I find comfort in that.

Ten minutes after the stewardess nudges me it is wheels down and a double thud on the ground. A few sun-worshippers clap in celebration of another day in a different city. Hooray for them. Hooray for us all.

I do not travel often; when I do, it consists of cross-country trips. I tend not to care about anyone, and the feeling almost always appears mutual. There was never a reason to venture out of my five hundred square-foot studio apartment. I require the basics for human survival and nothing more. The only person pretending to care about me is my mother. Is that not the role required of every individual with that title, though? She remains nearby to prevent me from doing anything drastic. That clearly did not work out in her favor as I taxi around the Fog City airport. Sorry, mother—not this time.

We arrive at our gate and the captain comes over the loudspeaker. "Welcome t'San Francisco. The weather's currently sixty-five degrees with light fog. Thank you for flying Trans World Airlines. We hope you join us again soon."

I hope for that, too, as my mental clock begins ticking. Every second on the ground is one closer to my return flight. Three days and I am on my way with that sweet reward from the Sun God of losing three hours on the flight back to the East Coast. Three days.

The fasten seatbelt sign flicks off and we are free from our prison cells.

"You from here?" the middle-aged woman next door interrogates me to break the awkward silence.

"No," I grunt, "just in town for the weekend."

She does not know I was forced to come here. The other option was far less ideal and almost guaranteed to be permanent. Do not get me wrong, I can appreciate a different city, its environment and its activities, but this is not a time for pleasure. I have been to this city half a dozen times throughout the last six years. Each visit leaves a bad taste in my mouth. It is not the salt in the cold, heavy air, but the person I am here to see.

"That's nice," the woman responds with a smile. "I live here. I was just in New York visiting my new grandson. He was born a few days ago!"

"Ah congratulations on the grandson," I mumble. Poor grandson. The forced response paired with a quick smile leads to a convenient moment to return my eyes to the seat in front of me. My tray table is in its upright and locked position. The stewardess is pleased.

We deboard one by one—cattle herded for slaughter. My shining moment arrives as I shuffle out of the jetway to find a group of impatient sun-worshippers waiting to roll the dice in the same metal machine we arrived in. They watch us pass as if we were science experiments.

Most travelers carry an excessive amount of luggage with them, the true definition of the over-indulgence of American culture. Then there is me, rushing toward ground transportation with nothing except a backpack on my shoulder. The pack is full of a few poorly folded items of clothing, a toothbrush and a water bottle. This is what remains of my personal possessions.

I am draped in the suit I wore every day for ten years. The suit has transformed into a wrinkled sweat towel over the last day and a half. The charcoal-grey fabric I spent so much money on is ruined. My hair looks like Walken's on its best day. I take one last look around at the cattle in the crowded airport and slide off my tie, making my way out of the automatic doors.

I forget why I am here for a fleeting moment, gazing up at a cloud-covered sky, and letting the symphony of cars honking and braking suffocate my senses. The sight transports my mind to a time in my youth. Lying on the roof of my family's suburban home and cloud-gazing for hours was the only hobby I can recall. I carry that memory with pride. Even as a child, I was intrigued by a cloud's ability to cover the sun. The white puffs rebel against the Sun God's unlimited power, trying their hardest before the Almighty inevitably prevails.

And then, flinging me back to reality, I see a familiar jet-black Porsche 944 Turbo blasting music. The driver lays on the horn. The tinted passenger window slides down. Here comes that cringe-worthy voice.

"It's about time man. Just toss your stuff in the trunk."

Three days and I will have done my time. Three days and I am free.

START THE CAR

Sam's wearing that sad blue tie again. It's the one barely past his chest that looks more like a sock that's seen too wash cycles. How does he get away with wearing that piece of shit so many days a week? I swear no one notices besides me. It's no wonder I'm stuck in this room with him.

The tie has yellow dots on it, looking like he ate a dozen hotdogs at lunch with a little too much mustard. It's draped over the table like a bib while he holds a pen in one hand and twiddles a cigarette in the other, a man caught off guard. He will feast on bad news.

The clock at the end of the conference table grabs my attention; it's more fascinating than anything blue tie guy has to say. I have ten minutes to get this over with. How do I cut that down by about nine minutes? I suppose these situations are why they pay me the big bucks.

I don't consider myself a man in love with his job. Hell, no one wants to work—anyone who says that's full of shit. Work sucks no matter what you do. What I do love is money. I'll do just about anything to make more of it, too. Life's about cozying up to the Green Goddess.

The last five years have been an uphill battle with these jerkoffs, but I've climbed the ladder. I have no intention of turning back now. Not even Sam's micro-tie can stop me. The yellow dots look like someone grabbed a highlighter and thrusted it on the tie with rage. Jab after jab until it was out of ink. Then they bought another and resumed the jabbing.

"Sam . . . I'm sorry t'do this. It's strictly financial. We can't make the business case t'keep you on board with everything goin' on right now."

My eyes shift from Sam—who fends off tears—to the clock on

the wall. Nine minutes left. The cigarette freezes and the fountain pen falls to the floor. How dramatic. Does he expect me to believe this is a surprise to him? The signs were there for weeks. He and his little tie knew about the cuts. He isn't pulling his weight—all three hundred pounds of it.

"I don't understand," he responds. "Is this for real? There's gotta be some misunderstanding. Is this about the pens? It's about the pens isn't it?" He's fumbling through every scenario in his tiny head to relax himself. The mind seeks rationalization even when there is none.

I feel for the guy. I'm not a monster. No one wants to get fired, especially under vague circumstances. I've not made it five years in this business because I'm a limp noodle, though. A degree from Stanford led to my first position as Associate Sales Rep. That title meant I was someone's bitch. Again, that's behind me now. I've fought my way to the top. Blue tie guy hasn't done that and that's exactly why we're here.

"No. It's not the . . . pens," I shake my head. "Like I told you it's been a tough year. We're all feelin' the effects one way or another."

He responds with heavy staring. The fat tie man stares into my soul, reading straight through the corporate bullshit. The frozen look morphs into tears. The guy cries in front of me and all I can think about is his pen comment. How many pens has he stolen to think that's why he's being fired? A pen costs no more than a dollar. He'd have to pocket a thousand pens to think anyone would bat an eye at the thievery. I'd press him for details, however, something tells me his response would involve me shoving some pens somewhere up my body.

A grown man sits in front of me crying Niagara Falls, a deer standing on an open road waiting to get struck. Only the smoke burning in his hand comforts him. The tears subside for a moment so he can tend to fogged-up, Clark Kent glasses. I use the opportunity to check the clock again. Four more minutes with tiny blue tie guy and it's sayonara. Back to business.

"You want me t'grab ya a coffee or somethin'?" I rattle off the first thing that'll kill more time.

He declines with silence, shaking his head so tears fly in the air like a wet dog in the house. It's back to nudging a box of tissues further down the conference table. Get this guy to stop wiping snot on that hideous tie and then get him out of my sight.

"Listen I'd be happy t'write you a letter of recommendation. I know you've been with us for five years n' all. We appreciate the work you've done n' the impact you—"

"Seven," he cuts me off. His face transitions from sorrow to rage. "I've been here seven fucking years. You wanna get rid a me because a some bullshit reason like that? I've been here longer than you!"

He leans over the seat, puffing out his chest like a gorilla wearing a hideous tie. This is his workout for the year and my brain continues to focus elsewhere. I wonder where this passion was at work. I guess this is what happens when your world gets turned to shit in minutes.

"You'll get the severance Sam."

No response.

"That should at least hold you over 'til you get back on your feet. In the meantime take a break from all the work. Go on vacation. Girlfriend? You have a girlfriend?"

More silence.

"Fuck you Robb." He closes the sales pitch of his career. "How d'you live with yourself?"

It's the conversation-killing response I dug for. Time to send him on his way. There are still two minutes to spare according to the clock, too. Early dismissal for the both of us.

"I needa ask you t'leave now." I keep my cool. He continues to stand over his chair in what's his idea of a threatening position. "If there's gonna be trouble I'll call security t'escort you out. You'll put the severance on the line too. Don't do that man."

Just as I think he's about to climb across the table and lay his fists of fury on my face, he leans back. He spins around and exits the room. The applause of a sitcom's laugh track plays in my head. I lean back in my chair and take a breath. One minute to spare. Glad that's over.

I collect my things from the room for the third time this week and head back to my office, locking the door behind me in one last safety measure against the volatile fat man who was sent packing his bags. I didn't like the look in his eyes and don't want a bullet to the dome.

My phone's flashing red light catches my attention not a minute after sitting down. Four missed calls. I pick up the handset to investigate. I know who's been calling. Superman doesn't have this kind of special sense. I hit redial and she picks up after a single ring.

"Hey honey. You called?" A gentle voice greets her. It's the complete opposite tone I just used with blue tie guy. I'm hoping for some reciprocity on the other end.

"Mike. Mike lands in five minutes Robb."

Shit. One crisis is averted and the next enters the ring to knock me out. I was supposed to leave for the airport twenty minutes ago.

"Can't you get him?" My tone shifts to a whine. "I'm in meetings all day. It's not really ideal for me t'—"

"How many times do I have t'tell you I'm working the day shift?" she yells. "This isn't my responsibility. Jesus Robb . . . have one other priority for once."

"Alright alright. I'll leave now." I avoid escalating the conversation.

Clink. I pull the phone from my face as a disconnected line fills my ear. This isn't my responsibility; he did this to himself. People need to deal with the repercussions of their idiotic actions. I'd never tell Meredith that, but it's the truth.

I grab my jacket and head toward the lobby. The rush out the building forces me to lock eyes with blue tie guy once more as he collects his things. Oops. A nod paired with an 'It'll be alright' expression come to mind. He flips me the bird in return, tracking it along my path across the room. I'm again impressed by his dedication to this new hatred.

It's twenty-five minutes to the airport assuming there's light traffic. The flight landed fifteen minutes ago. Some quick mental math and a turn of the key and I'm cruising to SFO. I'm cruising to pick up his sorry ass.

I appreciate family—I do. It's something I didn't have much of growing up, or at least until I had a mouth full of braces. That's why I married at twenty-one. That's why we brought our first kid into the world after twenty-two years. Creating a family of my own was my solution to a rather shitty upbringing. That doesn't mean these impulsive decisions were the right decisions in retrospect. In fact, they were far from smart choices. Call it overcompensation.

More family's not always the answer to lingering loneliness—another sentence I'd never utter to my wife. What does fill that gap is work. Money fills the gap, too. They say money can't buy happiness; that's a lie crafted by the poor.

I look at my three thousand square-foot home in this competitive city along with my Porsche. These bring a smile to my face. Cruising down the 101 with the wind blowing in my face is happiness. Money is happiness.

Thirty minutes inch past. I'm Tetris-ing my way through arrivals. Buses, taxis and friendly pick-up rides cram every lane. How can I complain with the nicest car around? The slow-moving road eventually takes me to Trans World arrivals. I know exactly who to look for thanks to my mom's detailed description on the phone.

Hundreds of people stand with luggage, poking their heads up and down to spot their ride like baby birds waiting for a worm. Many have smiles, excited about a vacation or the chance to reunite with a loved one. One person stands out from them all: a slouching, lifeless body in the crowd. That's him.

I roll the car up in front of the man. My sunglasses hang off my nose for a clearer view. I roll down the passenger window and lean over.

"It's about time man. Just toss your stuff in the trunk."

NO PLACE TO GO

My mother is old enough to be in a nursing home yet still manages to manipulate my life. She shipped me to Fog City as if I were luggage. I should appreciate a supportive person in my life. It is all an act at the end of the day, though. She is conditioned to adhere to the responsibilities set forth by mothers of the past. And their mothers. And their mothers. And so forth.

The Oedipus complex was coined by psychoanalysis founder Sigmund Freud. This refers to a child's unconscious desire for the opposite-sex parent. Doctor Polk speaks of this often, claiming I have a deep desire to be close to my mother. Sun-worshippers with made-up degrees created this concept. Master in Bullshit. Doctorate in Fabrication. The list goes on. They labeled this concept a normal stage of psycho-sexual development.

My own complex states parents are the first draft of their offspring, a test-and-learn of sorts. The trial run. A child takes what he or she knows about their parents and grows from it. The child learns from mistakes of the past. They are stronger because of these mistakes.

My mother was not responsible for my being here as there were countless factors at play. Everything traces back to decisions I made less than a day ago. How rapidly a life can change only to fall back into place. These decisions were made in an impulsive attempt to break free of routine. They are choices with severe consequences.

"Mike can you pass the potatoes?" Meredith asks.

Meredith is Robb's wife. The two sun-worshippers married an eternity ago. I cannot determine what constitutes a happy marriage, but their relationship is far from fruitful. It is chaos on most occasions.

"Yes of course," I respond. "I hate t'linger on this but please call me Michael."

I hate my name as it is one of the most generic names in the country. In fact, Michael was ranked the most common name for a newborn boy this year. Imagine that. Names are false identities society forces upon us. I drew the short straw out of infinite combinations of letters. Michael, not Mike. That is not Meredith's fault; however, she has known me long enough to realize that is a hot button.

"Hey let's not be a jackass at the table alright?" Robb scoffs.

"Honey watch the language in front a the boys," Meredith jumps in. She sends a tight-eyed glare Robb's way, a regular occurrence under this roof. The look is their equivalent of an average couple's kiss.

"I didn't mean t'ruffle any feathers," I add. The last thing I want to do is sit through another argument. "So Jackson . . . how's preschool? Have you learned a lot this year?"

I do not know the first thought that goes through a child's mind and do not care; any distraction is better than hearing this couple bicker. The boy responds with silence. It is a response often attributed to shyness. It is truly the undeveloped psyche avoiding meaningless interaction. Good for you, boy.

"It's okay . . . he's pretty shy," Meredith speaks for the child. "You like school don't you Jackson?"

The boy nods. Small talk is over.

"So mom told us about what happened at the office," Robb starts. "I'll tell you what . . . that sounds like somethin' I've wanted t'do these last five years." He laughs mid-chew. Potatoes and brussels sprouts slosh back and forth in his mouth.

Robb and I were never close. This is due to a combination of our age gap and that he was brought into the family around eleven years old. I am four years older than him. That is a big age difference, especially when growing up.

He stood out to my parents as the driven son between the two of us. Perhaps traveling between foster homes in his youth made him appreciate life; however, I can see through the happiness. It is a mask he wears well.

I had the stereotypical loving parents. They were the sitcom type. I received a respectable education and was financially well-off growing up. These are a few factors the therapist attributes to my unique mental state. How are you supposed to appreciate what you have if you do not know any other way of living? I did not ask for any of these scenarios. If it was my choice, I would have been raised a poor boy.

"Right. Of course she told you about that." I roll my eyes. "I was sick of the place. There's nothing else to it." It is much more complex than that, a fact they do not need to know. "I decided enough was enough after being there for years n' hearing the same complaining. Slave all day at work n' go home n' come back the next day. It's all the same crap in a loop. It's a never-ending cycle."

Wide-eyed stares fly my way as my mind comes out to play.

Quitting my job was one dramatic decision. Of course, quitting is not quite the correct word. What happened—according to the police report—was an 'aggressive meltdown.' This consisted of rising from my four-by-four cubicle and tossing objects across the office. I had no regard for others while doing this. Fear consumed my coworkers' eyes. At the same time, I saw flickers of inspiration in their eyes. Those sun-worshippers were blessed with a glimpse of what life could be like outside windowless walls, if only for a moment.

"That's . . . a fair point," Meredith responds, doing her best to relate. "I know we've all had those moments where we wanna get up n' quit. Isn't that right Robb?"

Robb's sitting there, eyes narrowed in on the distant television in the other room. It is incredible every man can conform to the cliché of being a sports fanatic. Robb is the epitome of that label. He wears it with pride. Here he is, a man with all the pieces to a 'happy' life: a wife, children and a high-paying job. Yet he takes everything for granted. That is not to say a life of that nature is desired; however, I understand the subconscious need for such components. It is a result of poor nurturing.

"Robb!" Meredith lifts her hand and shoves it in his face. One loud snap takes him out of the hypnotic trance that is football. A bunch of men grabbing each other for a ball. Great use of time.

"Yes . . . right. Of course. We're here for ya Michael," he responds.

He rattled the words off without a single thought. They are words sitting in the back of his head to ease his wife's frustrations. Robotic phrases to avoid confrontation.

We push through the rest of dinner without another word. Dessert follows in the form of more football in another room. It is not my type of dessert. Quality family time indeed.

Meredith hurries the kids upstairs for a forced bedtime despite the Sun God's lasting glimmer. Parents justify an early bedtime with many explanations. The actual reason is unspoken: silencing the little sun-worshippers.

Meanwhile, Robb and I stare at the television in the living room. We taste the discomfort in the air and channel our focus into the screen for relief. That bright, light-up box is our savior. Praise the television for it has saved us from conversation.

Halftime inconveniently arrives. More awkward silence fills the room as we are both aware that our stares into the screen are now mere distractions. He cracks open another Pabst Blue Ribbon with his feet on the recliner. He is motionless in a self-made coffin of sorts. This is happiness to him. This is what he has worked toward.

"So anything you wanna do while you're in town?" he asks.

We continue avoiding eye contact through the convenience of advertisements. Thank you, forty-inch light-up box.

"Nothin' really. I'm not here on vacation." I can feel him turning his head, looking at me while he takes a gulp of beer. He belches. The answer is not enough. His non-verbal cues press for more. "I guess I'd do some sightseeing if you have recommendations."

He turns back to the television. "Sure thing. We'll give ya the tour de San Fran. Maybe take you t'Fisherman's Wharf n' all."

We are too stubborn—too proud—to alter this affiliation composed of nothing. Our parents conditioned us to be brothers; it was not a choice. Silence reveals mutual acknowledgment of the fake relationship that remains protected. God forbid our mother sees us cutting ties, destroying what she built.

My second dramatic decision was making my personal assets vanish. Just like that. Doctor Polk and my mother called it a mental breakdown when it was really an attempt at minimalism—at least that is the way I think of it. The purge occurred half an hour following the scene at the office. The tight timeframe of both actions paints a much larger picture in their eyes. 'Something is seriously wrong with Michael,' they think.

The high of leaving my job in the dust faded on the drive home. I did not feel accomplished; I did not feel free. So, I walked inside my apartment and started with the common area. I tossed down chairs, a side stand and other furniture from the two-storied stairwell like it was a garbage chute. Everything landed on the curb—one big pile of me. I found myself in the kitchen when the common area was a barren wasteland. Then the bathroom. Then there was nothing.

No more wasted time deciding what to wear; no more cooking and doing the dishes; no more alarm clock. It sounded great. I could even say I was happy during the purge. The happiness fleeted as suddenly as it did when leaving my job, though.

Still nothing. I cleansed myself of routine and material possessions for nothing. The events culminated on the floor of my studio apartment where what used to be a loveseat rested. Dust and cobwebs outlined the seat's shape like a crime scene. The remaining items accompanying me were an old backpack and a telephone, still plugged into the wall. I had plunged to rock bottom and even that did not stop the fall. The phone began to ring. Was this hope?

"Yes?" I answered, hoping whoever was on the other line would do most of the talking.

"Michael . . ." a voice responded. "Your work called. They said you quit your job?"

It was my mother. My former employer had the audacity to dial my emergency contact. They let her know all about my tirade, informing her that the police were stopping by my apartment at any moment. On top of that, she was on her way as well. She hung up before I could state my case for independence.

The uniformed men were at my door now. Some officers entered the apartment while others inspected the pile of mint-condition furniture left curbside. My mother arrived soon after, questioning my every decision. She interrogated herself with concerns like 'Was it something I could have prevented?' and 'Was I not there the way he needed me?' The visit climaxed with no charges other than some small fines for damages. The larger punishment followed.

My mother insisted on my not being alone for the near future. The officers were sympathetic to her worries. I had two options: live with my mother, who would oversee my therapist attendance, or travel to Fog City to see my brother and his family for a 'mental health break' as my mother called it. Living with her was out of the question, so I chose to hop on a plane the following day to buy myself more time. A few days of freedom from her grasp. More time to discover a more permanent route of escape.

Here I am now, sitting in Robb's living room avoiding conversation. Meredith eventually reenters with a bottle of wine and three glasses. I am not much of a drinker, yet the bottle is a welcome sight after the last day and a half. She pours heavy glasses and makes her way around the room, landing on Robb's lap. How adorable.

"Kids," she sighs. "They're miraculous little things but thank God for enforceable bedtimes."

Robb lets out a fake chuckle, repositioning himself on the couch to change the channel. He needs a better view of the glowing box distracting the three of us.

"So we were just chatting Meredith." I pity the neglected wife. More small talk. "Robb says I'm gettin' a tour a the city this weekend."

"Oh is that right?" she laughs. A look of confusion spreads across her face. She turns to Robb. "I think the role of tour guide'll be played by Robb this weekend. I'm working double shifts again so I'll barely have time t'sleep let alone strut across the city. You two'll have a good time."

"Honey . . ." Robb's ears perk up for the first time tonight. "We have that big presentation on Monday. We're not nearly prepared for it." He leans across Meredith to meet my gaze. "Sorry we didn't plan this better bud. I'll be in the office all day. We don't mean t'leave ya alone by any means, it's just not as good a time t'do this as we thought."

Robb holds some high-ranking sales position at a company headquartered in Fog City. It is the type of role that makes him believe he is untouchable—a king in the office and out. He joined the company after college when the place was up and coming, working his way through the ranks over the last several years. Such rapid success has its consequences. One of those is his relationship with his wife and children. Of course, that never seemed to bother him in the slightest.

"It's fine. Putting bread on the table n' keepin' a roof over the family's head comes first," I respond. I know where Robb's true values stand and I am too exhausted to challenge them.

"You're family too Michael," Meredith lies. "You're just as important t'us as anyone else under this roof."

Worry consumes Meredith after I cannot quite find the words with which to respond. She mistakes a loss for words for disappointment. The same silence comes over Robb as he stares at his wife. It is a standoff. Who wants their psychotic brother-in-law near children all day?

"Nonsense . . ." she continues, "the sitter was already paid. Robb'll pull some strings n' get his coworkers t'cover for him."

She gives Robb an obvious elbow to the side in frustration, hoping it will force him to do the right thing for once. The dysfunctional couple continues to argue via non-verbal cues as if I was blind. An annoyed and frustrated Robb caves to an upset wife after her stares stab his soul.

"Right . . . yeah. I'll figure somethin' out. Might have t'pull a late-nighter n' do some work in the mornin' but it'll work out."

"Word around the office is Rodgers, Robb's boss n' the company's CEO, is set t'give up his seat t'pursue some other venture," Meredith adds. "Apologies for the back n' forth . . . just wanted t'clarify why Robb's work's particularly stressful right now. Does tomorrow afternoon sound good t'you?"

"Sure. That works for me," I reply.

It is pathetic how insincere this conversation has become. I am a child speaking with his separated parents. In this scenario, neither parent wants anything to do with the child.

"It's a plan then." Meredith buries the last nail in the coffin. She strikes the gavel. "Feel free t'sleep in, watch some television or spend time with the kids n' nanny 'til Robb's ready t'roll."

The curtain closes on the painful conversation. A peaceful silence comes over the room as the three of us gaze back at the screen. 'This is so uncomfortable,' Meredith thinks. 'How the hell am I going to get out of work?' Robb questions. 'How the hell do I get out of here?' I ask myself.

A quick look at the clock above the television reveals it to be nine o'clock. The long day of travel and significant time change form the perfect opportunity to call it a night. I stand up from the couch, clutching an empty wine glass. This is my evening toast. I hope they enjoy it.

"Well it's gettin' pretty late. I've been traveling all day n' had a long night yesterday so I think it's time for some rest. Thanks for dinner Meredith."

"Oh of course," Meredith responds. "You must be exhausted. There're fresh towels on your bed n' I changed the sheets. Goodnight Mike."

There it is again—Mike. I choose to bite my tongue as I am about to correct her for the fifth time this evening. Any remark risks continued conversation. I am one more sentence away from bashing my head into the glowing square box and Robb yelling at the sudden disappearance of his distraction.

I crawl into the neatly made bed after stripping down to nothing but underwear, my first time taking off this tattered outfit in nearly forty-eight hours. My eyes stare at the hypnotizing ceiling fan spinning above me. How did I get here? This is not where I am supposed to be right now. I am supposed to be free. What went wrong?

I spent yesterday destroying my life. I left my job and got rid of the material items that held me down. Tonight, I find myself in another full-size bed with not a full day having passed. A nightstand sits next to the bed and a wardrobe stands tall on the other side. The Sun God holds me captive, gripping me tighter than ever.

GET READY

Yesterday was a long night and there's a longer day ahead. I understand my brother needs some supervision at a time like this, but I have priorities. I can't shift important work at a moment's notice. I picked the guy up from the airport for Christ's sake. Meredith can lend a fucking hand now and then.

Like my mom, Meredith's always sensed something off about my brother. At first glance, he's a normal dude who's quieter than the average Joe. He had a stable job and afforded a place in that massive city. Hell, he even had a girlfriend at one point. My brother had a girlfriend; I still can't believe it.

After you get to know the guy, you hear him talk and you know there's a screw loose upstairs. I don't mean to talk crap, but it baffles me how someone with such a normal family could end up like that. I was the one with the awful childhood, passed around like a football until age eleven. Suck it up, brother.

I enjoy working on Saturdays because the office is a ghost town. My mind's too cluttered when there are keyboards clattering away. Distant chatter's everywhere. Most people disagree with my mindset there. We wouldn't have people like blue tie guy being laid off if people treated this job as seriously as I do, though. All I'm saying's the high turnover isn't a reflection of the company; it's a result of a lack of good work ethic.

"We all know why we're gathered here today gentlemen. We're finalizing this month's report before Monday's board meeting," I announce to my two right-hand men, Mark and Nate—real stand-up guys as far as subordinates go. I toss my bag on an open chair. "We needa work quickly. My brother's in town n' I needa deal with that for the rest a the day."

"That weird dude?" Mark asks. "Can't he take care of himself?

He's an adult."

"Yeah that's my only brother Mark," I snap back. "He's been through some shit. My mom doesn't trust him alone. Yada yada yada. Just suck it up, put your head down n' get this done while we have time."

My brother became a poor reflection of me when I entered the picture. That's not my fault. He was two giant leaps behind me at the start. I joined the football team in high school while he stayed home playing 'Space Invaders' and 'Pong.' In college, I snagged one job after another while he had the title of 'Scooper' at the local ice cream shop. He was jealous of my success and it still eats away at him.

"What're your plans?" Nate joins the conversation, distracting us from working again.

"Still not sure." I throw my arms up in annoyance. "We'll prob'ly end up doin' some touristy shit. I'll take him for a lobster roll or something. Doesn't matter. Two more days n' he's outta here."

"Gotcha. I've actually got family stuff on the agenda too," he replies as if I asked what he was up to this weekend. Keep your eyes on the table. You're not getting paid to talk about your personal schedule.

"What stuff?" Mark asks.

"That new museum opening up in a few months," Nate shares. "My sister worked with the guy who's puttin' the whole thing together so she invited a buncha us on this private tour. She's got a ton a connections t'historical hot spots around the city. We were actually plannin' t'visit Alcatraz Island for one a those island tours. Haven't been there since the National Park Service took control those years back."

"You need tickets for that thing don't ya?" I ask. Alright, now I'm guilty of indulging in the distractions. This might be a solution to my brother problem, though. "Did she grab tickets for you guys? Meredith's wanted t'go there but it's always so damn busy."

My ass is grass if I don't do something brotherly with Michael. My original plan was taking him to this seafood shack near

Fisherman's Wharf. What's wrong with a fresh 'catch of the day'? He can look at the sealions on the pier, too. A day-long excursion to a place like Alcatraz instead is a convenient opportunity to waste a solid chunk of time. The rest of the weekend's mine if I get something that monumental over with. I can work all day Sunday without worrying about entertaining him.

"Yep they're definitely tough t'come by," he adds. "People book these days or weeks in advance. Pretty nuts if you ask me."

"Does she still have the tickets? Your sister?" I pester him. We're all looking down at the table now, trading comments as our pens move and papers flip. "I'd be happy t'buy 'em from her."

I'm letting out what must sound like a desperate plea for help and I don't care. I'll do anything to pass the time with my brother. I can't have my wife and mom screaming at me.

"I have 'em. They're back at my desk. They're for a noon ferry so I'm not—"

"I don't care man. I don't care. I'll take 'em. How much?"

Michael and I don't get along. I'm not trying to dig into our hearts, find a soft spot and become best friends either as that's an impossible task. There's one memory I have of him and I can use that to my advantage here: his interest in true crime. He had all sorts of books and movies about some of the most fucked up shit. Murder, theft, sex cults. If there's an article about it out there, he's heard of it. The weirdo even minored in criminal justice. A trip to one of the hardest prisons in the country might just interest the man. The man with no interests.

"They're on the house for you buddy" Nate says. "She's the one who paid for 'em anyway."

He wouldn't be saying that if I didn't have my thumb pressing on his head. They're both kiss-asses. Who wouldn't be with someone as intimidating as me at the helm? They'll do what I say the moment I say it, which is why I feel comfortable leaving them to finish the report.

"Sounds like a deal. I'll owe ya one." I put on my 'approachable superior' hat. They don't need to know my real feelings.

A wave of silence returns to the room, a cue to get back to work.

This time, my stern face shuts any mouths about to open. They know I mean business. No talking. No eating. They don't even ask to take a piss for the next two hours. Imagine having this kind of power.

Still, I don't think I've worked this fast in my life. The hurried work will leave holes all over the report. Yet quick progress is the only option to keep us on track. Fortunately, I have Mark and Nate to bring this thing to the endzone. They'll scrub the report as clean as they can before it's in my hands for a final assessment. Bah-da-bing, bah-da-boom. It's a plan.

The clock reads eleven now. "Alright guys," I interrupt their focus. "If I don't leave now I won't make this ferry in time."

They hesitate to look up, both wanting my job when I climb the ladder to new heights after my dickhead boss is out the door. Maybe one of them will get it, maybe they won't.

Nate lifts his head. "Oh yeah . . . right. Completely forgot about the tour there. The tickets're in my desk drawer. We'll wrap this up n' leave the latest on your desk this evening. Sound alright?"

I thank the guys for their dedication to the report, reminding them of its importance. There's a lot to do. I agree to multi-task during the day out with my brother. I can't do much on the go, yet the work must move forward somehow. This will save me some time when catching up on their latest updates this evening. I'll keep it subtle so my brother doesn't notice.

I scoop up the tickets on my way out. He wasn't kidding—the tickets each read twenty bucks. Twenty bucks to look at some shithole left of an island? It figures this sort of stuff interests my brother. Two oddities attract.

My car screeches out of the empty parking lot. Mark's navy Buick and Nate's brown Toyota are the only other cars in sight. Sorry, dudes. You have to work your way up the ranks like I did for the sweet reward.

I punch the radio dial and it's back to a few more minutes of jamming to some legends. The plan's perfect. It's glorious. A couple hours with my brother and my mom calls me a saint; Meredith tells me how caring I am. Most importantly, my brother—

the leech—falls off my back for the rest of the weekend.

The entire experience is bound to be uncomfortable. I realize he doesn't want to be on the other side of the country; he's made that clear in the little time he's been here. No one wants to be treated like an infant. He might choke on something or he might not eat at all. This is the role I'm starting to play. I'm the parent and that can't go beyond today.

The shining Turbo rolls into the driveway. The windows are down. The music continues to blare. I hop out of the car, walk up the steps and burst in the front door. Twenty minutes until the ferry leaves. Twenty minutes and the countdown to solitude restarts. Tick-tock. I step into the kitchen and the nanny, Marybeth, sits at the table, a newspaper standing upright in her crusty hands while a steaming cup of coffee rests in front of her. And to think we pay her five dollars an hour for this type of work.

"Hey where're the kids?" I ask. There's no response. The newspaper continues to move. I step further into the room and cough. "The kids Marybeth. Where're the kids?"

The newspaper tilts down to reveal her huge glasses, giant like two magnifying glasses a kid might use to burn ants on the sidewalk. "Good afternoon to you too Robert. Check the yard. It's a lovely day outside."

The kids are in the back playing some made-up game the way kids always do. Marybeth ignores them instead of teaching them anything practical. One kid carries a stick while the other grasps a 'G.I. Joe' action figure. How are they developing from this? I don't have time to get into it with the nanny—at least not today.

My brother's on the patio, not far from the kids. That same sulk consumes his body. That same depressed look's plastered across his face. He stares off at the sky with his feet propped up on an empty chair. It's the same look he had when I picked him up from the airport yesterday and it's the same look he'll carry until the day he dies. There's no one home. He's off in the clouds again.

"Hey . . ." I clap my hands in front of his motionless body. He shakes his head, breaking out of a self-imposed trance. I'm sure he's scaring the kids. I toss the envelope on his lap to get on with it. "We have five minutes t'get on the road. If we don't leave now we'll miss the ferry."

"What? What ferry?" He looks down at the envelope.

"The Rock. We're gonna check out that island."

TROUBLE IN PARADISE

We turn another corner in line at the edge of pier thirty-three. A group of sun-worshippers bump into me, one after the other brushing my shoulder while I zig-zag the roped line. Incredible how some are so oblivious to their surroundings. They are preoccupied with routine.

"What will I make for dinner?"

"This was how much money?"

"There better be something for the kids to do on that island."

Empty thoughts from empty-minded individuals.

This trip fascinates me—I will admit that much. I get to witness history gone wrong. It is society admitting they screwed up with a maximum-security prison ripped apart and put back together as a misshapen place for tourists; a place for souvenirs. The officers' break room is now a giftshop. A lookout post was transformed into a scenic overlook. How embarrassing. Each ferry ticket spits on the graves of those who spent time on the island.

"So you got these tickets from a coworker?"

I am doing my best to converse with Robb. The more I blend in with the rest of the tourists on this boat, the sooner he will trust me to be on my own. I cannot spend another moment around that nanny and those children.

"Sure did," he responds. He wears a fake smile. "Actually I've never been there in all my years in San Fran. Sounds like we'll both get t'see somethin' new today."

We move further down the line as the boy up front clips ticket after ticket. Sun-worshippers make their way onto the massive, two-level ferry. Telling people to watch their step must be one hell of a summer job. If that is not the epitome of a slave to routine, then I do not know what is. The kid on the barstool is already trapped in that sense.

We make it to the front of the line. It is our turn now—our shining moment. The teen clips Robb's ticket. Robb looks back at me with a half-smile, aware we are both counting the seconds until we part ways. One last whiff of Fisherman's Wharf fills my nose in what is a combination of funnel cakes, day-old crab rolls and car exhaust.

Tourism fuels this area of Fog City. The same little knick-knack shops are renamed every two blocks: John's Yo-Yos on one block and Yo-Yo City on the next. It is all the same in the end, yet sun-worshippers are too blind to notice.

A pleasant seventy degrees at the pier plummets to the fifties as the boat pulls out into the bay. Each passenger reacts to the rapid temperature change sweeping across the boat, covering their bare arms or putting up the hood on their rain jacket. We have not reached the island, yet it is obvious the prison's security relied heavily on the brisk air. I suppose you cannot attempt to shank a wave.

The pier fades into the dense fog until we are left with a boat among an endless, thick cloud. Robb sifts through a folder full of work-related documents while I gaze in the distance. He could crash-land on a desert island with no food nor drink and the first thing he would look for is his briefcase. He is a twenty-seven-year-old child, closer to needing his own babysitter versus sitting at the top of a company. His behavior will not change even if he gets the promotion Meredith spoke of. He relies on the hectic nature of his schedule, thriving on not having enough time for his young family.

"What's it say in that thing?" I ask.

I can see the annoyance building in his eyes. He puts his work down and flips through the brochure the ticket-clipping teen gave us. He thinks this will entertain me. He thinks it will distract me from his working on the trip and ultimately provide more time apart.

"Just some quick facts on the island's history. A few a the most infamous convicts were locked up there. There's also the obvious special request for donations on the back. Cheap bastards. The prison isn't even operational anymore. Pretty depressing if ya ask me."

Depressing indeed, Robb. That is one thing we can agree on for once, even as you pull out your precious manila folder again. Depressing indeed.

The captain comes over the loudspeaker halfway to the island. He interrupts an otherwise peaceful experience with, "Hello all you convicts out there." This is going to be brutal. "As we make our way t'Alcatraz Island we wanna remind you that flash photography is allowed. Please be mindful of other people on the island though. We also encourage you t'check out our new audio tour. It discusses various moments, people n' places during the prison's history."

How many times does he recite the same garbage to inattentive passengers in a given day? He is no better than the ticket clipper.

"Return ferries will board n' leave hourly 'til five o'clock this evening so make sure you hop on that last one. If you don't you might become The Rock's newest prisoner." A brief pause follows as he giggles to himself. "I'm kidding . . . but please be cognizant of the time during your stay."

I whined about the captain of a winged wonder not being fit for such a powerful title, yet this clown spews the same information every hour while weaving in awful puns. He is a single, overweight blob living an unimpressive life. I do not have to see him to know this. He will perish under the Sun God and never be remembered.

"So you've never been here?" I question Robb again. I must spark some forced small talk to mask the sour-milk taste left behind by the fake captain's speech.

"Nope." He shakes his head. "Seems int'resting enough, just haven't had a lotta free time. Priorities n' all ya know?" He says that as if forgetting he is speaking to a man who dug up everything stable in his life and incinerated it all.

"Well surely Meredith or the kids mentioned wanting t'come here right?" I take an obvious stab at where his priorities stand. "I mean it's one a the most iconic things around."

"Sure . . . it's come up once or twice. It's complicated with our schedules. Let's just sit back n' enjoy this yeah?"

I throw him a half-assed thumbs-up in response. He returns to his pressing literature.

Robb's work enchantment provides me with a few minutes to slip away. I wander to the side of the boat. The sun punches through the clouds for a moment and a beam of light strikes my line of sight, a gentle reminder from the Sun God that it follows me wherever I go. It is a tap on the shoulder telling me regression is inevitable. I will soon unintentionally force my way back into the safety of routine. Not today, though. Today I am going somewhere I have not gone before.

The fog breaks near the bow and a cryptic rock formation exposes itself. That is it—The Rock. This place was the epitome of all society considers wrong; a single location brought together those who rebelled against the norms. These rebels were against the definitions of right and wrong—against the sun-worshippers' solid structure.

And still, society united these rebels under one roof. The prison system was created by the weak-minded sun-worshipper. These rebels were not executed; they were brought together. If there is a rat infestation, a clear head does not unify the rodents. A wise man poisons them. Society kept these scoundrels around, afraid of what the world would be like without their balance. They believed an uneven society was destined to tip over.

Balance. It was all about balance to these people and still is today. If the rebels are gone, society must find a new group to counterweight the right. The right does not exist without the wrong. I am on the side of the wrong. Of course, I do not condone senseless violence, but at least these rebels proactively work on breaking the balance. They seek to corrupt, murder and steal from the right. They make the right defensive and angry in return.

I will learn about some of these rebels during this trip. Hopefully, their spirits provide the insight required to break free from my own routine. Sun-worshippers try to pull me back in. I will fight them until my last breath. Perfect balance.

The island is fully visible now. Impatient passengers rise from their seats. They shiver from the constant draft coming from every angle. Those who fight the frigid conditions distract themselves by reaching for their disposable cameras, flashing away at the island as the sun shines over a guard tower. Good luck with your scrapbooks.

The Rock is an endless hill. There is no flat land in sight. It is the top of a mountain, torn off and plopped into the Fog City bay. It is a tight, crowded island, with concrete structures all around like the Big Apple itself. I thought I left that place in the past.

Dark green and grey are the only visible colors next to the teal water surrounding the island. The green fights the grey as nature sticks its fists up in rebellion of man's creation. Plants grow out of and up the sides of every structure. The island's Empire State building is the lighthouse, hovering above the rest of the island. This is man. Hear him roar. Then let nature get its revenge.

"Can you imagine livin' on that place?" Robb asks. He tosses his hand on my shoulder, taking a break from his heavy reading as the boat docks.

"Actually I can." We walk down to the first level of the boat. "It's just as much a prison as the rest of our lives. We listen t'some higher power. We're told when t'eat n' when t'sleep. What's the difference?"

"Listen man . . . it was a hypothetical question. Can you not speak like a moody teen for one day? Just for today n' we'll be good." He storms off the ferry and onto the dock before turning around with insincere regret. "Sorry. I know it's been a rough fuckin' few days for you but let's try t'keep that kinda thinking t'ourselves. You're on vacation . . . enjoy it."

My thoughts become dialogue and my mother speaks through him as a result. This mistake occurs more often as of late. A side effect from the lack of medication? Possibly. The more probable cause is the frustrating polarization between Robb and me. We reveal our true selves with every interaction while trying to remain civil.

We continue getting herded off the ferry. Red lettering on a building greets us as we touch land. 'Indians Welcome,' it reads. Prisoners were not the only individuals to occupy this island. I do not need giant lettering to reveal the history oozing out of every crack and crevice of Alcatraz. The smell of iron in the air is a mix of rusted metal and the pungent scent lingering after a bloody nose. How many perished here over the years?

Tourists scatter upon arrival, some touring on their own while others huddle, confused without their fearless captain. They need guidance. They need order. A child whines to his parents; a pathetic couple attempts to take a picture of themselves with the bay in the background; Robb has his face buried back in the manila folder, bumping into people every few steps while continuing to read.

The rest of the island remains a mystery as a giant curtain in the form of a building stands in front of us. Man prevails even after his failure. The other structure in sight looks like a former dock-house. Further inspection reveals it was turned into a bathroom. Society quite literally takes a shit on a piece of history.

"So looking at this guide it sounds like we can knock out the whole tour in a few hours," Robb declares. He looks around at the sun-worshippers, just now realizing we are off the ferry. "Not sure where we start so let's stick with some a these folks from the boat yeah?"

"Works for me."

Most sun-worshippers from our ferry huddle around a little podium—a soapbox—where an island employee stands tall as if prepared to deliver a revolutionary speech. We approach the crowd, remaining near the back for an easy escape.

Robb has looked at his watch three times since stepping foot on the dock. He is counting the minutes until he does not have to stand beside me. I peer over his shoulder; it is a quarter to one. We will leave by four if he plays his cards right. Do not worry, Robb. I, too, am counting down the seconds.

"Welcome to Alcatraz," the tour guide begins. "This moment marks your first stop at this former military fort. It's mostly known as a federal prison though."

She fumbles through the speech she rehearsed in the mirror this morning. Maybe she wanted to be an actress and settled for a few minutes of attention on this makeshift stage. The rambling is full of generic historical facts about the island. This information is already in our pamphlets. She explains how to go about our 'adventures' and soon struggles to remember the rest of her speech. Yikes.

"Let's go about this on our own," I tell Robb. "I don't wanna be stuck behind a buncha families the whole time."

Robb rolls up the folder tucked under his arm and shoves it in his back pocket as if hinting he is finished working. Fat chance. "Sounds good. I think the only way t'start out is up this route." He points past the group of spectators, toward the beginning of an inclined pathway.

The entire island is a massive ramp. I imagine a cripple rolling up the path to be rewarded with a giftshop. His wheelchair rolls back down toward the dock after losing control with him in it. He is fine with this due to his latest discovery at the top of the island. Life is full of disappointments—I should know.

The deeper we walk into the heart of the island, the more bird shit covers the grey pavement. These birds are the most recent occupants of Alcatraz. It is somehow a relief to see another color. Another work of nature fighting against man's creation.

Before we venture too far, I pull out my 'Visit Alcatraz' brochure, which includes a map of the island. My finger runs along the surface to determine our general location.

"Building sixty-four," I announce to Robb, who continues to pace ahead. "That's what this big building is t'our left. Looks like they used t'be residential apartments."

Robb rolls his eyes. "Alright then. Let's check it out. You lead the way boss."

If I am forced to spend time in Fog City, I am savoring the moments that are not complete wastes of time. This trip to Alcatraz is one of those moments. It may have the answers I need, offering a chance to learn the way of the rebels. I can learn about the wrong.

From what I recall, my fascination with crime began while watching 'The Fugitive' as a child. I remember my father melting into the recliner while watching television—a glass of scotch in hand—and falling asleep moments later. I scooted closer on the floor behind him to get my daily dose of crime when he dozed off. I have no recollection of the television show besides the core premise: Richard Kimble, a wrongfully accused man on the run, had his entire life shattered in days. A successful doctor turned murderous fugitive overnight. He was a man who saw his life flip upside-down. Successful to jobless. Wealthy to poor. Safe to on the run. From right to wrong in the eyes of the public in the blink of an eye.

The inside of building sixty-four is grim for staff housing. The giant curtain feels like a cellblock in itself. We are forced to bend over as we walk through the building's basement—an area where I imagine only maintenance traveled. The interior is all grey, with no white bird shit or plants growing inside to fight back. The black-and-white movie is interrupted by bright windbreakers on the tourists wandering around inside.

The first dark room we enter appears promising, yet soon hides another group of sun-worshippers. They are huddled around a tiny television. These fools stand on an island where all this history occurred and choose to experience it with celebrity-voiced narration. As if it were not already pathetic, the screen flashes 'Alcatraz 101.' I let out an audible laugh, causing a few heads to turn. I ignore them, turning my back to the group and moving onward.

"This isn't anything," I whisper to Robb. "Let's get the hell outta here. They have an entire island t'walk through n' they'd rather stand here watching a VHS."

"It's your trip pal. I'm just along for the ride."

I acknowledge the condescending response and brush past him in the tight quarters. His lack of interest puts him lower than those in front of the television—lower than the captain of the ship. Even lower than me.

"Hey!" he tries to catch my attention. "It's a giftshop. I needa get a magnet or some shit t'bring home. I'll never hear the end of it if I don't bring somethin' back for the kids."

I cannot say anything comes as a surprise after years of being disappointed by Robb's words and actions. In his mind, he is superior to conflict resolution. He would rather change the subject than leave an apology on the table. There is no subtlety in his actions.

I look back at him. "Go ahead. I'll be walkin' outside. It's better than hunkering down with the rest a these imbeciles."

Robb darts to the giftshop, which stands out like a sore thumb in the grim interior; it is lit and organized while a smiling cashier waits for his next customer. Meanwhile, I head toward the beam of natural sunlight back at the entrance of the building. It is polarizing to the damp, dark basement.

The heat from the Almighty and the chill of Fog City's wind create a constant state of feeling too cold while also too hot. Human bodies are not designed to experience these conflicting temperatures. Right versus wrong. Cold versus hot. I enjoy this observation while peering off the island, across the bay at the rest of civilization.

Whoever decided this place ought to be a prison is cruel. They had a little wrong hiding in their right. They designed a jail where prisoners spent the rest of their lives looking at freedom across the bay. The worst part of it all is that it is a mere mile away in distance—at least that is what the theatrical captain informed us on our journey here.

The echo of the icy waves crashing onto the rocky shore and countless species of birds cawing in every direction leave me in a trance-like state. I indulge the unfamiliar sounds, smells and sights. An opportunity to resume Doctor Polk's prescribed meditation. It is a chance to ship my mind back to where no one can reach me. Doctor Polk—that cocky prick—still has a grasp on me. The meditation, he says, is a way to escape reality. The worst part is that he is not wrong.

It has been two days since that dark evening. Two days and there has been no progress in breaking free of my metaphorical chains that are the habits consuming my life. The decision to uproot routine was a failsafe, and an unsuccessful one at that. What will be left when I return to the Big Apple? I have no home, no job and no one waiting for me other than my mother, who does not count.

My mother, Robb and Meredith all asked on separate occasions about the catalyst to my recent decisions. The cops did the same while making themselves at home in my former apartment. The truth is there was no catalyst. Of course, that makes it worse in their eyes. No catalyst means nothing tangible to point to as the source of my actions. This concerns them.

Any hope of understanding disappears if they require a catalyst to understand my decisions. I like to think of it as an unopened bottle of soda. Every day—every routine—is an immature child shaking the bottle. Shake. They toss it down the grocery store aisle. They bounce it off the floor. Roll. Bounce. A parent picks it up and throws it in their shopping cart in a rush to pick up supplies for a last-minute event. An unassuming guest grabs a plastic red cup not long after, heading to the bar to make a Jack and Coke. The victim twists the cap and the bottle explodes everywhere, a sticky mess now on the victim's ironed dress shirt he wore to impress Susan. The host's carpet is soaking wet, covered in the brown mess. Everyone's unhappy.

The bottle receives the blame in this situation while others claim the title of victim. The bottle did nothing wrong. It was pushed to the point of explosion. My mother, Robb and Meredith awarded themselves with the title of victim following my actions. My mother worries; Robb wastes his time; and Meredith's relationship with Robb is further strained. It is not my fault. I am the bottle and I am the one who suffered most.

A woman's voice pulls me back from the clouds. "Excuse me sir. Would you mind taking a photo of me n' my boy?"

She holds a disposable camera in one hand with the other resting on the shoulder of the young boy at her side. The boy smiles at me for no apparent reason.

"Uhhhh sure. Yeah that's fine," I respond, caught off guard by the request.

Interrupted meditation feels like someone shook me awake during deep R.E.M. sleep. I am groggy, irritable and on-edge. Everything comes with side effects these days. Thank you, Doctor Polk.

I grab the camera, give it a few winds and hold it to my face. The two reposition themselves so the cityscape appears in the backdrop. "Three . . . two . . . one . . ." I snap the photo and hand the camera back to the woman. She thanks me before continuing down toward the dock. Just like that, we are strangers again.

"Oh!" she shouts with a look over her shoulder. "If this's your first visit, the new audio tour's a must." She pulls the boy along as he stares back at me. Run, child. The conditioning has not yet set in. There is still time to break free.

We never did much as a family growing up. My father died six years ago. My mother gave up on a traditional familial relationship after that, yet she did not give up on worrying about us. She was always protective and rather overbearing, but my father's passing made it worse. That suffocation led to Robb remaining on the West Coast, one quality of his life I do envy now and again.

"You make friends?" Robb asks. He steps out of the dark building with a smirk.

"Not in the slightest. Just playin' photographer."

He carries a white plastic bag, having found some soon-to-be-disposed-of souvenir for his children. He reaches in, feeling around the bag while staring back at me. He expects suspense that never builds.

"Here." He pulls out a pocket-sized book no bigger than my palm. "Think of it as reading material for the plane ride home."

I grab it and read the cover aloud, "Alcatraz: Ninety-Nine Profiles."

I open the small brick—the little book—flipping through various sections. I stop as I land on several of the featured profiles. "Thanks Robb. Yeah great reading material."

It is a considerate gesture. I am positive the action served as an alternative to an apology, though. It is a flex of his fat wallet. Still, maybe this experience humbles him. The thought subsides as he whips out his manila folder and flips through its contents.

I tuck the little book in my jacket pocket as we continue the self-guided tour. I mention the lady I spoke with recommended the audio tour as Robb remains buried in his work. He appears oblivious to my comments, resuming in his own, odd meditation.

Dilapidated buildings and other structures are all that remain of the former prison besides the cellhouse and building sixty-four. Oh, and, of course, the dock-house turned shitter. As deteriorated and useless as this place has become over time, it still holds more history than any sun-worshipper on earth. Decade after decade it stands tall and proud. It does not abide by traditional routines or listen to the Sun God's demands. It is free from it all.

The place would be more magnificent if it was not littered with tourists. Strollers, whining children and slow-walking couples cover the pathway. Robb blends in with everyone else as he falls behind, trying to read and navigate at the same time. I would prefer to be a prisoner at a time like this—at least I would enjoy the obligatory silence.

"You think it'd be better t'be a prisoner or guard back in the day?" I ask Robb, knowing his response. I prepare to state my case for the opposite. Let us add some heat to the conversation to pull him out from that folder.

"How's that even a question?" he responds, tucking the folder in the white bag. "My answer's neither. I wouldn't wanna be a prisoner for obvious reasons but a guard'd be just as worse. They prob'ly got paid dirt too."

That is correct, Robb. They could not have lived a lavish life like you if they spent their days and nights on this island. They were balancing the right and wrong with great purpose rather than for monetary rewards.

"You're not looking at it with an open mind. At least the prisoners had guts t'do what they really wanted . . . actions that risked their freedom. I'm sure the guards envied the prisoners at times."

"Jesus you think murder's the definition of freedom? Did you feel that freedom when quitting your job n' demolishing your apartment?"

He is prying—attempting to get me to cave—to reveal my true mind through an emotional response. My mother's words continue to fly out of his mouth.

"I guess that's one way of looking at it," I humor him for a moment. "Answer me this though . . . why does having a steady job, cozy apartment n' stable network of family n' friends needa be the norm? Why can't I do what I wanna do n' not what society tells me t'do?"

We stand motionless, pretending to read a nearby sign to avoid making this a bigger discussion. The sign outlines the burnt remnants of another small structure in front of us. It was a social hall back in the day that burned down in 1970. The fire's origin remains debated. All that is left is a shell of its former self similar to my own. My shell attempts to recreate the man owned by routine. I cannot have that.

I cringe at the idea of exposing my mind to Robb. He does not deserve to hear these worldly observations. I am sure he feels the tension in the air as he breaks the long silence.

"I'm not about t'get all philosophical on an island with you man. Just forget I said anything about it."

"Well then don't go there t'begin with. Let's do this audio tour so we can get off this island. I'll be outta your hair in a few days."

Fortunately for us both, the cellhouse ends up being no more than another five minutes of winding elevation away. Back and forth on switchbacks on the bird-shit-covered pathway. This is the experience I came for—an opportunity to get in the shoes or cells of some of the most notorious thugs and mobsters to walk this planet. The most infamous rebels of all time. The wrong. A pair of headphones also provides an excuse to avoid further interaction with Robb.

Robb trails behind again. This time, he uses work as a reason to avoid conversation. He resorts to babysitting me. I look like the bad guy from an outsider's perspective. Here is my adopted brother, taking time out of his busy life to spend with a 'troubled' family member. He takes me to Alcatraz. I am ungrateful. With little context, I am the bad guy—the bad brother. I am what is wrong. He is the sham of a victim while I am the bottle.

If an outsider knew what I know, they would not be so easy on Robb. He does not contact me nor my mother; he rarely converses with his own wife and children. He does not spend time with me because he is the good guy—he spends time with me because he has no choice. It is the quickest and most convenient way to keep the spotlight off him so he can return to his money-hungry lifestyle. He is the wrong in a way, too.

The cryptic interior of the cellhouse drowns the sound of families and friends conversing with one another. It is a powerful sight. A certain beauty lies in the simplicity of the building. Its walls are bare. Everything around the large room is a different shade of grey. The black-and-white film continues. Walt himself could not make an experience this authentic.

It is cold inside—colder than outside. The frigid air finds a way to seep through the concrete walls, filtering through the broken glass windows, past the accompanying bars to hit my face.

Metal bars are everywhere and there is not a cell in sight on the ground level. This is the most important structure on the island. So much time was spent here. This was the house of all rebels and it needed protecting. These security measures leave little room for natural light to poke its head in for a look around.

"Welcome t'the main cellhouse gentlemen," an older man says, standing at a movie theater-esque podium. "Are ya here for the audio tour or int'rested in visiting our bookstore on the second level?"

Another bookstore—of course. We hike all the way up The Rock to be presented with another verbal advertisement for cheap magnets and a prison-themed deck of cards. The wheel-chaired cripple reaches the top and rolls himself back down in disappointment at the discovery.

"The audio tour," I respond. The smile is wiped clear off his face. "Just give us whatever we need for the audio tour."

"Great," he replies. "Please find your headsets on the rack t'my right n' proceed up the stairs behind me. Your tour'll begin up there."

We walk over to the rack of sweaty cassette players and oversized headphones. Another employee stands a few feet back wiping down a pile of recently used supplies. I grab the tape and headphones, handing Robb the two as well, who proceeds to tuck his folder away. He looks around the room for the first time since entering the building.

We plug in our headphones and place them over our ears. We walk up the rusted metal staircase. Our steps echo, the sound sliding in past the orange foam cushions on the headphones.

A large red sign greets us as we approach the top. It reads, 'Please press play on your audiotape to commence the tour.'

We follow its instructions and push down on the cassette player. We glance at each other and agree to extend our silence for a little longer. It is for the best. Our heads will be a little clearer the next time we speak.

"Welcome to the Alcatraz cellhouse guided audio tour," a deep-voiced older gentleman says through the tape. "Please proceed into the room on your right for our first stop."

JUST IN TIME

The guided audio tour was a genius addition to The Rock. It is comprised of all the useful information provided by a sun-worshipping tour guide without the lame, recycled one-liners and idiotic questions from inattentive adults.

This tour includes detailed instructions, guiding listeners through each warehouse-sized section of the cellhouse. Sounds of distant chatter, cell doors slamming and the footsteps of guards fill my ears. The noise drowns out another toddler crying in the distance. The surreal experience forces me to stop and remove the headphones every few minutes to distinguish reality from fiction. It is ingenious.

Robb trails behind again, beginning a new stage of the tour as I finish it. We started at the same time, yet he has already stopped to pause the tape twice to tend to his pressing work. He is a prisoner of his employer. He wants that promotion more than anything else—even more than he wants his family.

The cellhouse is large. Sound carries from one cellblock to another, bleeding through the headphones for added realism. It is menacing, a beast of a building that has seen too much to speak of. It holds secrets. It wears the blood of the lost deep in its cracks as war paint. No mop and bucket can make this place new again.

The interior is a light beige, unlike the grey exterior and similar structures. The cell doors are painted the same cream color as the walls, a dull tone up to par with the sad, grey concrete floor.

The large room is organized. One cellblock. Another cellblock. A second tier of cells rests on top of the lower tier like a stacked brick. A catwalk hovers above the ground cells. The ceiling holds a few skylight windows, likely intended to keep prisoners from going insane. These windows contribute to the frigid temperature as well.

Each pathway between cellblocks is titled with a clever street name from cities across the country: Michigan Avenue in the Windy City; Broadway from the Big Apple. Park Avenue. Sunset Strip. Times Square.

"If you look up at the end of this cellblock you will spot a red arrow pointing toward the floor. Walk toward it," the audio instructs me. A few others follow me, their tapes synchronized with mine. The voice continues, "Look just below the red arrow. The keys hanging from the hook on the gun gallery played an important role in a failed escape attempt. The event is now known as the bloody 'Battle of Alcatraz.'"

The voice spends the next several minutes unraveling the fatal escape attempt. Another group of men rebelling against the system, attempting to break free from the rules forced upon them. They battled society for the second time after their first attempts sent them to this place. They are the unsung heroes that history books ignore. The rebels. The wrong. They deserve the movies. They deserve the fame.

I pull out the little book while peering at the man who purchased it each time an inmate's name rings into my ears. Robb falls further behind. He is the heartless sun-worshipper I share a namesake with. He does not care about any of the rich history breathing out of these cell doors.

The man in my mind drops me off at the end of cellblock D after zig-zagging through the previous rows. It is the last cellblock on our tour, where broken windows shine light on the floor to remind me a return to reality is inevitable. I am the Sun God's slave. It is near the end of the tour and I do not wish to speak with Robb anymore.

"This is Sunset Strip and home to solitary confinement," the voice informs me. "This is where some of the most ruthless criminals spent many days on Alcatraz."

The man goes into detail about the most troubled criminals, dubbed 'solitary servants' due to the long periods they spent on this strip. Robert 'Birdman' Stroud. Alvin 'Creepy' Karpowicz. The legendary George 'Machine Gun Kelly' Barnes. These men spent significant time in solitude, which sounds like time well spent. Alone with nothing except the mind. How inviting.

"When you get to the opposite end of the cellblock, stop and face the cells on your left. These four cells served as the ultimate form of punishment on Alcatraz. This is known as 'the hole.' These dark, quiet cells punished inmates for days, sometimes weeks, on end. The hole was still preferred over the depths of the dungeon though."

The tape fails to elaborate on the alleged dungeon. Instead, it tosses it at the end of a sentence and moves onto the next quick fact to distract listeners. I would like to know more after that curious piece of dialogue, but I am left in the dark. I do, however, recall some information on the dungeon delivered through reading material back home. Another benefit of my obsession with the wrong.

The island was transformed into a military prison in the early 1900s. The Army chose to maintain the basement that remained from former brick barracks. The prison turned the area into a brutal version of solitary confinement. Rodents scurried across the floor. Inmates were chained to the ground and had a bucket to defecate in and a blanket to keep warm. They were stripped to nothing. Of course, neither the park nor the government would allow such a place to enter the ears of thousands of tourists each day. They censor reality. History is molded to fit a desired story.

"Proceed to walk in one of the open cells."

I spot an isolation cell that does not have someone pandering around inside—cell fourteen. I step inside the dark abyss. The tight room is pitch black. It is a kind of darkness mirrored by the deepest, most isolate pocket of the universe. This form of emptiness should not exist.

I hear sun-worshipper after sun-worshipper exiting their cell to continue the tour. They do not appreciate this level of darkness. I stand paralyzed in the room. I am hypnotized by my eyes having not adjusted to the blackness. A beautiful place that is frozen in one spot; frozen in time. The Sun God cannot reach me in here. The Almighty attempts to break through the doorway while darkness holds its ground, emerging victorious.

Facing the back of the cell minimizes the amount of light sneaking its way in. A man pokes his head inside the cell, asking if his child can enter. I do not respond. This is my time. I reach a level of calmness that parallels the darkness in the room. I breathe the salty air coming in and out of the cell. My feet dig into the ground, crunching the loose bits of concrete that fell from the ceiling at some point in the past.

The man in my mind has been silent for a few minutes now, an intentional strategy by the creators of this audio tour. The silence allows for true immersion. Knowing the end of the tour is moments away, I anticipate something along the lines of, 'Now exit the cell and head toward the stairway on your left. Thank you for joining us and enjoy the rest of your time on Alcatraz.'

Instead, the next sound that arrives is not the man in my mind. It is a powerful rumble in the distance. The Sun God turned the volume up on its estranged cousin, the Thunder God. How is this appropriate background noise at this stage of the tour? The violent thunder continues to crash into my ears. It grows louder until I am forced to remove the headphones altogether.

The thunder does not fade; it grows louder. I look down in the dark room at the faint shadow that is in the shape of the headphones in my hands. I am not wearing headphones. Thunder again. Again. It is not the audiotape. This is reality.

The opportunity to process the approaching roars passes as a new concern arrives. The floor begins to vibrate. It forces dust and tiny chunks of crumbled concrete to hit the floor. The pieces fall onto my hair, jacket and shoes.

I turn to face the front of the cell only to find the beam from the Sun God has vanished. I cannot gain my bearings. Pure blackness engulfs the room. The persistent roar suddenly merges with screams from outside the cell. Dozens of tourists stomp about in fear. I cannot move.

The increased rumbles throw off my balance, prompting me to reach out. I feel for something to grab onto, anything at all. No luck. A sense of security and balance is as barren as winter rain. The previous blissful state fades faster than it arrived.

Each attempt to walk across the room results in my falling backward against the wall. The endless quakes interrupt any train of thought making sense of this. It fuels a mentally and physically paralyzed position. I am trapped.

The occurrence culminates in a quake that fills the entire room. The beast has arrived, leaving me in the eye of its hurricane. Larger chunks of concrete crash to the ground around me. One strikes me on the head, and I topple to the concrete floor in pain.

In a haze from the blow, I use any remaining strength to cover my ears from the deafening rumbles. My eyes slam closed. I am overwhelmed. Sensory overload. Raw reaction. Throughout the madness, the child-like position on the floor reverts my mind back to youthful days.

Robb pushes his way through. Except it is a young Robb, sitting on the ground in the fetal position mirroring my own. Tears run down his face with a small scrape on his forehead. He looks sad. The smug look on his face is gone for once.

"What happened?" I ask.

He curls tighter into his body. Silence. This is the one time I bond with Robb—the one time he is not pretentious.

I am biking home from school and spot a group of teenagers shoving him to the ground. The forced empathetic nurturing from my upbringing sends me speeding over to the group. I crash into them. They flee while yelling back obscenities. A bullied Robb turns bully.

This is a memory I hold onto despite my desire to lose it.

My hands fall from my ears. The thunderous roars fade into infinity while my eyes remain shut. One sense at a time. The rest of my body shakes on a cold, damp floor.

Several moments of tranquility ease my mind. Just breathe. Remember the meditation. I peer out of one eye. It is still dark as night, only this time the single beam of light fighting its way through the doorway has vanished. Complete blackness. Was there a power outage? Did a storm cloud brew from above? The mind races to find any logical conclusion to cling to in moments like this.

Minutes feel like hours. As my eyes adjust to the darkness, one sense refuses to resume: sound. Silence swallows the building, letting out a quietness more painful than the loud claps that have subsided. Nothing adds up. Screams of terror should echo for miles after the bizarre phenomenon.

Touch—feeling—guides me through the room. I rub the new bump on the side of my head. Is this all a distant dream? My feet ache as I inch toward where the opening was once located. It was there—I am certain of that much.

A single thud bounces off the four walls as my body slams into a metal surface. The contact shakes the silence with an all-encompassing echo. The chilled wall is an endless surface of icy steel. It scales floor to ceiling where an open space once stood. Finally, a protrusion. Hinges. This is not a wall—it is a door. A locked door.

My heart buries itself in the deep confines of my chest. My fists pound against the door. Bang. Bang. Each collision leaves my hands stinging in pain. Terror wrestles discomfort and comes out on top.

I disturb the lingering silence. "Hello? Anyone there? I'm locked behind this damn door!"

No response. I am alone. Dazed and trapped and—for the first time in as long as I can remember—alive.

The mind can only ignore the body's cries for help for so long. I am soon left kneeling in front of the metal blockade begging the inanimate object to obey my commands. The solution rests in my mind, a place Doctor Polk sends me when other therapeutic methods fail. It is nothing more than a distraction; however, it is an alternative to broken knuckles.

Meditation sends me to a vault of memories from the last few days. Does this stem back to the life-altering choices implemented to break free of a meaningless life?

For the first time in what felt like hours in isolation, a single pair of footsteps clatter down the cellblock street, growing louder as they approach. The footsteps pair with a muffled clanking. Keys. A park employee must have evacuated the building and is now sweeping for trapped sun-worshippers. There is no chance it is Robb outside the cell; he is likely pushing past women and children to get onto the nearest ferry.

"Open cell fourteen!" a voice shouts from the other side of the heavy door.

The cell doors must have slid shut during the quake, explaining the darkness. A few tourists remained trapped inside while others fled the scene.

A clank comes from down the cellblock. The door slides open. Outside stands the outline of an island employee. They are dressed head-to-toe in full uniform—hat included. A park ranger stands before me.

"What the fuck was all that?" I ask the man. He stares back at me, maintaining his stiff stance. "And why the hell did the door close? You jackasses needa take another look at the safety of this place."

I feel alive. The adrenaline lingers. It all feels great and at the same time I am fearful for my life. Living is being fearful for your life. Is this the Sun God freeing me from his grasp for a moment?

I step outside the cell to get in the tall man's face. The internal fuel prepares me to let out more frustration. Instead, I am greeted with the swift draw of a baton followed by a strike to the stomach. A gut-punch. I feel like puking.

"What . . ." I struggle to catch my breath. I clutch my stomach and fall to my knees. "What the hell's wrong with you?"

"You'll speak when spoken to!" the man shouts. "Not another word! If this continues it's down to the dunge—" He freezes the way I froze in the cell. He pulls out a flashlight clipped to his belt, panning the light up and down my body. "Officer Douglas . . . who's assigned t'fourteen?"

The second shadow-figure stands tall at the top of the gun gallery, hovering a full story above us. He reads from what appears to be a clipboard. "Says here it's open captain. No logged inmates in that cell for over two weeks now."

I look up at the ranger. He must think I am involved in the origin of the quakes. "Listen I dunno what happened!" I peer up as he looks down in anger. "I was on the tour . . . the audio tour. I got locked in here somehow."

"What don't you understand 'bout shuttin' that rattlin' trap a yours?" He crouches to my level, looking me in the eyes before landing another excruciating blow on me. The baton slams into my face this time. "Now answer me this . . . where'd you get that ridiculous getup?"

"There must be some sorta mistake," I plead with the man while rubbing my face. I will not be struck again. This lunatic is beyond reason.

His face succumbs to a new level of fury as he grabs my jacket. He yanks me all the way out of the cell and onto the street. My body continues to recover from the paralyzed state while the ranger drags my corpse on the hard floor. I am a bowling ball destined for collision. I try to regain my footing to no avail, slipping and sliding across the ground.

I glance out the windows. It is dark outside. Not cloudy, but rather night-like despite it being the late afternoon. It is not later than four o'clock. Is this all a result of the quakes?

The falling concrete affected the unattended cells in Sunset Strip while the rest of the cellblock remained untouched. It appears spotless. My ears stretch to hear past the sound of my shoes squeaking across the slick floor. The screams of terror have vanished alongside the roars.

This does not feel right—not my corpse sliding across the ground nor this insane ranger. What feels off is the setting of the cellhouse. Most everything appears fine. In fact, everything appears better than it did before.

"You don't wanna talk?" The ranger looks back at me. The man in the gun gallery smiles as we pass. "You'll stay in the dungeon 'til we can sort this shit out." The ranger looks down at me every few seconds to ensure I am not trying to overpower him, a pointless effort if I tried with the way my body aches right now.

The ranger reaches down, jingling an army of keys. One key dives into an opening on the floor and the man rotates his hand. A small hatch flips open. We are still in D-block as he slides me across the floor once more. My body tumbles down a set of narrow stairs while the man continues staring from above. The flashlight from the gun gallery lights up his figure like something from a horror film.

"Strip!" he shouts. I look up at the tower of a sun-worshipper, confused by the sadistic request. "I'm not gonna ask again." I strip down to my underwear and toss the clothes up the stairs as requested, fearful of what he is capable of. He is not yet pleased. "N' the rest. I said strip didn't I?"

I follow his orders and toss the underwear up the narrow stairs. "Can I speak t'someone?" I am back in Doctor Polk's office pleading for another reasonable mind besides my own. "There must be a misunderstanding."

He acknowledges the desperation with a menacing grin. The metal hatch slams back down at the top of the staircase. The footsteps resume, this time moving away from my location and fading into silence.

I scoot my bare body across the wet, icy ground until I land in a corner. Emasculation defined. It is somehow more frigid below ground than it was in that cell. The dungeon—this must be the island's dungeon. Everything around is damp as if hit with a natural sort of morning dew found on suburban grass.

When stripped of one sense, others become enhanced. I press my ear to the ground. I can hear water dripping and what I assume are rats scurrying along the floor. This place is revolting. It is no wonder why they tried so hard to cover it up.

Strip. Why strip? The audiotape mentioned the rebels thrown into the hole were stripped bare with only a wet rag and a bucket to comfort them. There are no rags or buckets with me down here, yet I am very much nude.

If they blamed me for the quakes, a park ranger would have delivered me to authorities by now. This is something different, a step away from reality. Did terrorists infiltrate the island? Did a tourist group of mental institution patients overpower island authorities? Insane possibilities sound logical at this point.

Doctor Polk's meditation returns. I think a little harder about what is happening. A dream seems more logical than any previous theory. Perhaps the chunk of ceiling that hit my head left me unconscious. A few slaps to the face dismiss that idea. This is too vivid. Too real. I replay the loud rumbles in my head. Whatever is occurring now is affiliated with the violent quakes. I am certain of this.

My body is exhausted from a racing mind. It has been beaten and stripped as well. I begin to drift off, still huddled in the corner. A situation like this is ideal for me. This loneliness should feel liberating. There is something wrong about this experience, though. Even a flawed rebel like me cannot enjoy this. This is a new level of the wrong. Complete imbalance.

Splash. I am disturbed from my uncomfortable slumber as a frigid wave crashes onto my head.

"Wake up!" a voice shouts. It is the same man standing above. A tower of a man. He smokes a cigarette in one hand and rocks an empty bucket in the other. "Warden wants t'see ya. You better start makin' some damn sense a this or it'll get a hell of a lot worse before it gets any better."

I stare up at him. Water drips from my hair and onto my face. "Alright. Let's get to it then." I am a stray dog, hosed off and thrown into a kennel. Time for my checkup.

Fear and curiosity collide as the man tosses me up the stairs. Water drips to the floor while a light chuckling lingers behind me. My bare body slides across a few other cellblocks. Various whispers echo down the walkway. I must not be the sole suspect here.

The average person covers their genitals at a time like this in embarrassment. Not me. All I am concerned about is if Robb managed to make it off the island before all this unraveled. Bring the police. Bring anyone who will put an end to this situation.

The path leads to the control room, a place the audio tour guided me through earlier today. The room remains dark like the rest of the cellhouse while carrying a certain unfamiliarity within its walls. A like-new appearance engulfs the room. Various lights flicker on previously long-dead dead machines. Why would these rebels attempt to operate old equipment? Perhaps my memory of the room is warped, or more likely it is simply a similar location. A familiar dream. The baton-wielder whacks my back after catching wandering eyes.

Our painful trek ends outside with my feet shuffling across the concrete. We pause at the entrance of another building. The rebel knocks on the door. The man in my mind identified this area as the site of the home to former wardens. We were not permitted to enter during the tour, yet the knocking results in the door swinging open. Something is off. Someone is here.

Inside stands another rebel. He is covered in a white evening robe and holds a glass of golden liquor. His thin hair is a few shakes of pepper poured into a saltshaker. Wide glasses cover the many wrinkles holding his old face together.

He smiles. "Thank you Captain Peters. Please, both of you come n' join me."

He takes us through the foyer and into a living room. The entire house rises from the ashes like the control room; it is spotless. The baton-wielder pushes me onto a couch. My hands remain cuffed while my bare ass rubs against a frigid leather sofa.

"Really?" the robed man asks, looking at me while speaking to the man he referred to as captain. "You're gonna strip him down, dump water on his head n' let him dry off on my couch?"

"My apologies sir," the captain replies. "He's been rather uncooperative over the last few hours. Needed t'set him straight before comin' in here's all."

"Well I appreciate that, however you're no longer needed right now." He waves the man away like a fly lingering around a family barbecue. "Please remain outside while I chat with our friend."

He keeps his eyes locked on me while sitting across a coffee table. He tightens his robe. The captain exits the room, leaving me alone with the stranger.

"I don't recall meeting you," the robed man says. He gulps the remaining drops in his glass before setting it back on the table. "Whatever the case, I can't say it's a pleasure." He extends his hand. "Howard Madison."

My mind flashes to the audio tour and the man in my mind. Warden Madison—Howard Madison—was an Alcatraz warden some thirty years ago. He ruled this place from the '50s to the early '60s. The picture becomes clearer. These men are attempting to act out roles from long ago. They determined I am the ideal candidate for the role of prisoner. In reality, I am a hostage.

Battling this reenactment resulted in pain. Maybe they are more open to reason if I play along. Let them continue their game. They know I am a tourist, so there is no quantity of truth that will set me free. I will play along with the hope of identifying an opportunity for escape. No more pain right now.

"Yes . . . right," I reply, lifting my cuffed hands to wipe water from my eyes. "Why am I here though?" Give me something to work with. Slip up and reveal something useful.

He leans forward in the sofa. His hands clasp in front of him the same way Doctor Polk sits. "You tell me. You were cooped up in the hole making a fuss in the middle of a peaceful night. I like my sleep. It's in everybody's best int'rest if I get my sleep. Just ask Captain Peters. So let's start with your name."

A moment of silence passes as I stare at the hardwood floor. I feel the man's persistent gaze while I massage the idea of offering an alias. An alias does not matter in this game. They know what is reality and what is fabrication and they do not mind crossing those streams. The only way to win is to play their game.

"Michael," I respond. "My name's Michael Field."

The man sighs, leaning back in disappointment. "We figured as much." He reaches in the robe's pocket and pulls out a leather wallet. Thank the Sun God I told the truth this once as this is my wallet. "Except we don't have any record of a Michael Field at U.S.P. Alcatraz. You better start talking . . . n' I better hear where you got those clothes the captain brought t'my door in the middle of the goddamn night."

"My name's Michael Field!" I declare, slamming my cuffs on the coffee table. The guard pokes his head in to ensure everything is civil. The truth did nothing but worsen matters. "I don't know what the fuck's going on. I was part of that audio tour before I got locked in one a those isolation cells." He continues to shake his head while I plead for my freedom. My thoughts continue to morph into words. "I assure you whatever you're looking for or trying t'accomplish by holding me hostage n' stripping me t'nothing isn't gonna work. I have nothing. I'm no one. I'm a useless victim." I am the bottle, not the victim.

If Robb made it out before these lunatics grabbed the wheel, then rescuing me is the last thing on his mind. If anything, he avoided several more hours with me. There is no doubt he will spend the rest of his evening finishing whatever work he needed to accomplish. He does not have to speak with me and can fabricate any lie to my mother and Meredith without a second thought. He is good at lying.

The self-proclaimed warden eyes his empty glass. "I'm not sure what sorta game you're playing but I won't have any more of it. Mark my words. You were found tucked away in the hole. You were screaming bloody murder n' disrespecting my guards. Now you sit in my home sharing lie after lie. D'you take me for a fool?"

"Do what you needa do then." I remove my hands from the table and place them in my lap. I am at my most vulnerable. "Have your little moment of power . . . of rebellion. It won't change anything. I've already been there."

He desires what all sun-worshippers want yet are too afraid to pursue: freedom. Freedom—if even for a few hours—to live and die by his own rules.

He stands up and motions for the guard to come in. "Captain Peters . . . take Mister Field, or whoever this man is, back t'where he came. Take him back t'the dungeon."

The role-playing guard yanks me by my wet hair and shoves me to my feet, "Let's go bird. It's back t'the dungeon for your sorry ass."

"Wait . . ." the robed man requests. "Mister Field. Michael. D'you understand your lack of cooperation puts me in a very difficult position? I have a clean reputation. I spent years earning my way to the top." He sounds like Robb. "I'll go down in history as one of the greatest wardens in the country. The press'll have my ass if word gets out about your sudden appearance n' lack of documentation. The government'll have my ass too. That won't happen despite these continued lies. I'll make sure of that."

These two men are not open to reason. Whatever their goal is, they are sticking to it and positioning me square in the middle. This is the finest acting around; Oscar-worthy performances from mysterious individuals.

Their general appearance is spot on as well. The captain's uniform mirrors the historical images around the island. Their clothes matching the images is one thing—their hair and accessories from people of the past is another.

My mind visits the dark cellhouse lit up by the stars in the night sky. The windows are now repaired. The bars had copper rust that consumed them before this hostage situation, yet they are spotless now. Somehow these rebels were able to make all sorts of updates without being noticed. Has more time passed than I realize?

I find the role of Captain Peters particularly astonishing. The six-foot-four tank resembles a pit bull with incredible upper body strength while his thin legs make pants flow behind him as he walks, a sail for a tall ship. His face is pulled straight from a '60s movie. He is clean shaven besides a well-groomed, pencil-thin mustache resting above his lip. A traditional captain's hat hides greasy, slicked-back black hair.

The captain shoves me out of the house and back into darkness. The warden stands in the doorway. I cover my exposed skin with my arms as the icy wind hits from every angle. Perhaps out of fear—or sheer curiosity—I walk away from the captain as he continues ahead. What will happen when he notices? Another strike to the gut with the heavy baton? I choose to find out one more time despite the existing pain.

A look over my shoulder reveals the man has stopped walking. He observes me from right outside the cellhouse entrance. Is story time over? A few more steps forward and the answer to that question arrives in the form of a loud bang in the distance. A bright spotlight shines down on me. It is too late for the Sun God to come out to play despite his fascination with me.

"Not another step," a voice yells from afar. "You keep walkin' n' you'll find yourself in a body bag floatin' across the bay."

The voice emerges from the source of the spotlight. There is a third actor positioned in a guard tower. How many rebels conquered this island in mere minutes? Why is this all so elaborate?

My feet shift while repositioning within the spotlight to get a better look at the individual. Another bang echoes over the island, this time sending a piece of concrete flying up in front of me. These are gun shots. The second one hits about two feet from my naked body.

"Officer Bates!" The warden steps out of his home and onto the pathway. His glass is already full of two more fingers of liquor. "Don't you waste ammo like that. Captain Peters has this under control. Let me rest for Christ's sake." He tosses up his hand and steps back inside, slamming the door behind him.

The spotlight is swallowed by the night. Peters grabs me by the handcuffs. The obedient dog grabs the baton from his side, impatient with my slow pace. The next thing in my line of sight is the growing shape of the all-black rod headed toward my face. Lights out for a while.

I find myself in a familiar emptiness with a throbbing headache. A damp floor. The squealing of rats fighting over rotten crumbs. I am back in the dungeon. This time, I am uncuffed with a pile of dry clothes resting on my lap. It appears the actors expect me to take this a step further by playing dress-up. Acting the part was not enough. The average man protests and remains nude, yet the unusual situation continues to interest me in a peculiar way. That, and I am about one whack of the baton away from a concussion if I do not follow orders. I will assume the role of model prisoner.

Dressed and feeling somewhat rested, I stand up and limp over to where a ray of light pierces the emptiness. My greatest adversary is as mighty as ever, reaching me in even the most unreachable location. It is daytime. I must have been unconscious for at least a few hours considering there was no sign of the sun before the captain knocked me out. If hours have passed, where are the authorities? Surely Robb or others alerted someone by now.

I make my way to the other side of the room and step up the stairs. I press one ear to the cellar latch at the top while hunkering over. I am listening for tourists, employees or the police swarming through the cellhouse. There is nothing but silence.

I step up again, getting closer as if my ear was to melt through the latch. My foot lands on a block—a piece of wood or crumbled concrete. I fumble around in the dark trying to make out the object.

Smooth, glossy and rather flimsy. I know this feeling. It is the book. The little book Robb purchased rests on the step next to my foot. It must have fell out of my jacket pocket when I tossed my clothes up to the captain last night. It is a useless weapon in a predicament like this and still I find the discovery comforting. It is the first familiar item since this all started.

The book's pages stick together due to the room's constant wetness, so I flip through them carefully so as not to tear anything. My tired body cannot rest. My mind cannot retreat into the comfort of itself. The Sun God is not going anywhere anytime soon. This is why I read the book to pass the time. I may as well make complete isolation worthwhile. After all, in a way I asked for this solitude.

The heavy beam of white, yellow and orange provides enough brightness to fill the surface of the little book. It sends me scanning through various sections. A section for inmates; a section for guards; a section for wardens. The warden section —'Alcatraz's Finest'—consists of short biographies of each warden. Around thirty years and four wardens.

Each warden's profile is a few paragraphs with a headshot accompanying the text. Jackson was the first warden, then Samson, then Madison and finally White. Only one captures my attention, though. Howard R. Madison. Madison was the prison's warden from '55 to '61. That is not what captivates me; my eyes are locked onto the wrinkled man's headshot. He is older with wiry hair and wide-framed glasses. The glasses cover half his face. I have seen this man before.

The little book slides from my hands and drops to the floor. Another paralyzed state of disbelief. The headshot is a mirror image of the man I spoke with in the warden's home last night. This is the robed man who claimed the title of Warden Madison. Peters struck me over the head harder than I thought. Did this alter my memory? The entire encounter could be a vivid dream—a hallucination. I try to calm myself with logic to no avail. I met this man last night—I am certain of it.

My back crashes against the wall as my hands grasp my head. One hand cups the front of my face to blind me from reality while

the other tugs my hair in frustration.
    What is going on?

MIXED EMOTIONS

He seems to be enjoying himself. That's more than I can say about this trip as I've not had the opportunity to take a single break since we got here. Duty calls.

My brother's a kid running around in a candy store while I get the important shit done. I know he feels this, too. That's why we continue to walk in silence. He wants me to apologize which won't happen as long as he continues to act like a baby.

Focusing one hundred percent of my attention on this trip forces me to work all day tomorrow. That, and I'll have to deal with a very pissed-off wife for the rest of the weekend. But my brother's a grown man who might snap at any moment. Lord knows what I'd deal with if he did snap. There's no winning here.

Michael kept looking behind him throughout the tour. He noticed the increasing gap between us due to my frequent pausing of the tape to tend to work. I pressed him to open up a little—sue me. If he wants to act this way it's his own damn fault. Just because he's careless and useless doesn't mean the rest of us have to suffer alongside him.

Fighting against society's norms doesn't make him a rebellious person; it makes him a homeless person. He's digging his own grave. We came from the same upbringing, so I don't pity him. He had it better than me—much better.

"Now face the end of C-block and turn the corner," the audio instructs as I resume the tape and tuck the files in the bag. "This is Sunset Strip and home to solitary confinement. This is where some of the most ruthless criminals spent many days on Alcatraz."

The tape feels like a damn treasure hunt dragging us around the cellhouse. All there is to discover are useless historical facts and figures. Leave the past where it belongs. I don't have time to spend all day learning about a bunch of thugs. The annoying man on the tape eats at my patience, leading me to unplug the headphones.

I make it around the corner when a faint rumbling sounds in the distance. The sound isn't part of the audio tour. The roars are complemented with vibrations on the ground. My teeth chatter and my sight blurs while tourists scream. People run wild in fear, dinosaurs on the verge of extinction from a meteor.

I've lived in San Fran for years now. I've experienced several earthquakes that impacted the Bay Area in one way or another. Those didn't concern me then and this doesn't concern me now. Sure, this one's a little more aggressive, but it's the price of living on the West Coast. Deal with it or move out east with my whiny brother.

The vibrations last another thirty seconds. "What was that?" a man asks, standing with his wife. "Are we gonna be alright?" He sees my calm demeanor and mistakes it for comfort.

"Yes . . . we're fine," I respond, chuckling at their life-or-death reactions. "It's not the first quake here n' it sure as hell won't be the last."

The two stare at me as the man takes the woman's hand and powerwalks toward the exit. A bunch of babies. Although a precaution, island employees and rangers storm the building from every entrance. They console concerned visitors, sharing the classic 'drop, cover and hold' instructions they learned in their one-hour training session. Maybe they'll put us on a ferry and ship us home. The quakes could be a good thing if they can get us out of here. It's back to the mainland and back to work.

"Hey . . . what's the protocol when somethin' like this happens?" I ask a ranger with a smile on my face. I'm the only one who sees a silver lining in the quakes.

"Hate t'break this news t'ya friend. Standard procedure's t'evacuate the island."

A man like this thrives in these situations. What could go wrong at an old prison littered with tourists? An exciting time to work on Alcatraz. Now to grab Michael and get the hell off this ancient rock. He couldn't be more than a minute or two ahead on the tape.

"One more question for ya." I tap the guard's shoulder. "Where does the tour go after Sunset Strip? I have t'grab my brother before we leave."

"Not a problem. This's actually the last stop on the tour friend. If you can't find your brother up here he's prob'ly already headed t'the dock."

He went to the dock. The selfish bastard only acts brave and fearless. No doubt he pushed women and children out of the way to get a comfortable spot on the first ferry out. I can't wait to see the look on his face the whole ride home—that fearful kid.

A trip downstairs in the cellhouse leads to more screaming guests. A few fallen chunks of concrete rest on the floor, which somehow makes visitors think the world's ending. Rangers attempt to manage the funnel of people piling up at the cellhouse exit, a clogged drain of people waiting for some lubricant. I exit a few minutes later and proceed to walk down the winding concrete path, eventually sifting through strangers at the dock. It's the Titanic. Everyone's looking to toss their family on a ferry. 'I'll wait here. Go on without me,' a dad gets his fifteen seconds of bravery. Relax, man. It's just another quake.

My path weaves in and out of the dock's crowd. I push my way to the edge of the dock, then back toward the nearest building. I walk through the nearby bathroom—maybe he needed to take a leak. He's not in there either. Come on, brother. Show yourself.

A man comes over the loudspeaker to share news that the first ferry's arriving in a few minutes. No ferry has left the island since the quakes, meaning my sad brother's strolling around Alcatraz somewhere other than the dock. In the meantime, waiting will provide the perfect opportunity to get some work done. Uninterrupted work at a time like this. That's corporate loyalty.

It's calming knowing other employees respect me enough to grab the reins while I'm not present. That's what being on the management track's all about—delegation, organization and the right mix of intimidation. It's a competitive job market. That said, I still don't trust anyone on the team to get the job done the way I can. If I have a chance at getting that C-suite position, then I can't risk anything going wrong during Monday's meeting. It's still my time to shine.

Michael would be blue tie guy if he was at the company. He'd be Sam, buttons waiting to pop off his dress shirt while he looks like a deer in headlights; someone whose head's in the clouds. He's the person with the lack of drive, allowing everyone to step on them as they continue their climb without lending a hand to their stepping stool. This contrast between us forces my brother to see me as a man engulfed in his work. He's right, but for the wrong reasons.

I came from nothing. My parents dumped me off at a foster home and continued living their lives without the burden of a son. Bouncing from foster home to foster home each year's no way to live. I chose to stick my middle finger up at the world after turning eighteen. I graduated from a prestigious college. I married someone from that same prestigious college. I make more money than any of my friends. That's the way to live. If my real parents saw me now, I'd give them a tour of my million-dollar home followed by a peek at my bank account before sending them packing.

This is why I'm here, perched on a railing with my head buried in papers while others panic. All that's until authorities try to file me onto the first ferry at threat of imprisonment. Tourists board in a single-file line, allowing me to scan each passerby for a sign of my brother like airport security.

The first ferry departs while I slip through each ranger's fingers, reverting to sitting on the railing again. A second ferry arrives ten minutes later. More people proceed up the walkway and onto the boat. Still no Michael. The second ferry departs fifteen minutes later, and another arrives. The process continues for another half hour. Any remaining patience takes off from the island as the fourth boat departs.

"Sir we need you t'pack up your belongings n' line up t'board," an officer instructs. "The final ferry of the day's almost here."

"Trust me, I'd love nothin' more than t'get outta here." I stand up from the railing and tuck the folder under my arm. "I'm waiting for my brother. He's not from here n'—"

"I don't care who you're waitin' for. This's a serious matter n' safety's our only concern right now."

These guys are blowing this out of proportion. Even so, I have no choice but to wait for the final ferry. More individuals stroll down the walkway over to the dock. This dock ranger might lay down the hammer of authority, but the rest of these phoneys must not be as strict across the rest of the island if people are still making their way to bay level. The final ferry hasn't arrived yet. I have some time to track down my brother. He doesn't make anything easy. What'd I expect?

The growing concern for my brother's absence stems from the heat I'll get from my wife and mom if I lose him. I'll never hear the end of it if I arrive home without the leech at my side. I'd be on that first ferry if it was any other adult besides that wimp.

The most probable scenario is his lifeless body sunken on a bench or staring off into the distance at the edge of the island. He does that—letting his brain float off into oblivion. The cellhouse was the last place I saw him, so it'll kick off my game of hide-and-seek now.

Rangers continue to ask visitors to leave while they walk around with their thumbs up their asses. I blend in with the confused crowd. It takes me ten minutes of walking around to realize I'm doing laps around the cellhouse. Still no Michael. Goddammit.

A ranger notices my return to the front of the building for the third—maybe sixth—time. He requests I make my way to the dock as instructed. He takes it upon himself to escort me back to the rest of the remaining visitors without another person in sight in over five minutes. I'm his number one priority now. It's back to the dock.

The final ferry boards. Each passerby's a stranger. No Michael. My brother isn't here. Fear grows outward from my core like mold in the back of a fridge. I'm the very last person to board. There's no way he walked past me unless he caught a ferry before the quakes. That timing doesn't add up either.

A payphone awaits me at pier thirty-three along with a difficult conversation. My feet ache from wandering around the island as well as the ferry looking for the man. My eyes are sore from staring at these documents all day. This conversation's the last thing I need right now.

"Marybeth. It's me, Robb . . ." I start as the nanny picks up the other end of the line.

"Marybeth left," someone else responds. It's Meredith. "I came home after those awful quakes. Where are you guys? Headed home soon?"

Her questions confirm Michael didn't already make it home. The conversation can't wait any longer. Any further delay hurts my case.

"Honey listen," I respond. I'm unsure how to angle the strange situation. "I'm sure it's not a big deal or anything. I just needed t'tell you that . . . Michael n' I got separated when they evacuated the island. I waited at the dock for as long as I—"

"Where's Michael, Robb?" she interjects. Her tone's already elevated to the shrill I've grown to dread. "What're you trynna tell me?"

"He's missing. I mean not missing . . . he was with me n' then he wasn't. He's a grown man so I'm sure he's fine. Anyway . . . I'm headed home now. We can wait for him there."

"He's not a grown man," she argues. "He's a troubled man. Your mom expects us t'watch out for him." She gasps, taking a second to finish her thought. "You don't think he . . . you know . . . could've done something like that?"

My brother destroyed his home and job with a single toss of a stone. Is he capable of offing himself? He's a depressed man who thinks he's a philosophical warrior. He wouldn't question his own existence; he does that to society as a whole. Killing himself means throwing in the towel on the way his mind works. Jesus, even thinking about it gives me a headache. Not suicide. Never suicide for my brother.

I try to share these lighter beliefs on the phone. No words stop my wife from worrying. Her arguments are fair yet jump to outrageous conclusions. It'll work out. He'll show up and go back to his sad life. I'll go back to work. All will be right in no time.

My porch is a DMV waiting room in the evening. There's nothing to pass the time besides staring off into the street, waiting for my brother to stroll up. An hour passes. We go inside to eat, then it's back to sitting on the porch. Another hour flies by without any sign of him.

Meredith breaks a little after five in the evening. She storms into the house and I immediately hear the phone dialing. She calls the pier first—no sign of him. She dials the police station next—they don't have him. The hospital. Local hotels. He's vanished.

"We're telling her." She comes back outside. I put my work to the side to hear her out. "You're calling n' telling her what's going on. The sooner you do that the better."

It's my brother. It's appropriate that I break the news to my mom. Of course, I know what's waiting on the other end of the line. She'll get all confused at first, letting me know 'that's not like Michael.' That's not like her baby. She'll put on her investigative hat and state the obvious: 'Did you ask the rangers on the island?' She does exactly that.

What begins as curiosity transforms into anger. She blames me for what happened. The conversation sounds scripted as her reaction to any problem's already written in stone. It's the same formula from start to finish. I can envision her pointing a finger at me over the phone as she lets me know she'll be on the first flight out in the morning. Hooray. More distractions from work and more blame headed my way.

Are you happy, brother? Is this what you wanted?

This was his own choosing. Depressed or not, he's in charge of his decisions. He'll show up and we'll pour an unnecessary amount of attention on him. He wants to see us broken. He wants to tear us down, then show us the worrying was for nothing. This is the same as his job. This is his apartment. It's a desperate cry for help.

I won't let him ruin my life, too.

CANNONBALL

It's been three days. Three days without a call or a knock on the door from my brother. It's ironic how people experiencing the repercussions of a missing person are often the ones left in the dark. No answers. More questions.

The cops are no help. There hasn't been a single lead on his whereabouts since they opened a missing person investigation a day and a half ago. Everyone assumes he'll show up dead in a ditch or washed ashore. Three days and we're where we were the day he disappeared.

Worst of all? The meeting was a fucking mess. Mark and Nate—the dimwits—took control of the room on Monday. This 'family emergency' put the rest of the report in their hands while I tended to police visits, a nagging wife and a crying mother. This was my chance to stand out. It all crumbled at the worst possible time.

The story couldn't have been clearer to the police: a man with depression experienced a complete mental collapse. A total breakdown. He traveled across the country to tour a place that's every suicidal person's dream. Rocky shores. Steep cliffs. Sharp metal. The facts do add up—I'll admit that. It's hard for anyone to imagine another scenario. I'm not letting him off that easy, though.

They say Alcatraz was inescapable, a giant cell with hundreds of cells inside it. The hazardous conditions of the island are its guards. The icy water is its thick steel bars. According to the lead detective for my brother's disappearance, the current around the island keeps its victim sucked underwater until they drown. If the current doesn't end them, their body's sure to be crushed against the rocky shore. "It'd be like crushing an orange t'a pulp. There'd only be juice left." The detective's words, not mine. The prick actually said that in front of my mom, wife and kids.

"Remind me . . . he saw that therapist for how long?" the detective asks.

We sit around the very kitchen table where he ate with us a few days ago. No work and no television to distract me this time makes matters much more tense.

Everything the detective says is in past tense.

"He was how old?"

"When was his flight back t'New York?"

"You were his only sibling?"

I know he's not a doctor, but this isn't healthy bedside manner. He looks like he's holding back a chuckle after letting out each question. I suppose he thinks there are bigger fish to fry. His case is closed and I can see why he feels that way.

"At least four years." My mom answers every question for us. "He was seeing that therapist for four years or more."

She wipes away the waterfall of tears with a used napkin. Red pasta sauce from last night's dinner's crusted on the paper, so it looks like she's tending to a nosebleed. I'm doing anything to keep myself distracted at this table.

"But he's had on n' off blocks of therapy during his entire life," she continues. "Of course he's always claimed he doesn't need it. He knows the only way I'll leave him alone's if he continues t'attend though."

"N' were you under the impression he was still seeing this therapist?" The man resumes the interrogation. "N' taking medication as well?" My mom nods in response. "I see. Well I'm sorry t'tell you this. We spoke with Doctor Polk this morning. He let us know your son stopped attending his sessions three months ago." Gasp. And he calls himself a detective? "He also informed us the last refill of his prescription was filled two months ago. He was off his meds for quite some time now."

He's reached a silent verdict without a body. The questions he lobs across the table grow darker. They're all meant to force a theory down our throats. This dude doesn't care about any other scenario we toss his way.

Like a good officer, he assured my mom the search would

continue for some time. This was a complete lie that I can't complain about as it keeps my mom hopeful for a little more time. When the detective leaves, it's just me left to talk to. The kids are over at Marybeth's for a few days, so I'm stuck in a house overflowing with estrogen. Optimism—a dangling cat toy—keeps their attention. That, and taking frustrations out on me.

"You should've kept a closer eye on him!" my mom yells not a full second after the detective shuts the front door. "Are you sure you're tellin' us everything?"

Meredith questions my intentions, too. She sees my annoyance building like an active volcano on the verge of eruption and only fuels the fire. Both women assume I had something to do with my brother's disappearance. Their not-so-subtle remarks suggest I could've prevented this. Yeah, right. My brother couldn't protect himself and that's all there is to it.

"I'm not the one who went off my meds months ago!" I snap back. I'm losing it.

Life's problems require someone to blame, someone to take the heat like blue tie guy at work. A bad quarter at the company? Give someone the boot in exchange for a fresh, motivated face. I've never been in the hot seat before. Yet here I am, engulfed in flames thanks to these two women and my goddamn brother.

One argument turns into another until they make up an entire day's time. Then another day's time. And another. Days pass without an update. The lead detective drops by for a check-in and returns to busting teenagers at the mall. He's saving face and easing a guilty conscience. Meanwhile, fingers remain in my face. Big, fat fingers point at me. This leads to my work suffering again. When I can make it to the office, I realize how behind I am. The work moves forward while I remain stagnant. I'm trapped by my brother. My safety net drifts away as the current pulls me out.

The blame grows more personal with each argument. Stories from the past resurface courtesy of my mom. Meredith uses the whole situation to shine a light on flaws in our marriage. None of it makes sense anymore. It persists nonetheless.

The blame's a cancer that spreads like wildfire, eating at

everything that matters. My job. My house. My marriage. My kids. My brother remains victorious. He's somewhere out there. The police can have their theories while I feel my brother's sick smile from a distance. My gut tells me he's alive, but I'd never admit that to my present audience in fear of sparking another argument. The desire to prove my mom and wife wrong has subsided. I want answers for my own reasons.

Whatever happened to my brother was not my fault. Once he's found, this will be put to rest. My job will return. My life will come flying back like a boomerang tossed a little too far.

"It's time." My mom enters the living room one morning. Her arms extend like the Virgin Mary. The Virgin Mother has entered the room with a decision we anticipated coming any day now. "It's time t'put our boy t'rest. He deserves t'be respected . . . honored. Every day that passes shows our selfishness n' avoidance. The detective spread out everything in front of us n' we've ignored it. My son deserves our respect now."

"T'rest?" I ask, standing up from the sofa. "It's been two fuckin' weeks! I take vacations longer than that."

Meredith places her arm across my chest—a human seatbelt. "She's right Robb. This can't continue. This isn't an average missing person case. The facts add up. They're all there. His actions leading up t'this paint a clear picture. The detective said the case'll remain open for the foreseeable future. They'll do their due diligence t'find him but we all know what they're gonna find. Your mother's right."

They're exhausted—numb from weeks of tears, confusion and frustration. They've hit the breaking point. The pessimist detective's hypnotism worked. They've accepted my brother's fate. Give them anything to end this emotional rollercoaster. What they don't realize is they've dragged me through the mud along the way and left me there. This destroyed my chances of getting that promotion and I won't stand for that.

I try to state my case for holding out a little longer. They refuse until another argument ensues. A vigil of sorts is what brings them peace of mind. An event like that also throws me further under the bus I was wrongfully tossed in front of. I won't take the fall for my brother's disappearance. They'll deny blaming me yet carry the belief to their graves, easing their delicate minds.

Déjà vu sets in as we begin organizing my brother's arrangements over the next few days. Memories of my dad's passing resurface each time the discussion resumes. It's difficult to plan events like this knowing there's no body involved. The whole thing remains a mystery. It's troubling that everyone's okay with this. At least there was closure with my dad; we knew what killed him. We saw his body, proving he was dead. How can they say the same works here?

My mom insists the services should happen back home in New York. My necessary involvement in the charade adds another layer of complexity in reclaiming my job. I'm trying to Band-Aid the oozing wound that represents the time I've spent away from the company. Splashes of blood squeeze out the sides onto my khaki pants. It's a useless effort.

The uncomfortable services take place three weeks after the disappearance. Three weeks. Mark can barely close in that time. It's a thought that continues to trouble me. Three weeks of blame and a finale in the form of a vigil—a quaint, Chappaqua vigil. It's a big town, yet no more than five additional people show up to 'remember' the man no one knew. My wife, mom, kids and I fill most of the space. "Spread out," my mom commands. She's trying to make the open area feel full for her own comfort. My youngest son cries from across the room. I toss him a wave paired with a smile. He cries harder after the gesture.

There's not a shred of evidence pointing to death. Not suicide. If anything, the lack of clues warrants further investigation. This is what I tell my brother's coworker, stopping mid-conversation to tend to a nearly empty flask. How else am I supposed to get through this bullshit? I need a mask to hide my frustration.

The cross-country funeral stripped me from three more days of work. Three days closer to becoming blue tie guy. This is all I can think about at these laughable services. My mom smiles, comforted by nonexistent closure. I cheers her with a sip from the flask.

My brother managed to burn all his bridges; however, he was never big on human contact to begin with. He poured gasoline on his coworkers and family before tossing a match over his shoulder. He didn't look back. I don't feel bad for him. I'm surprised this place isn't completely empty right now. I suppose he failed in that sense.

A vigil's the intermission between life and death. It's a celebration of purgatory. Pictures from a decade ago bully a photo of my brother from two years ago. Let's remember a less pathetic version of him, please. My mom's closing words complement the visuals around the room—sad and empty. She talks to Meredith more than she talks to me. She relays strange stories about my brother—tales no one gives a shit about. This is why my wife's more involved in this act than me. She can wear a mask without a layer of liquor.

No one else speaks about my brother, so the other five people pass the time by asking where the coffee cake's from. "Not sure. My mom bought it," my record repeats.

"Why aren't you eating more?" my mom asks. She drowns her sorrow with another piece of coffee cake. It's not enjoyable, but it's better than the taste in the other room. At least chewing's an excuse not to speak. I take an entire piece and cram it in my mouth when a guest approaches me.

The God-awful experience can't end sooner. The charade carries on far too long. 'He's not dead,' I tell myself. Any verbalization of the theory lowers me deeper into a pit of blame. The idea remains my little secret. In the meantime, I'll keep my mouth shut with this horrible coffee cake and regular sips of liquor.

My ass is back on an airplane fourteen hours and twenty-seven minutes after the services. I counted every fleeting minute in my head until this point. It's the first time in weeks my mom isn't ramming accusations down my throat. The new assassin to avoid now is Meredith. She continues to aim her pistol at my head. I stick the barrel in my mouth in protest. I dare her to make matters worse. I know she won't do that in front of the kids.

The experience was supposed to end an exhausting month. I

should be free of my brother's tight grasp. Get me back to a busy life, the type I know best—a working life. I'm supposed to feel that motivational fire burn. Give me that fuel required to reclaim my job. The fire's fading, though; my brother pisses all over it.

The much-needed motivation's replaced by confusion. The cliché of 'unfinished business' floats around my head. I should be thinking about my career. Instead, the business calling my name is my brother. I shake it off only for it to cling tighter.

The following days fill with optimism—hopeless optimism. The confines of an enclosed office distract me from unwanted personal thoughts. The 'unfinished business' is buried with paperwork yet fights its way to the top at the end of the day. I can't catch up. I'm falling. The fire fades.

I pour a glass of whiskey at night, a liquid dinner for one. There are never any leftovers after this dinner. I down another glass while staring at the television. This is dessert. I can usually close my eyes after a few more splashes. I close them from that fucking 'unfinished business.'

Meredith doesn't take well to the drinking. She can smell liquor before I walk in the door every evening and before I walk out every morning. She takes an animated whiff of my suit jacket before I leave for work. I reek of betrayal courtesy of the bottle. The stench becomes an excuse to distance me from the kids, too.

"They can smell that shit on you," Meredith whines.

I'm numb to her complaining; it doesn't affect me. It can't affect me because he's not gone. My brother's not dead. No body, no evidence and no closed case. They blame me for this and the cure to the frustration's raising my fists to any form of emotion. A raw feeling soars upward from the depths of who the fuck knows where and tries to grab me by the neck. I drown it with alcohol. It creeps back and I shove its head under the golden liquid again. Stay down and shut up.

One brutal weeknight ends with more drowning than usual. An empty bottle of whiskey balances halfway off the nightstand, waiting to crash into a million pieces like my life. I sit at the edge of the bed praying Meredith's nightshift doesn't send her home early. This much liquor should leave me face-down on a pillow breathing in my own puke or lying dead on the floor.

A drunken brain explores. Mine decides to replay the last month on repeat. A perfect life shatters as my brother enters the picture, turning it to shit. A pancake's flipped and left to burn. He disappears and leaves me drawing the short straw for his grand finale. I was with him that afternoon. Not a single square foot of that tiny island wasn't littered with visitors. I couldn't get more than ten feet without a ranger getting in my face and telling me to head to the dock. A different fire grows inside me now.

My body tosses and turns throughout the night. Confusion. Dreams of my brother. Dreams of having my life back together. The night ends with a bright light shining in my face accompanied by a stabbing headache. This is how most nights end these days.

Most people go for a glass of orange juice with a greasy breakfast on mornings like this. Maybe two Tylenol to wash it all down, too. This isn't one of those times. The cute mug my kid made me in preschool's filled with whiskey. It called my name and yanked me out of bed. The booze, not the mug.

It goes on. Hangovers and sobriety hover above me, both waiting to strike like lightning as they're silenced with another drink. Each morning I fill my flask to the brim. Each evening a light nightcap turns into blurred vision as I stumble up the stairs, holding onto the railing so I don't break my hip. A judgmental wife awaits me upstairs when she's not on a late nightshift. She shakes her head and crosses her arms. None of it matters when I don't remember the argument by morning.

I watch myself become a shadow of the successful man I've created over the last five years. Each day I lie and tell myself change is around the corner. Just another day away. That change never arrives. Any fleeting moment of sobriety lets the demons back in. I know those insistent emotions are waiting for their chance to strike, prompting me to deal with reality. Is my brother really gone? This must be my fault. Those are sober ideas. A few more swigs and the weak theories vanish.

My boss is quick to observe the change in my behavior, too. The over-observant prick should've resigned by now, yet he lingers on my current state. He thinks he knows what's best for me. He introduced me to this place and will forever hold that over my head.

I leave Meredith in the morning to be judged by this asshole. He smells the booze on me like she does. He walks in my office at the start of each day to say 'Good morning' now. He never did that. He wants to check up on me, staring with those same judgmental eyes that rolled goodbye earlier in the morning at home. I don't remember getting married twice.

The prick calls me into his office for a change one afternoon. It's the first time in weeks he's wanted to meet with me and it's a promising change of pace. He's breaking the news. He's finally giving me that promotion to set me back on track.

"Thanks for meeting with me." He greets me with a frown.

My expectations are shredded into a bah-zillion strips of nothing by the mere tone in his words and look on his face. It's bad news; I'd expect a smile and a hand extended across the desk by now if it was anything else. I begin sweating and alcohol seeps out my pores, dripping onto his mahogany desk. He diverts his attention from my eyes to the suit jacket that hasn't been washed in over a week. Stains from whatever frozen dinner I ate last night color the brown suit an ugly tie-dye. I don't care about these judgments. My reputation defines me.

"Robb . . ." he pauses. He shakes his head the same way Meredith does every night before bed. "I'm not sure what the deal is but we've suffered because of it. I mean I've got Clarissa picking up the slack for Christ's sake. She's my damn secretary."

I revert to staring at him. I imagine telling him about my 'unfinished business.' I wonder if he'd take my side or everyone else's. The lingering eyes dismiss that idea and tell me his decision would be the latter. Prick.

"Listen . . . you know I'm aware of your brother's disappearance," he adds. Here we go. "It's an awful awful shame n' you have my condolences Robb. With that said, at the end a the day I'm running a company. This's your team. If the leader isn't in a good state a mind then . . . well it's like a chicken running with its head chopped off. So t'speak of course."

"You of all people know how much I've invested in this job," I respond. Desperation takes the wheel. Give me a blue tie and call it a day. "Just gimme a little more time t'get my shit together."

He sighs, rubbing his balding head. "I'm sorry Robb. I've already spoken with the board. They wanna have someone else step in 'til we figure out somethin' long term. You've been my right-hand man for a few years now so I'm willing to give ya the time you need t'get your head straight. When you're ready there's a spot in the ranks for ya. Nothing's changed in that sense."

It's a surprise and at the same time expected. I should care more about this, but the booze blanket makes me immune to any sort of news these days. The prick can go to hell. He has no idea what I'm going through. I've dedicated my life to this blood-sucking career and all it took was a few weeks to lose it all. The new flame roars and I don't care about the rest.

"That's fine," I respond, refusing to put up a fight. My emotions won't get the better of me. "Do I need an exit interview or something?"

He looks at me. "An exit interview?" He's dumbfounded by my lack of reaction. I won't be blue tie guy. I'll maintain my dignity. "No an exit interview won't be necessary. Best I can do's offer some additional leave time. Under the table of course. Take it n' use it t'keep you n' the family on your feet these next few weeks 'til we find somethin' else for ya."

"That'd be great." I close the curtain. Something else?

That's it. Five years of sweat ends with the few slurred words I'm able to spill out. I'll get a few more weeks of paid leave before needing to work my way up the ladder again. I decline his offer. I spit it back on his balding head.

Polishing off the last of the flask before the drive home leaves me in no condition to break the news to Meredith. She gives me enough shit on a daily basis. I crash-land on the bed minutes after stumbling through the front door. I'll pull off the illusion of a brutal cold that leaves me bedridden. She'll believe that. 'It's the flu,' I'll tell her. 'It gets around this time of year.' That's enough to buy some solitude for the evening.

"This's getting t'you isn't it?" Meredith peeks in the bedroom. She's still cloaked in her teal scrubs, about to leave for another nightshift. This is the only nightgown I've seen her wear in years. She shuts the bedroom door behind her to prevent the kids from hearing the conversation to come. "Robb I know this isn't you feeling sick. It might be enough for the boys t'believe but you've been acting up enough for me t'know something else is goin' on with you."

"It's all bullshit."

"What's all bullshit?" I feel her sit on the edge of the bed while my head buries itself deeper in the pillow.

"He ruined it all. He did this t'me . . . t'us . . . as some fuckin' move in a secret strategy t'ruin my life." The words are mumbled into the pillow.

"He's gone honey," she responds, resting an arm on my head that's still quick-sanding into the pillow. "I know you two weren't close n' that's prob'ly weighing on you. We need t'accept it n' push forward now. There's more family than him t'preoccupy yourself with at the end a the day."

There's not more to worry about besides this. He destroyed my life. He's out there somewhere reaping all the benefits. I feel him watching from afar. My career's destroyed. I haven't been sober in weeks. I'm defending myself to everyone. There's nothing else to preoccupy myself with.

"I know that," I mutter. "It's been a rough time. I honestly don't feel well either. I'm not lying about that." I'm lying about that. She doesn't need to know.

"Well have you considered therapy? I know you said you don't believe in that kinda stuff. I just—"

"No!" I cut her off. I drag my head out of the pillow. Why's this conversation still going on? "No, I'm not seeing a therapist. Lemme figure this out in my own way."

"This behavior ends now then," she complains. The good cop act's over. "I can't take care a this family by myself so you do whatever you need t'move on from this. You do it quickly though."

"I'll handle it," I assure her.

I'm not going back to work tomorrow. I'm not going to therapy either. I'll do as she asks and find a way to move on from this on my own terms—through my own methods.

Tomorrow I'm going back to where this started. I'm grabbing my life back from the man who stole it from me.

THE WANDERER

Heavy cigarette smoke interrupts the musty scent of mold growing on every inch of the wet dungeon. I am not a smoker, yet my nostrils welcome the odor. The natural scent down here is far more unbearable than that of exhaled tobacco. That, and the foggy smoke assures me I am not completely abandoned.

A few days have passed—perhaps three. I would not know for certain as my biological clock was unplugged the first few hours down here. So much time has passed that my eyes have adjusted to complete blackness. I would go blind if tossed in the Sun God's beams of light at this very moment.

The captain opens the latch above every few hours, sometimes to toss down scraps of food and other times to collect a pail of feces. On rare occasions he sends a bucket of water raining down on me for his sheer enjoyment. I should feel humiliated. Instead, every interaction piques my interest in this peculiar situation.

Curiosity reigns supreme while an aching body and empty mind fight for that same top position. Even a man like me, who thrives on solitude, breaks with enough time. I will not last down here for much longer if I do not appease the characters—the actors—above.

The item keeping me sane is the little book. The Sun God's sliver of power shines through to brighten the object, leaving me huddled in a corner shifting it back and forth with each line to remain within the Almighty's rays of glory. Its pages seem to freeze when Howard Madison's entry arrives. Warden Howard Madison. The resemblance is uncanny. That dead-eyed stare remains burned into my mind. I am certain I interacted with that man.

If this was a hostage situation it should have ended by now. Surely, a rescue mission would be carried out. Boats would land on the dock. Countless marines would come trudging onto land like the beaches of Normandy; meanwhile, my captors would use their hostages as leverage. Neither scenario has played out. At least three days have passed with nothing except this little book and the smell of mold to comfort me.

Attempting to catch someone's attention through shouting resulted in abuse from the captain's baton. My body continues to recover from the blows on my first night here. Fresh bruises and dripping blood are the last things I need right now. I must go about this strategically.

A sign near the dock informed me there was a time when American Indians took control of Alcatraz. 'Indians Welcome,' the hand-painted message read as we stepped off the ferry. Indians controlled the island for months without government interference. It took an island-swallowing fire to toss them out. Is a similar situation unfolding now? Not Indians, but perhaps a terrorist group. Theories leave my head aching while the rest of my body does the same.

It is time to crawl my way out of this sinkhole. I will claw my way to the surface if I must. I do not wish to live among the sun-worshippers of this world. At the same time, I cannot wither away in a damp basement at the hands of two or more lunatics. And to think they called me crazy for bidding farewell to an underpaying job and an overpriced studio apartment.

The Sun God rested the last time the captain came down. The subtle light on the little book hints at a few hours having passed. The man is bound to appear soon if this cruel routine resumes. Even the rebels cannot avoid the seduction of routine. When the latch does open, I must ensure they do not take the one item keeping me sane. They cannot seize the little book. Hiding it in this raggedy attire is no easy feat. Fortunately, time is all I have in the dungeon. It finds its resting spot in my back, tucked underneath loose-fitting underwear.

The uncomfortable lump remains there for a few hours. I can feel it leaving an imprint on my back until my skin goes numb. It stabs me with a papercut every time I shift to the side. I cannot lose this little book. The pain is worth it.

My instincts were accurate. The silence breaks as keys rustle above followed by the thick metal door creaking open. Light floods the darkness until a shadowy figure steps in its way. I put my hand over my eyes as if staring directly at the Almighty.

"Back against the wall if you wanna eat," the captain orders. "If you don't I'll personally make sure you watch the rest a the vermin down there enjoy it while you rot. They'll eat you next then."

I follow the madman's demands without putting up a fight. I am a compliant hostage. I scoot backward—the little book still stabbing me in the back—until I hit the wall. He makes his way down the stairs.

I greet him when his thick leather boots crash onto the dungeon floor. "Good morning Captain Peters. I've been thinking. I believe I'm ready t'speak with the warden. That's if he's ready t'hear the whole truth."

"You better not be playin' games here," he responds. He kicks the tray of food toward me. I scoot it to the side and look at him in the eyes as I remain cross-legged below the tower of a sun-worshipper.

"No games sir. Truthfully . . . a mind wanders too much down here. It's really getting t'me." A bit of truth is mixed in with the lies. The reason I am revealing this is to get to the man in charge of this charade. I must talk to the warden.

The captain obliges, slapping icy handcuffs on my wrists. He proceeds to shove me up the stairs. He uses the baton to push me along which I am grateful for as he could otherwise feel the little square lump pressed against my back.

The cellhouse looks different in the daylight. It looks more colorful, even cleaner. Would a group of lunatics—rebels—go as far as to refurbish every square inch of the cellhouse? Another consideration that does not sit well. Something bigger is going on here.

I peer to the side as we pass B-block on the route to see the warden. A group of men stand single file. They are draped in the same faded-blue attire I am wearing. More men resembling the captain pace down the middle of the two lines of men. I would rub my eyes if I was not cuffed. Hundreds of other men are being held hostage on this tourist-filled island. Why is no one coming to the rescue?

I am not able to process the obscure scene before the captain rushes me along, not wanting me to see what is going on. The cellhouse's surroundings change as we enter a section of the building designed for staff members. An officer's lounge and a few other offices look out of place in the otherwise grim building. The ground is carpeted and the walls painted a navy blue, a few shades below the blackness from the dungeon. The entire setup is as if two very separate buildings were smashed together by a blind architect.

Peters points toward an open door at the end of the hallway. He nods his head. "That's it. This's your meeting. You fuck this up n' it's the last time you see the light a day."

I walk down the hall as Peters follows a few paces behind. It feels like death row; however, I know this is my only option at this point. I must break free of the dungeon.

"Mister Field . . ." the man in the room greets me with a long pause. This was the robed man from the other night. He sits at a wide desk across the room. "Please take a seat. I had a feeling it wouldn't be long before I saw you again. I presume you're here t'shed some light on what occurred late last week."

This is the man pictured in the little book—there is no doubt about it. Either Robb is playing a sick joke with his present or this man believes he is Warden Madison resurrected. Another sharp stabbing hits my head as theorizing becomes too much to bear. I must first focus on why I am here.

The room is littered with papers—documents, folders and more—that make it look quite modern. It resembles an active office. Is this a park ranger's workplace?

The warden snaps his fingers at me, bringing my attention back to his familiar face. The moving face is an uncomfortable sight after days of looking at his small portrait in the little book. Howard Madison. The resemblance is identical.

"Yes of course sir," I answer to his delight. "You see . . . I arrived on a boat not long ago. In fact it was right around when the captain found me in that cell."

"But we didn't put you there did we?" He leans in with growing interest. "How'd you get there in the first place?"

I am flying by the seat of my pants. Robb does not lie this well. I suppose this is what happens when you feel alive for the first time in your life. Curiosity takes control; that combined with fear fuels every word spewing out of my mouth.

"No . . . you didn't put me there. They missed me. Those guards missed me on the dock when they were taking count that day. When I couldn't find a way t'escape I decided t'hide out in one a the vacant cells in Sunset Strip. It was dark, isolated n' provided an easy way outta the cellhouse. The door slid shut on me n' I was stuck there for days. That's until Captain Peters found me."

He ruffles through a stack of papers on his desk. I peer over my shoulder and the captain has exited the room. It is me and the warden, who is now flipping through papers on his desk the way I imagine Robb doing while at dinner with his family.

"Ah yes." He pulls out a single piece of pink paper. "The arrivals from last Tuesday . . . of course. However the list states everyone who boarded that ship for the transfer. Your name's not accounted for here. No Michael Field at all. Tell me . . . how's that possible?"

No words. The game is more complex than I imagined. He wants to play a level deeper. Documentation to go along with his story adds an exceptional layer of depth. Still no words. His stare sharpens with each second of silence. Tick. Tock.

"Captain Peters . . ." The warden looks past me, waving at the doorway across the room. "It seems we have more trouble with this fool than anticipated. It's been nearly five days since we came across Mister Field. It was another two since the last transfer docked." He shifts his eyes back to me. "Someone didn't do their job that day Michael. You slipped through the cracks n' the blame'll be pointed at me. Know that I will not be the one who pays for it."

"Yes sir. That's fair," the captain agrees. "What d'we do with him?"

"Lord knows where he came from. He's our responsibility now though." The warden shakes his head. I forget this is an act at times like this. I am convinced the man believes this situation is real. "Captain, please ensure we get some documentation for The Rock's latest arrival. Before that, get him acquainted with his new home. Drag him t'Broadway with the rest of the scum. There're a few open cells on ground level of B-block."

Astounding. The experience reveals itself to be more believable with each interaction. Again, I would clap if my hands were not cuffed. There are no words at a time like this. I have remained silent since the warden asked me that last question.

They are beyond negotiation. Any fraction of their past sun-worshiping selves has vanished. These are creatures much different than rebels. And yet, I continue to play the role of prisoner. I am silent and accepting of my inescapable new home. What discoveries await me in B-block?

"You heard the man!" Captain Peters slaps the back of my head. "Let's get you to your cell. I'm sure the rest a the cretins are dying t'meet ya."

The dark days in the dungeon were filled with my flipping through the little book. I memorized every word in that sixty-six-page brick. Some of the most famous—and infamous—prisoners, wardens and guards were present throughout its pages. One name never appeared despite my thorough search, though. There was no profile on a Captain Peters. If the older man chose the role of a powerful warden that complemented his appearance, then why would this other rebel not also choose a meaningful role? Why create something out of thin air?

Peters escorts me back to the cellblocks. The spotless concrete floor glistens; you could eat off of it. The cream cell bars, catwalk and walls remind me of a desert. Each cell we pass is full of items. Beds, blankets, clothing and more fill the cramped spaces. People are living here. If I remember the man in my mind, this was where most inmates spent their time on Alcatraz.

The line of men positioned down the length of Broadway from before are nowhere to be found now. Instead, various whispers echo around me like spirits. One voice yells from the second level, "Hey what ya do t'get such a long stint in the hole?"

Word must travel fast. It looks as if the other hostages have assimilated to the storytelling within these walls. They gave into madness, likely fearful for their lives. Was this their fallback after other solutions proved pointless?

Captain Peters tosses me into a cell on the lower tier of B-block. I fall to the floor, my legs still Jell-O from the extended time in isolation. He turns around and yells down the hallway, "Goddammit Douglas! Close one-five-four already will you?"

A lever cranks at the other end of Broadway. The cell door slides shut with the finale of a loud bang when properly sealed. How did they figure out how to operate the cell doors? Those rusted levers had locks on them and had not been operated in decades.

"What now?" I ask the captain. We are face-to-face across the steel bars. "What's the end goal? Money? Fame? Whatever it is you better act fast before the fun's over."

He steps closer to the bars. A hard snort precedes his head tilting back and a wad of spit flying across the bars. "You'll learn t'shut your mouth soon enough. You're one fuckup away from goin' back t'the dungeon." He remains in perfect character.

The cell is more cramped than I recall studying during the tour. I stepped inside an open cell near the beginning of the audiotape and it felt somewhat spacious compared to my former studio apartment. It does not look nor feel that way now.

Half the room is filled with a single bed tucked against the lime green walls. The green clashes with the beige paint around the rest of the cellhouse. The fighting colors remind me of key lime pie. A disgusting, concrete key lime pie. The little space the bed does not consume is occupied by a miniature toilet. A white sink, two empty shelves and two tray-like boards are attached to the wall. Add a hostage to the mix and there is barely enough room to turn around.

As tight as the room is, a dry cell with an actual mattress is a pleasant sight—a dark shade of a silver lining. Fresh clothes lay folded on the mattress, a replica of my current getup. At least these clothes are spotless. The comparison between the two outfits is a before-and-after study of a meth addict.

I find myself lying on the bed looking up at the beige ceiling despite creeping confusion interfering with the curiosity. The single light above me pretends to be the Sun God. It will never hold up to the standards set forth by the Almighty.

At least a dozen other men are playing this game with me, yet no one is complaining. No one is scheming to escape. There are no whispers across the street mentioning rescue. Not a peep from one of the self-proclaimed guards nor the hostages to comfort me.

One idea bounces around my head before being tossed out the window and welcoming another with open arms. Minutes feel like hours. Each idea becomes more absurd than the previous. This is what I wanted. This is the Sun God's sadistic way of shattering my routine. Why do I crave more answers after everything I have been through?

An uncomfortable lump pokes my back as I rest on the bed. I reach my hand between my body and the mattress. The little book. The last possession from a former reality has not been confiscated. Seizing it would not affect my current state; however, an inner voice tells me to keep the object hidden. 'Keep it a secret,' the man in my mind speaks new words. I listen to him, pulling the little book out from my backside and shoving it beneath the rock-hard block this place considers a mattress. I imagine the rebels overlooking this cliché hiding location.

"The tape," I whisper. The origin of the man in my mind. The little book was not the sole item in my possession when the vibrations arrived. The headphones, cassette tape and audio device were left in Sunset Strip—in cell fourteen. The more this act plays out, the stronger the connection I feel toward the little book. The audiotape now pulls me in as well.

Inanimate objects were the bane of my existence not long ago. I loathed them so much that everything in my possession ended up on a curb. The essentials were all that was needed to survive. That feeling—that urge to leave it all behind—has changed. I do not know why these objects call my name.

"Hey . . . you there?" a voice breathes from outside my cell. "You awake cherry?"

This is not the man in my mind speaking this time. This is a different voice, one I have never heard before. Perhaps it is another hostage prepared to divulge information on how he wishes to return to a normal life. The inevitable return to routine. I recall the tape stating 'cherry' was a nickname given to new inmates in any given prison.

The voice guides me toward the back of the cell. I press my ear against the green grate near the floor to listen closer. Continued curiosity muffles the aches and pains on my body. Is someone looking for a way out? Or did they already discover it?

"Who's this?" I ask the mysterious voice.

I will not risk a rebel testing my behavior. Peters could be on the other side of the grate waiting to lay a few more whips of the baton on me. I do not wish to give him that pleasure.

"Dummy up there," the voice responds. "There're screws patrollin'. They're always makin' rounds. In the grate . . . speak closer in the grate n' we'll be good."

I follow the request with doubt, denying my initial instincts to avoid contact. I press my face against the chilled metal surface. My lips poke through one of the diamond holes while my eyes squeeze through two more. I imagine myself resembling a fish at this moment.

"Alright . . . I'm here. Who is this? You know what's goin' on?"

"Never mind who this is," he whispers back. It is not Captain Peters' nor the warden's voice. "You get here in that chain the other week?"

"Chain? What chain?"

"The new class," he whispers. "The new prisoners from a week or so back. Listen . . . that doesn't matter. Just tell me what you did t'get yourself tossed down in the dungeon for so long. Better yet tell me what you did there all that time will ya?"

"What d'you think I was doin' there?" I raise my voice. "I was trynna figure out what the hell's happening. None of it makes sense. D'you not agree?"

"No bird's hit the bricks on Alcatraz. You really dunno much about this place do ya? People who've tried t'escape were recaptured or greeted with a bullet t'the dome. If they don't getcha that way the bay's current sure as shit'll claim you as its next victim."

"How d'you know this? Who are these guys n' what d'they want with us?"

A few moments pass with nothing to drown the silence except the sound of active pipes roaring from beyond the grate.

The voice answers my calls after all seems lost. "You musta been hit one too many times there cherry. These screws wanna make our lives a livin' hell. The name's Fred Wilson. Just call me Wilson though. Sounds like I just saved your life with that bit a knowledge."

Fred Wilson. A light sparks in my confused mind. I recently came across that name from someone—or rather from something. The little book mentioned the name. Days of sifting through the dry reading material imprinted most pages into my brain. Fred Wilson is one of those lasting imprints.

The conversation ends without notice as I scurry across the cell floor. My hand slides under the rock-hard mattress and digs around for the object—that small rectangle. I turn my back to the cell bars when there is no sign of an approaching guard. The little light reflecting off the ground allows me to flip to the book's prisoner profiles. There is one surname listed under W: Wilson. Fred T. Wilson. He was a prisoner of Alcatraz referenced for his attempted escape in '56, an otherwise forgettable rebel lost in time with the fabricated Captain Peters.

A few more whispers seep out from the grate, not surviving long enough to reach the bed. The sound comes through even fainter from the front of the cell. This voice originates from the cell next to mine. My neighbor is a hostage claiming the identity of Fred Wilson. Great.

I would attempt to read into the discovery if my eyes were not collapsing upon lying in bed again. I am motionless. This is the only way to make the aching cease. I am a decorated corpse at a wake, frozen in this position. My mind settles like the passing of a thunderstorm; it is calm and quiet. My thoughts go belly-up to the demands of its tired master. My body calls for rest. If I can slip away from this distant dream, perhaps I can think more clearly tomorrow.

Perhaps I am not seeing straight at the moment. Perhaps I will wake from the dream entirely.

A loud horn followed by a few shouting guards serve as a terrifying alarm clock. The sudden shouts are expected during public panic—a fire, an active shooter, a terrorist. Instead, they are used as a wakeup call. I am still in this reality.

Hostages across the street rise from their beds and stand at attention. I do the same out of fear. Blending in is a strategy that protects me from more pain—aching that leaves me mentally crippled as well as physically.

Several guards walk down the hall, inspecting each cell in some strange routine. The audiotape discussed similar counts from when the prison was operational. I recall that because it was the first time I noticed Robb falling behind. It appears his lack of interest proved beneficial after all.

A guard reaches my cell. I am at the end of the cellblock. To my surprise, it is a new face.

"Open one-five-four!" the man yells.

The rather husky rebel steps inside my cell, dressed in the same attire as Captain Peters aside from a missing hat. He glances around the room, making his way from one section of the box to another. I continue to reposition myself, standing in front of the mattress to protect the little book. We shuffle in the tight space.

"Outta my way." He nudges me aside with his baton.

He is not quitting. The object pats the surface of the bed while the man stares me down. He finishes inspecting the top of the mattress and transitions to searching its side. The little book is bound to turn up and there is nothing I can do to stop him.

"Whatcha doin' Bates?" a voice shouts, the same one from the grate last night. "How come ya never toss my cell? I try t'flee once n' our friendship turns t'shit."

The guard ignores the taunting. A look of annoyance lingers while he pushes the comments to the side to resume tossing my cell. He is sweeping the shelves now, which have a few books and magazines left over from the audio tour's life-like décor. In the rebels' play, I am sure it belongs to a former cell occupant.

"Givin' me the cold shoulder Bates?" the voice irritates the man. "Thought we used t'be buddies."

Several quips later and my secret appears safe—for now. The man referred to as Bates snaps, only a step away from flipping my mattress upside-down to reveal my possession.

"Dammit Wilson don't you ever shut up?"

Bates brushes past me and storms out of the cell. He stands outside the doorway, peering into the neighboring hole in the wall. He clutches his baton a little tighter. The furious grip leaves his knuckles white and fingers pressed flat from the pressure.

One more foul comment comes from the cell and the man lets out several swift cracks of the baton. The block quiets as every sun-worshipper's attention locks onto my neighbor. Bates reaches deep in the cell and tosses the occupant in the middle of Broadway. It is a two-man performance at a sold-out show.

The poor bastard's face is beaten—a cheek caved in like a crater on the moon. Bates continues to whip the baton at the man like a kid beating a piñata. He is smashing a cockroach. I also stare at the two men with my front-row seat. The man claiming the name of Wilson stares at me the entire time.

Bates walks away, exhausted from the effort. Wilson's face is covered in blood. His cheek rests on the concrete as a smile grows across the rest of his face. He has lost his mind. Does he prefer death over standing this hostage situation any longer?

The violent rebel walks around in circles on Broadway, pointing his baton all around the block to address every hostage at once. The encore. "If anyone else feels like makin' some smartass comments this mornin' you can spend the rest a the week in the infirmary! Everyone else step outta your cell n' line up for count!"

We obey the command. Even Wilson manages to get back on his feet to jump in line. He keeps a hand on his brow as blood drips to the floor. The trail of red stops a few feet to my side. The neighbor from beyond the grate stands next to me with his face distorted. Why did he distract the guard for me?

We file into the dining hall in the type of line formation a local parade has with its veterans, only everyone in this parade resembles a young man from the '50s. The rebels are taking this too far. We are quiet. We are serious. We march to the kitchen area.

The empty area near the back of the dining hall is a school cafeteria. It is not empty now like the way it was during the tour. More hostages stand behind metal bars, wielding spatulas and wearing black hair nets. This area was also empty during the tour. The rebels are forcing their hostages to cook. I will find my way back there, too, if they are impressed by a level of cooking talent that consists of not burning a Pop-Tart.

The hostage behind the bars slaps a thick pile of oatmeal in an empty bowl and hands it over to me. He breaks off a banana and tosses it on the tray as well.

"Here ya go," he says.

There is no look of sorrow on his face. He is not desperate to flee with a gun pointed at his head. He looks content with his spatula and black hairnet as though he has done this for years.

I look down at my brown tray—at my plastic spoon, napkin and side of room-temperature coffee in a Styrofoam cup. The big, sticky blob of oatmeal steaming out from the bowl does not smell too unappetizing despite its appearance. The final product is rather impressive for a kitchen that has not been operational in decades.

While the tray of food smells rewarding after days of eating stale bread off of a damp concrete floor, seating soon turns into an issue. I bring my tray to one table and a fellow hostage slides it away. It lands on another open spot and the surrounding captives glare at me until I move again. The uncomfortable experience drops me off at the end of a table closest to where we entered. It is nearest to the rebels standing in uniform watching over us.

Do the captives fear the same punishment I received? There must be a reason they will not allow me to eat alongside them. Solitude is a preference, yet days of complete isolation drive even the most introverted man to crave socialization. I need answers as well.

The silent meal does not last more than twenty minutes as we are hurried out of the dining hall. I did not touch the food on the tray. All hostages line up on command as if having years of training. I scurry over to the nearest line and scoot into an opening before being herded out of the room. This seems quite elaborate for only missing several days of conditioning.

"Get in your lines t'report for detail!" Bates walks out from behind a cellblock. "Move it move it move it!"

The man from the tape described daily assignments around the island that mirrored the structure of jobs held by most sun-worshippers beyond the bay. Take the human out of routine and the routine lingers. The prison had an obligation to abide by the laws of the Sun God as well. It is clear these rebels are choosing to recreate life in Alcatraz Penitentiary; I do not need an explanation from one of the rebels to reveal as much. Our captors do not have an end goal if this creation is what they seek. No motive. No reason. They are operating without a blueprint, taking it day by day.

The lines split into various directions. I have no direction except the back of the man's head in front of mine, so that is my guide.

Captain Peters steps in my path a few paces out of the hall. "Field . . . where d'ya think you're goin'? You move as ordered. These cons already have their assignments."

"Sorry sir. I was just following—"

"You'll be in the Industries Building." He stares down at a clipboard with a list of names. "Laundry detail'll suit ya well seein' as you're still dressed in that filthy uniform." He shakes his head. I did not have the strength to change clothes last night. "Jesus don't ya have any respect for yourself?"

The Industries Building, formerly known as the Model Industries Building. That piece of shit. A dilapidated home to tetanus was one of the final stops Robb and I made before cutting all communication. The setting of the cellhouse may look like an exact replica of how it looked back in the day, but I cannot fathom how they expect to revamp the Industries Building.

Peters continues to ensure all hostages are on their way to detail. The lines fan out like a marching band, fanning out in unison. Robb's beloved halftime show. My line moves toward the main entrance, passing through the control room and several nearby offices.

"So what've you guys been doing when they send you on

detail?" I turn to the man behind me as we are escorted out of the cellhouse to face the brisk air. "I mean what d'they expect us t'accomplish in the condition a that place?"

"Keep it t'yourself," he whispers. "I just got outta the hole a few weeks ago. Don't want your skinny-ass t'be the reason I'm sent back."

I suppose the average sun-worshipper fears returning to the depths of Sunset Strip. The depths of the dungeon. There is no possible way this hostage had it worse than me in the hole, so I push back.

"You're worried about being sent t'the hole again? Look where we are. It doesn't matter where they put us. They'll do whatever they want with us as long as they have the upper hand."

Officer Bates—the big-boned bull who beat Wilson to a pulp— walks over. "Field is it? Cap'n tells me you're one t'keep an eye on. Now I'm not sure what fairytale facility you came from but things run a little diff'rently 'round here."

I nod. "Yes sir. There won't be any problems."

The other hostages prefer to lean on the side of survival. Survival means silence. They follow orders out of fear. If not for that reason, they are crafting the perfect escape attempt, waiting for the right moment to strike. Not me. I require more answers before I can be at peace here. I am no one's hostage at this moment.

The conga line weaves down the winding road. We zig. We zag. We reach the bay's level in a few minutes. I glance away from the man's balding dome in front of me, an action no one else musters the courage to perform. We have reached a building—a parking garage with the same sandy tone as the rest of the structures on the island. Patches of moss—perhaps splashed-up seaweed—provide a little color to the otherwise dull building. This is not a place Robb and I passed during our tour. Of course, all the arguing could have forced us to wander by this sturdy, three-story building without knowing. The windows are as pristine as the ones in the cellhouse. The bars are free of rust with silver reflecting off the rods as the Sun God continues to rise for the day. This is a new building.

"Alright get your asses inside n' prepare for count!" Bates

shouts. He stands in the doorway, a bouncer to a nightclub no one cares to visit. Two more uniformed men stand at attention on each side of the door holding old-timey rifles. I would not be surprised if those weapons were empty. It is all a show.

My head turns in every direction, trying to gain my bearings on the island. The disorientation makes my mind throb again.

"What building's this?" I take my chances and try to converse again. "I don't remember this on the tour."

"Industries . . . it's the Industries Building," the same man whispers through his teeth. He stares forward, fearful of the three guards. "Now shut up 'fore they catch us spittin'."

I wrack my brain to recall what the outside of the Industries Building looked like last week. Too much time in darkness resulted in a fuzzy memory. My real-life memories disappear like evaporating water as I recall the most obscure facts from the little book and tape in their place.

The man behind me kicks his foot at my heel. "Move," he says. I look forward and the line of hostages is filing into the building. I follow the man in front of me. One, two. One, two. We are marching to somewhere unknown.

A different angle reveals the sandy building rests on the edge of the island. It sits on a cliff; a few feet further and the structure drowns in the bay. This must be the Industries Building. The similarities cannot be a coincidence. Robb and I toured the entire island as he grumbled all the way. There is no way we missed anything. My mind cannot define reality.

Inside are more uniformed men. The vibrations from functional machines make the thick, concrete ground shake as if the building was about to topple over into the water. The smell of an air freshener—perhaps some nearby flowers—fills my nose. The hostages walk up to a desk upon entering the building. One by one they receive orders and walk deeper inside.

Another look around and my memory reassures me of its latest theory: this is the Industries Building. I recall stepping into the large room as Robb darted to a nearby corner to work in solitude. I recall the way the Sun God pierced through the glass to rid the room of the brisk Fog City air. The outside looked spotless; the inside looks the same. The building has been remodeled in such a short while. The inside is cluttered with stations. Hostages fold shirts. They iron pants. They sew loose buttons and patch rips and tears on the same-looking outfits—those of the hostages and those of the rebels. The sea of two colors resembles a giant bruise—waves of black and a dark navy blue surround me. The first floor is one room, only cloth walls resembling shower curtains separating its various sections.

The sound of hardworking sun-worshippers and machines distracts my thinking. That, and someone addressing me.

"Name?" the man at the desk asks. "What's your name?"

So many questions wish to spill out of my curious mind. Instincts tell me to avoid asking this man anything. "Field," I respond. "My name's Michael Field."

He looks down and flips through the clipboard in front of him. "Field . . . Field . . . I don't see any Field on laundry detail. You sure you're in the right place?"

"Just add the damn name down!" a familiar voice commands. I turn around. Peters stands tall in the doorway, his hair greasy as ever below that ridiculous hat. "Assign him wherever there's an opening. It's his first day. You know the drill. Jesus Mason do I still have t'hold your hand?"

"Ah well laundry detail it is then. Welcome t'Alcatraz," he says, ignoring Peters' comment.

The man directs me to a bin packed with foul-smelling clothes. I am able to catch a name on his uniform before departing. 'Officer Mason,' it reads. He is the only man in uniform who has yet to physically or verbally attack me. A potential ally or simply a role he plays?

I wheel the bin across the room, studying the building with each step. Spotless glass rests where dangerous shards once obstructed an empty hole in the wall. The filthy remnants of an old office now hold a file cabinet and a cluttered desk. A man in the room notices my gaze and closes the blinds. A guard forces the cart to a halt and rolls it toward an empty machine. "Eyes up," he says, continuing his stroll.

I follow the lead of others and begin tossing the clothes in an industrial washing machine. This machine was not here a week ago. This is truly laundry detail. There is no way these crooks hauled laundry machines across the bay to the island. There is no chance in hell they managed to repair the entire building in that amount of time either. This is beyond mere theatrics.

I peer out a nearby window through the heavy bars that confine the rebels' hostages. Boats. Dozens of boats ride within the bay. They cruise as if nothing is wrong. One boat is headed toward the island. 'U.S.P. Alcatraz' lines the side of the ship. The boat glides past us and begins honking its horn, ready to dock.

A hostage situation turns into a nightmare, a welcoming thought as no other possibility comes to mind. That is much more plausible than any other explanation. Criminals—even terrorists—could not pull off this sort of elaborate, undetected heist.

This is the closest concept I can grasp—a distant dream. I am stuck in a distant dream that transcends all other slumbers. I turn to the man on my left, dropping a pile of clothes in the process.

"What year is it?" I ask. He looks at me and laughs, shaking his head and returning to work. "I'm serious. What year is it?"

He leans over after confirming no uniformed men are nearby. "You're for real? Damn how long you been cooped up here?" He studies me. "Wait a second . . . you're that fish the cap'n caught in the hole. Tell me man, how'd you hide for that long? We're dyin' t'know." I glare at him. He can sense my impatience. "Alright fish. I get it. Calm down." He taps his hands in the air, attempting to get me to relax. "It's '58. Least it was when I woke up this mornin'."

My hands tend to a frazzled head. The aches and pains are back. I attempt to force myself awake, slapping my own forehead. I close my eyes and open them. Nothing changes; the man still stands in front of me. I try it again. Nothing. Doctor Polk's meditation will not stick. My theory of a hostage situation does not pan out. A distant dream approaches.

"What the fuck's going on?" I shout through the room.

The sound carries as men everywhere stop working to observe the screaming. I yank my hair. My fists punch the washer. The man next to me backs up, not wanting any part in this meltdown. He is wise.

It does not take long for uniformed men to rush over. I continue punching the machines. I kick the pile of blue and black clothes on the spotless floor. I remove my shoe and chuck it at the window, breaking a piece of glass before the object hits the bars and bounces back.

A pile of black clothes jumps on me. They are not pleased with the outburst. I am not keeping the peace. This is not a hostage situation. They must realize this is something much different. I cannot be the only one feeling this way.

I continue screaming as more bodies pile on my back. I throw myself at every object in sight to try and shake them off. I am a child in a grocery store throwing a tantrum.

"Tell me what's going on!" I scream. "Tell me now!"

Captain Peters approaches, standing behind the several uniformed men. I recognize those leather boots every time they come into sight. He takes my head and lifts it from the ground.

"You shouldn't've done that." He grasps the baton at his side.

Emptiness.

DREAM ALONE

I awake to the sight of cuffed hands in my lap. My vision is blurred and my head pounds worse than ever. The distant dream I hoped to wake from persists. It is tireless.

"Michael . . ." A man snaps his fingers in my face. "Michael d'you know where you are right now?" It is Warden Madison.

"Howard R. Madison. Alcatraz's third warden," the man in my mind replays the tape.

Everything is double vision. Madison's two heads tilt sideways. Two desks. Two black pantlegs stand at my side—two Captain Peters.

Madison's look of disappointment surfaces as my vision improves. His wide glasses scrunch against his face as his brows shift down and his nose wrinkles up. He wears a full suit, the man looking much more put-together and professional than the first two times we met.

"Huh? What happened?" I ask, knowing what occurred. I want to hear it from him. "Alcatraz Island. I'm on Alcatraz Island. It's where I've been for over a week now."

"No Michael," he responds, reaching forward and lifting my resting head. "You're in my prison. U.S.P. Alcatraz. This isn't some tropical vacation either. Now I've been very lenient with you after these last few outbursts. My patience is wearing thin now." He looks to my side. "Captain Peters, what was this inmate doing again?"

"He was screamin' sir," Peters responds. The warden's pet—his servant. He is not a sun-worshipper; he is a warden-worshipper. "I came over n' three officers were already holdin him t'the floor. He continued t'yell 'til we were forced t'knock him out."

A vivid dream or not, the physical beating is taking a toll on my well-being. I cannot handle another blow to my body. Something must change. If I must spend more time in this dream world, I will do so intelligently.

"I lost it," the first thing that comes to mind flows out. "I dunno what got inna me sir. I think it's all that time in the hole. It went to my head. I just need t'adjust t'routine again." Routine. There is that dreaded word.

The warden bends down to my level, blowing a puff of smoke from a pipe in my face. "Last chance Michael. One more screw up n' this's it. God himself isn't gonna fly down from heaven t'save you. I promise you that much."

"Yes sir. I understand sir."

I am back in my cubicle speaking to a self-righteous supervisor. I thought I quit that job. I left this in the past. The status quo is resurfacing. Is this my mind battling my own actions in a twisted metaphor?

Madison orders his servant to toss me back in my cell where I will spend the rest of the very long day ahead. Madison claims some healthy sleep will ease my mind. Truth be told, the reason he did not punish me further was because he knows I do not belong here. He knows that and continues to work through his pressing problem without a long-term solution. All three of us—him, Captain Peters and I—realize this and continue playing our never-ending game.

Rest sounds pleasant. I cannot argue with the suggestion. A chance to further escape this dream world. A level deeper. So, that is what I do. My body crashes in bed, slamming against the hard mattress. This darkness is prompted—welcomed, even.

My eyes stretch open moments after closing, distrusting of what has already resulted from this deep slumber. The longest dream continues and I have nowhere to go. A strange representation of the routine-filled life that I am trapped in? No, this is more than that. I do not give my mind that much credit.

The vibrations. The thunderous roars outside followed by a locked cell door. Darkness. Everything was so real—so raw. The road from there brought me to this very cell where I spoke with my neighbor, Wilson. Fred T. Wilson.

The thoughts send my hand digging under the mattress for the little book. While other figures in my dream tend to their detail assignments, I am alone in the light and free to read. My fingers flip through until I land on Wilson's profile. There is already a permanent opening in the little book where the profile rests; I slam the book closed and it creaks back open to the same page without effort.

Wilson's picture mirrors the man who took a beating in the middle of Broadway this morning. His face was deformed, but he appeared to be the same individual shown in the little book. I move past the distracting image and force myself to read the full profile again. I read it again. And again. I read it until a line jumps off the page.

"He tried to escape," my thoughts verbalize.

Wilson attempted to flee from the island a few years back in this distant dream. Does the dream end with my escape as well? It is a dream the average sun-worshipper categorizes as a nightmare. I wish to vanish yet fear regret from moving onto my former reality.

The Sun God fades into darkness over the day. I read the little book five times through until an officer brings a meal to my cell at suppertime. A brown tray packed with a warm roast, fresh vegetables and a side of mashed sweet potatoes is a welcoming sight. The meal is once again enjoyable. It figures my sense of taste in a dream is superior to reality's.

"Lights out!" a guard interrupts my thinking.

The bright spotlights attempting to rival the Sun God's power vanish in a second. A loud thud of a switch leaves the cellblock in total darkness. That is enough literature for the day.

"Hey Field," the cell grate speaks to me. "Hey . . . you up?"

What is there to lose at this point? This is not the ridiculous hostage situation I believed it was this morning. There are no rebels coming to put a bullet between my brows. There is me, this cell and the voice calling from beyond the green grate.

I indulge in the distant dream, scooting off the lousy mattress and pressing my face against the cold metal surface.

"Yeah I'm here. What d'you want?"

"No need t'get snappy," Wilson whispers. "You need a friend. Someone on your side ya know? I've seen the way the screws treat you . . . 'specially that big bastard. This isn't a place for the weak-minded. I can be that friend for ya."

"What's that s'posed t'mean?" I am tired of everyone beating around the bush. I force my dream—or whatever this is—to reveal more. "We're locked up in a maximum-security prison. We can barely talk t'one another for Christ's sake."

"You'd be surprised," he argues. "Tomorrow. Find me durin' grub tomorrow. Second table t'the kitchen on the window side a the hall. I've seen you havin' trouble out there. You can't even find a spot to eat. Sit with me if you wanna make it another day."

The proposition leads to another brutal attempt at resting. Why rest in a dream anyway? Morning shines through the cell bars in no time. I am grateful for that. The Sun God leaves a pattern of stripes on the concrete floor from the shadows of the tall rods locking me in this cell. They are the type of stripes my mother had on her living room rug growing up. I lose my appetite thinking back on that memory.

Another bell sounds followed by shouting. We are soon lined up outside our confined homes. Routine is kicking in. We file into the dining hall with the rest of the dreamers who seem to lack any emotion. I can relate to someone for once. They are versions of me projected from my subconscious. This is the way I choose to interpret the beings for now.

The line leads to a tray full of the same soggy oats and fruit as yesterday. "Enjoy," the hostage behind the kitchen repeats, a broken record. Routine is as rigid in here as it was out there. I must find a path of escape.

I follow Wilson's verbal map to the table near the window. One odd spot is left open across from a man with dark black hair that stands as if it were electrocuted. The hair on the side of his head is buzzed off like the barber quit halfway through the job. Burly brows shift up and down as he speaks to those around him. His eyes lack life, remaining droopy despite his active hands and clamoring mouth. This must be the man I am looking to speak with. If his general appearance does not give it away, then his punched-in cheek certainly does.

The oatmeal finds a home in the spot across from the electrocuted man. This is Wilson. The inmates around the table look offended as I sit down. They stop talking and watch me as if they have a rifle in their faces, confused as to why this stranger interrupted their conversation.

"Field," the man across the table whispers. It is the whisper from the grate. "Field that you? I know that lost stare. It's just like the hopeless sound a your voice on the other side a that tiny grate."

"You're Wilson then?" I ask.

He smiles and steals a scoop of mush from my tray. A historical figure in the flesh. A dreamer I spent many dark days studying. The little book is accurate for the second time. I can thank Robb for once.

"You're taller than I imagined," he proceeds. "N' you're sure as hell a lot scrawnier for that matter." My neighbor looks around the table at the other cons sticking their noses in the conversation. "Oh where're my manners? Field, this's my crew."

Wilson proceeds to introduce the three men around him. He is a storyteller and the center of this supposed crew. He is its stable mast. He takes it upon himself to reveal the members' life stories and how they all united. The leader tries to spin it as a mutually beneficial crew despite the group's silence, their obedience indicating he indeed recruited them as his followers.

"I carefully pick my crew," he confirms. "Loyalty's the only thing that matters. Someone loses my loyalty n' that's it for us. That's all we've got on this rock anyhow."

The crew consists of four escape-hungry birds. 'Birds' is a term Wilson uses—a term I rather like. "Talk like you belong out there n' you'll piss a lotta people off," he said. Each bit of prison slang thrown onto the table is followed by a definition from him or a crew member. He must notice I do not belong on this island. I do not belong in my own dream.

Wilson's at the top of the chain. He embodies everything I dislike about Robb, yet he remains a resourceful person. I need to stay close to him—for now, anyway. I can learn from my neighbor as long as I am stuck here. This is a dream with pain carried over from reality. Fear is real. I must protect myself at all costs.

Across from Wilson is Lens, who received his nickname from the large glasses swallowing his forehead. Wilson claims they do not allow inmates to wear glasses; Lens is one of the few exceptions. The nickname also comes from his apparent talent of knowing where any guard is at a given time. "He's got all the right connections," Wilson pats his ally on the back. "You want anything from him n' he's your man. Weapons, booze or a letter to your gal 'cross the bay. Don't matter. He can get it done."

Ronnie is next, sitting at the edge of the table sporting a violent expression. Ten minutes pass and he still sports the same face. That sinister glare. As the black sheep of the crew, Ronnie contributes one value: physical prowess. "Ronnie doesn't do much talkin'. He has other ways a gettin' his point across."

Then there is Sykes. If Ronnie was a pirate, Sykes would be his parrot. He is a translator of sorts who does most of the decision-making between the two of them. Five years together at U.S.P. Leavenworth forged their bond. "A dangerous duo." Again, Wilson's words.

"N' why've you taken an int'rest in me?" I drill down to the reason I sat at the table. "I mean you got your ass kicked just because these guards were tossing my cell."

Wilson drops his spoon mid-bite, offended by the question. "Listen you spent over a week in the dungeon." He raises a bushy brow. "Not the hole . . . the dungeon. As if that wasn't enough t'catch my attention you also stayed outta sight for over a week. I've seen a lotta shit go down on The Rock. I've seen everything imaginable. Plen'y a men tried t'escape over the years yet none stayed hidden for as long as you. Not by a long shot."

He does not know the truth behind my arrival; I do not know it either for that matter. I am in a dream somewhere far away—the type that flies away from memory minutes upon reaching reality. My mind cannot distinguish fact from fiction. And yet, I am comfortable with that notion. This dream world drives me forward.

It provides a purpose—a reason to exist rather than survive like the rest of humanity.

There are two choices now. Option one is breaking my way back into reality. Option two is to continue playing along with this dream. Feeding the dream. It is not a hostage situation as I theorized. It is different—beyond explanation and only viable within a fabricated reality. However, a third path reveals itself with each passing moment. That last path is much more complex. It gives meaning to this world, making it real. A blend of two realities.

"It wasn't easy . . ." I buy myself a few seconds to craft a story. "It's not my goal t'escape . . . at least not yet. My goal was t'prove this place has its weak spots. It's not an unconquerable fortress as they claim. There's an open wound n' I started picking at it. A wound like that takes time n' patience t'dig at."

A stream of consciousness pours out into words. Wilson and his crew are alert, their ears perked up like dogs begging for table scraps. I am convinced they would not move if the breakfast bell rang. The words are bullshit—ones I know the crew wants to hear. They view me as an asset for escape. They want me to lead them to freedom. How long can I keep up the act? These inmates are hardened criminals. They are members of a small, dangerous community consisting of the nation's most notorious convicts.

Do I desire allies? Absolutely not. Attention from others—minds to entertain besides my own—is at the bottom of my slim wish list. My path—option one—requires assistance. These rebels can teach me the methods required to return to reality. If I study them, they will provide an exit strategy. If this is a dream, those around me will slip. The work of fiction cracks with their stories, awaking my mind to where my body truly rests. If this is the third path, an added wall of protection is beneficial. All three roads point to developing my relationship with this crew.

The dining hall bell sounds. The rest of our conversation is put on hold until the next meal or grate interaction. Routine buys me time to anticipate their forthcoming interrogative questions. What is my backstory? What crime sent me here? So many opportunities for my cover to shatter to a million pieces—landmines buried across the island.

I am not going to lie, I was relaxed conversing with Wilson and his crew over a simple meal. My time wasting away in the dungeon and yesterday's private meals left me in the dark. I cannot remember the last time I craved human interaction like this.

The birds are swift in cleanup with screws monitoring every action. The cons line up near the kitchen with their brown trays. They toss the clump of oatmeal and the banana peel in the trash and leave the tray on the counter for other prisoners to clean. When cleanup is complete, we form another line outside the dining hall for count. Routine.

The most unrealistic aspect of this dream is the food. My clever brain perfected every component of this world. It built sun-worshippers who dramatize my rebellious position on life. It created realistic feeling, touch, scent and sight. The Sun God burns my face every morning while the winds of the water do the same in the afternoon. The food, however, tastes like it came from a Michelin chef.

I give myself too much credit on the food rating. When your diet consists of half-frozen T.V. dinners and a can of soda, it is easy to imagine any other meal tasting as savory as the lumpy oatmeal. Or the still-steaming roast beef with mashed potatoes. Even the bananas taste as if they were plucked by the hands of a self-made Costa Rican farmer who delivered a bunch to the dining hall that same morning. The detail of the dream tries to suck me further inside. It wants me to explore it, maybe even act on it. I must remain grounded until I know the truth.

A short break in routine allows me to flip through the little book. Stay focused. Breathe. I skim through the pages as if spinning a zoetrope. Lens, Ronnie and Sykes all lack profiles. Meanwhile, Wilson's profile remains lengthier than most. Irrelevant criminals or another flaw in my mind? I made these characters. Yet the little book has earned its validity until I know which path I am traveling down. The object is worn—a shirt passed down from one sibling to another.

The tape has still not seen the light of day—at least to my

knowledge. Perhaps it sheds more light on Wilson's crew or even Wilson himself. If I can understand who I am joining forces with, I can discover the truth. The tape remains out of reach, though. The hand-held device hides in the confines of cell fourteen; I left it behind in the hole. It dropped to the ground the moment the rest of my body fell from the quakes. At least I hope it traveled to this world. If not, this experiment will be for nothing.

Lens works his crafty little brain one day at dinnertime. I suppose it reflects my own cluttered head in a sense. He theorizes I hid from the guards for so long due to the location of cell fourteen. That dark, empty cell. It is the untouched crevice between the couch and television. It gathers dust and dirt and mold, and everyone forgets about it. No one cleans it. Cell fourteen is the last cell in solitary confinement. It is therefore the last place to house a bird besides the dungeon. They call it the strip cell due to the common theory that they leave your bare body to sit against the icy, dusty floor for days on end the way Peters did to me in the dungeon. They let cuts get infected and bacteria climb all over you. It is this place's attempt at making its prisoners one with the hole.

Lens can brainstorm all he wants; he can have his theories. That is all they will be: fictional stories to help his busy mind sleep at night. His observation is to my benefit, though. If the tape made it to this dream, the chances of it resting on the floor of that cell are exceptionally high. I believe the tape is necessary. This is my chance to shake my body awake. I anticipate its discovery resulting in that falling sensation. It is the trigger required to unravel this story. The dream keeps me curious, luring me in with interesting projections. It is a cruel disguise imposed by the Sun God—the man behind the curtain.

The most realistic method of ending up in the hole is to be thrown in it, kicking and screaming after some intense altercation. But what if this is more than the distant dream I hold onto? It is difficult to justify such extreme measures to reach D-block—Sunset Strip—when this all feels so authentic. Three paths and one answer. I cannot make up my mind. The Sun God tricks me to its delight.

Unfortunately, a rude comment to a guard does not toss a con in the hole, especially not in the strip cell. All it takes is a few swift cracks of the baton to resolve an issue like that. Inmates do not end up there by disobeying orders either. Violence is almost always required. They reserve cell fourteen for extreme, dangerous violence. This is what Lens tells me.

The Almighty rises and falls as rigidly as the rules and regulations of U.S.P. Alcatraz. Hours of contemplation transform into days while an impactful strategy does not cross my mind. The blank slate forces my hand to fall victim to the routine of the prison system. I trek to the Industries Building for detail each day where I fold clothes and iron the guards' dress shirts. My little spare time is spent on food and sleep. Food, sleep and rumination of how to get my hands on the tape.

My relationship with Wilson and his crew grows stronger each day. In turn, I lend more of my trust to them despite not knowing the other members' fates. I strike down the sharp objects they throw my way in their tests of loyalty. Lens requests I smuggle obscure items from the Industries Building back to my cell. Magazines. Cigarettes. I drew the line when he asked me to sneak a pipe down under for a gift Wilson wanted to give one of the guards. He was not serious, but I considered it for a moment. I am putting everything on the line while avoiding attention from Peters and the warden.

Sykes requests I steal food for his giant pet, Ronnie. He sits at the dining table pointing and staring as he picks out new victims for me to rob. Ronnie sits alongside him, chuckling at the tasks conjured by his parrot. I try to steal from new inmates—new birds—when I can. This makes the challenges easier. A new arrival will do just about anything to survive his first week.

These are mindless tasks for the crew's sheer enjoyment. At the same time, I am aware Wilson is behind each assignment. The puppeteer. The ringleader. Nothing gets past him. He continues to befriend me by letting his minions assign the difficult tasks, a strategic move on his part to gain my trust. I do not need to return the favor. They are all projections from my mind that offer an opportunity to learn. They will show me the path to cell fourteen and guide me to the tape, allowing me to return to the life I desperately desire to change.

Yes, my instincts tell me this is fabricated. It is an infinite mental prison designed to keep me locked up for years. Perhaps Doctor Polk sent me here. Part of my brain believes that is the truth while another part holds onto the other theory. There is a tickle in my throat that refuses to vanish and worsens when tended to. That tickle is reality grabbing my attention.

Reality. Not my own reality, but rather another I stumbled upon. This world has the correct components to make up such a place. My mind has never experienced such a phenomenon. The alternate reality theory climbs its way to the top of the list with each human interaction. Each meal I eat convinces me that I am not dreaming and every sleepless night in my cell mirrors the same insomnia I have experienced for years.

An opportunity arrives to my surprise during yard time. Rec time. The yard. The boneyard. Recreation time is the closest a prisoner gets to flying across the bay to freedom. It is the chance to mingle with nearly any con that does not reside on Sunset Strip each weekend. The yard even allows for pick-up games of mindless athletic activities like baseball. Of course, there are no wooden bats allowed, those risking a blow to another inmate's head. Instead, they carry a flimsy sort of plastic one used at a toddler's birthday party. Every aspect of life in these walls is childproof. They do not even trust us with silverware. Spoons put in overtime to play the role of forks and knives.

"Who's that?" I ask Wilson. I point across the concrete jungle to a tall, lonely man. Half-grey hair tells me he holds the title of oldest man within these thick walls. He is at least a contender for such an unfortunate award.

The opportunity to learn about this place and its creatures outside of the little book is through the word of others like Wilson. He tends to know a lot about this place. I do not have a reason to trust the man quite yet; however, he is the only other resource at my disposal.

"That guy?" he laughs. I nod. "That's Creepy Karpis. He's had the longest stint in this place's history . . . so far that is. You heard a Doc Barker?"

"Sure. He spent some time here n' was shot in the head while trying t'flee," I respond. I read Barker's profile several times. The tape also made a big deal about the timeless wrongdoer.

"You know your fellow birds. I can respect that." He pats me on the back. "Well he ran with a tough crowd. He played a big role in that Karpis-Barker gang everyone blabbers about. I say whatever. Keeps to himself for the most part these days."

Most profiles in the little book are from the early days of the prison. Big shots like Capone and 'Machine Gun' Kelly are awarded numerous pages compared to others who have a few sentences. It is unfortunate as nearly all those birds are now gone from this place. There is a certain darkness in that literary preference. The author researched every inmate and determined which ones were the most exciting. The most thrilling. She chose the ones that caused the most destruction simply to make an extra buck.

I am gaining Wilson's trust, slowly and surely. It is my failsafe should this place prove to be something other than a distant dream. I attempt to go through other members of his crew for intelligence, but they fear the head of the snake. They stick to their assignments. Wilson puts on a rather tough act for having such a straight-forward story in the little book outside of his pitiful escape attempt. The little book—of course. The quick insight kickstarts my mind and sends it into overdrive for the remainder of the day. My brain latches onto an idea until my hands can search through the literature at night.

I flip through the little square pages when the lights clunk off. I must find anything about Karpis, the lifelong rebel dubbed 'Creepy Karpis' by Wilson in the yard. The closest name my fingers slide past is Alvin Karpowicz. This criminal arrived at The Rock in '36. Karpowicz rotted away in Alcatraz for thirty years until the prison closed in 1962. If he was to see this little book—if anyone was to for that matter—it would spark chaos.

Karpowicz served his time relatively under the radar on Alcatraz. The only way to survive a long-term stint within this concrete box is by keeping to oneself. Karpis does just that. I can appreciate a desire for solitude. His date of birth is 1907; he is over fifty years old in this dream. I doubt a sun-worshipper at his age is capable of inflicting physical violence. Prison cannot treat the body well, let alone the mind. I do not know enough about other current Alcatraz residents to draw similar conclusions, so this must suffice.

Karpis' fate is in writing. He is an old man. He is destined to see the sun rise and fall each day until it goes on without him. He is of little risk if I am to get tossed back on Sunset Strip—my opportunity to wake from this dream. If the other path is instead true, my actions will reveal reality. They say you cannot die in a dream; Doctor Polk tells me as much each time I share a cryptic vision. I hope his blind teachings are accurate this once.

Thoughts come and go until dusk becomes dawn. No sleep. This cannot be a dream, yet it is too distant for reality. The irritating sound of the bell and violent shouting by Officer Bates reveal last night's minutes were not wasted by my being awake. Progress. Routine replayed in my mind dozens of times from start to finish last night. Every detail. Every interaction. It is all predictable. Routine is on my side this once.

Yard time provides a window to make a move on Karpis. He is on special detail thanks to his long-standing residency. An ancient bird. Executing a plan during detail is an impossible mission and pushing the Creep off the edge in the dining hall is not ideal either. Any number of utensils or dishware could be fashioned into a weapon. The physical power of a spoon is underestimated and the Almighty knows I am not cutout for a confrontation.

My short time here puts me at a disadvantage. I do not have the mind of a criminal—of a true rebel—quite yet. Karpis has the high ground in both the dining hall and detail. I must strike during his weakest moment—his most vulnerable state. It must take place in the yard. Karpis was in the yard the other day, so no special privileges appear to exist in the playground. That combined with the hopeful support of Wilson, his crew and attentive guards all provide an extra line of defense. It is a failsafe against death. Against reality. It is a seatbelt should this dream screech to a stop to reveal its truth.

No doubt can exist if I am to go through with this approach. Karpis must be the right victim the first time around. If he is not how the little book defines him and reality arrives, then it likely costs my life. Every word from the author must be accurate. I am trusting a sun-worshipper.

My life—or whatever this is—comes into focus with each passing moment on The Rock.

WIND OF CHANGE

I'll track his ass down myself if he won't show his face. The cops weren't with him when he vanished. The rest of our family wasn't with him either. I was with him. My mom and Meredith are wrong, and I'll prove it.

I lied to Meredith when I told her I'm going back to work today. She'd freak the fuck out if she learned I'm returning to that island. It's a white lie—big deal. She doesn't understand what happened and neither does anyone else for that matter. Bodies don't go missing, least of all my pathetic brother's. He's a smart dude, although I'd never admit that to anyone. Most stuff coming out his mouth seems insane with a light splash of logic in there. I can see past the clutter and pull out a few insights every so often. I'm a translator of sorts.

I flew back home to New York the day my dad died. The first thing my brother said when I walked in was, "It's inevitable. That's the last stop on the train for all of us." It's inevitable. Was he serious? The average person calls that denial, one of the first stages of grief. I grew up with the guy, though. I was closer to him than anyone by default. He wasn't in grief; that's just how his wild mind works. If his mind's that out of whack, his actions must be, too.

These thoughts distract me as I return to Fisherman's Wharf, the tourist-filled hub of San Fran. The warehouse for fun hats and magnets and t-shirts that spew out the same crap.

I'm not sure what's back at Alcatraz that'll lead me closer to finding my brother. Still, it's the sensible first step in this one-man investigation. A head-first dive into a sea of unknown depths. Maybe I'll call it quits if this doesn't pan out. Who knows?

"Hey there," I greet the unsuspecting kid working at pier thirty-three's ticket booth. It's eight in the morning on a Tuesday. I'd be startled, too, if I was in a reasonable state of mind. "I wanna get my hands on a ferry ticket for today."

He judges me in silence. I'm in my clothes from last night. I look like my brother when he first arrived a few weeks ago. A pair of loose-fitting sweatpants, a red Stanford sweatshirt and a Giants cap hide a disgusting mess of a man. Pathetic.

"Sir these tickets sell days if not weeks in advance," he responds. It's the pimple-faced brat's convenient chance to show power over an adult figure and he knows it.

"Alright I know these tickets are hard t'come by," I change my aggressive tone. It's time for the soft sales pitch. "Can't you make an exception this one day? From one salesman t'another. We both know there're extra tickets back there. Name one thing money can't buy kid."

"These tickets," he snaps back. Great response, I'll give him that. He's about to throw a temper tantrum if I don't turn the other way. "If you don't get lost man, I'll call my supervisor n' she'll call the cops." Yada-yada.

I'd like nothing more than to pull him off that little stool, take his ponytail and drag it across the pier, throwing him into the water like a lifebuoy. I only don't do so because that'd leave me in a much worse position than I'm already in. I can't do much investigating in prison. The action won't get me on the island either. He wins. I turn around as his pubescent heart desires and leave the pier—for now.

I won't get arrested, but I'll deal with the shame of being a beggar. I wish blue tie guy could see me now, hands waving around at people like some drugged-out hippie. I plead with each individual, family or group of friends who turn from the sidewalk to the pier. If the tour won't sell me a ticket, I'll get someone else to give me their ferry ride.

Intoxication lingers from last night, leaving passersby beelining in the opposite direction. I can't get a few words in their ear before they start powerwalking away. It doesn't help that I look like a mess. Fearful tourists. "I'll pay you a hundred dollars!" I shout at one person after another. One hundred fucking dollars and zero cents. The homeless look suave compared to this.

The wise-cracking kid at the edge of the pier notices me. He squints in my direction, raising a hand to his forehead to get a better view like the captain of the Titanic. I continue to hound tourists for tickets as the teen leaves his post. His fat ass remains carved in the black barstool's cushion as he waddles over to the closest building.

I get a few more minutes of pestering pedestrians before a pier officer comes storming out of the same building the teen had entered. Dammit. The teen stands in the doorway with a smug look on his face. This is the most excitement he'll see all year.

"Alright alright! I'm leaving!" I shout at another young adult hustling toward me. He's either carrying a baton or pepper spray and I'm not dealing with either of those right now.

I could've given a shit about my brother the first time we walked up to this pier. That's not changed much, yet somehow my life now centers around him. I drown that realization with booze around the corner of the building that touches the pier. A flask full of whiskey hides in my jacket for these glorious occasions. It's time for a few swigs to ease the frustration. I can't wait any longer for this celebratory failure.

A few layers of cheap gold liquid waterfall down my throat. The tingles set in a few minutes later and I'm able to muster enough courage to head to the car. Maybe another day. It can wait. My brother's not going anywhere and neither am I without my precious job.

One hand remains on the flask tucked in my jacket pocket while the other leans against the stoplight pole. I'm waiting for that little glowing white man to light up. Give me the little man and send me on my way. The liquor cabinet calls. The booze is already wearing off. I shake it off like a snake shedding skin only to leave behind a layer that's raw.

More passersby stare, watching me pace around the never-changing light. No little man except the one waiting at the crosswalk. An elderly woman waits to cross, too. At least I'm not alone. She's not running in the opposite direction like everyone else. A not-so-subtle look my way and she inches closer. I stare at her from the corner of my eye as her wrinkly arm touches my shoulder.

Is she about to kick me out of here, too?

"I said I'm leaving!" I scream. Enough harassment. I said I'm leaving. These people have nothing better to do.

"Just breathe," she says to my surprise. "Close your eyes n' breathe."

She remains calm despite my vivid, boiling rage. Her arm doesn't leave my shoulder after a few twitches try to shove it off, so I give up. She watches as I take a deep breath. There, is she happy? In and out. In and out.

"Alright. I appreciate that," I respond through my teeth. It was an annoying gesture, yet it's nice to have someone on my side. "But ma'am I'm just trynna get back t'my car at this point."

"You look like you've been through quite the day," she smiles. Try a month, lady. "I've been eating my lunch on that bench for the past twenty minutes." She points to a bench near the pier. "I watched you pester every individual who strolled inna that pier."

The lady must be in her seventies. She's draped in a plaid scarf and big, black earmuffs; she's wearing a cape in the form of a grey peacoat. Her short, curled hair pokes out the earmuffs like thick mud squeezing out the side of a heavy shoe after hitting the sidewalk. There's too much flair for a woman her age.

She reeks of an entire bottle of flowery perfume. It's that certain flowery and musty scent all old people somehow carry. I'm one to talk, though. My whiskey cologne crawls out every pore to punch people in the face. I'm sure our combined scents would send tourists running for the many hills of San Fran.

"That's great you get t'eat your lunch outside," I reply, saying the first thing that comes to mind. How am I supposed to respond to that? "Glad you also enjoyed the free show. Hey, don't try t'go on that ferry by the way. It's practically impossible . . . especially for someone your age."

She stares at me. That shriveled hand still rests on my shoulder, flashing a large diamond ring. The object catches her attention for a moment before she snaps back to reality. I can imagine the dementia setting in. I'll let her enjoy herself while she can. Have your fun, ma'am.

She cracks another smile. "That may be so . . . but I have a ticket right here I can't use today. It's only good for one day as well."

The woman holds out her hand and flashes the ticket, the same paper dozens of others carried as they walked past me. It looks like a winning lottery ticket to me; I wouldn't know the difference at this point.

"You can't go?" I ask. The intrusive woman has my full attention. Only a bottle of booze would soothe me more. "Are you headed t'hand it off t'someone else?"

"Quite the opposite," she pauses. She takes a moment to meet my unfocused gaze. I look around to see if anyone's waiting for her. Nobody approaches. "I wanted t'see if you'd give it your all t'get on that ferry. That or just give up. Looks t'me like it's the latter. Whatever the case I'd still like for you t'have this if you'd like."

She removes her hand from my shoulder and slides the white paper into my jacket pocket. I pull the ticket back out, wary of the encounter. It's not a receipt or a piece of notepad paper. I've set my expectations lower than low. It's a ticket to get on that ferry. It's a real ticket and it's mine.

"Don't you want money for it? Why're you giving this t'me?"

I'm still staring down at the ticket in disbelief. I lift my head in response to the silence and it's just the light pole in front of me. The woman's gone, already halfway across the street and not looking back.

"Thank you!" I shout, hoping she hears my gratitude yet not wanting to risk the ferry departing without me. Thank you.

Do old people go around planning activities and backing out at the last minute? Either way, it appears my luck's starting to turn around. The remaining hurdle's the half-empty flask in my other pocket. A few healthy gulps remain in that metal container. A few swigs to coat my craving throat and intoxicated state for a few more hours.

I sprint over to the end of the pier and weave under the empty, roped line. There's no going back. If I'm investing in this, I'm investing everything. The ponytailed teen shakes his head as I shove the ticket in his face. I won the battle. He reluctantly clips the piece of paper and unhooks the indestructible rope keeping the ferry protected, a tight operation headed by a deadly agent with acne and a ponytail.

Every sight, sound and smell on the two-story boat leaves me with déjà vu. I'm living in a recurring dream. My eyes instinctively study the water over the side as we drift off, entranced by the mesmerizing pattern of waves pushing out from under the boat. What I'm really doing is scouring the sea for my brother. At least I'd have some closure if his scrawny body floated to the top. Of course, nothing ever surfaces as we glide closer to the enlarging island in the distance.

The boat slides up to the old wooden dock not more than twenty minutes later. I shove and squeeze my way down from the second level of the boat to the exit. It's Christmas morning again. My elbow greets men, women and children. It doesn't matter who's in front of me—they're just obstacles.

The bathroom calls me over the moment my feet touch land. This is my chance to take a few more pulls of the liquid gold. The island's already crawling with tourists, so the drinks keeps me focused. They keep the nerves and what-ifs from grabbing the wheel, blocking the emotion that's trying to build up.

Where to begin now that I'm here? The police claimed they closed this place down for two full days searching for my brother. Two full days and they gave up. They had full access to the island for those two days, an opportunity I don't have today. My investigation's limited to the same area as the tourists. I'm still confident I can discover more than that goddamn detective.

Retracing my steps is the most logical thing to do. Yet instead, I venture to areas we didn't pay close attention to during our first visit. It's selfish to make it about the both of us; however, there's a reason he chose to run while he was with me. The visit to Alcatraz provided the perfect opportunity to disappear. He was in the right place at the right time.

Every sight's new. I spent the last trip buried in sales reports; buried in a folder with a pile of paper. It's refreshing to stop and read signs or observe crumbling pieces of history. This could be the booze talking again, although it doesn't matter as I'll take what I can get when it comes to staying distracted.

"You been here before?" a man next to me asks. We're both staring at the sign in front of the island's former powerhouse.

"Nope. First time," I lie. No small talk. He doesn't leave, so I flip it back to him. "How 'bout you?"

"You bet!" His ears perk up. Here we go. "I've been comin' here every year since they opened it up t'the public." I'm already here, dude. Drop the cold call. Relax. He continues despite obvious disinterest. "You know people really sing about that audio tour up top. The real treat's near the sally port if ya ask me."

"What's near the sally port?" I ask. Another stranger finds a way to lure me in. Where's he going with this?

"Ah that'd be the little gallery," he whispers. "But don't go shoutin' it from the mountain top." He complements the comment with a chuckle.

I despise this family man. It's all an act. It's a mask glued to every dad's face the moment his first kid pops out. A happy-go-lucky camper thrilled to drag his whining family cross-country.

I follow the suggestion despite his depressing state. An hour ticked away on this rock and I've learned nothing new outside of useless trivia. Maybe this trip was a way to provide closure. A journey to the last place I saw my brother gives him a proper goodbye.

The liquor holds the microphone at this point. I'll roll with whatever it's telling me as I'm too lazy to fight back. Denial—is that what my brother experienced when my dad passed away? I've internally mocked him for years for his idiotic comment about death; however, it's not more ridiculous than running my own investigation on this island.

Meredith and my mom were right. The grief drove me into a state of allusiveness. It resulted in an unhealthy drinking habit and ongoing family arguments. Verbal violence. Even my kids know to steer clear of me. They're smart kids raised well by the nanny.

Maybe my supervisor was right. I've been distracted. On edge. Dangling. Personal matters crawled their way into a professional environment. They consumed the successful career I've always cherished. My brother was an irregular part of my life that can't compare to the importance of my job—one that provided so much more than he ever did.

The detective in me turns tourist for the rest of the trip. I tell myself this is the last time I'll linger on something that should be tucked away by now. It's time to check out this 'little gallery' near the sally port. This last stop takes me through the rest of the grieving process—through the proper wake my brother never had. Just because I'll say goodbye to him doesn't mean I've settled on the man offing himself; it means I shouldn't give a shit about what happened at this point. It's tearing my life apart.

The little gallery's above the sally port in a structure plucked from the middle of a quaint, suburban neighborhood. It looks like a house. I step inside to creaky wood floors following each step and the same musty smell that lingered on the woman at the pier. It's packed with people, too. My new dad-friend told every passerby about his prized destination. Secret my ass.

The visit's underwhelming. It's a gallery of objects behind glass accompanied by silent observers who keep their hands folded behind them as if at a prestigious art show. The lights are as dim as they can get without leaving everyone in darkness. It's a scrappy showcase the government tossed in to encourage tourists to stick around a little longer.

A bathroom sign at the other end of the room's a welcoming sight. It's an appropriate opportunity to finish what's left in the flask. The golden liquid. Cheers. I raise the flask after entering an empty stall. That's the sendoff my brother deserves. That doesn't make me insensitive. Besides, I'd get less from him if the roles were reversed.

The flask's vertical, floating above my tilted head. I've hit bottom. The buzz doesn't take long to kick me back into gear. All I've eaten today's a bowl of oatmeal. The liquor flows through my veins in minutes. The feeling leaves me calm with a warmness nothing else seems to provide.

I can last a little longer. Several additional minutes reading up on forgotten history can't hurt, so it's back to the gallery—back to the dark room occupied by floor-to-ceiling glass display cases and lingering tourists. The next ferry leaves in twenty minutes. There's time to kill. The buzz lingers as I wander out the bathroom.

Each person's as silent as a church mouse. They stare at various artifacts as if picking out a new car from the lot. The layout of the room doesn't have much order, making it difficult to study any displays. There's no pattern. My vision starts to get crossed after shuffling along the glass for five minutes. I'm seeing double of everything and I feel invincible.

I leap in front of the first object I see that doesn't have people swarming around it to take a moment to breathe. Breathe—just as the old lady suggested. This is my last opportunity to try and appreciate this place before I bury it alongside my brother.

"Dining hall spoon," I read aloud.

The utensils prisoners used during meals. Riveting. The self-guided tour proceeds with me laughing at the ridiculous objects being showcased. Silverware, magazines, clothing and photos are now captivating artifacts. They have meaning because this glass wall says so. My hammered mind makes this seem hilarious. It is, after all.

A few rotations around the first room and a theme starts to pop up. There's actual organization to these crappy artifacts. The first room consists of objects prisoners used during incarceration. A fucking spoon. Imagine letting a prisoner know the spoon they used would be on display behind a glass case. Hundreds of people study it daily, and for what?

I catch my laughing breath. The second room's full of old photos taken during the prison's operational years. Stern faces fill each fading picture collecting dust behind a glass wall. What does a criminal have to smile about, after all? The pictures look staged, like prison photos you'd see in a movie. The criminal version of the stock family photo that comes with every picture frame. A few prisoners throw around a baseball. Others look up in sadness while dining. Several unlucky inmates are caught in action doing the laundry of hundreds of filthy criminals and lazy guards.

I wipe my blurred eyes as a familiar sight comes into frame. More déjà vu. My head shakes back and forth attempting to refocus. I'm hammered. That's nothing. The clockwise cycle around the room continues. Maybe I've had too much. Another fifteen minutes until the next ferry. Take it easy, Robb. Look through this next room and go home.

My feet freeze at the open entryway. I'm stuck in place. 'Go back,' the booze whispers. 'Just make sure. There's no harm in making sure.'

"Excuse me," I mutter, tapping the shoulders of a line of people behind me like a game of duck-duck-goose. I'm a fish swimming upstream. Traffic jam. "Think I missed a photo back there." They sigh, groan and roll their eyes.

My finger runs across the glass of the last display case. It scans every photo for the fleeting observation I caught a few minutes ago: the photo that entered my drunk eyes. More eye rolls and groans come from tourists who now have to deal with a streak lining across the glass. The precious, three-foot darlings alongside them can't see.

Bingo. That's it. That photo—the one from the Industries Building. There's a man in the background folding a pair of pants on a table. Sober eyes couldn't fix the out-of-focus man, yet I'm able to discern enough detail. That forgettable expression. The lanky, tall frame. It's the familiar hunch I've seen so many times.

"Michael?" I ask.

The tourists stop to peer over at the man calling out a name who also just swam upstream and smudged an entire glass pane. I say it again—louder this time. Families scurry out the room as if I have a bomb strapped to my chest. Parents gather their children and push them along. None of that matters as my eyes fixate on the figure in the photo.

A few rangers enter the room; I'm positive a concerned parent called them over. I'm already making my way to the giftshop by the time they all enter the first room. I purchased a few souvenirs for the kids last time I was on The Rock. I remember there being disposable cameras at that giftshop, too.

I sprint across the island. I'm fleeing from a predator; I'm zig-zagging past strollers; I'm playing 'Red Rover' with elderly couples clutching hands. My clothes become drenched in sweat. It's sixty degrees outside and my shirt looks like someone dumped a bucket of water on my head. I storm into the giftshop. More heads turn as cash flies across the counter. "This disposable camera. Hurry up," I demand as if the photo was to disappear in broad daylight. I won't take that chance after all this wasted time.

I rush back to the little gallery near the sally port—the little home perched above a bridge of sorts. It feels like a dream again. I'm counting the seconds before I rise up in bed next to a frustrated wife. That won't happen if I can get to the photo.

"Excuse me! Sorry!" Insincere apologies. Get out of my way. "I need t'get t'the next room."

People look at me as if I've lost my infant child. The rangers already left the building, disappointed the potential excitement disappeared. Convenient for me. My luck prevails. I fly into the room that has all the photos, careless of people in my path. I couldn't control my body if I wanted to. I'm Noah parting a fucking sea of humans.

There it is. It's still sitting there, right where I last saw it. It rests on its small metal stand behind half an inch of glass. I don't know who's behind this and that doesn't matter as I'll have enough proof to show everyone something else is going on. I'll show Meredith; I'll show my mom; I'll show the police. I'll toss it in front of my kids if I have to. They're all wrong.

The camera tears into the silence of the room with its repetitive winding scratch. It's fully wound—click. Another flick of my index finger. Click. Click. Click. I make sure the entire roll of film's empty. I position the camera at every angle—near and far—to make sure at least one photo doesn't have a reflective glare. It must be clear. And then, as suddenly as it started, the photoshoot ends. I leave the original photo behind like a one-night stand. A few moments of intense interest followed by a stood-up date. I don't need the photo with this camera roll.

I can't miss the next ferry. The path forks outside the little gallery. One walkway leads to the dock while the other path leads to the cellhouse where authorities claimed to have spent most of their wasted time. What's that bullshit about the road less traveled? Everyone looked in the wrong place.

I was fearful the last time I boarded the ferry, concerned about the repercussions of misplacing my brother. Turns out those concerns were valid. My feet get a second chance to walk up the walkway to the boat. This time, I'm determined. Angry. Confused. I feel everything besides fear.

The island fades into the bay's mystic fog. Satisfaction sets in. I'm not sure what good these photos will bring, but it's still better than going home emptyhanded. I can't believe I was about to accept the denial—the lies—everyone's spewed over the last month.

These photos aren't closure and the trip to the island wasn't a symbolic farewell to my brother; they were the fuel I needed to convince me I'm not in the wrong. I'm not crazy. My job belongs to me. My life belongs to me. I'll prove everything can't be so easily stripped away.

The satisfaction buries other ideas trying to swim up from the depths of the bay's water. This satisfaction is temporary. There's a much larger obstacle forming. These photos are proof of another story behind my brother's disappearance. I don't know what that is, but it's on me to figure it out.

Memories from the first trip to Alcatraz accompany my view of the fog-swallowed island. That dreaded weekend with my brother; that dreaded trip to the island. The coldness between us during the tour leaving the frigid air feeling too uncomfortable to bear. Even the image of him looking back in dismay during the audio tour sticks to my mind.

Sobriety hits like a wave crashing on the shore. I reach in my pocket and pull out an empty flask. There's nothing to contain my feelings or justify these impulsive actions. It's a lengthy trip across the water without any distractions. I deserve a drink. Another celebratory discovery.

A clearer head tries to wrestle with the notion of showing anyone these photos. I can't keep this discovery to myself, though, as it'll eat at me like the disappearance of my brother already has. The world needs to see these. It's the only way to get my job back and return everything to normal.

SAY IT ISN'T SO

Why's it that everything you see on T.V.'s too good to be true? Why can't it reflect reality for once? A slow buildup, a climax and a resolution create a formula built on deceit. It feeds us lies and expectations that'll never come true.

A little reality isn't asking for much when it's a cruel bitch anyway. The buildup's steady, drops, then rises again like a roller coaster. There's no climax in sight; I'm learning that after another month and a half of digging for answers. One drop of water ripples across the pond, shaking everything that was once calm. The hero loses it all in the blink of an eye. Let's see that on an episode of 'Cheers.'

I'm doing everything I can during the hero's conflict, but this is much darker than anything an executive producer would dare keep in their film. It's raw. I've nursed a bottle of whiskey for a few hours now. Tiny bits of tissue loft across the motel room toward the garbage. I invented this one-man game. Every time a piece misses the trash can, a light swig from the bottle follows. It's two heavy pulls if the piece goes in. It's a win-win, lose-lose game.

Everything's gone. My motivation to wake up's the very monster that destroyed my life. That monster's my brother. That photo. My wife, my job and my kids have vanished in the blink of an eye. The path ahead's one that finds my brother, proving this wasn't all for nothing. Everything that's broken will mend if I can find him.

Meredith wasn't hard to lose. She threw in the towel on our relationship the moment I came home without my brother. The nail in the coffin was showing her—and the kids—the blurred photos of a man in the ancient photo from the little gallery. Looking back, getting the kids' opinion was a mistake. What else could I do when she wouldn't give the picture a second look, though? My inebriated state didn't make matters any better.

She came home from work and I sat on the living room floor with an empty bottle of gold. The photos from the disposable camera were spread out on the floor with both kids sitting next to me, studying the indistinguishable prints. It looked terrible in her eyes. I was so obliterated that I couldn't find the words to defend myself at the time and just went to bed.

Most photos on that cheap camera reflected the price I paid for it: two dollars. The dark room either resulted in a flash across the original photo or the unfortunate reflection of a drunk man with a camera. A single snap grabbed the photo behind the glass. It grabbed the man within it, too, and still wasn't enough to convince anyone I was right.

It's a vicious cycle. When I've reached a low, I end up finding the motivation to kick my life back into gear. That moment of clarity makes matters worse. Emotions flood my mind, sending it to retreat to a safe place. That place is looking into the top of a bottle as it tilts toward the heavens. I couldn't shake the cycle if I wanted to, so I embrace it instead.

It's not a high-quality photo, but everyone knew what they saw. I don't need to be a detective to call their bluffs. My brother stands out like a sore thumb. The reality is these jackasses couldn't pull out a realistic explanation for what they saw in the photo. Why reopen an investigation when they've closed the book? The detectives can go home early for a nice family dinner and my own family can stay free of further worry and grief.

'It's a blurry photograph' or 'Everyone has a doppelganger.' Every excuse is a copout. That's what drove me over the edge. I couldn't put this to rest as the lies forced me to protect the discovery—the truth—at all costs. People don't deserve my respect if they can't in turn respect the truth.

My mom, who lost her one biological son, wouldn't return my messages. The considerate, maternal instincts ingrained in her couldn't keep up with what she labeled 'delusions.' She supported her impulsive, emotionless biological son over the years despite his actions and turns a blind eye when it comes to the justifiable beliefs of her adopted child.

A fed-up wife and a fragile mom joined forces—a recipe for disaster. I made a ground-breaking discovery and they responded by flushing a flawless life down the toilet. Quick collaboration on their part sent me packing my bags for an indefinite stay at a nearby motel. I'm still at that motel. I haven't made matters any better. They're waiting for my mind to return to normal for the sake of my health and the kids.

The motel trash game, dubbed 'Whiskey Tissue,' is a break from my core focus. It's a chance to refuel a wandering mind. Adult recess. The real spotlight shines on the opposite wall. Newspaper clippings. Maps. The detective-esque lines of string look strategic. I'm not quite sure they mean anything yet. All these objects convince me of progress, fueling the vicious cycle.

Photos litter the wall, serving as homemade wallpaper covering the fading white paint behind it. In the center of everything's the picture of my brother. He's the star of the show, appearing everywhere and nowhere at the same damn time.

The truth is, there are no solid theories from this—I admit that somewhere deep down. I've looked at him coming to San Fran; I've spoken to his former employer about his behavior over the years. Nothing fits together. Alcatraz continues to provide the most information, always at the burning core of this investigation. I try to look elsewhere for answers and the cycle eventually pulls me back to studying the island. It's the only constant.

Most research on the motel room wall investigates the prison's history. The '60s—that's the decade the original photo was captured. I study the prison during that decade. Is there a reason someone took the photo and branded it as being from a different time? What's to hide?

The most far-fetched theory's a government coverup. The island's considered a national park, a protected landmark with government history and interference. Did my brother come across something he wasn't supposed to? Are they holding him hostage? Did he leave that subtle photo as a cry for help? The ludicrous theories provide another reason to pour a fat glass of gold.

I ask myself what he'd think now—what my brother would think in his analytical mind if the door swung open and he stood in its place. I'd like to think he'd be the sole person who doesn't hate me. Maybe he'd pity me. The shred of actual logic clinging to my mind tells me he'd stand there and laugh. He got his way after all these years; he flipped the script. King him.

When theories don't consume my mind, I find myself at public libraries around San Fran. I wouldn't be caught dead in one of those lifeless structures a few months ago. A different man resides in this body now. Motel. Library. Bar. Repeat.

The San Francisco Public Library kicks off the week. UCSF Library powers me through the middle of the week. The Park Branch Library carries me through the weekend. What I do at these libraries is something I'd never admit—not publicly, anyway. I book it to the history section. It's the most abandoned area in every library and home to all things Alcatraz.

San Fran tends to toot its own horn, meaning libraries carry rows of books about that stupid island. Literal rows of biographies, notable events and stories from Alcatraz. It's tourist bait, or bait for anyone in my position. It was built for me.

I absorb the information without context. Useless facts and figures fill my mind yet never spark insight. The photo's at the center of the maze for answers and the library visits are coping mechanisms. Still, they're a hell of a lot better than drowning my concerns as a full-time profession.

At this point, I've cleaned out every library in the Bay Area. So much information and so little action. I could give a tour of the island blindfolded. It can't be a coincidence this happened on that rock.

"Excuse me," I greet the librarian. She doesn't need to look up to know who's addressing her. "Any new books come in?"

The woman tilts down her reading glasses before responding, "No Mister Field. There're no new books relevant t'your studies. You were here a few days ago."

A few days ago? The days are blurring together. I peek over the counter to glance at her desk calendar. It's Sunday. I never go to the public library on Sundays. Why am I here?

I tell every useless librarian I meet that I'm writing about Alcatraz Island. A thesis, a short story, maybe a novel; the exact lie doesn't matter. I don't want anyone to know the real reason for these visits. I'm screwed if word gets out to Meredith or anyone else.

"Can you just check again?" I plead despite her insistence. "You didn't even check the damn system."

A careless person like her would be sacked in any corporate position. She wastes the day playing sudoku and turning a valued community member away, the female version of blue tie guy. I'm her client.

"Sir I work here six of the seven days a week," she snaps back. "I've seen you come in over half a dozen times this month. I assure you there're no new books on that subject. Now please keep your voice down n' respect the other individuals in the building."

I slam the stack of returned books on the counter. The impulsive action turns a few heads. I'll look on my own then. If I can confuse days of the week, I could be off the mark in other areas. Maybe there's something I missed during the last visit. I'll look at anything to pass the time.

An internal alarm ticks every fifteen minutes. The incessant ringing doesn't subside until I'm in the bathroom taking a swig from the flask. Alcohol's a depressant to most. It makes people tired and foggy-headed. For most, a library's the last place they'd want to be while inebriated. For me, it's the opposite. It's a necessity now. I started this quest fueled by booze and I'm not slowing down until it's finished. The rest of the journey starts with finishing this flask in a public bathroom. No matter how many books I've read, blueprints I've studied or photos I've viewed, something inside always urges me to search for more. An empty flask and full belly fuel this feeling. More useless information; more time irritating the librarians.

I like to sit cross-legged on the floor. I take up as much space as possible. Books sprawl out around the faded carpet like a kid's mess at daycare. If anyone enters this section, they either turn around in fright or roll their eyes in annoyance. I don't care. I laugh at their frustration.

I reach out and grab a paperback from the shelf, noticing a familiar cover. "Someone Is Hiding on Alcatraz Island," I read aloud, letting out a quick laugh before placing it back on the shelf. That's the one book every library seems to have. It's one of my favorites despite its fictitious nature. Even the fictional novels leave my head spinning.

"Sorry . . . can I get by?" a man asks over my shoulder. He has the audacity to walk down my section. Can't he see there are all sorts of books scattered on the floor? This is intentional. It's my area. Get lost.

"Yeah sure thing," I reply.

I can't get kicked out of another library. Besides, his persistence strikes a chord. He's determined to make it to the other side of the section despite the minefield of books. I can respect that. He'd make it far in my former world.

"Thanks." He passes. The middle-aged man stops in his tracks when he reaches the end of the row. His head turns back. "You must really be inna Alcatraz huh?"

"Oh right . . . the books," I realize. "Just a little historical reading. I'm in grad school. Doin' my thesis on the psychological effects prisons have on inmates." That boilerplate story's engraved in my vocal cords along with several others. The lies feel natural; even I believe them.

"That's fascinating!" His interest piques. "What university?"

My patience is wearing thin. I let you pass, man. Don't linger. "San Fran State," I reply. Another scripted lie.

"Ah no kidding," he laughs. "I'm a former Gator myself. Don't mean t'age myself but I was in an introductory criminal justice course during my undergrad years in the '70s. If my memory serves we had a former Alcatraz inmate speak t'the class."

A former inmate. Why didn't that enter my intoxicated mind? I'm wasting away in a library when I could be getting a history lesson from someone who experienced everything firsthand. Alcatraz closed in the early '60s. This guy claims to have heard a former con speak in the '70s. It doesn't take much mental math to determine the con in discussion's an old man by now.

The comment from the passerby justifies a response, so I dig for a little more info to make it worth my while. "Huh how 'bout that? I would've thought most guys locked up in there were dead or contained elsewhere by now."

He steps back in the row and bends down, picking up one of the dozens of books scattered on the floor and flipping through its pages. "Well it's not like it was Big Al. I'm still damn sure the guy was from Alcatraz though. The chilling stories told me that much. That shit sticks with you."

He's getting in my personal space. Put that book down. This isn't Sherlock and Watson. Watch yourself.

"Thanks for the info," I dismiss him and bury my face in a nearby book. He takes the hint and vanishes. I appreciate the help, but he was prying.

There's finally a reason to leave this second home. A random stranger's what moves me along this self-destructive path. The most useless people of all were those buffoons on the island. Tour guides and park rangers—self-titled experts—pushed me a few steps back with their lack of info the last few times I visited. The only nugget of knowledge I yanked from those clueless professionals involved the photo. One tour guide claimed to know the person responsible for preserving all the island's artifacts. The guy the woman spoke of developed a personal interest in preserving new objects as they arrived on the island. One of those items was the photo I carry in the form of a blurry copy in my jacket pocket. It was a glimmer of light shining on the pitch-black photo for a minute.

"This picture's from the late '50s or possibly early '60s," the woman informed me. "We got this a few years back along with a whole collection a photos from that time. It was right around the close a the prison so a few a those pictures fit well within the gallery." Beyond that insight, those who spend their days on that island are idiots. They're also people who'd be fired to hell and back if they worked for me.

The Civic Center's library will have what I'm looking for. This location keeps local newspapers on record going back decades. I glare at the librarian on my way out, pulling the flask in my jacket out from my pocket and taunting her as I walk past with the bottle tilted upside-down in my mouth. The liquor drums against the metal container, disturbing a few more peaceful readers. Bitch.

The sun's closing in on the day as I travel across town. There's a little kick to my step right now. It's the first time I've changed this routine in weeks. Two libraries in one day. I'm not headed to the history section this time either; I'm on my way to the archives. It brings a fleeting smile to my face, an expression that disappeared months ago and one that feels foreign. It's a Sunday, so only the ancient and homeless hunker down in the Civic Center with me. Both groups are probably here for better reasons than my own. Still, the search must go on.

I strut over to an empty microfilm reader. Local papers would surely cover a story about some dried-up prisoner. My search will narrow from there. The San Francisco Chronicle. The San Francisco Examiner. The process begins, continuing for hours as the stack of microfilm piles up on the desk. The search goes on, day-by-day—paper-by-paper. There are three hundred and sixty-five days in a year. That's searching through at least twenty years of news. Some more math and it equates to over seven thousand papers to sift through within a single outlet, let alone numerous publications.

Hours at the library turn into days. I don't skip a single paper. Another furious librarian paces nearby with her arms folded. I can't remember the last time I showered, although library visitors can take a guess based on their quick trip in and out the room. The odor from my body mixes with the stench of stale fast food and booze as a warning to all who enter.

I flip past another story about crab recipes in the Chronicle. Who reads these? There's been at least one crab recipe per hour as I sit in front of this machine. Crab rolls. Crab bisque. Crab cakes. Forget broken bread—crab belongs at The Final Supper or whatever that thing's called.

Soggy Italian beef drips over the desk while I readjust the microfilm with my other hand. Multitasking at its finest. My eyes study the latest film until an eight-letter word catches my attention: Alcatraz. My heart races. I toss the rest of the sandwich in the trash to get a better look. "Inside the Mind of a Former Alcatraz Inmate," I read aloud in the afternoon of the fourth day of searching. The words are mumbled as beef and bread slosh around my mouth like a chunk of chewing tobacco. The mixture drips on the desk as I continue to read. "Jeffrey Park, who spent fourteen years on Alcatraz, now lives a peaceful life in Napa Valley. He prefers to spend his days in solitude."

This is him—this is the man my library pal told me about. The date reads 1972—around the time the man in the library attended college. I absorb information like a sponge, knowing I can't take the slide with me and still know what it says. I scramble around the room for a pen; a pencil; give me a crayon. I'll write with my own blood if I have to.

Park was fifty-nine when the article came out. Following a fourteen-year stint on Alcatraz, he was paroled for good behavior. According to the paper, he wasn't considered a threat to society. He'd be pushing a few years shy of eighty today. That's not very reassuring for my investigation. He's probably spoon-fed mashed carrots if he's still kicking. Still, the discovery sends me darting out the door. I leap toward a nearby payphone, repeating the same few facts in my head like a skipping record. Where can I find this mystery man? He'll be able to shed some light on the blurry photo.

Quarters leap out my jacket pocket, jingling all the way to the ground only to roll off on the concrete. I don't need them. I still have three in my hand and that's enough for the call. Clink. Clink. Clink. Dial. My nails tap against the metal box before the call starts ringing. It doesn't take more than a single ring for the other line to pick up.

"Hello operator," a woman answers. "Where can I direct your call today?"

"Yes. Yeah," I stumble. I'm too impatient for pleasantries. The name's already starting to slip away in a storm of drunken forgetfulness. "Can you put me through t'the residence of a Jeffrey Park in Napa Valley? He should be between . . . between seventy n' eighty years old."

I'm waiting an eternity in anxiety.

"Yes . . . here you go," the voice responds. "The phone number for this residence is 707-555-8988. Is there anything else you nee—"

I slam the phone down. Sorry, operator—there's more important information to remember now. More figures are crammed into my fuzzy mind. I repeat the number aloud as I fumble to collect three more quarters from the pile reflecting off the ground.

Ring. Ring. Another ring. I'll lose my mind if I can't move forward today. A high like this can't come crashing down. I can't waste the evening in that shitty motel. No more 'Whiskey Tissue.' No more staring at that meaningless map on the wall with the strings of yarn that were added for aesthetic appeal.

"Hello?" a raspy voice picks up the other end. It's a woman. Panic sets in as I wonder if I misdialed. I don't have time to call the operator again. It's slipping away upstairs.

"Hi ma'am," I respond. I'll give it a chance. It's better than hanging up and starting from the beginning with a blank memory. "My name's Robb. I'm calling t'speak with a Mister Jeffrey Park. Do I have the right number?"

"Oh Jeffrey," she says. "Yes. Yes my Jeffrey."

This sounds promising. The screaming into the phone and shaking in her voice tell me she's as old as Mr. Park, if not older. She must be his wife. What condition's he in if his wife sounds this frail? I press on anyway.

"Ma'am can I speak with Jeffrey?" My patience wears thin with another innocent individual. "Can you put Jeffrey on the phone?"

"Jeffrey doesn't like talking on the phone," she responds, then has a brief coughing fit. I hear the saliva and mucus splashing onto the speaker. "He only speaks in person. No phone for Jeffrey. He gets nervous you know?"

"Thank you so much for letting me know that ma'am." This is going to be more difficult than I imagined. I give the man waiting for the phone behind me a finger in the air to inform him this'll take a while. I turn back to the phone. "I'm one a Jeffrey's old friends.

He knows me ma'am. He doesn't need t'be nervous." I'm desperate.

She responds with heavy breathing. A hard clank follows. This woman shouldn't pick up the phone if it risks her keeling over. If she's checked out, how bad can Jeffrey be? Is it even worth speaking with him? I'm more worried about my potential conversation than the well-being of this woman.

"Sorry mister." The heavy breathing resumes. "I was retrieving our address book. Our address's 2652 Pine Grove Avenue. Pine like the tree mister. You're coming t'see Jeffrey?"

"Actually I just wanted t'speak with Jeffrey on the phone. Can he—" I cut myself off to gather my next words. I can't lose her now. She's with it. She provided the address. I've come this far—what's a little farther? "Alright that's fine. Pine like the tree . . . of course. When can I come see Jeffrey?"

I'm done wasting time. This needs to be done right. A visit to Napa will take at least a few hours. A drive with the windows down for some fresh air and clarity will do me well. If I'm face-to-face with Park, I'll have a better understanding of his current state; I can assess if his responses are dipped in dementia or entirely accurate.

"Today," she speaks as if the phone was in her mouth; it's all fuzzy. "Why don't you come see my Jeffrey today hmm?"

This woman's full of surprises. Can she sense the urgency? I figured I'd have another sleepless night waiting for a drive first thing in the morning. Instead, I can get this over with tonight. Tonight, my answers won't be in a dusty history book. I'll have first-person observations.

I manage to shake Mrs. Park off the phone after some mindless chitchat. She started talking about her dead cat. She told me they buried it in the backyard under a red willow tree. This was seven years ago. I had to listen for three minutes so she wouldn't rescind my invite to come over.

I pick up a few more quarters from the ground and pat the man behind me on the shoulder. "Keep 'em." The rest of the shining silver is his. He's at least a buck richer. All I need's enough to get back to that filthy motel room. I'm in a good mood for once.

The bus stop's a block away. It's around twenty minutes from here to the motel. There's a long night ahead of me—a long night on the move. I need to refuel with a flask that'll carry me through the entirety of tonight's investigation. Prime rush hour bumps me back an extra twenty minutes, too.

The sun's setting on San Fran as I jingle the key to enter the motel room. Just a quick pitstop. The headache's starting to kick harder than a mule. I won't make it long without some fuel, so I fill the flask to the brim in fear. The liquid waterfalls over the side proving it can't hold another drop of gold. Two fingers remain in the bottle, providing an excuse for me to finish it off before hitting the road. The car's a few stumbles away from the door and it's off to Napa.

The headache fades while crossing Bay Bridge. I'm whole again. The road takes me through Oakland. The vacant evening road and Roland Orzabal's voice manage to block the unwanted contemplation. The duo of distraction swats it away while the booze blanket does the heavy lifting.

I zoom past Richmond. The money-hungry business leader morphed into this guy, the one sitting in the driver's seat with a flask in one hand and roadmap in another. A washed-up artist. I hit the charts and slide into irrelevance. The businessman elbows his way back to centerstage. He stomps his feet and moans, folding his arms in protest the moment he gets escorted away. This new man doesn't give a shit about any of that. He ignores the businessman. A few months pass and the reputation I built for years shatters. I'm a one-hit wonder; the greatest magician who ever lived. The man in the driver's seat desires temporary control. He'll leave the stage when all's right. He must get to the bottom of this first. Acceptance isn't closure for this man. Closure's telling acceptance to fuck off. It's taking matters into my own hands. Closure's spending months becoming a subject matter expert for no reason, losing your job, and living on golden liquor and items E4 and D2 from the vending machine across the hall. It's taking a trip to Napa at a moment's notice to meet a stranger.

Jam after jam blasts through the stereo. The music combined with the wind keep my eyes open. The car rolls through Valona with a personal concert blaring through the speakers. The music gets softer with each song. This piece of shit radio; this piece of shit car. Meredith stole the Porsche, leaving me with this broken box on wheels. I flip the volume knob, but the music doesn't get any louder. I pound the dashboard with my fist, hoping the stereo responds to violence. It doesn't. My fist continues to pound the dashboard, the radio dials and the car door. I'm assaulting this piece of shit car. I glance up every few seconds to readjust the wheel. I'm sliding— shifting into other lanes. The rough vibrations from the wheels hitting the side of the road further infuriate me. Bump, bump, bump, bump, bump, bump. I slam my fist back on the dashboard. Bump.

One particularly heavy thud from my hand sends a series of bright flashes reflecting off the dashboard. Red and blue flicker from the faded plastic surface. My pounding didn't fix the audio; it created these flashes. No. No, you idiot. This isn't what it looks like. The flashes reflect off the rearview mirror and into my eyes upon looking up. The lights get brighter. Closer. It's a police car.

"What the hell?" I hover a hand above my eyes to block the lights.

The music isn't fading. It's a day of eating a single greasy sandwich paired with an entire bottle of liquor—maybe more— coming for its revenge. The intoxication rams into my skull like Charles Haley leaving a QB curled up, face-down on the grass. I shouldn't be driving. I look down from the mirror and back at the dashboard. The piece of shit car still swerves from one lane to the next. This is all wrong.

My foot slams on the brakes and the officer almost rear-ends me. I roll off to the side of the vacant, pitch-black road, my fist still pounding the dashboard in frustration. Piece of shit car. I somehow blame the vehicle for my intoxication. The lights flicker as a door slams shut from behind me. The trot of an officer approaching the window's louder than the music. I slam the dashboard. My priorities are out of whack.

Two knocks of a flashlight strike the window. My eyes shift from the dashboard to the source of the sound. The man motions for the window to roll down. I strike the dashboard with one hand and crank down the window with the other. Multitasking.

"Let's see some license n' registration sir."

"Huh? Was I speeding officer?" Slurred words slip out my mouth. That can't be good. "I mean . . . it's the stereo!" My blood-red fist crashes against the dashboard. "See? It's the damn music!"

"Alright I'm gonna need you t'step outta the car." He steps back and shifts the light from my eyes to the ground. He does this a few times.

"Sir I wasn't speeding. My—the cassette player—" I don't have time for this. Let me off with a warning, asshole. This piece of shit car's the problem.

"I'm not gonna ask you again." He takes it upon himself to open the door this time, clutching the side of his belt with the other hand.

"What're you gonna do? Are you gonna shoot me? I know my rights. I'm—"

Blackness—further than blackness. The tape ejects from the stereo. The car crashes against a wall, sending bits and pieces in every direction. My mind shuts off, one hundred to zero with no caution sign.

My eyes are glued shut as my mind turns back on. Faint conversations surround me. My face rests on a hard surface and my body's freezing. Unpleasant sounds of groaning and coughing fill my ears, too. It takes every effort in my body to open my eyes from a coma and the resulting blurry sight's far less appealing than the sounds around me. It's a war zone. Men clutch their heads in pain. They reposition themselves to try and get comfortable in the grey room.

We survived a personal war tonight, ending up in the drunk tank. The smell of vomit, body odor and booze leaking out of everyone, everywhere confirms my theory. I and a dozen others are in the same state, waiting to return to normal lives as we're stuck in this little box of shame. A man dives across the room to puke in the single toilet. Everyone watches, asking themselves when it'll be their turn to be neck-deep in the metal vessel.

"Hey." I struggle to utter a single word to the man next to me. "You know where we're at right now?"

My foggy eyes peer to the side. A large black man's torso towers next to me. He sits upright, staring forward and cracking a smile as another man spews a mix of liquor and his dinner onto the ground. My neighbor turns and grabs me tight by the shoulder, a friendly yet intimidating grasp, the type an older cousin greets you with at a family reunion.

"You're in Solano." He turns back to the free show. "Welcome t'Solano brother."

"Solano?" I repeat his word, trying to imagine the roadmap left in the car. "That near Napa?"

"Why?" he asks, chuckling as a second detainee stumbles to the toilet, pushing the other man's head out of the way. "You lookin' t'turn up once they let you loose? Ya better think again brother. I saw 'em drag your ass in here. Boy was that a sight."

The other drunkards in the tight room glance at the two of us and shake their heads. The loud talking's too much for their fragile state.

"Drag me in here? What're you talkin' about? How long've I been in here?"

He grabs my shoulder again. He's bored with the vomit show now. "If you've got questions go poke your head out them bars. Ask a pig for answers."

I'm out of options. I'm supposed to be on the way to Napa right now. Depending on the time, I might have already arrived in Napa, already speaking to Jeffrey Park at his home. This was my opportunity for answers.

The large man's my guiding light. It's his advice or the inside of a toilet bowl. My feet struggle to stand from the rock-solid bench that cradled me for God knows how long. I'm learning to walk again as I waddle over to the cell bars in pain.

"Hey," I cough. Phlegm flows up from my throat to my mouth like an erupting volcano. I clear my throat again. "Lemme talk t'someone! I've got somewhere t'be!"

The rant continues. Officers ignore me and other detainees interject with 'Shut up' and 'Don't waste your time.' They can beat the shit out of me if they want. I won't stop yelling until someone comes over. I'm supposed to be in Napa with Jeffrey Park, so the other detainees are forced to listen to the yelling for another thirty minutes. My voice grows coarse yet seems to find enough strength for another obscenity.

"Let me out you lazy assholes!"

"What in God's green earth are you goin' on about?" a voice yells from down the hall.

I turn toward the rest of the drunk tank to ensure it wasn't another smartass comment from in here. All heads are down as if deep in prayer. The comment came from outside the cell.

"Mister Robert Field." The voice shows a face. It's an officer. The man stares at a clipboard, glancing up and down from the sheet to me.

"Yeah that's me," I whine. "Jesus I've been screamin' here. Aren't you guys s'posed t'have respect for other human beings?"

"Respect?" He steps closer. The clipboard's at his side now. I have his undivided attention. "That's a bold request comin' from the guy who assaulted my partner. I dunno who you think you are but you better count your blessings. You're on track t'rot behind real bars if this is your lifestyle." The man shakes his head, writing on the clipboard and turning to his left. "Ma'am . . . you're sure about this?" He turns back to stare at me in disgust. "Looks t'me like this one deserves the rest a the night in here."

The officer steps to the side, his eyes tracking someone moving down the hallway. Clattering heels echo toward the cell bars. A woman takes his place several seconds later.

"Meredith?"

ONE FINE DAY

Nine hours. Nine out of the twenty-four hours the Sun God rewards us with are wasted in the yard, library or confines of a cell. This is time designed to be spent away from routine, yet it forms new habits—at least for me. I spend this time rereading the little book, praising its pages at night. I recite information in the dining hall or showers. The time is also dedicated to monitoring Karpis. He sits alone during meals, revealing that he does not have a band of misfits like Wilson. He heads to detail like any other inmate. He is an old man going through the motions of prison life.

The Barker-Karpis Gang was one of the most notorious gangs of the 1900s. I know this because of the little book. Creepy Karpis was the gang's leader. The group did not limit themselves to bank robberies either, adding kidnapping and murder to their lengthy resume. Karpis holds the impressive title of 'last person to ever be on the FBI's Public Enemy No. 1 list.' Yet he remains docile and lonely in this dream world. Is the little book wrong? Perhaps it is his old age or a spiritual awakening that makes him keep to himself. He is everything except the man historians document him to be. He putters around the yard alone with a solemn look. The system caught up with him after all these years. In Alcatraz, the Barker-Karpis Gang is a one-man band.

This is all an effort to calm down, an attempt at convincing myself I am making the most intelligent decision. Those lucky enough to have their names written in the little book are worthy of my attention. Sure, I can place the target on Wilson's back. I know as much about him as Karpis, but I already made an ally of my neighbor. An ally is my failsafe should this dream world flip upside-down. Besides, Wilson's crew is too loyal to allow him to suffer at my hands. That leaves Alvin Karpowicz as the catalyst to send me to cell fourteen.

"So Wilson . . . I heard you orchestrated a pretty foolproof escape a while back." I lean over to my ally during supper. "How'd you think a that anyway?"

He pushes his tray out of the way to make room for his elbows. He lifts his hands and cups his head, shaking it in disappointment. "And where'd you hear that?" It is as though he is a Hollywood star approached by an irritating fan. "Be careful a the things you talk about that you've got no business bringin' up in the first place."

"Some of the guys brought it up a few days ago," I lie. "From what I heard it was a genius plan . . . escaping from the dock n' all. Most guards expect escapees t'dart off near a cliff or another vacant part a the island. You did it in a heavily guarded location."

Wilson raises his head, tilting it sideways to study me. He is trying to assess my intentions—reading me like the little book. I do not have his full trust. I am still trying out for the crew. The audition of my life. Wilson is cautious in his words as well as in his actions, maintaining the upper hand with exceptional strength.

"It wasn't easy," he says, leaning back. He pulls the tray toward him and takes a spoonful of steaming stew to the mouth. The self-centered wrongdoer is too proud to keep his trap shut. He looks around to make sure no one besides his closest confidants tune into his words. "It took months a preparation n' detailed plannin'. Garbage detail put me in half a dozen places a day. That was an edge I had from the start."

He carries on for several minutes, continuing without interruption like a schoolgirl with the gossip of the month. I am already a paragraph ahead by the time he finishes another sentence thanks to the little book. I continue to act intrigued nonetheless. This is me earning his trust. Ten minutes pass and he is still blabbering on—a wind-up toy that carries on and on. The whispers soar across the table with pride. It is a wonder how he has not broken out in song yet. He stops to catch a breath. The moment forces him to quiet himself and raise an eyebrow at the one-way conversation.

"Why you grillin' me on this anyway?"

"No reason. I'm impressed by it is all." Another lie to maintain his trust. "I had t'hear it from you t'know the truth. If I'm being honest it's actually inspiring."

It was an idiotic plan—mindless. The dock is perhaps the worst location for escape. He had plenty of options with garbage detail, yet chose one of the most-guarded areas on the island. My interest serves one purpose: luring him in.

Simple curiosity transitions into a cold glare. "Keep your voice down Field. Dummy up. This isn't the place t'talk about that type a shit."

I have his full attention. He sunk his teeth into the bait; I have him hooked. The final step is to reel him in. He looks around at his crew, shaking his head again, but not at me this time. He realizes he flew too close to the sun, revealing a deep secret and realizing the knowledge is now in my possession.

"I know . . . I'm sorry." I resurface the drowning conversation. "It's just I think with your experience n' my new perspective we could do it all over again."

He is humbled by the remark while insistent on my silence, so he does not acknowledge the soft offer. He cracks a fading smile and shakes it back into its cave. He is aggravated by the lack of secrecy, yet optimistic about another chance at freedom. The idea of freedom is the pornography of the prison system; it is a representation of the unrealistic.

The bell tolls before the conversation can progress. We are sent filing out of the dining hall into our various lines for final count. The sound was convenient as I was running out of words to keep Wilson engaged.

Wilson spends most of his life behind bars. Again, this is not a fact I dare reveal to the man as a tornado of reactions would soon follow. It does let me know that he is not one to consider as a true partner in crime, though. There is no long-term alliance between us should this be reality. If that is the case, I will jump ship from this temporary craft. It is doomed to sink.

Another sleepless night is spent staring up at the blank ceiling and at the green grate across the cell. Weeks have passed in this dream—in this reality. I dream of a different freedom now with the

Sun God shoving routine down my throat and expecting acceptance. Sleepless nights provide the opportunity to center my thinking. I channel the internal radio dial back to its original station. The audiotape. The more time I spend dancing with routine, the more I drift from my primary goal. Everything starts and ends in cell fourteen. The tape.

Vivid nightmares become frequent when your life revolves around existential thinking. The world explodes; I plummet to my death from a steep cliff; Robb stabs me in the back in the middle of the night. He stabs me until my back looks like a cheese grater with holes everywhere. These are my nightmares, yet I cannot die. I replay the scenario. If this is a nightmare, an encounter with Karpis awakens me like any of the previous encounters with death. Is this what I want? To wake up in Robb's million-dollar home with a life still in shambles? I wish to escape from this routine—one from a dream—while I simultaneously crave more of this false reality. It is a tug of war between waking up and accepting this new world. It is a satisfying predicament, leaving me in a state of fear that drives me forward. I owe it to myself to get to the bottom of this one way or another. No more accepting routine—no matter where it originates from.

I face a wall. I face the other wall. Back and forth. I toss and turn the entire night until the Sun God rises again. No sleep—that cannot help. I am at the point of no return. Today is the day. I am checking out of this cell and moving into cell fourteen. Nothing can stop that and a healthy eight hours of sleep would not change anything.

The false seed of escape is planted in Wilson's ear. That is a story I do not wish to further fabricate without additional thought. I have his attention. A final move on the board led to my unofficial membership in Wilson's crew. They are my allies; they are my crew and they will protect me. If they do not, Wilson's plan risks reaching every inch of Alcatraz.

It is Saturday, which means it is yard time. Every murderer, thief and other rebel on The Rock cherishes Saturdays. They carry a cheerful attitude that knocks the miseries of this island unconscious, if only for a moment. Take a man's freedom away and he still finds joy in the weekend. Our ancestors laugh at us. I could care less about the day of the week as something else keeps me occupied. I count down the minutes before yard time arrives for other reasons.

I push around the food on my tray, full of over-cooked eggs and soft toast, with a spoon in the early morning. No sleep and no food. I am on edge.

"I'm not feeling so well," I tell Wilson and his crew.

They have sent stares my way since we first sat down. My mask is slipping off. It all comes down to my actions today and keeping up the act falls second to that no matter how hard I try.

"That's the slammer for ya," Sykes laughs as he flicks my temple. "If ya feel well at any point there's somethin' wrong upstairs. The food ain't here t'keep us alive. Why ya think it's so tasty? No . . . they're poisonin' us. It's untraceable in them low quantities ya know. Yep we're all dyin' here."

Commentary from Sykes and Lens carries us through breakfast, following us out of the dining hall and landing in the yard. Just like that, the moment has arrived. What felt like months of time for preparation dwindles like a bomb destined for detonation. Wilson must trust me. I have done all I can to keep him on my side.

The five of us stand in our usual spot. That is the way yard time works; it is territorial. We are lions protecting our turf. The steps are for the power-hungry cons—the most senior or the ones with the most intimidating rap sheet. Our spot is in the northwest corner. This is our turf. Everything has gone as expected today—the rigid routine does have its benefits in that regard. I know what to anticipate. It is the same re-run of 'Miami Vice' every week. We get so used to it that we depend on routine. That is why these territorial disputes exist in the first place.

The crew argues with Sykes over the validity of his claims from breakfast, providing an open field of vision for me to monitor Karpis. The loner Creepy Karpis is in his personal corner of the yard as a one-man pride. This is my target today. I am on my own if I wander into his territory without rhyme or reason. This punches routine in the face. The crew will not understand nor come to my rescue without proper cause.

"Baseball!" I blurt out.

A few lobs of a baseball interrupt my view of Karpis. Baseball—that stupid sport Robb wasted his time watching. An opportunity to venture out of our usual territory and a neutral area for any and all prisoners.

"Why don't we play baseball?" I elaborate. The crew stops arguing, all members turning my way. They look offended. Sykes, who has rambled on for half an hour now, is silenced. I continue holding the microphone. "Listen I'm all for standing here chatting every moment we're outside. Really I am . . . but it's as damn nice a day as it'll ever be on this rock."

They continue to stare.

"I mean the weather that is. Let's do somethin' diff'rent for once yeah?"

My Robb hat goes on. Years of hearing his bullshit sales tactics and success stories bubble up after being repressed. It takes a few more insightful comments until Sykes expresses interest. When one crew member is in on an idea, it causes a domino effect. Ronnie agrees with his parrot. When both Ronnie and Sykes are in, the tides turn and Lens is open to the suggestion. He even removes his glasses and drops them in his shirt pocket to prepare for the activity.

"So what d'you think?" I ask Wilson.

The four of us stare at him in anticipation, forcing him to respond in a timely manner. "Have it your way then," he lets out a dead chuckle. It is obvious he despises the idea. It is the first time he is not calling the shots and he is threatened. "You guys deserve a little relaxin' for once."

He knew this was not going his way. He spun the situation to wrestle me for the microphone, convincing the crew this is their reward for longtime loyalty.

This is not Robb's baseball; it is not his virtual escape from reality. This form of baseball consists of plastic bats that could not break a piñata if someone's life depended on it. Soft, underhand pitches are required on the gravel. No birds run in fear of getting shot, every con jogging from one base to the next. It may be childish, however, it is the closest activity the rebels have to a real sport. This child-proofed form of athletics received the stamp of approval after an inmate went at another with a makeshift knife. He proceeded to shank the opponent over the outcome of the game— over the stupid, pointless baseball game. From there, this hollow substitute for the game was incorporated to limit anyone's success with the bat.

Sweat sticks to my denim clothes as we linger near the bleachers. The uncomfortable perspiration intensifies the more I attempt to cool down. The crew stares at me. I pull my pants away from my legs after each step like soaked swim trunks.

"It's hot out," I tell them.

It cannot be more than sixty degrees outside, yet nerves get the best of me. My body reacts without warning. We stand near the concrete steps waiting for our turn to take the field. The sweat continues to stick.

Each game consists of two innings. We can thank the previous violent outburst for the short length, too. The two innings last several minutes as the weak bat sends every ball floating into a glove sooner rather than later. My heart pounds a beat faster as each group is called. We inch closer behind home plate. Second on deck. A few minutes pass and we are on the line, ready to step onto the field.

"Next up!" an officer shouts from atop the bleachers. "Next up I said! Field that means you!"

My trance is broken. Time is up. Everything culminates in these next few minutes. This is it. The five of us march from behind home plate in a straight line. The failing rebels from the other team hand off the flimsy plastic stick. There is no going back. No more time spent with the little book. I cannot earn any more of Wilson's trust.

Each member of the crew parts ways, moving into position. The only reason I know a damn thing about baseball is due to Robb's obsession with the sport growing up. He carried the godly title of an all-state warrior in high school. My parents ordered those little magnets of him in his uniform, smiling with a fake backdrop. They posted them on every metal surface in our home; they ordered mugs; they made screen-printed t-shirts. I threw the extras in the garbage. I imagine my mother still has them somewhere in a box in the attic.

Wilson hovers over the mound, his final effort to exercise power. The crew agreed with me for once and he was in the minority. Taking the mound is his way to maintain dominance. I anticipated him accepting no other position and was correct.

The powerhouse Ronnie stands behind home plate. He crouches down, his fat ass already touching the ground. His large face fights the catcher's mask, skin popping out over the little metal fence covering his forehead. The batter stands tall, yet his head barely rests above the watermelon balancing on Ronnie's neck.

Sykes takes center field. He stares at Ronnie, looking uncomfortable and exposed. This is the furthest the parrot has stood from his master's shoulder—Ronnie's broad shoulder. His hand punches the brown, worn leather glove. It is a form of stress relief— the equivalent of those useless foam balls on every desk in every workplace. I am sure Robb had one, too.

Lens wanders around right field. He paces back and forth, crafting a theory to prove Sykes' beliefs on the poisoned food are wrong. He pushes his glasses up every few steps as they slide down his nose. He is not cut out for athletics either.

The stars align as left field is mine. This is the closest position to Creepy Karpis. The entire yard cannot be larger than half a professional baseball field, including the concrete steps and the corners of solitude like the one Karpis claims. Still, this being my position must be some sort of sign.

An officer reads a few scripted rules aloud. Each crew member jumps into at-the-ready stances like dogs waiting for a tennis ball to be thrown; they are prepared to please their master. Wilson stands proud on the mound, the rest of his followers behind him. The game commences with the blow of a whistle. Wilson begins by throwing a few brutal pitches. The hollow ball cannot travel far with an underhand pitch, leaving two men to walk to first base after the wind carries the white cylinder far from home plate.

"This wind's bullshit!" Wilson complains.

He looks back at the crew and shakes his head. Other birds

chuckle from the steps and his middle finger skyrockets in their direction. A guard shouts at him in response. Wilson is frustrated, maybe even embarrassed. Is this why he avoided specific yard activities? Fear of failure in front of his men is too much to bear. The con's patience dwindles. The white ball ends up everywhere besides the plate. The rainbow toss has a short trajectory. These are environmental factors every prisoner is aware of besides Wilson. His vision remains tunneled in frustration. He sends a third rebel walking after the light sphere strikes the man on the shoulder. Strike. Ball. These are baseball terms I can again thank Robb for jamming into my life.

The fed-up pitcher turns to the outfield. He addresses his team— he addresses me—with a not-so-subtle wink. That look on his face—I have seen it every day. He is plotting something in his sensitive mind, unaware of my own plans for this game. He will not throw in the towel and send his crew walking off the gravel onto more gravel that carries less pride. The men would not dare make fun of him to his face, but he is intelligent enough to know they would do so behind his back, or at least in the confines of their minds.

Wilson winds up the sphere. This time, his arm goes straight backward behind his head. He whips the ball overhand, one final middle finger to prove he is the boss. It happens so fast. Guards do not have time to digest the forbidden pitch. The laser is a bullseye headed toward the plate. The sphere crashes into the plastic bat, pivoting in the opposite direction like a pendulum. The ball soars through the air. The yard is silent as every breathing body watches the dinky orb float onward. To them, it may as well be a U.F.O. on the verge of abduction.

"Field!" Sykes yells. The sound is muffled as I, too, stare at the ball. Is this how Robb feels watching this ridiculous game on television? "Field . . . get the ball dammit!"

The crew's persistent shouting pulls me back from the clouds. I am back in a dream. The sphere continues to rise until it reaches its inevitable climax. For a piece of plastic, it goes an impressive distance. Hats off to Wilson and the batter for the accomplishment.

The ball descends and I sprint toward the object. Its path has a trajectory that will leave it near the corner of the yard. It is bound to be in the Creep's general area. This is no coincidence. This is as close as I will get to Karpis with Wilson and his crew within shouting distance. This is it.

Time moves slowly with each step echoing on the gravel. The falling dove loses my attention as Karpis becomes the new target. He stands a mountain tall with his back to the yard flipping through a magazine. His time of solitude is closing in. Does he deserve what is headed in his direction? Perhaps not, but I carry with me his unfortunate long-term fate. It does not matter if this is a dream or reality. No action changes his fate. He perishes in prison.

My strides draw closer to the infamous rebel. Nurtured instincts of safety and protection whisper in my ear, 'Stop.' They are ignored. A few strides later and Karpis' head turns from the pages of the magazine in complete confusion at the sound of gravel kicking the air. He hears the stomping closing in on him—a bull charging at red.

I glance up at the sky in a last-ditch effort to appear distracted. The ball already struck the ground and a quick glance in front of me indicates Karpis did not notice as much. If he believes the inevitable event is an accident he may not try to murder me in cold blood for disrupting his peace.

Boom. Thud. Pain arrives as my body smashes against the mountain that is Karpis. The six-foot-three-or-larger monster slightly stumbles without toppling over. My body, on the other hand, crashes to the ground. The tree stands tall several feet away from me, attempting to process what just occurred.

Whistles blow from every angle as guards meet the fallen meteor back on earth to respond to the escalating situation. Cons yell and run about in every direction. The shouts are of enthusiasm; they hope a fight ensues. Their wishes may be granted based on the look on Karpis' face. I attempted to topple one of the biggest monsters within these tight walls.

Karpis steps closer. He lets out a few growls steeped in pain and rage. A wild animal awakens from its slumber. He bends down, pulling back his balled-up fist and tossing it at my face. Stinging pain. I try to envision his fist as the baseball soaring through the air to distract myself from the present. His fist grows farther, then it enlarges. Closer. Farther. Closer. Take me away from this distant dream. He pulls me up by the collar and pushes me down with his fist. Each punch sends thick red iron skyrocketing out of my nose and onto the rest of my face like fireworks in the night sky. My head feels a little less cluttered with this painful anesthesia. Send me away from this distant dream to show me where I stand.

My eyes swell. I try to finish the job by closing them on my own terms. I accept this fate. I try to determine what is next in this bloodbath. What is the grand finale? The sun beams into what remains of my swollen eyes; the Sun God's glare bounces off Karpis' hip. It is a knife—a rigid, makeshift knife he has carried around for such unpleasant encounters. The rebel accepts his fate, too, pulling the object back and pausing for a moment. His body vibrates with rage. He closes his eyes, preparing to indulge in the forthcoming action. One final blow to my body and this will end. Reality will reveal itself.

"Get off him Creep!" a familiar voice shouts.

It is Sykes. Wilson and his crew of crooks made it to me before any of the guards. The plan is working. The loyal band of bandits are by my side; they are in this now. Bring me to the tape. The last image that comes into frame before the light switch flips off is the meathead standing behind Karpis. Ronnie yanks a fuming Creep off of my bloody body.

Darkness is too familiar as of late. This is the only time my active brain is silenced. Nothing matters for a moment. It is what I imagine death is like. No thoughts. No worries. Emptiness that cannot be described. It is rather peaceful in a sense.

My body aches from top to bottom. A car struck me and sent my corpse tumbling down a ravine. This must be what happened. This happened on the way back from the airport in Fog City. My eyes remain swollen shut. The pain is more real than that in a deep sleep. The firm surface assures me this is not one of Robb's thousand-dollar mattresses. The lingering taste of blood tells me enough. This is not Robb's home and this is not a dream. The pain from Captain Peters' baton in my distant dream did not feel this real—this intense.

"You're lucky t'be alive son." The sound of a chair rolls across the ground as a voice welcomes me back to reality. "A fight like that in the jungle isn't something most men live through t'tell the tale."

The jungle? I muscle enough strength to squint out of a single eye. It is a doctor—or some sort of medical professional. The cheap uniform, ancient mustache and slicked-back hair are out of style. The getup is acceptable for Halloween or a Broadway musical set decades in the past. The doctor paired with the icy handcuffs strapping me to the bed put another concern in my head. The last thing I recall from the distant dream is the crew coming to save the day. The meathead Ronnie was pulling Karpis off my body. This doctor—these handcuffs—paint a complementary picture to what went down in the distant dream.

"What happened? How'd I end up here?"

Each syllable hurts. It is a deep pain originating from my chest that slithers its way up to my head. The pain ripples like a stone tossed in a pond.

"Well you obviously made it outta there," the man responds. He wipes blood from my face before placing a fresh bandage over the sections that continue leaking red jelly. "I dunno many details, however someone kicked the bucket out there. You best get on your knees n' thank the Lord Almighty it wasn't you tossed in the body bag."

"Someone died?" I ask, able to utter a few more words. "Who? Who died?" The distant dream is somehow reality. This is no act.

"I'm not at liberty t'discuss specifics with you," he starts. He looks down at a file in his hand. "That said I will say a Ronald Yantz drew the short straw out there. He passed just less than an hour ago from fatal knife wounds. Now get some rest . . . I have no doubt you'll have enough time by yourself t'think this over in the coming days."

The man slides his chair across the room. He puts a file on the counter and walks out of sight, leaving me cuffed to the bed like a psychiatric patient. Doctor Polk would be happy to see me getting such help.

Sykes always referred to his big bodyguard, Ronnie, as Ronald. That must mean he was the Ronald who died out there. I want to wrap my thoughts tight around how and why this is a new reality, but something more pressing takes precedent. Ronald was stabbed, meaning this was not a result of a guard's action. An officer would have clubbed him to death or gunned him down if they felt the least bit threatened. Creepy Karpis found a way to shank the meathead during the attack with that makeshift blade. This is what occupies my mind.

The doctor implied I will end up in confinement. The first path proved empty; it brought me back in a circle. I would pat myself on the back for including a failsafe if my hands were not cuffed. I should be able to get ahold of that tape once I am healed due to my actions in this twisted reality. The death of Ronald Yantz adds a new layer of complexity to an already confusing reality, though. Does Wilson know my actions were intentional? Will Sykes want revenge for the death of his big bodyguard? Is Karpis now a looming threat?

I dreamt of Robb while unconscious. The close dream centered around him arriving in this twisted reality, too. How would he fare in a similar situation? I dreamt of him crying when the guards stripped him of his business suit and manila folder. Despite the pain, despite the conflict, despite the uncertainty, one thing leaves me with an internal grin: I survived longer than Robb would have within these walls. My self-absorbed, adopted brother would crumble in a place like this. That eases the pain pulsating throughout my body like an injection of morphine.

THE PRETENDER

The Sun God waves hello and goodbye over my three days spent healing in the infirmary. Impatience dissolves as those days blur together due to medication and a constant state of exhaustion. My body continues to ache. Three days of silence and solitude. I am unable to explore this newly discovered, twisted reality.

Captain Peters enters the room on the morning of the fourth day. He is swift to lay his paws on my bruises as he uncuffs me. He does not say a word. Instead, he rolls me out of bed, almost tossing over the firm mattress in the process. He points to the doorway while keeping a stone-cold expression. The waiting game ends as I am shoved from one room to another. He is sending me to confinement; he would not be so quiet if we were heading elsewhere.

The walk mirrors the first few days in this prison. I went from room to room, speaking with Peters and Madison on a regular basis. I waited for the dream to reach its curtain call as I proceeded to blindly explore it. This time, Peters has another screw meet us in the cellblock. The crew introduced this as the double-team escort. Double-team escorts are reserved for troublesome inmates. Guards are too fearful to handle these prisoners on their own. A whining boy proclaiming innocence no more. I am dangerous in their eyes.

The guards push me past B-block; they push me past C-block. They escort me all the way to D-block. Sunset Strip. Solitary confinement. My failsafe swings into motion despite feelings of uncertainty. Three of the four cells referred to as 'the hole' are closed. The heavy, windowless doors slammed shut sometime during my recovery. The hole is never this congested. The cells were vacant when I first arrived in cell fourteen.

Cell eleven. Cell twelve. We continue to walk. Cell thirteen. I am thrown into cell fourteen again—the strip cell. Lens described cell fourteen as the ultimate form of confinement, even above the damp, dark dungeon. It is where prisoners' minds go to rot before their bodies.

"Let's see how two weeks in the shitter treats ya!" Peters shouts, attempting to speak over the sound of the cell door sliding shut.

I am home.

All four cells are now shut. In my months here, those hard cells occupied one individual at a time, possibly two. Karpis claims one of these cells while the other two could be home to any number of cons.

My theorizing is interrupted with recollection of what brought me here in the first place: the tape. That man in my mind. The long-lost audiotape traveled to this reality. I drop to my knees and feel around the dusty ground for the artifact. Panic sets in as the flat surface continues. I no longer have a leg up on everyone in this joint if they discovered the tape before me.

My hand brushes across an object in the back corner of the room. I grab it without hesitation. Here it is—that fax from a previous dimension. That calm voice brings me back to where I left off the moment I drape the headphones over my ears.

"Misbehaving inmates were tossed in one of these four solitary confinement cells as punishment for wrongdoings," the voice informs me. "Some inmates were said to have been in these cells for over two weeks straight."

Two weeks. Peters said I am locked in here for two weeks. I am one of those inmates the man in my mind mentions. The lack of mobility does not pose a problem as the tape continues, spilling new information that even the little book does not provide. Months of living within these walls allows for a painted picture of every corner of the island. Time vanishes as I immerse myself in the dialogue. The tape is the constant maintaining my sanity. I pause the audio sporadically to let information digest despite anticipation whispering for me to complete the recording. This is my entertainment for two weeks, so I must make it last. That, and I must study it. I cannot take it out of cell fourteen and risk screws or birds getting their hands on it. Two weeks to memorize the tape and it is good riddance—once and for all.

Days blur together more than they did in the infirmary as a symphony of darkness assists with that feeling. I can hear guards making their rounds in the flats above Sunset Strip a few times each day. When that happens, the tape gets tossed back into the corner. The light of the door opening for a quick meal delivery follows the footsteps. The light cannot reach the tape in the cell's blackest corner.

The sun rises. It falls. It rises again. I do not see any of this with only blindness and solitude to accompany me. One day this routine is finally shattered. A pitter-patter of dress shoes outside the door sneaks its way into the cell. Someone is approaching—someone different than the guard who brings me food based on the sound of their shoes alone. I toss the tape aside and lie in the fetal position. This is me dramatizing my physical and mental state that the tape has managed to keep intact. The heavy door slides open for more than a few seconds this time. What can this mean? The sun's powerful rays blind its prisoner. Shadows step in to cover the light, blocking the beams to produce god-like silhouettes.

"Get out here n' come with me," a voice orders.

I know that voice—the warden's voice. Two months have passed since I last saw the tyrant. He promised to have me executed if I did not agree to his story. His message was clear. Peters accompanies Madison, towering above him as a personal bodyguard. The servant steps into the cell, grabbing my bruised arm and forcing me on my feet. He throws a shirt and pants at my face.

"Cover yourself," he says.

They stare into the cell, arms folded while watching me clothe myself. They stand with pride in the doorway, their way of feeling superior. We proceed to stroll down Sunset Strip. Madison remains silent during the journey and a submissive Peters bites his tongue as well. The silence indicates we are headed to another mysterious meeting. Another chance to speak with me in silence. More threats of death. I have come to expect the worse.

Peters steers me alongside the warden like a shopping cart going down an aisle. We eventually end our trek at the dining hall. Peters gets an opportunity to flex his bottled-up anger and pushes me onto a seat in the empty hall as the warden walks around the table and sits across from me the same way Wilson did. He reaches into his suit pocket and pulls out a piece of paper.

"You see this envelope?" He holds it to my face. "This is a request for Alvin Karpowicz's transfer t'U.S.P. Leavenworth."

"N' why am I s'posed t'care about that?" I share fighting words.

So much time in the strip cell removed any and all inhibitions. I feel untouchable. This forces the warden to drop the good-cop act and let out a true beast.

"You know damn well why you should care about this here envelope. Your foolishness sent three men t'the hole. It killed another. You see this is the sorta thing that draws attention t'my prison—attention t'me as the warden of this place." He puts the envelope back in his pocket. "I've told you how important reputation is t'me. You've disrespected that."

"It's a prison," I add. "It's full of convicts fighting n' murdering each other. It was a simple misunderstanding. I don't see what the big deal—"

"The big deal's this whole thing revolves around you!" he shouts.

He slams his fist on the table, the gavel vibrating across the long surface. Peters motions to calm him down. This little meeting is our secret and the servant's job is to keep it that way.

"As you know by now . . ." The warden takes a deep breath. "the Federal Bureau of Prisons doesn't know you're here. They don't know we have a convict amongst us who slipped through the cracks. Using the records we forged is a last resort. We're keeping it that way as long as we can. You belong to U.S.P. Alcatraz now. This whole thing with Ronald Yantz? We're labeling it an accidental death on account of his own violent behavior. The fat bastard got in a scuffle with Karpowicz that he initiated. That sound like a good story t'you?"

"What about the guards?" I refuse to accept this ridiculous fiction. "N' the other inmates? They saw everything that went down in the yard. They know I was involved."

"What about them?" he laughs. "The guards answer t'me. The

prisoners answer t'me. You answer t'me. That's the benefit of running this place don't you see? I'm untouchable." He stands up from the table and yanks his suit pants a little higher. "In the meantime Karpowicz is transferring for six months 'til this whole situation simmers down."

It is clear Madison will do anything to save his own ass. His mind revolves around his and the prison's reputation. He will maintain that reputation even if it requires complete deceit.

"Use the rest of your time in the hole t'think about how you wanna act," the tyrant says, walking out of the hall. "Nothing'll go your way. Get used t'it or this'll end in misery."

The journey back to the hole is led by a free Captain Peters. A solo Peters means he can indulge in a variety of vulgar nicknames accompanied by a few cracks of the baton. He aims for the purple spots on my skin and the healing cuts on my neck, a servant in the face of power and an abuser in the face of the weak. I have more respect for the warden than this man.

I decide to listen to the tape for another few minutes upon returning to the cell, a lullaby to ease my mind before more time in an empty void. It is a distraction from the unfortunate conversation with Madison. The old man's voice from my mind morphs into a new therapist of sorts, someone I attempted to get away from months ago. Desperate times.

The tape does quite the opposite of calming me. Several minutes in, the voice touches on a few of the most hardened criminals who did time on Alcatraz, rebels the little book chose to spend an excessive amount of time lingering on. Where was Ronald Yantz in the little book, and where is he in the tape? One name suddenly stands out among the rest as if it was my own. The name of a ghost continues to haunt me. "Alvin Karpowicz," the new therapist whispers through the foam headphones. The consideration I continue to avoid steps into the spotlight.

"While Karpowicz did the longest stint at Alcatraz in the prison's history, he was briefly transferred to Kansas' U.S.P. Leavenworth. He returned to Alcatraz six months later."

Karpis was always going to Leavenworth. I think back to his

profile in the little book. The profile had two time stamps beneath his name, which never made sense until now. He did two stints at Alcatraz over the years, with one period ending in 1958. The other kicked in for the monster in 1959. He was always going to Leavenworth.

If this is not an alternate dimension, perhaps this is a time from long ago. The concept of fluid time seems more realistic than any other possibility with this discovery. Have I spent too much time in this cell? If this odd theory is true, the little book holds the past, present and future within its pages.

I pause the tape for the rest of the night for that minute of dialogue is enough to occupy my mind for now. If the little book knows all, does it mean its pages are written in stone? Or rather, am I capable of altering its content through my actions? If I cannot alter the little book's—and the tape's—matter, then I can immerse myself within it. I can blend into it like cream in black coffee. I have the opportunity to play a crucial part in the story. Karpis was sent to Leavenworth, but he arrived there because of my actions.

The tape plays through time and again as my days in isolation resume. When my mental clock has neared a two-week timer of solitude, I smash the tape along with its components against the cracking concrete wall. I smash it beyond recovery. When it is destroyed, I take a fallen piece of concrete and stab the pieces before sweeping everything into a corner. I am finished if anyone locates this device. These efforts ensure that will not happen.

One curiosity persistently pokes the back of my head: why am I not represented in the little book if I can impact its contents? Where is my story?

BIRDS ON HIGH

No tape nor book can illustrate what reality can. For instance, few people know who the Birdman truly is. Robert 'Birdman' Stroud studied law within Alcatraz. Of course, anyone with a history book knows that. At the same time, he sold his knowledge to inmates who were hoping to beat the system. The man found a way to monetize his education while held captive.

Countless stories written by unknown historians or authors tell a small fraction of the full picture. Huge chunks of reality go undocumented. These are collections of history—a 'Greatest Hits' of sorts. Society chooses to report on what it labels newsworthy while half the story is abandoned, left in time where it originated.

Taking time to memorize the tape from beginning to end before crushing it to smithereens was the right decision. No evidence exists beyond my enclosed mind. It is locked in a place much darker than cell fourteen now. I will carry that knowledge on my shoulders for whatever time I have left on this island. There is no doubt I would have been gutted by a fellow inmate if I relied on that tape over the last few months. Stuck in the belly like a pig. That, or shot in the head by Peters at Madison's command. I needed to learn about this prison's system first, everything from learning who to avoid to minor observations like what meals lead to sitting on the toilet the entire night. I needed to struggle to be born again.

Do not get me wrong, I have used the knowledge obtained from the little book to my benefit from time to time. After all, the tape would not end up in my possession if it was not for the little book. Consider it my getting up to speed with the life of a bird. Slang, a bit about various inmates and a list of island rules brought me this far.

The most obvious variable in this reality stands in my own steps;

it is me. There is not a single sentence of my being here within the tape nor the little book. What is an anxiety-inducing observation is soon explained in my forever-turning mind. Even if there were records of my presence here, Madison would ensure anything and everything disappeared for good. This is an obstacle I will deal with when the time is right. For now, there is work to be done. I need to assimilate back into the dreaded routine I spent so many years attempting to destroy. It is a routine I must pursue.

"Field!" Mason, one of the Industries Building's detail guards, yells over the sound of roaring laundry machines. "You're needed in the receiving room. Drop what you've got n' come with me at once."

Mason is a pushover, bullied by other guards. Even birds manage to get under his skin. It is a common scenario among newer screws contributing to high turnover. Inmates claim you can pick out new officers by the way they walk and the way they talk. They tread with an unnecessary cautious tiptoe as if a jailbird was about to jump out from the corner and stick them in the belly with a bar of soap carved into a pointy shank. These guards are often terrified at first, fearful for their own fates upon arrival.

This is not my first encounter with Officer Mason, so I know what the cherry guard has in store for me. I have known this since my first week out of cell fourteen. However, I must melt back into the prison system without turning Peters' nor the warden's head in my direction. I must remain as quiet and as orderly as possible even if that requires sacrificing my health. My bruises never heal.

Mason escorts me to the receiving room, a room that is typically empty in the afternoon. The last of the day's laundry is received at noon, so the guards and birds stationed in this room leave it open for all sorts of trouble in the late afternoon. This is my fourth time here in the last month. How long will it continue?

"It's a glorious Thursday isn't it?" a familiar voice steps out from the shadows.

It is Wilson, my former ally and neighbor. His crew follows, which acquired a fresh fish to fill the void of the deceased Ronnie. The dead meathead. Rest in peace.

Getting my hands on the tape did not come without consequence. I obtained the object by breaking the rules and regulations of the system as well as the law of the bird. It is times like this I much prefer the consequences of the former than the latter. The deal, at least from my perspective, is that the crew can beat me just shy of putting me in the infirmary in exchange for their protection over Mason. If anything goes awry amongst inmates, the crew keeps the weak screw out of harm's way. The officer sold his dignity for an extra line of defense. That coward.

Word spread like wildfire of every rebel locked in the hole during my stint after my return to Broadway. Two cells held Karpis and me while the mysterious other two residents of Sunset Strip were revealed to be Sykes and Wilson. Wilson and his fellow crew member were tossed in after tussling with some guards following Ronnie's death. They were furious over the loss of their fellow member and managed to land a few punches before getting themselves tossed in the hole for a week.

It did not take long for the crew to put the situation together following their reunion. From every inmate's—and guard's— perspective, the attempted tackle in the yard was intentional. They are not wrong—no amount of wordsmithing could convince Wilson and his remaining followers otherwise. They needed someone to blame, and they picked the winning ticket by choosing me as a human punching bag; a meat sack of black and blue and red from irritated bruises and sliced stitches. I forget what my skin looked like when not spotted with purple blotches. These are the consequences of obtaining the tape.

Mason turns a blind eye in the corner of the room. The wimp cannot accept the result of his pathetic actions. At least I am owning what I have done by allowing the crew to kick me on the ground. They take turns kicking my sides while the ever-observational Lens stands afar watching it all go down. My stomach retracts into itself; my ribs bend inward in a way they were not designed to move. My actions killed a man. I earned the tape while Wilson and his crew earned their revenge. When the beating is over, the crew returns behind the stage. This part of the ritual provides Wilson with an opportunity to address me alone.

"When we're finished with you you're gonna wish you were dead." He bends down to rustle my hair. "How's my route off this rock comin' along genius?"

He vanishes into the shadows with the rest of the crew. Mason approaches, ordering I stick to his story. The story, crafted by Wilson, is that I injured myself on a piece from an industrial laundry machine. The other guards care less what happened to a scumbag like me. Mason continues to fabricate his stories for his own safety nonetheless. At this point, I am convinced it is to feel better about what really happens down here. He spins his own truth to sleep at night.

I call cell one-five-four my home now. It is satisfying to return after another encounter with Wilson and his minions. I am flung into routine like the rest of the birds, spending the evenings in peace. A mattress; a toilet; even the little book under my bed. It is a suite compared to cell fourteen.

A man does anything to keep his mind occupied in Alcatraz, making it a good place to pick up hobbies. For some, it is reading. For others, like the Birdman, it is studying. Even Wilson and his crew created a hobby of beating me to an inch of death. My distraction is deep thought. None of that therapy bullshit either. An actual, unfiltered mind. This is not a dream; this is real. Is it happening for a reason? Does a phenomenon like this occur often? These questions keep my hope alive. The alternative situation is this was a mere slip in reality, a simple coincidence that caught me in its tide. A side effect. An accident. Deep, uninterrupted thought prevails.

"All rise!" the alarm clock of a guard shouts. The lights hovering above Broadway flip on. All peaceful evenings end in another day of routine, interrupted every so often with a meeting with Wilson and his crew. "Up n' out your cells in thirty seconds!"

Wilson steps out of his cell—still in tandem with my own—and studies the bandages and bruises covering my body. He smiles with a sense of pride, letting off that familiar, menacing wink. Captain Peters strolls down the corridor, inspecting each prisoner's cell in another random morning search. These infrequent occurrences leave every bird shaking in their blue pants when announced. Peters stops when he gets to Wilson and me.

"Jesus . . . you look like you got thrown in a blender," he says, breaking eye contact with me to stare at Wilson before turning back to me. "You're headed t'garbage detail today Field. This's at the warden's request. Don't you stir up any more trouble or it'll be a lot worse than two weeks in the hole this time. Got it?"

I nod. Mason must have cracked under pressure from Peters. I know Madison has Peters watching me for he has certainly spotted these reappearing bruises. The screw spilled at least a fraction of the truth to prompt Peters to send me to garbage detail. The warden is keeping me out of the spotlight at all costs, although in this instance it is to my benefit.

"Now get in formation!" he continues. All inmates proceed to turn ninety degrees in choreographed fashion in preparation of breakfast.

This was not a random search and seizure, but rather my release from pain. Just like that, the routine beatings are over.

Garbage detail is the average con's dream as the job requires prisoners to travel all across the island. Those assigned to this position receive more freedom than most. Plus, they are outside for most of the day. Even I can appreciate some fresh air for a change.

Officer Bates is my new detail guard. No more Mason—that coward. Bates is a middle-aged screw who has spent upward of a decade serving this prison. Wilson told me many months ago that Bates is not a family man. "He was born a screw," he revealed. In fact, the officer dislikes people in general so prefers to live on the island. That is a preference I can relate to and one that shouts independence. No need for illegal bird protection with that mentality.

"West!" Bates shouts across the dock as Peters dumps me on the officer like a bothersome rodent. "West! Get your ass over here when I'm talkin' t'you." The officer turns to me. "Christ, you'd think these fuckers'd know their own name by now hmm?"

A rather short man struts our way. The man's dark-brown hair points straight to the sky as if waiting for an incoming radio frequency. He carries a certain cockiness with him despite Bates' obvious frustration. The officer motions for the man to speed up. The con mocks him by jogging at a snail's pace.

"Yes . . . sorry sir," he apologizes upon coming over. "Just gettin' in my workin' zone on account a how much I love it."

"Cut the horseshit West," Bates grips the baton on his belt. "It's too early for this shit. I didn't ask how your day was goin'. We've got ourselves a fresh garbageman here who won't quit beatin' his gums with questions. You've been on garbage detail for a while now so why don't you show Field here the ropes this week."

"Oh . . . right. My pleasure chief." The man continues to test the officer's patience with insincere responses. Bates walks away, relieved to be done conversing with us. The bird turns toward me. "Well don't jus' stand there playin' with yourself. I'll show ya what t'do n' you can pull my slack for the day. Sound good?"

I hold out my hand, hoping he will do the same. "The name's Field."

He sneers at me, looking down at my hand. "I dun care what your goddamn name is. If I'm stuck with ya all day it's in your best int'rest t'keep your head down n' get shit done."

I oblige, not wanting to butter the wrong bread on my first day of garbage detail. I need to remain under the radar. My body could use the opportunity to recover for once.

There are only a handful of prisoners assigned to this position, so each time we exit a building or turn a corner I can feel eyes on my back. Not West's eyes, but those of guards watching from afar. Every guard tower monitors us as we make our way around the island like deer being hunted for sport. What is worse is that the guards use their rifle's scope as binoculars. In other words, they wait for a sleight of hand from a passing bird to justify a pull of the trigger. They are bored way up in the fog.

West, the prisoner I have been instructed to shadow, is a talker. He is not looking to have a two-way conversation either. Instead, he enjoys talking my ear off and keeping me silent. Stories of his time in different prisons across the country, crimes he has committed and women he has slept with make their way to my ears. Whatever flies into his spinning little mind comes out in dialogue without hesitation. I am already familiar with this rebel and it is only my first day with him.

"Then the other guy," he continues one of his stories, "the other guy's sittin' there the whole time. So I turn t'Peters n' blame the whole damn thing on that guy. Cap'n smashes the shit outta this guy's face n' he ends up in the infirmary for a month. Got transferred t'some hinky-dinky prison in Florida after that." He laughs to himself while looking back on the fond memory.

"Sounds hilarious," I interject after what seems like hours of silence from my end. The response prompts him to turn his head toward me in confusion, maybe even in offense. "I mean the guy deserved it. Some mama's boy like that doesn't belong here if he can't handle his own ya know?"

He goes back to grabbing garbage bags from a nearby dumpster. "Yeah you get it . . . but what ya know 'bout handlin' yourself? Those cuts n' bruises all over your skinny ass tell me somethin' diff'rent."

He has a point. Why listen to the guy covered in bandages? He does not know the story behind these war wounds, though. No one does for that matter. I decide to let my guard down and toy with the idea of spilling a microscopic fraction of the truth.

"Well I'm the son of a bitch who got Karpis transferred." That sounded much more impressive in my head.

"Yeah right," he responds. He is already hooked on the conversation. "Karpis was transferred 'cause a health shit. That bag a bones's ancient compared t'the rest a us fine folk. That whole issue in the yard? He was just defendin' himself."

"Was he?" I get him thinking.

"I know there ain't no coincidences on this island. Still dun see what that scuffle's gotta do with you. Wilson n' his crew were the ones in that rumble."

"It's got everything t'do with me." I smirk. "I started the scuffle in the jungle that day. I trucked myself at Karpis during the middle of a ball game n' got that 'bag a bones' riled up. I'm sure you were in the yard that day . . . remember the game?"

"N' why would ya up n' do a stupid thing like that?" He tries to contain a look of disbelief. "Sure . . . I remember some jackass runnin' at Karpis. I'd hardly call that knowin' how t'handle yourself."

"I did it for the thrill. A man does anything it takes t'keep his mind occupied in here. I'm sure you of all people can appreciate that given the stories I've heard today."

A two-way street of communication opens. I no longer listen to West mindlessly vomit random tales from his past. There were not many stories that I was unaware of, especially the more newsworthy ones—I can thank my bibles for that much.

West is a name I came across more than once while immersing myself in the little book and tape. A legend of Alcatraz. A few of these stories were included in the tape and West even earned a full-page profile in the little book. Good for him. He is cocky and arrogant, though. He does his time here and is paroled down the road only to end up back behind bars. Another crook destined to rot away. Still, I cannot afford to cause any more trouble right now. I need to keep the peace and could use a new ally.

"So you're the West everyone keeps talkin' about then?" I fuel his ego to pull the conversation away from my own dealings on the island. I am unsure of the man who took the wheel of the conversation just then as it was not me. I am too cautious to reveal as much, yet I proved myself wrong.

"Sure am!" he exclaims. "The one n' only West . . . none other like me out there. N' you bet your life I've seen more shit than a damn scuffle in the yard."

He proceeds to pull a few more stories out from thin air. In the meantime, my mind goes back to what I learned about this hothead in the little book and tape—my undeniable sources; the keepers of truth. I can view his page in my head. Allen West. Allen Clayton West. Imprisoned on Alcatraz in 1954, and again in 1958. He was sentenced ten years for interstate transportation of a stolen vehicle. It all floods back to me as if the information was locked in a mental cell of my own design. I keep that cell's key protected.

West is notorious for stirring up trouble. The little book also said he organizes the most elaborate escape attempts in Alcatraz history. The plan to hit the bricks, which does not pan out for him, resulted in the disappearance of three men. None of those men were ever found. I cannot imagine how West will feel when it all goes down in the years to come. He is left behind, tortured with the sight of freedom in a few years only to end up back in the clink. It is no wonder he spends the rest of his life getting revenge on society. A rebel for life.

The first day of new detail comes to a close this Friday evening. No work tomorrow means I can enjoy the evening without worrying about putting on an act—at least not one that is as exhausting as usual. When it is lights out, I use the dim light coming through Broadway to read the little book, which rests behind an open copy of 'Popular Mechanics' as a fake cover should a guard present himself on the other side of the steel bars.

I read through West's profile once more to fact-check his claims. The little book is tattered and worn from such repeated use. The pages flip open out of habit when the cover is closed. The only thing keeping it shut is the bottom of my mattress. West's profile touches on both of his imprisonments on The Rock. The one fact that does not sit right with me, though, is his involvement in the 1962 escape attempt. Perhaps he will claim a role in the masterful plan he cannot take part in for mere bragging rights. My day-long encounter with the man assures me he is not capable of organizing such an error-free jailbreak. The words on the page do not sit right with me despite reading them dozens of times.

The tape said there are four involved in the escape attempt. There is Allen West, who never makes it out of his cell during the night of the escape. Poor bastard. There is Frank Lee Morris, who is also said to have a large role in the plotting of the plan. Then, there are the Anglin brothers. John and Clarence Anglin—two men the prison decided to put next door to each other. The brothers—along with Morris—are the three individuals missing thirty years from now. These are the individuals who deserve my full attention.

According to the little book, West is the only one of the four who resides on U.S.P. Alcatraz at this moment. The other men arrive over the next few years, leading to the inevitable escape in 1962. That leaves a long block of time to uncover the real mastermind behind this plan.

A new target is in clear sight. A new goal—a purpose. My focus diverts from establishing the persona of a straight-arrow convict simply to maximize my time in this reality. I have years to watch this escape unfold. I can get to know each of the escapees and be the sole bearer of truth about what happens to them that mysterious night.

ROUND AND ROUND

I don't know why she drove over an hour to bail me out. I know better than to ask, though—especially in my current state. An angry wife was one thing. An ex-wife bailing me out of jail's on a monumental level. She crafts a new definition of hatred.

I walk outside in the rainy night after some bullshit paperwork's done and I settle on a court date. I trail behind her like a disobedient puppy. She's smiling on the inside, knowing this is a win for her and another reason to keep the kids away from me. I should feel bad about her coming all this way; I should feel bad for trying to deck a cop and losing my license. Instead, all I can think about is how much time's been thrown out the window. Hours have passed and I'm still not in Napa. I can't drive the rest of the way either. This is what concerns me over anything else.

"You came all this way for me?" I rub my forehead as intoxication morphs into a hangover. I need a bottle if I'm going to think any straighter.

She stares at me, her eyes empty as can be. It's a look of disappointment—full of pity. "I didn't come here for you. I came here for the children. I'm still your emergency contact you know. They were worried about you in there. Jesus Robb, how messed up were you this time? Where's it end? You needa get your life together if you ever wanna see your children grow up."

"I've been trynna be better," I say while fighting back nausea. "It snuck up on me . . . you know how it is." I'm living lie to lie.

"No, I don't know how it is," she argues.

We stand outside her car in the parking lot. It's pouring rain. And I'm still not in Napa. I glance over her shoulder, spotting a tow truck's red lights reflecting off a puddle. The truck's transferring that piece of shit car to God knows where. In front of me sits my former 944 Turbo, which is now Meredith's vehicle of choice. She rubs it in my face. Just the sight of that beauty brings back nostalgia for what I had: a powerful position at a thriving company, a picture-perfect family and an unlimited cash flow. These things have vanished and that thought will forever sound strange.

"I'm here t'give you your last warning," she continues. "You deserve that much as the father of our children. I will not have them around this person. You can ruin your own life obsessing over whatever this is. You won't ruin ours. Nothing'll bring him back Robb. We've all moved on n' it's time you did the same."

The headache biting between my ears convinces me she's transforming into my mom again. The same shit came pouring out her mouth from across the country the last time we spoke. Meredith can threaten me all she wants. She won't take the kids, though, and this won't stop until it's over. She can't win.

I stop myself from lighting off a rocket of rage in response to her threats. Pour a few drinks in me and this would be a different conversation. I look down at my watch—it's eleven. It's eleven and I'm not in Napa. Every second I spend speaking with my ex-wife is a moment I'm not speaking with Jeffrey Park.

"Okay . . . you don't have t'associate with me," I respond. "I'm getting better. I really am. It was a temporary lapse in judgment that's another wake-up call. I still love the kids n' I still love you. None a that'll change . . . ever."

She can't stop me. I do care for the kids; however, these words are sprinkled in to get my way. It's just a shortcut. After all, I know how to sell just about anything. Can't say that aspect's changed much these last few months. There's her acceptance. It's my lie of moving on.

"One last favor," I continue. She's halfway in the car already. "Ya see I was actually on my way t'Napa t'see a therapist tomorrow morning." White lies grow arms and legs. "I know you suggested it a while back. Well I'm finally seeing it through."

She looks at me with a 'go on' glare. We can't see eye-to-eye on anything, yet I can read her expressions better than ever. That's the magic of marriage.

"I could really use a ride there since they stole my damn license. It's another thirty minutes north. I'd go tomorrow but I'm not able t'drive n' I'd rather spend the night there than call a cab in the morning from here. Just t'clear my head tonight n' all."

She agrees. To her, it's me doing the right thing for once. The fuck-up husband's attempting to turn his life around for the betterment of his family. How heartwarming. Maybe that's in store for the future. Right now, there's a parasite that must be flung off: the disappearance of my brother. Nothing will change until I'm at peace with what happened to him.

The car ride's silent; not a word uttered, nor song played on the radio to ease the tension. We could break the crippling silence if we wanted to end this battle of stubbornness. We could remind each other of good times—a joke or a lovely memory—to put us on a friendly page. Neither of us is giving in tonight, though. Whoever speaks first comes out on the bottom.

Meredith and I were seldom on the same page. We knew this for years yet decided to marry and have kids anyway. "You grew up too fast," my dad told me. That's latched on more and more over these last few months. I married because adults did that. My childhood—a blurry mess—deserves to stay buried under a layer of cement topped with a steel plate. I leave it buried in the past where it belongs.

The ride climaxes with the sound of a door swinging open and Meredith nudging my shoulder. I fell asleep. She drove me all this way and I fell asleep in the goddamn car. In my goddamn car.

"Couldn't even stay awake for your taxi ride Robb? Come on . . . we're here." She loses our game by breaking the silence. How could she pass up that convenient remark? She shattered the noiseless night and I'm still at a loss for words.

I muster the courage to leave her with what I can after grabbing my bag from the trunk. "Thanks for this." Thanks for this. Lives destroyed and her willingness to drive an hour and a half out of her way result in an emotionless statement of gratitude.

She sees through the bullshit, gunning it out of the parking lot to go rescue the kids from the nanny. The tires skid out of the lot and exhaust floats in its place. A magic trick. She's gone as suddenly as she arrived.

She dropped me off in a motel parking lot. Napa's a beautiful area, yet she managed to pick the most revolting motel in town. Chipped paint gives the exterior a camouflage pattern of brown and white. Only a few of the two-story hut's various sections are lit thanks to dead lampposts management doesn't care to change. There's a single car in the parking lot, which I imagine belongs to an employee. Of course, none of this matters. I won't be staying here for more than several minutes.

A payphone's my single destination. I pan around the road to make sure Meredith isn't spying on me—waiting for me to slip up again. It's all in my head, yet the concerns seem valid.

"Yes . . . hello. I'd like t'order a cab." My jacket sleeve covers the greasy telephone. The state of the phonebooth's an unpleasant cosmetic touch to match the crusty appearance of the motel. My temporary residence in San Fran's a five-star resort compared to this shithole.

The operator asks me for my location. I look over to the four-way intersection and provide the cross streets. "Make it quick," I demand.

One car zipped out a motel parking lot and another takes its place. Why does this sound like the beginning of an awful joke? At least this ride won't stare at me in judgment.

"2652 Pine Grove Avenue please," I direct the driver. "N' step on it. There's someone I needa see tonight."

"You're not from around here are ya?" He tilts the rearview mirror to get a better look at me. The bearded man looks like he hasn't left the driver's seat in days. It smells like it, too. "You know where that address is friend?"

"No. I don't know where it is," I respond. Just drive. "Is it far or something? Fare won't be a problem."

"Nah it isn't far at all." His eyes straighten out to the dark road. "It's just I think ya may have the wrong location. That's the Parks' house." He looks in the mirror again and notices my blank reaction. I could care why?

"Yeah I know that. I'm meeting with 'em. That's why I'm headed there. What's the big deal?"

"Nothin' my friend. It's none a my business. It's just no one 'round town visits that nut job. One too many loose screws up top if ya catch my drift."

I didn't think I'd visit a legend of Napa—maybe someone infamous. I interrogate the driver with more questions while he remains a closed book. Maybe he's trying to scare me, or maybe that's actually all he knows about Mr. and Mrs. Park. They shouldn't have a problem with me strolling up to their doorstep at midnight if they're as crazy as he claims.

The drive's another five minutes. Five minutes of bouncing questions off the bearded bastard and all I get from him is, "You'll see for yourself." Does he drive around all day freaking out his passengers? The car whines to a stop. Yellow and red meet on the sidewalk as the headlight and taillight clash.

The driver leans back and holds out his hand. "That'll be ten fifty-five." I see him from my peripheral as my eyes remain focused on the one-story home that's a front yard away.

The street's consumed by darkness; there's not a streetlight in sight. The yellow and red crawl from the sidewalk to the home, a strange form of Christmas lighting covering the house. Weeds run ragged over the pathway to the front door. The grass is a jungle that hides the lower half of the home. In a few words, it's broken.

"I see what you were gettin' at," I tell him, reaching in my pocket and tossing him a twenty. "Keep the change n' your car phone on. I may need you in a while."

I slam the taxi door. He waits until I hit the walkway to the home to pull away, thinking I'd otherwise disappear in the dark forest for the rest of eternity.

"Good luck," his voice fades. "If you need a ride back call this here cab company n' ask for my vehicle number." He points out the window to the side of the car. "I'd love t' hear whatever comes outta this visit."

He takes the only streetlight with him. The moonlight now shines off the house a few yards from the curb, fighting off enough darkness to light the way toward the door. The ground's damp from a storm I must have missed. These are all pieces of a haunted house's definition.

2652—this is the place. My tired eyes operate with dead batteries while trying to get a closer look at the crumbling structure. It's a shadow of a creation that was once a peaceful home. I don't blame anyone in this town—I wouldn't visit this place either. I'm left with no other option, though.

I clench my fist and bang on the wooden door. I knock again. Still nothing. Knock. Knock. With each knock an empty future becomes clearer: no answers and a life fueled by the bottle. My fist pounds harder. I fight through the pain until a sound finally echoes back. The doorknob shakes and flings away from me. Someone's there. My fist remains raised in disbelief, prepared to knock again. Someone's there and they're welcoming me in.

"N' who might you be?" A pair of eyes creep from the crack in the doorway. The raspy, weak voice follows with a coughing fit. I recognize that cough—it belongs to Mrs. Park.

The door opens wide without response to her question. I'm in. A distant light pouring out from another room reveals a daytime sundress on the woman. I can count the white hairs on her head that stand frightened in the air. The moonlight crawls from the front door to her skin. The ghostly color is complemented by a texture mirroring the roughness of an elbow. Her cheeks are caving in on themselves.

"Hi ma'am," I greet her in my most pleasant tone, the one I use with my kids. "My name's Robb. I called you earlier today n' spoke t'you about your husband Jeffrey . . . Jeffrey Park. Is he home?"

The empty stare grows into a soft smile. Her ears perk up like an attentive puppy. "My Jeffrey? You wanna speak t'Jeffrey? Jeffrey's home . . . you can speak with him inside."

It's murder or a warm glass of milk and cookies. It can't get worse than the rest of my night. I'd welcome murder before going home emptyhanded. I accept the invitation and step into a home that's on the verge of a pile of rubble. The interior's as tattered as the exterior. The walls are draped with flowery wallpaper in a design that looks inspired by the woman's sundress. She putters down the hallway until we reach a living room.

Her frail hand points to a plastic sofa. "Sit there."

The room's full of knickknacks, little thrift shop gnomes dressed in festive outfits I imagine they've collected for years; cheap souvenirs picked up at an airport giftshop that they cared about for a day. After these souvenirs make it home, they collect dust for a lifetime. They are garage sale items the right buyer purchases for no more than a dollar. Needless to say, it's crap-overload.

"So you said we spoke on the telephone young man?" she asks, leaning her cane against the side of the couch before she collapses on a plastic cover. The couch crinkles the way a noisy blue tarp goes while being folded.

"Yes ma'am. I spoke with you earlier about your husband Jeffrey. Am I able t'speak with him? I can speak with the both a you if you'd like."

"Jeffrey?" she asks. "Jeffrey? Jeffrey!" Her tone morphs into faint shouting. She turns toward another room. "You come in here this instant n' talk with this young man."

I can smell the answers from here. I'm a few moments away from unraveled truth. I can taste it. Of course, it could also be the taste of the black mold hiding in every corner of the room.

"Thanks honey," she continues. She glances to the other side of the couch. "Yes honey. This man came all the way from . . . young man, where'd you say you came from again?"

The cab driver's concerns start making sense. All of a sudden, the entire room—the entire home—seems a touch creepier. Mrs. Park continues to whisper over her shoulder. Her voice grows fainter with each comment. She pauses. A ticking clock's the only sound keeping us company, which has Hawaiian-looking flowers where the numbers are supposed to be. More tropical décor in a Napa Valley home.

"Ma'am . . ." I interject. My folded hands clank onto the wooden coffee table to grab her attention. "Is your husband here? Is Jeffrey here right now?" The answer's sitting right in front of me.

"Oh yes dear," she responds.

Fuck. She's useless. This is useless. I pray she takes her cane and whacks me across the head. My mind begs her to take the plastic cover off the couch and wrap it around my head to end it all, a final feat of strength before she keels over.

"He's right here!" she laughs. "Don't be a stranger honey. This young man wants t'speak with you."

I rise from the crinkling couch. I'll investigate the matter myself. Mrs. Park remains seated, eyes now closed as she grasps the cushion next to her. She thinks her husband's there. The air flowing through her fist is his hand. She's beyond senile. The cab driver knew what I got myself into and left me here anyway.

The rest of the house is as broken as the living room. It's all chaos. The kitchen has a wooded theme to it, the type you'd find at a cabin in the thick of the Rockies. Small prints of evergreens camouflage into the dark-brown walls made to look like wood. Pots and pans scatter across every surface as if a grizzly ransacked the place many years ago. The small kitchen comes full circle as another doorway leads back to the living room. A small home that doesn't make much sense. It shares Mrs. Park's lack of logic in that way.

The pale woman remains on the couch, unaware of her surroundings. I peek around her only to find her eyes closed. She's either meditating or dead.

The unlit fireplace catches my gaze next. A house full of knickknacks and the mantle's untouched. A single object—a perfectly centered vase—rests up high. There aren't any flowers on this object, just a charcoal-grey vase standing by its lonesome. No Hawaiian patterns. It doesn't fit in with the rest of the room's items. I step closer to find the object's engraved.

"Jeffrey M. Park," the withered woman's voice startles me. "That's my Jeffrey over there."

It's not a vase, it's an urn. Jeffrey Park died in 1987 according to the engraving. Mrs. Park's been alone these last few years. It's a wonder she doesn't have his body perched up stiff on the couch with her current mental state taken into consideration. This trip was for nothing.

"Did your husband pass away Missus Park?"

Give me the nail in the coffin.

"Jeffrey?" she asks. I nod. "Yes dear. He went away. But he's still here. He didn't leave us."

Doctors call this some twisted form of denial. It's the type of denial my brother had back when our dad died; or the type Meredith and my mom think I have right now. Can't say I agree with that classification when it comes to my thinking and Mrs. Park's doing something right if she's able to live on her own for years on end. Maybe she isn't clueless after all.

"Oh . . . hello Jeffrey." I play along. What's there to lose? "It's nice t'meet you. D'you mind if I ask a few questions?"

She looks at me then glances over her shoulder. She turns back and says, "He says it's fine. In fact he says it's been a while since he's had anyone t'speak with besides me."

"Great. I'm glad we can chat Jeffrey," I continue to address the empty air next to her. "There's plen'y I wanna talk about. I'm particularly int'rested in the time you spent on Alcatraz Islan—"

"Oh no no!" she shouts, cupping her ears and shaking her head the way a psych ward patient does. "Jeffrey doesn't like t'talk about that. We can't talk about that."

She reaches for her walker. I leap toward the couch, sensing the conversation dangling off a cliff. My hand lands on her own with a gentle touch. Her eyes calm and her tense muscles relax. She put every ounce of strength into that little show. Brava.

"Hold on ma'am. I'm sorry . . . it's just that well . . . I also spent time in that prison back in the day. I thought Jeffrey n' I could swap stories about our time there."

If we're going to play pretend, I'll give her exactly that. A broken mind reaches for what it knows. In her case, it's Jeffrey Park. I fuel that desire as a moment of clarity mends her scattered brain. She leans forward, eyes squinting so tight they're almost closed. She's judging me—determining if I'm telling the truth. I was paid to wear a million different masks. This is no different.

"He says he won't talk about any a that," she pauses, looking around the room as if there were others listening in. "He says I can though."

"That'd be wonderful," I respond. Where to start? "I'll keep it brief. D'you know what years he was locked in that prison?"

"Do I ever!" she raises her voice. She's lost in memories as the moment of clarity peaks. "He spent three years on that darn island. They only let me visit once a week. Can you believe such a thing?"

I'm working through a cold call. Positivity, personalization and patience—our sales department lived by those three P's. They'd be gone quicker than they could say 'blue tie guy' if they didn't. The P's also come in handy outside the office.

"That's great you got t'see him once a week at least. It must've made his time there much more manageable. You said three years ma'am . . . which years were those?"

"Hmm . . . I believe they were 1956 . . . yes, 1956 to 1959." She's a bright light compared to the woman I pleaded with a few minutes ago. How long will this clarity last? "Yes those were some tough years for us. Weren't they Jeffrey?" Her hand sweeps the clear plastic on the cushion. "But they made us stronger."

This is it. She's as clear as she'll ever be. I reach into my pocket and pull out the worn photo captured on the island. The tattered, blurry photo that's haunted me for months. The island employee said the original was from the late '50s or '60s. That'd be around Jeffrey's time on Alcatraz Island.

"You see this man in the background?" I move the photo closer to her wrinkled face. She reaches to the coffee table and grabs a pair of reading glasses, putting them on. "This man right here . . . this was one a my friends on that island. Someone I was very close to during those years. I'm trynna get in touch with this man."

She pushes the glasses up her nose until they send skin flowing over the frame like Play-Doh. "You mean Mikey? That there's Mikey. Mikey's a good friend a Jeffrey's. Isn't that right honey?" She looks over her shoulder and tilts the photo toward the empty cushion. "Look at Mikey there honey."

Her frail finger lands on the ghost I've been chasing. My heart races. There are two other blurred figures in the photo, yet she identifies the one I'm searching for. Sure, it's a small, blurry image, but if I knew who that was at first glance why shouldn't Mrs. Park, too?

"Yes . . . Mikey. Michael. Michael Field right?" I press for a full name. "Is that Michael Field ma'am?"

"Field? Who's Field?" She frowns, rubbing her head in confusion. I'm losing the moment of clarity. She turns to me after facing away. "Jeffrey says you're thinking a the wrong man. That's Mikey Kimble right there. We know Mikey Kimble."

She's senile. She spends her days alone in this cluttered house with a brain rotting into oblivion. Mrs. Park doesn't know what she's talking about. A first name's a lead—enough to feed my addiction.

"Sorry . . . right. I meant Mikey Kimble," I cave, trying to resurface her lucid state. "It's been so long . . . so long that his name escaped me. What can you tell me about Mikey?"

"Oh Mikey liked t'keep t'himself," she whispers, keeping the secret to the only two people within shouting distance. "Jeffrey n' Mikey weren't very close on that island. They didn't even meet 'til years following their time at that awful place."

I've gone so far down the fucking rabbit hole that I don't know where I'm digging anymore. Digging in the dark. It's beyond the lazy S.F. Police Department. It's actually come down to flirting with the idea of some conspiracy theory, maybe a government cover-up. Sobriety continues to test my patience. It challenges my beliefs.

My fist clenches at my side in escalating anxiety. The cravings remain bottled for the sake of Mrs. Park. It'll burst the moment I step back into the night. I crave another drink.

"Is there anything else you know about Mikey?" I'm interrogating her now. "Did . . . does Jeffrey keep in touch with him?"

"No . . . no he wouldn't do such a thing." Her head sinks into her chest, the skin from her neck flattening like a baker kneading dough. "I'm afraid Mikey moved on many years back before my Jeffrey moved on. We stopped hearing from Mikey long before that. Yes it's all very sad."

"He's dead?" If he's dead this trail's heading back to the steep cliff. "Missus Park d'you know where I can find a little more information about Mikey? I lost touch with him a long time ago too. I'd really like t'connect with him the way you bond with your husband."

"Oh no!" she shouts. She grabs her cane quicker than I can react this time, her slippers already shuffling away from the couch. "No no no no. We're not able t'talk about Mikey. Not even me. He told us—"

"Hold on . . . why aren't you able t'talk about him?" I plead for more information, following her as she heads toward the living room doorway. "Like I said, we were good friends. I'm looking t'reconnect with his spirit. That wouldn't be so bad would it?"

"I said no." She stops in her slow tracks, staring at me standing in her way. Her expression moves from confused to upset. "We told you no. Jeffrey's tired now. We're tired. I think it's best you leave young man. We don't want any trouble now."

She resumes her lengthy journey across the room. I managed to keep her calm for this long and blew it with a single request. Why's she so protective of the man in the photo? What does she know that's so important? Forcing more pressure on her weak mind won't get me anywhere now, so I keep these questions to myself.

"Ma'am . . ." I tap her shoulder as she approaches the front door. "Ma'am I . . ."

Her head turns back to reveal a complexion that's a shade paler. Her eyes open as wide as her mouth; she's terrified. The cane slips out her hand and crashes to the creaky, wooden floor. Mrs. Park's body follows the cane's lead and slips backward. She stumbles until landing ass-first on the floor. This is happening and I'm standing motionless in disbelief.

"What?" she cries out. "Who're you? What're you doing in our home? Get out! Help!" She continues to scream for help that won't come. Her worn voice doesn't carry more than half the hallway. She scoots toward the front door in terror.

"Ma'am . . . Missus Park . . . you let me in your home."

I reach out my hand to help her up. She moves further backward, rolling into a ball like a defensive roly-poly, safety that's as logical as protecting herself from monsters with a comforter. Her brain's deterioration is worse than I thought. I caught her during a moment of complete clarity. She saw her true past. She knew where and when she was. It's turned to shit now. She doesn't know who I am, a stranger in her house. A burglar. A murderer. Any of those options are easier explained than the truth.

I'm at a loss. Who knows when her mind will be sober again? Sober from the cancer that I'm sure riddles her body; the dementia that consumes her more each day. It's not worth it. I risk more jail time if a neighbor suspects any wrongdoing in Mrs. Park's home. An unforgiving ex-wife follows that jail time.

"I'm sorry Missus Park. I came in t'use your phone." I look out the small window at the top of the door. It's pouring rain. Lightning illuminates the cluttered house for a second at a time and thunderous cracks follow. "It's raining out. Look outside Missus Park. You let me come in t'call a taxi. Can I call a taxi n' be on my way?"

She peeks out her cocoon. The woman's crying. Tears roll down her cheeks in different paths thanks to the many wrinkles redirecting the flow. She lifts a trembling hand and points to a side table against the wall down the hallway where a phone sits atop.

"Please make it quick. Please don't hurt me."

My fingers can't dial fast enough. I call the cab company and spit out the driver's vehicle number. I throw the address at the dispatcher on the other end of the line. "Tell him t'step on it," I order. The handset crashes back onto the stand.

"I'm sorry for this ma'am," I tell Mrs. Park. I walk toward the door, stepping around her as she curls up further into herself. I want to leave on a good note. "Thanks for your time Missus Park. Please forgive me for this."

The door creaks open. She reaches for the cane, putting all her effort into standing back up. I look at her over my shoulder, nodding and closing the door behind me. It's the least I can do to leave her in peace.

My hair showers in the rain; my jacket's next. My life's ruined and there's no reason my attire shouldn't crumble, too. It does, and it's what I deserve. I take one last glance at the frail home. Mrs. Park stares at me from the doorway. Disappointment covers her face while embarrassment covers mine. I can tell she pities the man standing in the rain despite him being a stranger in her eyes. What did I do to this old woman? It's the first time my head's been clear in months. No fog from the bottle nor from the addiction that is this investigation.

Mikey Kimble? Michael's one of the most common names in the country. I start repeating that to myself. Everyone has a doppelganger. My mom was right—they were all right. He never went by any name besides Michael either. He hated every nickname we tried to give him over the years.

Denial must transition into a stage with greater purpose: acceptance. I did time in the drunk tank, frustrated my ex-wife, put a life with my kids on the line and almost killed a senile woman in a single night. I'm a cancer. I'm lost forever if I can't shift into acceptance and leave behind whatever I'm searching for.

The cab rolls up in front of the house, the same lights now illuminating my drenched body. The driver looks to the back of the car where I'm seated, soaking his torn leather seats with what must be pounds of water. A human washcloth.

"Figured it wouldn't be long." He lets off a 'told you so' smile. "Where to now friend?"

"Couldn't tell ya." I sink into the seat, giving one last look at the home that once contained a healthy, happy life. "Just drive."

STAND

It's remarkable what a few days of sobriety can accomplish. The physical effects are one thing—more energy, fading headaches—but the mental recovery's on another level. My mind went from a clogged drain to a free-flowing stream. I'm awake.

The last few months were from a dream, vivid nightmares I couldn't shake; they clung tighter the harder I tried. Every time I climbed out from the abyss I was dragged deeper into despair, a pointless fight with the bottle calling the shots. I chased the phantom of my brother to put my life back on track. It seemed necessary at the time. Answers were the key to freedom, or so I thought. The intoxicated logic put my detective hat above everything else. The most ironic part is it ended up costing my identity. At least I admit all this much. That's my acceptance.

That's not to say Meredith, the kids nor work will take me back with wide-fucking-open arms. Quite the opposite. Some things are irreversible. There are mistakes that can't be undone by pouring the rest of a bottle down a sink.

The one aspect I can control is money. The green, glorious goddess. It's a motivation that can push me forward. It was the most important aspect of my life a few months ago and it's the catalyst that'll slingshot the pieces back into place.

"Pancakes?" she asks, welcoming me into the kitchen. "I can make those pancakes you like. I have the whipped cream n' all."

I hopped on the first flight home the morning after nearly scaring Lucille Park to death. New York—my old stomping grounds. They say home's where the heart is. Mine drowned in the San Fran bay. Instead, home welcomes recovery. If my mom can't scare me into a straight-edge lifestyle then no one can. This is a last resort as I had nowhere to go that rainy evening in Napa. Having no car and no family didn't help matters.

"Sure. Pancakes sound great."

I walk into the kitchen. Fleeting flashes from my days growing up in this house follow close behind. My brother was never one for breakfast nor any other family meals; he did his damnedest to avoid eating with the rest of us. My parents chalked it up to troubled teenage years. Mood swings. They lied to themselves. Their biological child wanted nothing to do with them. They avoided these front-and-center facts their entire life.

My fingers press against my temple. I'm punishing myself. I can't resurface those pointless flashes. Memories are meant to stay in the past. I need to wipe him away. This house isn't a haven if it tempts me into reverting to my previous way of thinking. Mental relapse leads to cracking open a bottle and bathing in it until I've come full circle.

"You've had quite the past few months Robert." She sits next to me at the circular table, sliding over a plate of eggs that could feed a small village. I roll my eyes at her comment. This upsets her. "Don't gimme that look. You know Meredith always kept in touch. I wish you'd do the same."

Here we go. "Are you worried about me or something?" I grab a fork and stab the center of the plate. "I'll be fine. People have diff'rent ways of handling this type a shit. Why the hell's she keeping tabs on me anyway?"

"Watch your language," she snaps, lunging at the opportunity to resume parenthood. She rises from the chair to flip pancakes on the stove. "I'm always worried about you. Meredith's updated me since the day you got that job n' moved inna that home."

"You don't needa know every time I go t'the bathroom mom. I'm not Michael." There it is again, another subconscious slip into regression. Relapse. This can't keep happening.

"At least your brother was only a short drive away." She points the spatula at me. Not a single pancake's done and her pink, ancient robe's already covered in flour. It's obvious she gave up on cooking—among other things—after my dad and brother passed.

"You know the two a you really aren't that diff'rent," she

continues. "You both had this fantasy of living life on your own terms. You were afraid a what might happen if you actually took the time t'relate t'those around you. Neither of you enjoyed this beautiful life."

"Really? We're gonna do this over pancakes?" I laugh a distorted cackle. The fork drops to the table and dings before settling. She pouts, turning around and flipping another pancake. She's upset, so I try to bandage the wound a little. "Listen . . . I enjoyed what I did. I enjoyed being successful n' makin' a name for myself."

Smoke floats from the pan. The grey San Fran-like fog wanders to the table and the scent of burnt flour and eggs flies up my nose. She can't even cook a fucking pancake anymore. She's living in the past, too. My mom needs to move on in her own way.

"Just because your kids moved on with their lives doesn't mean they're unhappy."

That sentence wasn't supposed to reach her ears. It was supposed to sound pleasant—encourage her that she can take a step forward with her life. It did the opposite. I appreciate her trying to identify the source of how I fell this far—that's the goal of a mom. She's doing impossible math to figure out how I wound up in her kitchen eating scrambled eggs on a Wednesday morning.

The unpleasant scent fades as she shuts off the stove. She makes her way to the sink to act busy with dishes instead. "We don't have t'get inna this Robert. If you're not here t'talk t'me you better figure out why you did come back."

She sure as shit knows what I'm doing in her house if my estranged ex-wife has provided her with a play-by-play during these last months. I'm not going to fuel this heated conversation anymore. I want to sit in silence enjoying these eggs and burnt pancakes.

The first step to recovery's reclaiming my job. It's mine. I spent more time in that office than at home. The observation's enough of a confidence boost to convince me to pick up the phone after the filling meal.

My fingers instinctively dial my old office line. I let it ring anyway, assuming some secretary or intern will answer in my absence.

"Hello . . . Mark speaking," a voice greets me.

"Uh yes . . . h-hello," I stutter. I know that pathetic voice. "This's Robb Field. Who am I speaking with?" I already know the answer before the man responds.

"Robb! Get outta here man!" I pull the phone away to let my ear recover from his reaction. "It's Mark Dent. This's awkward huh? I mean talkin' t'you on your old desk phone in your position n' all." He waits for a warm reaction that never arrives. "Hell, say somethin'! We've been worried about you. Nate thought you might've . . . ya know. I knew you were doin' fine though. You're doing solid right?"

I knew the position would be filled by now, I just never wanted to accept it. The truth was left on the backburner for an extended period. I'm not an idiot. I know how a company operates, especially one I helped build. I was the steel beam that made it stand over the years.

My disbelief's thanks to that clown picking up the phone. Mark Dent—a man who's been there a fraction of the time I have—now holds my position. My goddamn position. He rode the elevator to a floor that took me years to reach. What a disgrace. I'm embarrassed for the company, yet at a loss for words.

The conversation doesn't last another two minutes; how can it when I want to climb through the phone and punch the lucky bastard in the face? He offers to transfer me to HR. That lights the final fuse. He pities me. He'll toss me in the ranks below him and bask in the glory that's my office; my salary; my parking spot. It all belongs to me.

"I've got your back man," he says. "There'll always be a space for you on our team."

Bullshit. He doesn't hire me. I hired him. I make those decisions. Call it greed or label it denial again—either way I spit the opportunity right back at him. He reports to me.

I slam the phone against the wall. It takes everything I have not to raid my mom's liquor cabinet. If not booze, I need something else to take my mind off this mess. Give me something to blow off some steam. A workout. Yes, an intense, mind-numbing run to forget the conversation ever occurred. That'll do.

Suburban New York isn't much for sightseeing, but a run around the neighborhood serves as another trip in the past, full of the same fleeting flashes I saw at my mom's house. This time, the flashes guide me to my middle school days. My mom, just as controlling as now, forced my brother and me to take the long path to and from school. It avoided busy roads, which meant her little darlings were safe. I fight off the memories as sweat drips onto my brow. I pick up speed and steer my body down roads less traveled. I run down that busy road. I need to avoid these haunting memories. Home's proving to be a field of blossoming temptations that encourage me to pluck one from the ground. Not a chance that'll happen.

It did the job—a workout cleared my head of that weasel Mark, the latest of my concerns. It prevented me from gripping the bottle. This is working. I'll be alright. I reward myself with these optimistic considerations as I walk up the front porch steps. I'm drenched in sweat. Sweet relief. This is my new coping mechanism. Clean, healthy coping until my return to normalcy. I can keep this up.

My mom's mouse-like voice mumbles somewhere in the house. That sense of knowing home like the back of my hand vanished the moment I left this place for the West Coast. The faint sound now whispers around every corner, coming from vents and traveling through doorways until it crawls under my skin. She's talking to someone.

"Hey mom!" I yell from one room to the next. I'm lost in my own house, playing a game of hide-and-seek. "Are you looking for me?"

The mumbling subsides the moment I start yelling back at the whispers. She doesn't want me listening to whatever she was saying. Sound travels like wind in such a small house.

A glance up the stairs reveals her standing at the top. She holds a phone to her ear in one hand and cups her mouth with the other. I inch up the carpeted stairs to avoid being detected.

"No. I'm not sure how much longer it'll be. He just got here so I can't imagine anytime soon."

The whispers become more audible with each cautious step.

She's talking about me. My slow tread turns into a dash, jumping three stairs at a time to catch her before she can react. She's caught red-handed.

"I was calling your name mom. Who's on the line?"

"Hold on a second," she whispers into the phone. She pushes it against her chest, a dear baby being protected from abduction. "It's not for you Robert. Now can I please continue my conversation in private?"

"It's her isn't it?" I pester her for the truth. She's not getting off so easy. "It's Meredith. Gimme the phone! Hand me the phone!"

I wrestle her for the handset as a muffled voice comes out the speaker. We're both wrapped in the coiled cord in a few seconds. The tug of war soon ends as she lets go, her feet dancing backward on the carpet the way Mrs. Park's did not long ago. She tosses her arms over her head in anger and stomps into the bedroom. The door slams shut.

"I can't do anything without being yelled at!" she screams.

Am I supposed to feel bad because I caught her talking behind my back?

"So . . ." I put the handset to my mouth and clear my throat. "You still needa keep tabs on me even when I'm thousands a miles away? When's it end Meredith?" I'm throwing her own words right back at her. Where's her acceptance?

"What your mother n' I talk about's none a your business Robb," she hisses. "Besides, aren't you s'posed t'be in therapy right now? That's what you told me right? You were going to some sorta therapist in Napa. Why the hell'd I drop you off there if you were gonna continue t'make these impulsive decisions?"

I clench my fist. I'm on the verge of shattering the phone. I picture chunks of plastic buried in the shag carpet beneath my running shoes. No more phone calls if there's no phone. I watch myself run around the house destroying the other two handsets, kicking them off the wall until black holes with colored wires are left in their place.

"I changed my mind." I'm caught off guard by her memory of the recent drive to Napa. I was shitfaced at the time, after all. "I don't report t'you. I am getting better Meredith. How I do that's up t'me." I take a deep breath. The euphoria of the run has already disappeared. "Now listen to me . . . my mom's no longer family t'you. You needa stop treating her like family. Stop filling her in on my whereabouts. I'm not a child. I'm an adult. You're outta my life."

"I've been looking out for you," her voice cracks a desperate tone. She's holding back tears behind the handset. She did this to herself. "Your mother's been looking out for you too. Not everyone's out t'get you. Sometimes it's good t'have someone watching your back."

The tears pour out the other end of the line. I move the phone from my face, half expecting a waterfall to pour out onto my shirt. She did this. Those tears aren't for me—they're for her. She messed up and blew this out of proportion. The hypocrite held onto her relationship with my mom. She never let go either. Where's her acceptance?

"I don't care!" I yell back. Her heavy emotions are shoved aside. "I don't care what you're trynna do. You've been on my case since we first met! I've provided for our family. You left every night trynna be some nurse! This family ended when I stopped takin' care of it. Stop calling my mom. It's done!"

I slam the handset against the wall the way it went down with Mark. My hand shakes in pain. Blood drips from my knuckle onto the floor as another droplet rides down the white wall. I went a little far, but I'm comforted with a blanket of knowledge that it had to be done—ugly or not.

The door opens behind me. "What happened?" my mom asks. She acts like she didn't have her ear pressed against the door. I'm not going to answer that question.

At the end of the day, all tension breaks when a parent sees their child in need. It's instinctual; she can't control it. If she could, she'd be yelling at me the way Meredith did. Consolation's the last thing I need right now. I can't believe I was out to make peace with that witch. It was next on my to-do list during recovery and she shot that possibility dead in the face. It wasn't my fault this time. She's in the wrong for once.

That's zero for two today. I'm once again leaning toward a step forward before getting pushed back further than before. I fell on my ass this time, making myself bleed. The physical and mental anguish resurface.

I place my head on my mom's shoulder in a vulnerable moment. I don't know how to react. I lose myself when this happens. Tears rain down my cheeks the way I imagine Meredith's across the country right now. This isn't a light mist of tears, it's the insane crying that makes snot and saliva seep out everywhere without warning. The man in me fights back to no avail. I can't remember the last time I've had an affectionate moment with anyone, let alone my mom. I despise it, yet it continues. I don't feel anything, yet my eyes leak more liquid.

"I think I'm gonna go lie down." I muster the strength to push myself from her grasp.

Freedom sparks instant regret, the type of feeling following a hard blackout where I don't want to speak to anyone. Regret—how embarrassing. I grab my sleeve and wipe it on a leaking nose. "It's been a long day," I end the moment.

If I'm being honest, it's been a long couple months. Something has to give over these next days or I fear losing myself again. The only factor I can impact if my family and career won't budge is myself. I've spent my entire adult life slaving away for my family and my company. I'll focus on Robb for once. Put me at the center of the show. This is the safety net allowing me to rest my eyes in my old bedroom. I pissed the bed the last time I lied here. I've not grown. The bothersome thought rocks me to sleep, an infant man lying on his piss-covered mattress.

There's a heavy uncomfortableness in the air when I wake, another feeling reminiscent of long benders—too many whiskey ginger ales. Time after time, I woke up in a drunken haze wondering what I did the night before. What bar kicked me out? Who'd I pick a fight with? My head's clear this time and that makes reality more terrifying. I can't blame liquor for feeling this way. I've done this without a bottle. I shouldn't have let my guard down around my mom. She wasn't an advocate of my recent behavior and went behind my back to speak with Meredith. She called me crazy when I needed support on my self-destructive path. I revealed my most vulnerable self when I should've shown resistance. An emotional cleanse left her feeling superior, grinning on the inside while masking it with consolation on the outside.

I pass my mom in the dining room and the shameful afternoon hits a new low. She sits on the floor, legs folded pretzel-style like a kid. She's flipping through various books sprawled out on the shag carpet the way Alcatraz books were fanned out on the library carpet. I guess disorganization runs in the family. Her books are photo albums. She's holding onto memories, diving head-first into them like an addict in a pool of narcotics.

"What, you didn't get enough of seein' me like a child earlier?" I try to lighten the mood only to find the joke makes me cringe. I roll my eyes at my own comment. Add it to the list of embarrassing moments in this house.

She peers up from the wilted, glossy pages, acknowledging my presence with a soft twinkle in her eye. The flipping continues. What's worse, losing a brother and a father or a husband and a son? She can think that one over on her own. I leave the room to avoid any more unnecessary interaction.

"You know your brother weighed nine pounds ten ounces when he was born?" She catches me in the doorway, turning around a picture of an ultrasound. I turn around, too. "When the doctors took him away for the first time I asked your father 'What if they mix up the babies?' He said 'That's impossible . . . we've got the fattest one in there.' He always knew how t'ease my worries."

The comment's a desperate cry for attention. I drop myself to her level after shuffling back in the room, taking the hint that she wants me to stick around. My legs are pretzel-crossed and all now. I've never looked through family photo albums as the foster kid inside me steers me away from childhood memories. Rightfully so, too. An accident left for some other family to look after—that's all I am.

Still, curiosity sticks like glue. "Are these all pictures a him?" I ask. She nods, placing her hand on each photo as if he can feel her warm touch. She pats one photo before moving to study the next. "You think about him often mom?"

"I think about both of 'em often. I think about them every minute a my life."

My pretend family was demolished long before my dad died, a wrecking ball followed by a stick of dynamite. My dad tried to keep the remains together until he passed. The attempt was obvious and messy, like he was the only one who cared enough to hold us all in place. I suppose every family requires someone like that. 'All these individual characteristics intersect to form something greater.' His words, not mine. He believed our differences made us whole. I'm paraphrasing the dinner-table bullshit I vaguely remember yet don't care to dig for. My dad was a philosopher like my brother.

She rewinds to the first album, pushing over a stack of three other bursting books to get to the bottom. She wants to walk me through the journey of my brother's life with her own narration. It's a story with a traditional beginning and an obscure ending; the writers were bored halfway through and changed the tempo.

"How come you n' dad never told me about my past?" I interrupt before her story begins.

I thank them for sparing me from the details when I was a kid. They wanted me to feel loved—a part of 'something greater.' Except I'm an adult now who deserves to know the truth.

"What d'you mean?" She plays dumb. The look on her face reveals an uneasy reaction to the question. She's looking for a way around it, maybe in the form of a question answered with a question.

"The past . . . the history beyond the lovely Field family," I elaborate. "I know I was a kid when you n' dad brought me in but don't I deserve t'hear my own history at some point?"

She grabs me by the cheek. "Now you listen to me Robert. There was no Field family before you. It started when you walked in the door for the first time. We were always waiting for you don't you see?"

Dramatic. We're not in one of her favorite soap operas. This crap might've made me feel better fifteen years ago, but it's too late now. She'd prefer to keep me blind than come clean. It's the last memory she's trying to preserve as her single remaining family member looks for a way out. Meredith doesn't count in that regard.

I pop into pictures like a paranormal Polaroid after three albums. Despite the many captions and descriptions at various points in my brother's life, all that disappears when I come into frame. No 'Welcome to the family, Robert!' or 'Robert's first day of school!' captions. No fun stickers or doodles around the photos of me. Just photos. I'm tossed into the family like I've been there from the start.

I could really use a beer right now.

"Alright . . . one last question before I leave ya to it." I put my hand over the book to draw her attention away from her ritual. She's hesitant to look up as she knows something unpleasant is coming. "I realize this's your attempt at memorializing my brother. It's just that these photos still have me thinking beyond that. Why'd you n' dad decide t'adopt someone in the first place?"

"Yikes, now that's a question!" She laughs. She's frazzled—at a loss for words. "Well we always knew we wanted two children. Somewhere along the way it made sense t'care for a child in need. Just because someone isn't a newborn doesn't mean they don't deserve a home."

There's a line of sincerity in there somewhere. I don't feel like digging for it. The response is scratching the surface of the story, though. She has a terrible poker face.

"I'm sure you guys didn't up n' decide t'go the adoption route right? I mean honestly, what drove you t'that point?"

"There wasn't some hidden agenda Robert. We discussed the idea many times in the past despite your theories on what happened." She pauses, hesitant to proceed yet realizing I'm too stubborn to drop the matter. "In fact your father n' I had a close friend who guided us through the process. She was a huge advocate for us . . . one a those state-certified caregivers. If we didn't have her you'd never be in our lives. We were so grateful. So no, we weren't positive about that route at first. That doesn't mean we'd change the decision for the world."

"You knew where I was locked up all those years? Why wouldn't you at least tell me that much?" My blood boils for the third time today. "I spent my entire youth repressing those memories . . . goin' t'therapists n' pretending I was part of a happy family. I can't avoid that gap in my life. I could do it then. I can't now."

"Relax sweetie." She fails to calm me. "We weren't hiding anything from you. We wanted you t'always feel like you were at home is all. If you're that curious, your father kept the adoption paperwork in the attic. Go digging through cobwebs n' you might find some more up there though. Not everything deserves t'come outta the dark."

"Appreciate the words of wisdom." I rise from the floor and head toward the stairs. I don't look back this time. "A third a my life's missing. I'm thankful for the other two thirds. I still need t'at least acknowledge the first part. I'll never let it go otherwise."

There's a new endgame. This is why I came home—the solution to my problem if I can't make amends with my family, wife or employer. I can't win back my old life, so I'll craft a new one. Independence. A free spirit takes me to new limits.

ADRIFT IN A WORLD OF MY OWN

I did not have a purpose. There was no little book in the palm of my hands guiding my every action. I was a slave to the Sun God, or whatever entity may be out there. I withered away with the rest of the world with no great purpose. No calling. That is not to say this place—my new reality—did not force similar slavery on me. Alcatraz shoved routine down my throat. It forced me to abide by its celebrated micro-society, only it failed. My actions have substance now, even if those actions revolve around routine.

One routine I have mastered is garbage detail. West has not taken a liking to my obvious efforts to befriend him during our time together despite my successful integration. If anything, he believes I am making advances on him. A queen, as birds say. The last inmate whose homosexuality was revealed got stuck in the heart. How inhumane. Fast forward thirty years from now and the stigma remains. More rebellious humans are forced to conform to a society that believes only heterosexuals are worthy of the great reward that is an afterlife. Let the people live, I say. Society requires rebellion. I keep these observations to myself. There must be a more appropriate way to win West's trust. He must perceive me as an ally based on merit, not mere friendly interaction.

"Field!" Bates shouts during morning dock count. "You're needed for a special project in the warden's office. You'll report back t'the dock when the job's done."

I have remained a law-abiding prisoner; there is no reason for Warden Madison to suspect otherwise. The last time I saw the tyrant was in the kitchen months back. A stern threatening was the only dialogue he had to share. My stomach drops quicker than an elevator snapped from suspension after Bates' comment. What does he want with me? Did West speak to someone about the Karpis story I revealed? If so, this is a threat I am not prepared to navigate around. The little book cannot guide me out of a mess like that.

"Aw man . . ." West leans over as Bates continues count. "What'd ya do t'get a meet n' greet with the king screw?"

His sudden interest suggests he is not a fink. He has higher standards than stooping to a rat's level despite his hotheaded nature. The game of 'Clue' is cut short as Captain Peters strolls down the path to the dock. It is never a hopeful sign when the whipped servant comes to escort me. If West did not speak to the warden, then what is the meaning behind this summoning?

A few questions to Peters on our walk to the warden's office do not shed any light on the matter as he shoots them down with rapid fire. He yells at me to pick up the pace. The suspense soon leads us to an open office door. I can already see Madison's feet perched on his desk. King of his island. The king screw, as West labels him.

"It's a pleasure seeing you again Michael. What's it been . . . several months since we last spoke?"

"At least," I reply. Peters takes a seat across the desk while I remain standing. "I've held up my end a the deal. No one knows my story. I'm blendin' in with everyone else. Why am I here?"

He puffs a thick cigar double the width of his thumb, leaning across the wide desk and blowing a heavy cloud in my face like trailing exhaust in the stands of an active raceway. "Well how 'bout that? Time certainly flies. There's no deal Michael. There was your obedience n' your survival." He motions for Peters to leave the room. "See that's why I brought you here. It's been over five months, so our old acquaintance Alvin Karpowicz is set t'return in a short while. Does that name ring a bell?"

"Set t'return?"

The little book continues to be impenetrable; although I can shape events, the writing is carved in stone. It has been static for all of time, an object drifting from the future to the past. It has no origin. No source. It is cycled through time and through realities. The chicken or the egg?

"Yes. He's being transferred back t'my prison . . . for now. Here's where matters become curious. A public defender represented Karpowicz following the death of Ronald Yantz. While nothing substantial came of that trial this individual requested t'speak with you."

"T'speak with me?" This is confusion I do not have to fake. "Why would someone wanna speak with me?"

It does not make sense. I am not represented in the little book, a ghost floating through these events without an origin. My name does not make it off of this island.

"Well from what we can tell Karpowicz divulged a good amount of information on what occurred that day. Now even I'm not able t'get my hands on that information. However something tells me it shined a light on a certain Michael Field. It wasn't in Karpowicz's best int'rest t'reveal his truth with Yantz's death ruled an accident. Are you following?"

"Sure . . . I'm following. So my name was never brought up in the case?"

"No, that's much too risky." He sifts through folders on his desk. Connections across the bay have fed him any and all information. "I've asked the judge t'dismiss any sorta outlandish claims from the defendant." The line of corruption goes on for miles. "I've asked you here today because the public defender's waiting for you in visitation at this very moment. They refuse t'depart until meeting with you. If we don't grant that they've threatened t'go public with other information."

"You're askin' me t'lie?"

The man has his bases covered. Who knows where other loyalists hide if he has connections across the bay? I do not wish to find out.

"No. I'm telling you t'lie." He lifts the folders, hitting them against the desk to align them before tucking the stack in a drawer. He locks it. "I've said it before n' I'll say it again: you know exactly what I'm capable of doing t'your future. I'll make you disappear faster than you can snap your fingers. Poof." He snaps his fingers for dramatic effect.

The easiest option was murder. He knew I did not belong on this island yet was cowardly when it came to pulling a trigger. He could not locate the strength to get rid of his problem for good. That time has since passed, and he regrets it. He can make threats on my life, but I have leverage if this public defender is aware of my existence.

Hopeful Howard calls for Captain Peters to return. An obedient dog. There is no time to think this through. I am used to a trail of breadcrumbs guiding me from one measure to the next. This requires quick, critical thinking. I cannot reveal the truth yet must maintain the public defender's attention.

Captain Peters pushes me toward a visitation window after entering the core of the vacant cellhouse again. The only option is to play along with Madison's game. He made his move; I am not quite ready to make mine. If there is no record of my being here, then a slipup could leave Madison no other choice than to execute me. My leverage is the illusion of a threat in the form of the lawyer's knowledge.

For the first time in a year, the abandoned cellhouse mirrors the setting of the audio tour thirty years from now in my other reality. It is simply a large room without meaning. Emptiness fills the void of prisoners moving about in their cells and of guards pacing up and down the catwalk. All other birds continue their various detail assignments, unaware of my forthcoming meeting.

A few chairs facing the windows are separated by wooden blocks below the east gun gallery. It is the same ineffective setup proctors use with folders to prevent cheating during college exams. I suppose a gunman pacing up high is an effective scare tactic not found in a university, though.

"Right there . . . at number two," Peters says, pointing to the window.

Madison put significant trust in Peters to accomplish this task. The monster is sweating, his eyes pacing back and forth, ensuring no other guards can listen in on the conversation. From his perspective, this is another test of his readiness to take over as warden once Madison retires. Of course, that will never happen. The little book and tape are my sources for that fact.

The wooden chair creaks as my denim pants first contact the surface. I stare at the empty seat across the glass. That seat is freedom while this seat is prison; an inch of glass is the border.

Peters taps his foot in impatience and I claw beneath the plank in front of me in anticipation.

"Mister Field." A woman enters the foggy frame and sits down. She leans closer to the small holes in the glass like I am a fish in an aquarium. "Mister Michael Field? Is that who I'm addressing?"

My brain freezes, doing its best to process the simple question to no avail. This is unexpected. "Yeah that's who you're speakin' to. N' might I ask who you are ma'am?"

"Good. That's good t'hear Mister Field." She studies me the way Doctor Polk did. "My name's Rebecca Tillwell. I'm the legal representative of Mister Alvin Karpowicz."

"N' why're you here Miss Tillwell?"

She writes away in a notebook as if sketching a carnival portrait, her eyes shifting from the page to my face every couple of seconds; or maybe she is doodling to pass the time. It makes me uncomfortable either way. The intense attention to my every movement or word leaves me paralyzed. What is she aiming to accomplish?

"I'm afraid I'm not at liberty t'disclose much more than I've already said." She looks up from the notebook for more than a second. "I simply wanted t'meet face t'face. With that said I'd like t'ask you a few questions of my own. Is that alright Mister Field?"

She presents an insincere smile that we both realize is fake. She is attempting to befriend me. I can read these fake reactions like the little book under my mattress. I am the creator of these fraudulent emotions. I nod at the smile anyway, feeling Captain Peters' presence not far behind my chair. His foot taps the ground in worry. He cannot wait for this to end, and neither can I.

"Michael . . ." I answer. "You can call me Michael."

The sight of a woman is peculiar. It does not help that this woman fascinates me with both her words and appearance. She has short, brown hair and bright-red lipstick drawn with care so as not to touch any other part of her face. I imagine her looks mesmerize even the most invulnerable of men such as myself. Expressive brows give off a calm yet intimidating perception. She was designed for this career choice—placed upon the earth for this purpose.

"Alright then Michael," she humors my request. "Did you ever meet my client, Mister Karpowicz? It's possible you know him by the unfortunate nickname given by fellow inmates: Creepy Karpis."

I hesitate again, thinking through what the monster to my backside is pushing me toward saying. Madison shared that the public defender suspects some form of affiliation between Karpis and me, so I leave her with another nod. She leans back in relief. In her mind, she did not venture across the bay for nothing. I will ensure she does not receive what she desires.

"Right . . . n' were you incarcerated on U.S.P. Alcatraz during July of this past year?"

I wave my hand about in the air so she moves onto the building question—the elephant in the room.

She looks at her notebook then back at me. "Michael were you present in the prison's recreation yard on the second Saturday of that month? T'be clear this was the day my client claims t'have been attacked."

It could all come to light at this very moment. I envision spilling the truth and hearing her reaction. A simple 'Yes' would pique her interest—it may even get me out of here. Peters coughs behind me to set my mind straight.

"No. I was sorry t'hear about the incident with Karpowicz. I didn't witness it. I wasn't there that day." A look of confusion across the glass sends me digging for more inaccurate details. "I work in garbage detail ma'am. That task requires me t'work durin' yard time too." That is not true in the slightest. "I remember bein' on garbage detail that day."

Her stare persists. She is non-verbally pleading for the truth to come forward, putting one hundred percent of her energy into this moment. "I have t'ask . . . are you lying about this?" She leans in as if Peters was not hovering over my back. "There's no one here that'll know any margin of truth you share. You could save a man from spending the rest of his days rotting in a cell. Don't you want that?"

Another opportunity for honesty. Lay it all on the line, part of me says. That is what she wants without realizing the conversations going on behind the glass. Madison and Peters use me as a puppet. Any truth I share with her reaches them as well. I doubt she would care about my fate even if she did get her fill of facts.

"I'm not lying Miss Tillwell." There must be a more ideal moment to ensure my name is not lost in time. "I wish I could be of more help. I wasn't present durin' the attack. I can't help ya there."

It takes every effort in my body to maintain a poker face. She continues to dig for information, a dentist probing my mouth for imperfections. I am immune to her words. Suppressing emotion is my specialty—ask Robb or my mother and they would agree.

She looks off to the side and then to the other. The ever-observant, rather stunning woman knows I am hiding a deeper truth. "It's quite unfortunate t'hear that. Your knowledge could play a crucial role in ensuring Mister Karpowicz never has t'return t'this dreaded place." She rises from the seat that so many sorrowful visitors have sat in, wiping her hands on a handkerchief. She stops in her tracks halfway toward the door and peers over her shoulder. "Michael . . . just because you have t'suffer doesn't mean the rest of the world must too."

The departing comment sticks with me even as Peters yanks me from the chair by my shirt collar. It does not matter what I tell her for she does not know Karpis' destiny. I was never going to tell Ms. Tillwell the truth if Karpis is destined to return to Alcatraz. The little book is written in stone.

That was the first time I spoke with someone from the outside—someone beyond these walls. My name may not perish on Alcatraz Island after all. On the other side of the coin, I opened the floodgates for Creepy Karpis to storm into The Rock with a vengeance. Karpis. Wilson. Mason. The enemies are piling up. If that does not change soon, my story and fate are sure to be carved deep in stone as well.

Enemies require allies. Madison has them in the form of the law. Wilson has them with his crew. The box of rocks Allen West is the only prisoner on my side at this moment. The hothead. A man like me, in a rock—The Rock—and a hard place, is in no position to get selective.

"I spoke with the warden." I greet West upon returning to the dock. Opening with that forces my own hand in moving our partnership along. "He told me Karpis's comin' back next week."

A look of fear surfaces on his face. The curious reaction is dismissed as he realizes the display of vulnerability. "Huh . . . how 'bout that?"

I let him sweat for a moment before responding, attempting to read his body language the way Ms. Tillwell somehow managed to read mine. The information simmers. "He'll be back within the next few weeks," I share.

Officer Bates cuts in the conversation before I can relay additional knowledge. Let that news soak for a while, Mr. West. The only person capable of getting in his thick head is himself. A mutual problem with Karpis draws us closer. It is no longer my problem, it is ours.

Anticipation gets the better of me throughout the day. I picture Madison planning his next move and Ms. Tillwell forgetting about me. She leaves me on this island along with any respect I earned in her eyes. Karpis prepares his revenge and Wilson waits for his chance to strike again. You do not have time to spare when threats loom around every corner; therefore, I bother West again at supper.

"So about Karpis comin' back . . ." I resume the conversation where it paused.

He mutes my words, slurping a plate of noodles while staring off at a conversation next to him, one he has no part in. He is silent for once. Tension builds as I respond to his lack of words with a blank stare. He can feel my uninterrupted focus and that bothers him. I picture 'Karpis' or 'Creep' racing through his mind like flies on raw hamburger patties. He imagines Karpis returning and getting placed near his cell. The conversation next door cannot distract him for much longer.

"God dammit!" He cracks. "What the fuck you goin' on about? Dun ya have enough time with me durin' detail? You comin' onna me or somethin'?" His friends laugh while my blank stare lingers. I am a deer in headlights prepared for collision.

"Karpis," I repeat. The same fear from earlier sweeps past his face before reverting to annoyance. "Karpis's comin' back in a few weeks. Fuck, the Creep could get dumped tomorrow for all we know." I pause. He raises a brow with interest and waves his neighbors' attention away like a fly swatter. I continue once he is engaged, "I have issues with the guy. Somethin' tells me you do too."

"N' what're you some sorta mind reader?" He grasps his spoon a little tighter. Red pasta sauce surrounds his mouth like poorly applied lipstick. "Who's t'say I dun have an issue with you? You're always annoyin' the shit outta me n' all."

"That may be true . . . but I'm willin' t'bet that man keeps you up at night. He's someone you consider a threat. Someone who could end your life at a moment's notice. I'm the one bird who can make those worries disappear."

He raises his fist, catching the attention of a nearby screw. An inevitable punch to my jaw transitions into a wide stretch. The guard steps back to his post. West is aware of what he is doing—at least he thinks he is.

"Alright boys . . . suppertime's over." The hothead turns to the birds around him. "Why dun you shift down a few while I deal with this twat?"

The three men at the otherwise empty table gather their trays to do as instructed. Months of studying West's personality has shown me his true colors. He keeps useful individuals at his side, but deep down he is not loyal to anyone. Those around him fear him. While Wilson's strategy is loyalty, West capitalizes on his violent past, which strikes fear in the eyes of those associated with him. This is why I need him.

"Karpowicz's what birds 'round here call an original gangster." He pushes his tray aside to clear the stage for another animated story. "Stupid-ass nickname for a piece a shit like him. He's been on this island longer than anyone far as I know. He's carryin' more than a nickel if ya catch my drift. It's that all-day sentence. The Creep's a real quiet son of a bitch too. That dun mean the guy's not a problem. That amount a time comes with a certain . . . level a cred. He may not have other birds coverin' his ass like the rest a us but the guards've always looked after him."

My instincts were correct. West is rolling over, revealing his agitation. Fear is not a difficult emotion to yank out of someone's core as it consumes them, taking control of the mind and defying reason. I learned that the moment I landed in cell fourteen. Society ceases to exist without fear.

"N' he's used that privilege t'his advantage?" I ask. "Did he undermine you or somethin'?" I work to identify the source of his fear and the reason he knows so much about Karpis.

"Undermine? You been spendin' too much time in the damn library." He laughs a nervous laugh. I forgot I am speaking to someone with minimal education. "You keep up that smart talk n' you'll be someone's June bug in no time."

I take note of his harsh advice; I did the same with Wilson. Traditional education does not equate to knowledge within these walls. Knowledge is defined differently on Alcatraz Island and West believes he is the most intelligent man in this prison. This is him trying to change the subject again rather than educate me. I will not let that happen.

"Alright, I get it West." I prepare to boomerang the conversation. "Just tell me . . . what was the deal between you n' Karpis?"

"Right . . ." He rubs his head. He now confides in me by his own choosing. The last time this happened was with Wilson. This occasion must have a different outcome. "He's untouchable now. 'Bout the first six months a my stint here they put me with a small gang that prevented this place from lookin' like more of a shithole than it already was. You know the salt from the bay eats these fuckin' pipes right? Anyway we did some bigger gardenin' n' paintin' jobs. The Creep worked 'longside me. He must've caught a whiff a the prison's fresh catch n' preyed on it. He told me t'pick up his slack. I refused 'cause I'm no one's bitch. I didn't know who the tall motherfucker was at first. When I refused t'do his work the Creep made the guards leave the room we was in. I mean the old bastard actually convinced the C.O.'s t'scram."

"Why'd they listen t'm? He's a con . . . a slave t'the system. How'd he pull off somethin' like that?"

"I'll get there." He motions for me to calm down. He is right, the story is getting the better of my emotions, too. "When a bird's 'round longer than any screw they become the system. When the officers scurried out the Creep looked at me for a minute. Ya know . . . sorta got in my face n' all. He's a fuckin' tree so I'm down there starin' up at him. I knew what was comin' next. It wasn't my first time in that type a rodeo. So I grabbed a paint bucket n' flung it at the monster's skull. The guy caught it mid-air n' whipped out a knife. Next thing I knew I'm lyin' there with blood soakin' so far through my blues there's a puddle a my own red poolin' 'round me. Can't make this shit up."

He lifts the bottom of his shirt, revealing a thin scar traveling from his hip to his abdomen. I envision the knife piercing his skin and landing in that exact position; I picture Karpis pulling out the sharp object to open the floodgates holding back a tsunami of dark-red blood, and finally West dropping to the concrete floor from a combination of pain and disbelief.

"N' he got what for doin' that? What'd they do t'him?" I demand answers.

He sweats, reliving the violent moments while massaging his side as if the blade was still inside his skin, shoved in so only the handle remains exposed on the oozing surface, a cork waiting to pop out at midnight on New Year's Eve.

"What'd they do t'him?" he mocks me. "I'll tell you what they did . . . nothin'. Those spineless sons a bitches told the warden the whole thing was an accident. They said I fell on some broken pipe stickin' outta the ground. They didn't even check t'see if there was a pipe in the room. Unreal I tell ya."

West revisits the story for several more painful minutes until the bell sounds. Suppertime is over. The look on his face is that of a man who has confessed all of his sins—he looks relieved in his own, hotheaded way. I follow the rest of the room's symphony of birds rising from their seats in synchronized fashion. West will not roll over despite the bell sounding and screws shouting. He wises up— something Wilson never did—to demand answers. He let his guard down around me for the second time without context.

"No ya dun get that shit for free!" he argues with a hissing whisper. He stands behind me in line as we prepare to file out of the dining hall. "You sit down with your mind games n' all n' you dun give me anything. What you got on the Creep that makes you keep spittin' his name? I swear t'God I'll put you in the infirmary myself if you peep a word 'bout this."

"Relax . . . there is somethin'." I attempt to ease his mind.

My tired brain is unsure of what that something is. I needed to leave him with hope—hope and fear to keep him at my side the same way he operates with others. Another lure hooked into the cheek of a con. This time the benefits are bound to be mutual, helping me rest my eyes later tonight.

A guard steps over before West can dig deeper. Our conversation is cut short. Still, I have managed to loosen up a wild West during our quick chat. He is not a wise man by my observation, yet he is motivated. A spark winds him up and throws him into action.

The rest of the inmates shuffle down the cellblock while I walk with pride. I am left with a sense of accomplishment. A potential ally is in the mix after months of operating alone and tallying enemies. This is an opportunity to dispose of a massive, inevitable threat. Things are looking positive for a change. The successful interaction calls for celebration in the form of an evening of uninterrupted sleep. Peaceful, much-needed rest—a chance to let my mind wander. There is no need for therapeutic meditation for a new method of calming wraps me in its welcoming arms. I accept the challenge of putting Karpis on his destined path with West's assistance—a path that leads to life imprisonment.

"Field . . ." a whisper echoes through my cell grate. It grows louder with each word. Not more than ten minutes of solitude is flushed down the drain. "Field . . . I know you can hear me."

I recognize the despicable tone like the back of my hand. It is Wilson, my inevitable neighbor. His voice bounces through the cell, calling my name on repeat. This is an emotion I do not have to hide: fear. The same fear West felt at supper.

I let the whispers drift through the cell several moments longer, hoping for another distant dream to reveal itself. This must be a deep sleep on the narrow mattress. I slap my face and the noises do not cease. The mindless taunting takes a turn for the worse as echoes of substance pour through the grate.

"Ya know I was never much of a reader . . . but this's a real page-turner."

The tone is taunting. He has something of mine. The little book? No, that is not possible. The only personal item I possess is safe and sound. I lift my mattress, fumbling around in the blackness waiting for my hand to land on the small lump—the tumor under the bed. The surface is as smooth as it has ever been—no lump. I am certain the little book is not there, yet I toss items about the cell anyway. It is gone. It was under the mattress this morning and now it is gone. It disappeared. Vanished. Poof. It cannot be true. Another dream, maybe. My palm continues to slap my forehead, punishing myself for not thinking faster.

"Tsk tsk . . ." his voice leaks through the grate again. "Under the mattress . . . really? I took ya for a smarter fish than that. It's a wonder a turnkey didn't turn it up already. You really are the dumbest crook in this joint."

"No no no no . . ." My whispers of worry travel to the grate. I crawl toward the green, holed plate and press my face against it. My face squeezes through the diamond holes. "Wilson you don't understand. It's not what you think it is."

"I don't give a rat's ass what I think it is. All I know's it's important t'you. Don't you think I heard you shufflin' over there lookin' for it? You're scramblin'. The tone in your voice says it all. This here's important t'you . . . n' it's mine now."

My accomplishments with West are tossed into a raging flame to burn as Wilson dangles the little book in front of the same mass of yellow, orange and red. He has it now; the source of knowledge is in the hands of an enemy, and an intelligent one at that. I flip through the little book in my head. I rewind the tape and recall the old man's voice guiding me through the cellhouse. The man in my mind. I try to remember every crime-based television show I watched growing up. No solutions. My shattered mind remains in infinite pieces. The all-knowing bible was stripped from my hands due to carelessness. What did I expect?

I do not know what is more terrifying: the idea of Wilson using the little book to his advantage or the object never reaching public light. It would be well-documented thirty years from now if it is to be confiscated, on display for tourists to admire behind a dusty glass wall. Then there is Wilson, who is bound to bounce from prison to prison until he is paroled in the far future. He cannot use the new knowledge to escape—I am certain of that much. So, what happens to the little book?

Whatever tomorrow holds in store, one destined path will remain untouched: I will not be sleeping tonight.

TWILIGHT TIME

Wilson's clever hands have possessed the little book for two days. Two full days of dread and desperation as I sweep my mind for any opportunity to reclaim the personal possession. The efforts are useless. The most nerve-wracking part is the loud silence. I have yet to hear a peep from Wilson or a member of his crew since the reveal of his discovery through the grate. Dead silence.

The only plan with any traction is stringing West along to gain his trust. This is a focus so that I do not lose my mind over the absence of the little book. The strategy is like my befriending of Wilson, yet I pursue West's allegiance with true purpose. I am in it with him until the end so long as I am careful until that time.

"Listen Field," West whispers, intercepting me on our march to the dock. "I said it once n' I'll say it again . . . if you're some sorta fruitcake lookin' for a good time you can jump right off the dock n' swim inna a shark's mouth." There are no man-eating sharks in the bay. Of course, he does not know that. "I meant what I said 'bout sendin' ya t'the infirmary."

"You n' I both know there's more t'this, so cut the cry-baby routine." I am on edge. I do not have time for the foolish hothead to test my patience. "This isn't the place t'have that talk. We'll both know when it's right."

"One day." He flashes his middle finger in my face as a substitute for the index. "I'll give ya one day t'spill what you're holdin'. After that we're strangers." He leans in closer to keep the nearby birds from listening in. "The Creep comes back in four days. One a my buddies heard a few screws chattin' 'bout it. Four days n' he's back so know you understand my itchin'."

It is a reasonable ultimatum. He divulged more than I asked for that evening in the dining hall. I owe it to him to provide some level of detail behind Karpis' departure from the island. I do not have enough to please him yet, though. The plan is not fleshed out to his—nor my—satisfaction.

Another day inches by without development. In the blink of an eye, West goes from making his threats at the dock to awaiting my response the next morning in the yard. A sleepless night drained my mind of any energy to craft a plan. I am a walking zombie. Time is up according to West's timeline. No progress leaves me with no option other than to play my current hand. A sliver of truth will satisfy him, pulling him further into a partnership. A few drops of honesty without dumping the bucket.

Wilson and his crew sit on the far end of the yard, claiming Karpis' previous section as a power move over the Creep, the equivalent of a dog pissing over another dog's urine. Their territory is marked before Karpis' inevitable return. A line in the sand. They spot me entering the yard, continuing their 'Where's Waldo' routine to track my every move. They stare but do not approach as it becomes clear I am headed to West's area. Wilson wishes to talk about the little book, yet I have nothing to give him at the moment.

"You talkin'?" West asks as I enter the circle consisting of him and his usual three other men. "I dun wanna see your face 'less it spits somethin' I wanna hear. I told ya one day n' it's well past that time by my count."

"That's why I'm here Allen. I'm ready t'continue our conversation."

He steps in the center of the circle. We are gladiators prepared for battle. "Allen? You're pressin' your luck pal." He spins around to address the colosseum. "Well ya heard the runt. Take a walk. Lemme tend t'my business."

They obey his command without question. My eyes bounce from West to the distant Wilson and his crew. There are too many moving pieces, so the little book sits on the backburner for now. Getting rid of Karpis is a priority with his return creeping up following the weekend. I cannot juggle both obstacles for much longer.

West and I walk along the tall, beige wall in the opposite direction of Wilson's new corner. We kick gravel to muffle our conversation in what is common practice during yard talk. Dust flies up from the ground in front of our path as the conversation commences.

"D'you remember me tellin' you about how I threw that ball at Karpis in the yard?" I try to jog his memory with a familiar place to start.

"Sure. What's that gotta do with anything?"

"That tussle led t'the death of Ronnie Yantz. The papers n' warden declared it an accident. They claimed Yantz fell on a sticker he made in his cell."

"Yeah I heard that. So what? Whole prison knows that. What's your point?"

I take a deep breath. Once I dive into the abyss with West, there is no coming out. He will carry more information than anyone else in this prison. Even Madison does not have the full picture despite his manipulative ways.

"It was Karpis' sticker . . . not Yantz's." I breathe out. "You said it yourself, Karpis could get away with anything. D'ya really think they'd believe Yantz kept a knife outta sight all that time? Madison knew he wasn't the sharpest tool in the shed. Yantz's death was intentional. Karpis killed the man in cold blood n' got away with it."

He stops walking and the air clears of dust. His internal lie detector runs at full force. Even if the readings claim bullshit, which they will not, he knows I have nothing to lose. There is no other reason to associate myself with him.

"N' what's a guy like you know all this for?" Curiosity becomes doubt.

"Because the warden n' I have history."

The conversation, a walk-and-talk, swallows the entirety of yard time. We walk the wall, back and forth, for over an hour and West's suspicions fade as each reveal proves to be more extreme than the last. He is baffled by these tales, as am I.

When the siren sounds, it is off to supper. West is locked in at this point. The hothead's demeanor changed; it is not full of the rage he often carries nor the fear he flashed in the dining hall. It is of pure interest—maybe even trust.

Change the count of impulsive life decisions from two to three. Two failed, but this action was successful—for now. I quit my job with a performance that makes an A-list actor look like a wannabe amateur; I tossed my belongings to the curb; I failed at making life any more tolerable. Putting my trust in a hotheaded con, however, can be chalked up as a win. I will take whatever victories I can obtain right now.

"Field!" a voice vibrates from behind us. "Field, you're needed in the library." It is Captain Peters again. Another meeting with the king screw is more than I can handle with everything else going on.

"Can it not wait 'til after supper sir?" Give me more time to anticipate what is in store at the library.

"Excuse me?" he coughs. "I don't wanna hear so much as you breathin' 'til you're in that goddamn library."

He walks closer, his leather boots squeaking on the floor. He is prepared to drag my body across the dining hall the way he did down Sunset Strip when he first found me in cell fourteen. I lift myself off the seat and walk toward him to his delight. The ever-obedient servant.

Peters escorts me all the way to the library entrance. There, standing hunkered over the entryway, stands a whimpering Officer Mason. This is not a meeting with the warden. Madison has no use of Mason as far as I am aware. The lowlife moved to library oversight a month ago following his lack of order in the Industries Building. That, and his obvious lack of enacting any disciplinary measures.

"Get the trash taken care of then bring the sad sack t'his cell," Peters orders. "Shouldn't take more than fifteen minutes so I'll come find ya if it's any longer. Don't piss your pants there Mason."

Mason shakes his trembling head in agreement. Peters' shoes stomp down the block back to the dining hall, a soldier marching to his next battle. There is no trash in the library. It is a wasteland seldom traveled by birds. Mason, the fearful son of a bitch, guides me to the back of the library. He does not utter a word. When I am out of sight, he steps aside to make room for the meeting's true organizer.

"Been a minute hasn't it?" Wilson chuckles. Sykes soon follows the leader, blocking the other end of the row of books. "Take a walk Mason. I'll holler if you're needed." The shameful puppy wanders off to his crate. "Now this's a good read," Wilson continues, holding up the little book like a priest worshipping sacred text. The object does not look out of the ordinary in the library should any other officers arrive at the scene, a clever consideration on his part. "Tell me . . . what were you doin' with this in the first place?"

"I told you it's not what you think it is."

I am distracted by the vision of coughing up blood after the two finish interrogating me. I believed this was over when reassigned to garbage detail—a foolish belief indeed.

"Yeah ya said that the other day," he reminds me. Sykes steps in front of him. "N' now I'm thinkin' it's pretty fuckin' useful."

"It's what's takin' ya down ya back-stabbin' bastard!" Sykes cuts in.

"Easy. . ." Wilson places a hand across his subordinate's chest to keep him from lunging forward. The parrot lost his protector. He is still angry—bent on revenge.

"Now Field, if you explain t'me what this book is we may be able t'work somethin' out," Wilson lies. "One thing I know for sure's this isn't yours. Sections on sections of practic'lly every man who stepped foot on this island are on these pages. There's one place you could a gotten this from n' that's the king screw's office. We see you walkin' t'his place with Peters every now n' again. So what's the meanin' behind this? There're dates in here that don't make sense . . . dates yet to pass."

He is fascinated by the little book; however, there is no chance in hell those pages see the outside of his cell given the literature's secrecy thirty years from now. I will call the bluff. I am not discussing anything—not a single page. There is one way to get out of this conversation and it leaves my skin purple and face torn open like it is in the midst of a surgical procedure.

"For the last time, that's not what you think it is." I inch toward one of the bookshelves at my side. I am trapped between walls of writing and the two crew members. The shelves will not budge—I already know that. "The book isn't meant for you. Someone as fuckin' stupid as you can't understand that. Just try t'get that through your thick skull Wilson."

The comment lands on a trigger button. Wilson bolts my way, little book in hand. Sykes plays catch up a few trots behind. I do not flinch. Instead, Wilson gets two feet away from me before my hand lands on a hardcover from the shelf. It swings with full force—a rocket blasted into orbit. The corner smashes his skull, sending my neighbor tumbling to the opposite shelf like a domino. He clutches his head on the floor, dazed from the blow. I reach for the little book in his moment of weakness. The mesmerizing object consumes my attention, blocking the sight of Sykes trucking his short, stocky body down the row. He crashes into me the way I crashed into Karpis in the yard all that time ago. We topple to the concrete ground—all three of us now flat on the floor.

The little book remains in Wilson's hands. Action scenes in films got it right; everything plays out in slow motion. I am McClane, fighting off villains out to destroy the world. Sykes rolls on top of me, identifying an opportunity for payback without Wilson controlling the spotlight. My eyelids swell with each fist to the face. Wilson rises to his feet to tap Sykes out of the ring. He stumbles in the process, disoriented from the deck to the dome. His arms lean against a shelf for stability. The two men hover above me, staring at each other while having a mental conversation about what to do next. They cherish their tender moment of victory.

Wilson does not let off two swings of his fist before a frantic Lens flies around the corner, arms waving in the air. He is sweating and his glasses have steamed up. The most reasonable crew member yanks the leader off of me while simultaneously trying to catch his breath. I spot a quivering Mason poking his head out from the end of the row, too.

"Quit it! Quit it!" Lens yells. "The captain's headed back. I heard him stompin' around the corner out there."

A cranked-up Sykes stabs the air with his fists while the other two pull him down the row, a real-life 'Rock 'Em Sock 'Em Robots' figure dragged between the shelves. The trio vanishes with no time to spare. No consequences for the wicked and no little book for me.

"What in God's green earth's goin' on here?" Peters storms through the doorway. My unavoidable groans guide the captain to my location. "Jesus Field . . . what the hell happened t'you?" He looks around. "Mason! Mason where the fuck are you?"

The coward circles the shelf, presenting himself on the opposite side from where he previously stood. He does his best to act surprised. "Field . . . what happened here? I can't step away for a second without you causing a ruckus."

I stand up, using the shelf for support the way Wilson did. I wipe my nose with my blue sleeve, turning it an odd shade of purple. The sight is boring after regular violence. Another prison routine. This is a form of desensitization man was not born to experience. What is one more session as the crew's punching bag? I kept quiet for this long; there is no benefit to folding now. I would be branded a snitch. Besides, that would draw the warden's attention toward me. I cannot risk that with Karpis' return only a few days away and the little book still in my neighbor's hands.

"I . . . I think I . . ." I stumble for the right words while waiting for the room to stop spinning. "I thought I saw a book up there. I wanted t'read it. I couldn't find a ladder so I tried climbin' the shelves. Next thing I know I'm flat on the floor, my back achin' n' face turned bloody as a slab a raw meat."

Mason breathes an audible sigh of relief behind Peters. He is safe for now. The captain folds his arms in disbelief. Only a subordinate witnesses the confrontation, so his worrying transforms into laughter. The real captain is out to play. "Since when'd you learn how t'read?" He slaps Mason's back to draw attention to the joke. "Mason tell me you saw this jagoff fall from way up top." Peters is as trigger-happy as any other guard without the warden around.

"I didn't see it captain," he admits, stepping into the middle of the row. He notices the captain's fading laughter and attempts to fuel it. "I sure as hell heard it though! Fell like a ton a bricks he did!"

"I dunno what I thought captain," I respond.

Bending over for them is better than having a conversation with Hopeful Howard. I am already on the warden's narrow radar thanks to Ms. Tillwell. Any extra attention from him and my plan to deal with the Karpis threat is incinerated. There are no second chances.

"Well clean yourself up n' get back to the fuckin' dining room already." Business resumes for Peters. "It's almost lights out." He nudges my shoulder with his own while walking past. "Mason make sure the klutz makes it back in one piece."

I stare at Mason down the narrow row. The limp noodle cannot make eye contact. I guide myself back to the dining hall in a display of dominance over the coward. He trails behind—a sulking Charlie Brown realizing how pathetic he is.

"Missed a spot," West greets me as I sit back down. There are only a couple minutes left of suppertime. "Reckon things are a hell lot worse than ya say."

A slice in my upper lip drips to my collar like a leaking faucet. I grab a napkin from West's plate and press it to my face. "None a that matters," I reply through the red napkin. "All that matters's your commitment. Your commitment t'the job. Nothin' changes . . . no matter how bad this gets."

"What d'ya take me for, some cherry like you?" He punches my shoulder. "I'm in it. Bet your skinny ass I'm still in it."

"Good. That's all I needa know. There's one more thing too. Even with Karpis outta the picture . . . we're gonna have an Officer Mason problem."

SMOKE GETS IN YOUR EYES

Wilson's mouth remains a closed book despite our encounter in the library. A man of reasonable intellect like him is aware the little book is valuable. The question is: how long does it take him to release its details to others? How long until he puts its contents to the test? To Wilson, an alternate reality is out of the picture, a laughable concept to anyone except me. According to his comments in the library, he believes the warden is behind the object's very existence.

My neighbor is a threat, but the problem still requiring immediate attention is the Creep. Karpis made a triumphant return three days ago—much sooner than anticipated. The phantom of Alcatraz passed through the heavy metal cellhouse doors once more. Every bird and screw awaited their first glimpse of the madman with anticipation. Peters followed Karpis' lengthy steps down the block, showing off his latest catch to the entire cellhouse. Anticipation verbalized with 'oohs' and 'aahs' as Karpis walked past each cell in a parade of one. The zoo animals were met with swift banging on the bars from four other officers guarding the convict. Some cons viewed the extra protection as the captain being fearful of the monster. In reality, sheer curiosity brought other officers along. The energetic scene did not faze Karpis, who did not bat an eye throughout the ordeal. He was a braindead patient plucked straight from 'The Ninth Configuration.' Worst of all, he now sits across from my cell, undoubtedly another one of the warden's scare tactics to keep me in line.

I stare across the shadowed block to a motionless Creep most nights. The lack of sound and movement from his cell is from nightmares. When daytime arrives, West and I dissect the plan again and again. We discuss our roles. We discuss backup options should a certain stage not succeed. The preparation continues while Karpis reintegrates into the system. He lost the faithful connections he built with screws over the years, taking on detail assignments like any other inmate now. The one exception to that assimilation is his solitude during detail. The warden isolates the Creep during the day by making him mop the cellhouse. West claims this is a temporary assignment until the screws feel comfortable enough to have him near other inmates. I hope for both our sakes he is correct.

Tomorrow is judgment day. Three threats are scheduled to be neutralized. The road is clear of approaching obstacles. If all threats were handled separately, the warden's eyes would fly from his criminal activities to another concern—me. All three rebels must fall in a single motion, and a week's worth of sleepless nights is bound to pay off tomorrow. I do not know what I will do if we are unsuccessful.

Wilson is smart. Mason is weak. Karpis is not the smartest of the bunch, however, his raw strength cannot be ignored. There is no little book to use to my advantage. There is no dialogue from the tape to brush these obstacles away. I am counting on West to follow through; my fate is sealed if he does not do as much. He has his instructions and I have mine.

The schedule I monitor—my primary task—sends considerations fluttering up like white specks in a snow globe. It is difficult to act like a model inmate for the warden while getting notes on Karpis' whereabouts throughout the day. Fortunately, a previous acquaintance of West serves library duty, providing us with a spy of sorts not far from the core of the cellhouse. Library duty requires little supervision as it is one of the most vacant places on the island—Wilson knew as much and preyed on the fact not long ago. Now, I prey on it as well. The acquaintance is an older crook pushing fifty. He has done his time and is considered a low risk based on his internal track record. According to West, the man has a few weeks left on this rock before hitting parole. This is how I am able to keep tabs on Karpis without drawing too much attention.

"What kept him in line all these years?" I asked West.

"A woman," he responded. "Some floozy back home. Can ya believe that?"

Why a soon-to-be-free man assists a hothead and his unknown accomplice is a curious thought. Either way, this would not be possible without the help of this old bird. I will thank the man for putting the possibility of freedom on the table if I ever find myself out of this hellhole. I am certain it was not an easy decision for the man to put his parole on the line. It will not go forgotten.

I am a child waiting for Christmas morning on this final night. My gift is the plan's successful execution, keeping me alive for the foreseeable future. If any action goes awry it will end with my demise. That demise originates from the hands of the warden or the knuckles of my enemies. It is a roll of the dice I wish to avoid at all costs.

My eyes collapse after hours of tossing and turning in the uncomfortable bed. Sleep is crucial for a clear head, yet my vision is as clear with closed eyelids as it is with them open. No counting sheep. No meditation. Full concentration on the plan. The insomnia sticks around for the long haul. It rewards me with fifteen to twenty minutes of rest every few hours before jolting awake again. And again. Another night wasted on tending to a cluttered mind.

The torture ends as the drum of lights flipping on fills my ears. A baton playing an out-of-tune melody against cell bars follows the unwelcome alarm. Morning has arrived sooner than anticipated.

"Up n' on your feet ladies!" an officer orders.

The block is exceptionally bright. The sun's rays beam from a window on the east side of the building and fill the cellhouse with deceiving warmth. The light is an illusion disguised as freedom. My former self despised everything the sun contributed, the worst of it all being routine; however, I appreciate routine today. Routine is my ally for once. The plan fails to exist without the careful observation of the prison's rules and regulations.

West and I remain separated during the morning. I spend breakfast on the opposite, empty side of his table. He socializes with a few allies while I toss my food around the tray. I have no appetite. No sleep and no appetite. Time stands still and moves too fast. I savor every moment of planning—rehearsing—yet find time slipping through my hands.

The breakfast bell sounds—another alarm clock, but this time for work. The gun fires at the starting line, sending the plan into full motion. Full speed ahead, as it is often put.

"Officer Bates!" West bolts out of line the moment we reach the dock. He catches an unsuspecting Bates leading the conga line of cons. Precisely on cue. "Yeah. Hey boss. I talked t'Officer Mason n' sounds like he needs some extra help in the library again this afternoon."

"What, again? Can't that bag a bones on library duty do anything useful?" Bates asks. "Jesus the guy gets stamped n' puts in for retirement."

That is a fair observation from the officer as this is the second time help has been requested in the last week. Believe me: an alternative location would have been chosen if it presented itself. Making the library the meeting ground is not ideal, yet it stands as the most desolate location on the island. Nowhere else will work— I played it out in my head countless times. Besides, we must stay near our primary target.

"Not sure boss," West replies. "Somethin' 'bout a new box a books comin' in. I dun give the orders. I just follow 'em. All I know's he needs some hands in there n' told me t'tell ya. I think Jeff can't handle it by his'self's all."

Bates studies West before responding, "Fine. Officer Maxwell'll take ya there in that case t'make sure this isn't bullshit. N' take Thompson with you if he really needs that much fuckin' help. For Christ's sake you'd think the toughest crooks in the world'd have some muscle on 'em."

West looks back at me, paused in line with the rest of the detail crew. I glance back in silence and he continues to stare, waiting for a line delivery. He must think on his feet for once. He is a criminal and one of the greatest storytellers around. This should not be difficult.

He turns back to the officer. "Honestly I dun do well with Thompson. I dun vibe with him. Figured ya knew that. We've bumped heads one too many times on our own." He uses his infamy for trouble to his advantage. West's strength is through his enemies.

Bates lets off another curious expression. The tense moment is soon interrupted by an impatient bird wandering off from the line. The officer pushes West aside. "Sure. Fine. Grab someone else from line then. Just make sure Maxwell takes note a your absences or it'll be both your asses. Tell Mason he has your help for an hour. There's trash all over this island. One hour n' you're back here doin' the work you were assigned t'handle."

The officer hustles over to the wanderer, unleashing a fury of verbal punishment. 'You ass-stain.' 'Dumb twat.' 'Melon-head.' The colorful words provide the perfect distraction for West to signal me over. Non-verbal cues yank me out of line toward a distant Officer Maxwell.

The guard takes note of our new assignment and we are on our way. The three of us part from the dock and head to the peak of the island—toward the library. My mental clock ticked the moment Bates informed West of the one-hour deadline. It takes five minutes to climb back up to the cellhouse, leaving fifty-five minutes for execution. Fifty-five short minutes.

Officer Mason slouches in the doorway of the library, timid as ever. He holds a clipboard in one hand and rests the other over a pallet of cardboard boxes. The book donation was not a clever lie. The shipment was planned and proves the validity of our need to be in the library. The officers exchange a few words and Maxwell walks away, leaving us with Mason. The little man stares at us, waving the clipboard in a motion to follow him.

Fifty-four minutes.

"Did ya hide the shit Jeff brought?" West gets in Mason's face the moment we are alone. "You grabbed that stuff right? Tell me it's here ya sleaze-ball."

I dissect West for his stupidity, but the man deserves credit where it is due. He makes useful connections. These occasional glimpses of intelligence fade with comments like the previous, though. I again recall the only factor driving him to complete this plan: fear. A tough guy who exudes cockiness goes a pale white when Karpis' name is mentioned. He fears for his pathetic life and that is what keeps him in line for now.

"We're dead men if this goes south. All of us. You know that right?" Mason's voice vibrates as he walks us to the back of the library, a death march in the weak-minded officer's eyes. He keeps a hand on his baton, a laughable sight knowing how easily we could overpower him.

"Well you're screwed no matter what by my count bug," West spews the vocabulary he knows best. "How a screw can be a criminal at the same time beats me. If the jailbirds don't getcha the skipper'll bend ya over his desk 'fore ya know it."

"Keep your voice down," I try to diffuse the tension between the two. I am mediating an argument between Robb and Meredith. My former reality returns.

Mason is screwed no matter how this ends—West is correct in that sense. Still, we need him now. His status as a guard is critical to our scheme and our being in the library. This would not work without the help of an officer. It does not matter if that officer is a coward or not.

The officer glares at West while pulling out a busy keyring to unlock the closet door. He turns back to West before turning the knob.

"Doesn't matter what side I'm on," he shares with the hothead. "It's every man for himself on this rock. I intend t'do what I must t'stay alive. I've got my whole life t'live."

Mason's statement was at the center of phase one of the plan. Mason is a chameleon, adapting to his environment in response to terror. Fear fuels his actions. He does not have the stomach nor the courage to survive on his own, so he focuses on appeasing those around him.

Another one of West's acquaintances helped bring Mason on board. All it required was a pack of smokes. West instructed the man speak with Wilson during laundry detail. He planted a seed in my neighbor's ear that others know about the little book's existence. Wilson's crew would never betray him as they are sworn to secrecy about this object. Wilson is aware of this so turns his suspicions on

Officer Mason next—the officer that is loyal to only himself. The rest is history. Wilson confirmed the little book was safe in his cell, then confronted Mason in the Industries Building. He did not need to be convinced of Mason's betrayal, more so welcoming it—even embracing it.

Mason's transfer to library oversight was the talk of the town. Wilson's fury resulted in the officer crying his way to Captain Peters and the warden. He was on library duty the next day—the safest location on the island. The safest location until today, that is. Mason soon realized his problem was not resolved as Wilson remained a threat to his survival. Of course, West and I played a role in feeding him those worries. Putting our arms around the officer needed little additional effort after that. We became his new safety net. We are his protection. He is our servant.

Here we stand in the library, a scared screw next to an open closet, a hothead destined for life in prison, and me, the man from another reality. All the components to a successful plan, I hope.

Fifty minutes. Back to business.

The open closet only has a few items on the floor, the majority of the space being taken up by cobwebs. The items are ones an average screw does not bat an eye at. They are safe in a locked closet, maybe belonging to an officer or confiscated from an inmate at one point. It does not matter their origin as any will suffice. A broom. A rope. A small lighter. We can thank our soon-to-be parolee for these generous donations. "Departing gifts from one con t'another," the acquaintance told West.

"This's everything?" West asks me. "You're sure it's the only crap we need t'get this done? We can get us a real nice sticker too. Just gonna take a couple a more days."

"We're not stickin' anyone." I stand my ground. This cannot end the way it did with Karpis in the yard. "Stick t'the plan. Everything'll fall inna place if we stick t'the plan."

West sighs. He swipes the items from the closet as his eyes roll to the back of his head. The hothead will not have his way—not this time. He tosses the three objects in front of us, clueless as to the next step even though we discussed it on countless occasions.

"Well what're ya waitin' for?" I snap. Forty-eight minutes. "Tie him up n' let's get started."

West smiles an evil grin. This is a nibble to keep his hunger for violence satisfied. He pushes Mason to the ground before the guard can pull out his baton, as if the coward would even dare swat at us. West flings the thick rope around the officer and proceeds to tie both his hands and his legs together. The coward is a pig ready to roast, a fitting look for what he has done and the violence he has let go unpunished.

"What the hell's this?" Mason yells. His legs try to kick free off the floor before West smacks them back down. "You said you needed me t'put this stuff aside n' keep it hidden!" He struggles more, fueling the hothead's elation. "If they find me here I'll be screwed! I'm done for!"

West grabs the man's baton and whips it at his back. He whips it again, the second time for enjoyment. Shouts of pain are silenced as West uses the remaining rope to gag Mason. The officer is silenced, and the first phase is complete.

Forty-five minutes.

"Calm down Mason," I plead. Tears drip from the officer's cheek, soaking into the brown rope that he chokes on. "This must happen. You'll be alright when it's all over. I promise you that."

We are done with the officer. He sits in a cell of his own; the empty closet is now his resting place. He hides our supplies and we hide him in the same location, another fitting punishment for the two-faced twerp. Now it is time to tend to the Creep. It is time to wipe Karpis out of the picture once and for all. Peters does not trust him next to another bird quite yet, so he continues handling daily detail by his lonesome along with an attentive Officer Douglas. His routine remained constant over the last week—the slime-ball Mason informed us as much, as did West's acquaintance.

West and I grab the broom and lighter, slamming the closet door on Mason and tiptoeing out of the library. The core of the cellhouse is at the center of phase two.

"Alright . . . you remember your role here right?" I test his failing memory. "You can't screw this up."

"A course. Played it out in my head all science-like 'bout a dozen times. That's the trick t'this Field. Stay focused n' you'll never fail."

Put his quote on a postcard and every recipient discards it. He is the brute in this scheme. I do not trust his claims, so I will continue to challenge his memory until I feel good about it. After all, he is not so unconquerable if he often ends up behind bars, destined to remain trapped on The Rock.

Karpis snakes up and down the cellblocks in his own daily routine. He cleans every inch of the floor on each block—both lower and upper tiers. He scrubs blood from altercations or punishments; he mops shit puddling out from overflown cell toilets, a result of an unsettling meal or simply a revenge-driven bird. The Creep is dragged from the interior of the cellhouse to the perimeter in the afternoon, so we must be swift in action.

Thirty-seven minutes.

Officer Douglas follows the bird like a shadow, not more than two feet behind him at a given position. He is a newborn duckling waddling after its mother. The benefit of this scenario, however, is the absence of another body in the gun gallery. There is no eye-in-the-sky needed when only one con roams around the cellhouse. This leaves West and me free to wander from one cellblock to the next without fear of bullets from above.

West prepares for a realistic game of 'Battleship.' He must figure out which cellblock Karpis is scrubbing at a given moment. From there, he is to lure Douglas away from the Creep.

"I did this all the time in Leavenworth," West told me the other day. "Only it was t'pull away a snitch. Needed t'put him in his place. Beat him bloody ya know?"

My ally and I part ways. My path leads to B-block—to Broadway. My home. An exuberant West hides at the end of Park Avenue. Whispers are far too loud at this distance, so we resort to hand signals. A peek down Broadway reveals Karpis. The giant shuffles down the opposite end of the street as Officer Douglas trots a few feet behind, attempting to read a magazine while walking. Minutes tick by and the two do not move more than a few feet. A large mess or a slacking Karpis—the reason for the lack of movement is unclear.

I leave my post, venturing to Park Avenue. I am worried. West stands around the corner, his back to the wall. A wave of my hand grabs his attention, ordering him to get moving. The clock ticks. The hothead responds with character-defining action. He holds up Mason's baton, pointing it above his head like a psychopathic villain with a knife. His shoeless feet inch down Park Avenue, making his way toward Seedy Street. The sound of the baton vibrating against cell bars commences the moment he is out of my sight.

"Stay here!" Douglas shouts at Karpis.

I sneak over to Broadway to find the officer slapping cuffs on the Creep. One cuff tightens around his hand while the other clanks onto the closest cell bar. Douglas ventures over to the source of the noise near the end of Seedy Street, where West will await. He grips his baton as tight as the hothead did on the other side. A battle of batons.

The clock above the gallery continues the countdown. Thirty-four minutes. Karpis is still on the floor of Broadway. Put him anywhere except Broadway and all would be fine. There must be another way around this.

A heavy thud travels from Seedy Street to the edge of Broadway before I can think of a solution to get rid of the cuffed Creep. Another crash follows as a body hits the floor. What just happened?

"Now! Do it now!" West's shouting echoes across the cellhouse. The sound of a banging baton resumes after he provides the all clear.

We are far behind schedule, so I reveal myself to Karpis. His dead eyes lock onto me the moment I step in the middle of Broadway. Matters worsen as I approach his position—he is locked to the cell next to his own. The odds are one in three hundred and thirty-six, yet I drew the short straw in a terrible miracle. The Creep stares without emotion. There is no curiosity in his eyes; they are as empty as the day he returned. He does not shout for help nor reach toward me in brutality. He simply observes.

I take the broom and shove it inside Karpis' cell. It moves around the cell like a rogue paddle, banging into the wall or ground every few seconds as my hand struggles to control it. A locket rests on the cell's far shelf. Karpis is known for keeping this item with him, the only personal item in his possession. The little book shared this fact. Every bird knows about this locket, as does every screw—it represents all that he is. It takes a few minutes of repositioning before the end of the broom reaches the shelf. I shove the stick forward and it knocks the locket to the floor. Karpis does not say a word throughout all of this. I am infiltrating his cell—stealing his possession—and he remains motionless.

West turns the corner the moment I stand up with the small, silver object. He wields a souvenir of his own—a bloodied baton. The stick drips a trail of red droplets from one cellblock to the next.

"What'd you just do?" I yell down Broadway.

He walks toward me with the same stupid grin he always has plastered across his face.

"He saw me," he replies, waving the baton in the air. "What was I s'posed t'do . . . let him cuff me too?"

"So you continued t'swing at him even when he was out?" I step toward him in rage. "Jesus why didn't you just cuff him? I heard him fall. It was done from there."

West was to provide a distraction. Get the officer's attention, sneak up on him and knock him out, a blind attack that leaves the two of us to our business and a guard with a large bump on his head. I trusted a trigger-happy bird to get the job done without issues. That was a mistake.

"He woulda gotten us caught!" he defends himself. "It'd ruin everything. I saved us!"

He deserves to be on the other end of that dripping baton; however, there is no time for punishment. Any attempt at disciplining him would send us both to the hole. This is an issue I will deal with at another time. Focus. Time does not stop.

Eighteen minutes.

Regular body and cavity checks infiltrate detail every now and again. The little book is tucked away in Wilson's cell without Mason as my neighbor's extra set of eyes. This is the most important stage in the plan and another reason Mason was a crucial ally. My neighbor's cell is a hop across the cellblock. What started as an initial alliance resulted in hatred. From neighbors to enemies. A smile brushes my own face in a strange thrill. I have not smiled in months—not like this at least.

West taunts Karpis from a few feet away. I grab the broom with one hand. The lighter from the closet ignites in my other hand and the two objects meet in front of Wilson's cell. The broom's end is swallowed by flames—my very own torch. I am a one-man mob infiltrating the home of a town's clichéd villain. The flame enters the cell and touches down on Wilson's mattress. The final step in this satanic-like ritual is tossing the locket on the cell floor. Karpis' precious locket. My precious little book. Wilson's precious leverage.

Twelve minutes.

The bed rises in flames until the beast covers every surface in sight. The view is beautiful. The heat warms my face and my eyes squint as the flames grow brighter. For a minute, I am at peace, shaping history before soon being reminded that the plan is not yet complete. Karpis still poses an unforeseen, peculiar problem. A cuffed Karpis does not equate to a guilty man. If anything, it provides evidence of his innocence. A likely deceased Officer Douglas makes matters even worse. Officer Bates will know the only other individuals in the cellhouse during the struggle were West and me, so it must be obvious that this was Karpis' doing.

West turns around after feeling the roaring flames kiss the back of his head. He looks panicked, preparing to sprint away. I leap across Broadway and grab his shoulder before he runs into the distance.

"Where're ya goin'?" I ask. He wiggles his shoulder free from my grip. "We have t'deal with him first."

We look over at Karpis. The Creep stares at us, waiting for the proper moment to pounce on his prey. We are a pair of monkeys taunting him for months on end. This is what I imagine flying through his head despite a rather calm demeanor. We step toward the monster in unintentional synchronization. West winds up the bloodied baton once again. I stretch out my arm and aim Douglas' key toward Karpis' corpse-like hand. This is the closest I have been to the man since he sent me to the infirmary. This was all for nothing if we do not uncuff him. I take a deep breath and insert the key into the lock. The cuffs clank to the floor. West holds the baton a little tighter and I step back. Karpis does not move a muscle. He remains kneeled on the floor, his hand resting between the cell bars as if still cuffed or praying to the Almighty.

Seven minutes.

Despair fills the Creep's face to the brim. For a moment, I empathize with him. He will rot in prison. He has a brutal past, yet the look in his lifeless eyes tells me he is exhausted. I suppose everyone has their breaking point—has Karpis reached his end of the rope? We leave him in his praying position as we jog down Broadway headed back to the library. I look back at the man and he stays in the stone-like state. He has given up for reasons unknown.

The last phase of the plan is one I have dreaded since it entered my mind. I did not think this through as sincerely as I had the other two phases. To be fair, any further consideration on the matter would force me to second-guess the forthcoming actions. West does not know about this phase for he would slit my throat if he did.

"Gimme the baton," I plead.

We run into the library. Sweat drips from our every pore, exhausted from the rushed, sloppy work paired with the heat from the growing flames in the cellhouse's core.

"What?" he asks, shifting the baton from one hand to the other as we continue to run. "Let's untie this bug n' make him bring us back t'the dock already!"

"No, we can't do that!"

We reach the closet, hands resting on our knees as we catch our breath. Four minutes—even less if Karpis decides to move a muscle.

"Noise like that's sure t'have echoed through the cellhouse, inna the library n' everywhere else by now. The flames're roarin'. It's over if Mason brings us back t'the dock. All a us are fucked . . . Mason included."

"Alright then let's take care a Mason n' make it look like Karpis did it t'the rat," West argues. He reaches for any logic he can provide. The baton. Violence.

"That's the plan," I assure him.

He hesitates to follow my request but realizes how much we have accomplished. He trusts me. This plan was my doing and it is my job to finish it. I tell him as much and he hands off the bloodied baton like a relay race. Two minutes until the hour mark hits. I can picture Officer Bates sending Officer Maxwell to grab us from the library.

West rushes to the closet to grab Mason. He grasps the doorknob to swing it open, the hothead's back to me. I punish West for what he did to Officer Douglas before he turns the knob; I punish him for the pain he caused countless birds and officers over the years, a taste of his own medicine. I punish him again and again. The baton was destined to crack against the side of his skull even if he did not beat Officer Douglas today. He had it coming, and the display of violence only made me more certain of that. One heavy blow sends him flying backward, swinging the closet door open to reveal a cowering Mason. West is on the ground, motionless.

I gaze at the weapon in my hand. Mason suffered, Douglas suffered and Karpis suffered; even West suffered. There is a single action left that brings this all to a close. It solidifies our innocence. This will make everything worth it in the end.

I look at Mason tied up in the closet, holding the baton above my head as if prepared to bash him bloody as well.

"You know what you have t'say. This was Karpis. This was always Karpis. Tell 'em that n' everything else'll fall inna place. Everything'll be fine if you stick t'that story."

Mason nods his head in agreement. Fear fills his eyes as they water again. There is a puddle spreading out from beneath him—he pissed himself. He prepares for a beating that never comes. Instead, the baton strikes my ribcage. It clashes against my arm. It whacks me in the chest. Each strike to my body is harder. I grow weaker with each collision yet find enough strength for another hit. The officer watches in awe as he witnesses a bird beat himself.

I am numb.

I am drained.

I am on my knees, weak and suffering.

I take the baton and use the rest of my energy to swing it at my head until I am lying on the ground, flat on the dusty floor like West. We suffer alongside each other, allies who are soon to be anything but that. The hothead will not understand what happened—he never will. I embrace the exhaustion—the nights of restless sleep combined with the pain coursing through my body—and shut my eyes. I can rest. No meditation. No worries. Just rest.

Footsteps trot from afar as my eyes stay closed and warm blood pools around me. The red concoction is a mixture of three men's internal goop, exposed for the world to see.

Footsteps and shouting fill the cellhouse. They soon fill the library as well.

I go away for a while.

ALL THIS TIME

Chappaqua's larger than people think. It was my own Manhattan as a kid since we'd only travel to the empire once a year. Another opportunity for my mom to remain an over-protective bird keeping its younglings in a cramped nest. My hometown's one of a few rural pockets outside the Big Apple that go unnoticed. Rural's an exaggeration, but they're rather dense when standing next to the city which tends to cast a shadow that goes on for miles.

The little I remember about foster life was being in Chappaqua for a good chunk of that time. I was a tyke after all, and these are memories I've learned to erase over the years. They're the sort best remembered as dreams, if at all. Shitty, meaningless dreams. Repression becomes a burden at times like this. It's the song title on the tip of the tongue that can't find its way out of the mouth. That sort of memory loss grows hazier the more time's spent remembering.

A few useful items have surfaced within my mom's organized chaos. Files and folders fill the house's dusty attic and, with just a flashlight handy, it's damn near impossible to find what I'm looking for—not that I even know what that is. The most curious item I've found is a photo from my first few months in the Field family. The photo includes my mustached dad and my mom's massive head of hair rivaling the blue-haired woman's from that new cartoon. And my brother's there, too, sitting off to the side with a common frown. In the center of the photo's me, a confused child trying to fit in where he doesn't belong; a puzzle piece that made its way inside the wrong box. It was all pretend.

"Oh hey honey." My mom catches me going through another box. "Are ya still looking at all this stuff? You should take a break already." She wants me to give up—to accept this life that forced me into assimilation.

"I'm not done yet," I snarl.

Somehow this reaction prompts her to step further into the room. "Come on. I'll heat up something t'eat," she insists.

"I'm not hungry," I protest, a child refusing his vegetables. She lingers, staring at me. I make use of her presence. "You mentioned you n' dad knew the woman who talked you inna adoption. What'd you say her name was again?"

"I didn't say her name." Her arms fold to prepare me for another lecture. "She didn't talk us inna adopting you Robert. That's the last time I'm gonna tell ya that. Her name was Samantha. Samantha Eldridge. Why d'you ask anyway?"

"Well I was thinkin' I owe her a personal 'thank you' ya know? It'd be nice t'have a positive experience like that with everything else that's happened lately. It'll put me on the right track. I mean I don't even have a goddamn job anymore. I need some motivation here."

"I haven't spoken t'Samantha in ages." She puts a hand over her forehead, trying to jog her own memory. "In fact no one has. She passed away some years back. I'm sure you thinking about her puts a smile on her face way up in the clouds. That'd be enough for her. Now come eat will you?"

I wave her off. She tosses her arms in the air and leaves the room. I'll worry about reconnecting with her after I have the answers I need. Putting my life back in order takes precedence over repairing relationships. My focus is me.

"Fine . . . then I'm headed t'the store!" she shouts from the other room. "When I get back I expect those boxes t'be back in the attic. If you won't be pleasant I'm gonna ask you t'stay elsewhere until you're in a better state a mind!"

She knows I have nowhere else to go and that it's to her advantage. This is an attempt at forcing me to make amends with her and the rest of the people I've wronged. She continues to steer me off track. I won't allow it.

"They'll be gone!" I yell. I'm a compulsive liar now. "I'll finish up by then. I'll find somewhere else t'stay if they're still out. You have my word on that." Blah, blah, blah.

The front door closes and the sound of a car starting follows. I stand up, peer out the window shade and watch her peel out the driveway. She thinks she has the upper hand—she's wrong. I walk over to the nearest phone when she's clear and far away. We'll see how truthful she is about this woman. I dial and an operator answers.

"Samantha Eldridge," I request. "Can you tell me if there's a Samantha Eldridge in the Chappaqua area?"

The operator shares a woman with that name resides in a nearby nursing home. My mom said Samantha Eldridge passed away years back. Either this is another old woman with the same name, or my mom's hiding something.

Hoffman Senior Living—the nursing home calls to me. The home's a fifteen-minute cab ride away. That's enough time to discover if I'm being fed lies or not. I'm not leaving to prove her wrong—that's a bonus. I'm leaving to start over. An outsider views this as impulsivity while it's actually pushing the few chips I hold into the center of the table, embracing my origin. It's the final bet before I'm lost again. My brother did the same not long ago. It'll work out better for me—I'm sure of that.

The cab rolls up five minutes later and I'm off. The nursing home's in a part of town no one cares to explore. Cracking buildings. Homeless people wandering with shopping carts. It makes sense society would dump those with minimal time left on earth into a place like this.

The nursing home itself's out of a fantasyland, a towering advertisement calling all old people to it. The tall, well-kept structure looking down on the rest of the crippled area summons the elderly. Freshly trimmed hedges wave hello in the breeze. A new layer of paint on the deep-maroon exterior resembles a summer cottage. There's even a doorman standing out front—a pleasant cherry on top. It's a welcoming place to die. Samantha Eldridge's years working in foster care in the same area paid off, assuming this is the lady I'm looking for.

"Good afternoon," I greet the receptionist. She's a refreshing face after months of speaking to librarians. I tell her I'm visiting

Samantha Eldridge.

"Oh are you one a Miss Eldridge's children? You're all so kind t'her. The love her children still carry for her after so many years just warms my heart."

"Right. Yeah. I'm one of her children," I hurry the conversation along.

She senses my rushed tone. "She's scheduled for television time now. Sign in here n' take a left at the end a the hall. You can't miss it with the television turned up so loud."

They kept this place looking alive on the outside, but only so much death and decay can hide in the shadows. This is the inside of a dying patient. The hall leading toward my destination's filled with people who'd kill for a brief interaction with an outsider. The smell of stale urine and other bodily fluids circulates in the air. The stench is paired with that of T.V. dinners and hospital gloves. These are scents that were never meant to be mixed.

The cryptic path guides me to the sound of shouting voices. The television's so loud that it fills the entire first floor—the receptionist was right. The sound peaks in volume as I enter an open room. A group of white-haired individuals sit in a trance, staring at a black-and-white television playing in the corner. They saw the show or film in their youth and reminisce about livelier days. That, or they're fast asleep and I just can't tell from here.

"Excuse me sir." I poke a staff member. "Is Samantha Eldridge here? If so could you point me in her direction?"

"Not a problem. Can I check your visitor's badge first?" He flexes useless security power. I flash the paper credentials at him. "Thanks. Yes, Missus Eldridge is over there in the corner. She doesn't care much for television time."

I could've walked in this room a hundred times and never noticed the woman in the corner. There she sits, staring out the window toward the parking lot. Her head moves back and forth as she watches people enter and exit the building. That's got to be her.

"Hello Missus Eldridge." I rest my hand on her shoulder. She turns her head. "My name's Robb . . . Robert Field. I'm Louise Field's son. D'you know who I am?"

She looks back to the window before responding. "Louise. Yes, I know your name. Excuse my frail state Robert." She looks down at the wheelchair she's sitting in and grabs one of her pajama pantlegs in disgust, flicking it back down onto her leg. The rest of the room's occupants wear the same outfit. "I'm all there upstairs. Don't let these wheels give you the wrong impression."

She doesn't seem to belong in this room nor this home. Others gaze at the television with empty eyes while she observes the real world. Her hair's dark black while other heads are a snowy white. Her skin lacks wrinkles. I wouldn't care about her physical state even if she was frail. She says she's clear-headed and that's all that matters. It's more than I got from Lucille Park in Napa.

"Oh of course not." I take my hand off her shoulder. It's clear she doesn't desire my pity. "Well . . . I spoke with my adoptive mom n' she shared your name. I thought I'd drop by n' personally thank you for all you did when I was a kid."

Her eyes don't break from the window. "That's very sweet of you Robert. However I can't say you're one of my children. It's nice t'see you again after all these years but I don't wanna get your hopes up for whatever you're hoping t'accomplish here."

"I'm not one a your children? What d'ya mean? When was the last time you saw me?" I take a breath. I can't scare her away with a flood of questions right off the bat.

"I can't recall the last time I saw you." Her head shifts up to the ceiling as she thinks. "It must be over a decade ago now. I've had a lotta children over the years. That said, none had an origin quite as peculiar as yours."

We're getting somewhere. "What was so strange about my situation?" I kneel beside her to level the playing field. Give me more. "I mean why was it diff'rent than the other children's upbringing?"

She laughs, finally looking my way. Her eyes are a light blue, the only ones in the room that aren't fogged over like a San Fran morning. "Like I said, you were never one of my children. Sure, I helped along the way with your road t'the Field family. That was the extent of our affiliation though. You weren't one of my children

Robert."

She motions to the employee at the entrance, who does a light jog over to Mrs. Eldridge's wheelchair. "Marcus . . . we'd like t'go t'my room now. Please take me n' my friend there."

"If I'm being honest ma'am, I didn't come here t'hear about a quick handoff t'my adoptive parents. I'm just happy t'meet someone who knew me before my life with my adoptive family. I'll let you enjoy the rest a your day Samantha."

I don't want to waste either of our time with a silly story about how I stumbled into the arms of Mr. and Mrs. Field. That's a story I've heard secondhand through my mom. My mom, the liar. The fraud. The phony. She didn't tell me Samantha Eldridge went away; she told me the woman was dead. That's an issue for later this evening.

"Nonsense. Join me!" she shouts.

The employee pushes her across the room, past the brain-dead group of white-haired bodies. The chair's rolled down a long hallway until turning to enter a private room, the wheels squealing as it completes the ninety-degree shift. I follow a few paces behind.

The man lifts Samantha Eldridge from the seat and plops her onto the bed. The look on her face is of utter embarrassment as the employee leaves us alone.

"Sorry . . ." She scoots herself up in bed. "You have one stroke n' you're stuck in this prison for the rest of your life. The 'ole walking sticks are useless these days. Funny how life works isn't it?"

I sit in a chair next to the bed. We're in the shadows now, a darkness that masks the crusty sight of this place. Samantha Eldridge reaches for human connection that isn't forcing food and pills down her throat. Human connection that isn't in a funeral home within the next week. Genuine connection. I choose to continue our conversation with a relevant subject: me.

"Yeah . . . funny. So you said my situation was strange," I pick up where we left off in the television room. "How'd we meet? From what you said it sounds like it was pretty brief."

"Yes. Right . . ." She rewinds her brain to a few minutes ago.

Mrs. Park would be gone by now. "Your mother prob'ly told you this, but I was a caregiver t'over two dozen foster children throughout my lifetime. Impressive hmm?" I nod. "My passion for helping young ones is the reason I don't have any children of my own." She looks around the bleak room. "It's really not bad in here when you know all your children are somewhere else living their lives t'the fullest. They're happy." She can tell I'm unsatisfied with the response, feeding my question with another. "What d'you remember before the Fields?"

"That's incredible. I'm sure those children are appreciative of everything you did for 'em." Now it's back to business. "I don't remember much about my past. In fact I've always tried t'avoid it so most of it's disappeared from my memory. Every kid wants t'fit in . . . forgetting was my way a doin' that."

"That's not uncommon," she comforts me. "You think you're the first person t'stop by n' ask about this stuff? Plenty've expressed the same feelings in secrecy over the years. I'm their confidant." She twiddles her thumbs together, uncomfortable for the first time in our short conversation. "As for you . . . I know nothing about your existence before you entered the foster system. No records n' no story. Nada."

I could leave now. She doesn't know about my past; it appears no one does. I was a child tossed from one foster home to another until dumped on the one family that'd keep me around. This trip was supposed to be about proving my mom wrong—finding a new sense of purpose. Why's it sinking me into further frustration?

"What's the big deal about that? Aren't all foster children coming in the system without a history?"

"I would've loved having you as one of my children." She tries to derail the matter. I'm referenced like some collectable action figure. "In all my years of fostering never has a child been so carefully passed from family t'family. I must've heard about you being moved half a dozen times over the years. I was never able t'give you my home though."

"What d'ya mean I was carefully passed?"

"You were diff'rent," she clarifies. Her foggy blue eyes stare into my soul. "You were diff'rent thanks t'the wonderful woman who found you. She didn't leave your side from that first day until you found a permanent home. She was a hawk watching over you with complete care. At the same time she refused t'watch you herself. She kept her distance like that."

"She found me?" One comment sticks. I ignore the bullshit, wholesome story she stirs into the pot. Focus on the important details, Robb.

"I don't recall the fine print. A couple passing through town saw a few of this woman's foster children playing in the front yard. From what she told me the couple grabbed their infant son n' dropped him in her hands that day. They never said a word either . . . didn't give the poor child a proper goodbye. This was you Robert. What sorta monsters do that t'their own flesh n' blood?"

I should've left five minutes ago. Instead, I have to live knowing a couple dumped me on a porch. I'm nothing more than a bag of trash. The truth doesn't sit well at first; however, it digests with ease over the next few silent moments. It's truth that provides me with a new appreciation for my current state. The couple that left me on the porch—and the Field family—don't matter. I carved my own path thanks to this mystery woman's help. I'm the reason I'm sitting here right now.

"So Miss Kimble continued t'care for you," she continues. "Maybe it was the glimpse of your previous life in that couple's hands that made her so dedicated t'keeping an eye on you. Or maybe—"

"Sorry . . . what'd you say her name was?" I interrupt.

I need to hear it again. Kimble. My mind reverts to a previous state. That familiar name. Say it again, Samantha Eldridge.

"Miss Becky Kimble. She was a rather unpleasant woman when all was said n' done. When it came t'children though, she was always warmhearted . . . compassionate."

Kimble. She said it again. Fucking Kimble. The old lady in Napa referenced a Kimble—Mikey Kimble. This can't be a coincidence. It's been less than a few days since the encounter with Mrs. Park. I've known no other Kimble in my entire life. This is a surname never uttered at the office nor with a client. Two references in the same week is an impossible coincidence.

Samantha Eldridge notices my pondering and interjects. "Why, d'you remember her? You know memory's fascinating like that. One trigger n' the thoughts come flooding back like a broken dam."

"Yeah . . . I think I'm remembering somethin'." I provide her with part of the truth. "You wouldn't know where she's at now would you?"

"I wish I could help you there Robert." She frowns. Her years of reading children's emotions goes to good use today. I'm still a fucking child, after all. "The last anyone heard of Becky was around when Louise n' her husband adopted you. She heard their names around town n' knew the two were looking t'adopt. Not t'take credit but I did serve as a reference for your parents. Becky knew I met the couple so she encouraged me t'discuss adoption with them. They needed a little reassurance was all. Anyway, she saw something in 'em n' knew almost immediately you belonged in that home." Her face lights up. "Once they saw your eyes for the first time they lit up with joy. You're lucky t'have 'em when all's said n' done."

"So you really have no idea where she could possibly be these days? Becky I mean." Another adorable remark goes ignored as I press for more. "People don't just vanish like that."

I can feel myself slipping, reaching for forbidden fruit. At least it's not a bottle this time. That observation keeps me moving forward in conversation despite the uncertainty coursing through my veins. I'm sober yet still desire answers. This is a new feeling.

"The last time I heard from Becky must've been about fifteen years ago. She sent a very generic postcard thanking me for all I'd done for her through the years. Specifically, delivering you inna the arms of your parents."

Parents—what a funny word considering mine lied to me all these years. My mom continues to lie, too. What other information has she kept in the closet? I'll soon find out, whether she wishes to unchain that knowledge or not.

Samantha Eldridge rotates her head toward the window—this

one's blocked by the blinds. "If you're thinking of finding her I'd advise against it. She left this town t'turn a new leaf. She didn't want any piece of her past lingering around. She made that crystal clear in the postcard."

"N' you're saying that includes me." I finish her thought. "D'you have any idea where she went? Any idea at all?"

"Sadly I do not," she insists. Is she lying, too? "For all I know she passed through some town when sending that note. It's no easy job you know . . . taking care of these children n' watching them move forward without you. Heck I'm about the only one left in town of the bunch n' that's because I'm stuck in this damn wheelchair. Sometimes you needa start over. I don't blame her for it n' never have."

I understand the desire to be born again more than anyone. I've chased the dream of a fresh start for months now. I thought the catalyst would be answers to my brother's disappearance or a magnifying glass into my past. The wind sweeps these efforts away whenever I turn over that new leaf for myself. I'm left with nothing and it's back to the beginning. I envy Becky Kimble for leaving it all behind without looking back.

"Right . . . I'd never try t'contact her. I get it. Seems like a difficult life t'live."

It's the perfect opportunity to close the curtain. Instead, I blurt out a final question. The answer to this serves as the coinflip to my next destination. Heads, I continue my path to Meredith's 'acceptance.' Tails, I jump onto another path.

"I'd like t'thank you again for speaking with me before I head out. It's a relief t'finally hear about my past, even if it's just the bare bones. I have one last question for you if you don't mind. D'you remember where that postcard came from?"

"Yes . . . I do remember," she sighs. She sees through my front of simple curiosity. My craving for more is obvious. "It was from San Jose California. It was one of those real colorful prints with flowers n' palm trees n' whatnot. Such a strange, unexpected card . . . that's why the memory's stuck with me all these years. Like I told you, one memory comes back n' the floodgates burst open. I suppose a healthy brain's a curse of sorts."

More logic has poured out of Samantha Eldridge's mouth than anyone else's blabbering trap. I've spoken to countless leads in my little investigation and each one fell flat—until now, that is. I owe this woman a few minutes of light conversation if I'm going to toy with the idea of picking up where I left off. Back into the storm without a life jacket this time.

The woman basks in the sunlight of stories from her past as the 'floodgates' open. She lingers on her relationship with the lonely Ms. Kimble. According to her, Kimble didn't reveal much about her own origin, a mysterious woman who channeled her energy into healing children. Yet she also had none of her own. Do I obey Samantha Eldridge's request to leave Kimble alone? The coin reads tails. I'm not done.

The building fades into the night as I walk to a line of cabs. I picture the old lady's bliss back inside. She soaks up a fleeting moment of significance in her rather paralyzed state. Memories are her friends. She thinks she helped another former child today, and she's right—just not in the way she thinks. The ride to my childhood house—my final one—turns into my own moment of bliss. I share this moment with Samantha Eldridge. I reach into my jacket pocket in the backseat of the cab and a folded, crinkled photo falls onto my lap. Wear and tear from rain, wind and the rest of my travels leave the paper looking like an ancient artifact. I continue to lie to myself that I've moved on while this photo follows me from one destination to the next. It haunts me.

The practical man inside leans toward disposing of a meaningless past. Another part of me pulls from the opposite direction, telling me to explore the unknown. The Kimble names aren't a coincidence. That postcard coming from San Jose isn't random at all. That puts Becky Kimble in the same vicinity as Mikey. I already flipped the coin; the decision has been made.

I look down at the photo. "I'm not finished with you Michael."

I'm able to utter his name again.

UNDER MY SKIN

Self-harm is frowned upon—at least it was in a previous reality. Society perceived it as a sign of weakness and the ultimate form of failure. Wave the white flag. It was even unappealing to my flawed mind not long ago. We are blind to its potential. The strong—the brave—are capable of this form of meaningful failure if executed for the right reasons.

Consider a blood ritual. The ancient practice stood the test of time across European and Asian cultures. I can thank 'The Devil's Rain' for this knowledge, a poorly executed horror film with a thought-provoking premise. Two or more individuals cut themselves—draw their own blood—to unite them in spirituality. It is viewed with value and meaning. That practice in my former reality leads to widespread disease. Still, my point remains the same, pushing aside all other considerations traveling through my mind. This is a coping mechanism for self-mutilation and it is working. It convinces me this was necessary. The pain was crucial to success. How bad is an action if it saves a life?

Two stretchers leave the red library; West and I travel to the infirmary. I am unaware of my surroundings nor Mason's fate. Dozens of guards' footsteps echo like an orchestra through the cellhouse. My body travels from cellblock to cellblock. It floats. My role in this performance has ended as I am summoned backstage.

"Well get the fuckin' hose then," a guard orders. "These fire extinguishers are meant for campfires!"

Another voice yells something inaudible besides a mention of Officer Douglas, which is quick to fly into my ears. I keep my eyes closed for show and envision the scene in the cellhouse. Peters shakes his head; screws run around putting out the fire in Wilson's cell with every bucket of water and faulty extinguisher they can find; medical officers tend to an unconscious Douglas. The only relevant name not traveling through the air is Karpowicz. Creepy Karpis. This worries me. Would an 'original gangster' like him turn snitch? It is unlikely given what my bibles told me before they were destroyed.

I get dumped onto an infirmary bed a few minutes later. I have spent too much time here since I arrived—a record for this prison if I was ever mentioned in the little book. I can already read the fun fact in my head. My involvement will not go down in history, yet it is enough to raise further suspicion from the warden. Plus, the act involved Karpis. Madison knows Karpis and I have unpleasant history. It does not take a genius to view the larger picture.

"Wha—what happened?" I mutter, dramatizing my body's current condition.

I peel open a single eyelid. As anticipated, it is not a mere doctor at the bedside; Madison and Peters hover over me as well. The fire. Officer Douglas. Karpis. Of all places to stand right now, they are next to this bed—next to me.

"Welcome back Michael." Madison smiles. "Are you feeling alright?" He walks around the bed, studying the fresh cuts and bruises covering my body. This is him playing detective. "Looks like you were knocked up pretty bad out there."

"What?" I maintain my ignorance. "The last thing I remember was . . . was West n' me. We were with Officer Mason in the library helpin' him with some trash n'—"

"I'm quite aware of what you were doing there," he interrupts. Peters stands behind him, his arms folded during their traditional 'good cop, silent cop' routine. "What happened in there you ask? Seems t'me you're the only one in a sober state of mind t'provide any useful information. If I were a betting man your buddy West won't wake up for some time after the injuries he sustained."

"Well . . ." I swallow. My body flinches from the self-mutilation. The pain is not entirely fake. "It's all fuzzy now. What I remember's Officer Mason leavin' t'check on some sorta yellin' in the cellhouse. Next thing I know I'm lyin' on the ground. A moment later I'm wakin' up here talkin' t'you."

"So you can't say if it was Alvin Karpowicz who came at the three of you with the baton?"

"All I could tell was it'd been a tall figure. He had a baton . . . I know that much. My body can't forget that." I draw more attention to the evidence in front of him, repositioning myself in bed. "Karpowicz you say? How'd he get in the library?"

The warden continues his examination. The human lie detector sees through the blood on the sheets, convincing himself I had something to do with this. He knows it. I know it. This is no coincidence. He tightens his tie and snaps his fingers at Peters to exit. The two slam the door behind them. Madison's roaring voice seeps through the door, punishing Peters with words. After all, the servant approved the detail transfer request from Mason. The conversation ends with the two vocalizing their belief of West and my involvement. Frustration gets the better of him as he realizes I can hear all this firsthand.

The warden's desire to keep me in the dark is challenged for a second time. The risk of someone putting their nose in his business—in my business—is far more probable than ever before. An officer was gravely injured and a bird's cell burnt to ashes. Those ashes will float their way over to Ms. Tillwell in no time, maybe even reaching a reporter. Heads will turn. Karpis can claim what he wants. Madison can believe what he wants. At the end of the day, the evidence cannot go ignored: Karpis' locket was found in Wilson's cell and two bloodied, battered birds lie in the infirmary. Even Mason, the fearful ferret, will realize he is best off remaining consistent with our story for his own well-being.

Karpis was discovered in Broadway if he remained in the emotionless state we left him in. He cleaned the cellhouse while supervised by Officer Douglas as well—written logs will prove as much. The only better scenario is a false confession from the Creep.

This confidence dwindles over the next several days as I am locked in the infirmary with West. Our injuries healed well enough after a day, implying the investigation in the cellhouse continues with the two of us at the center of it. This is more so isolation than recovery, an extension of D-block from my point of view.

Anticipation builds with each passing second and each lingering worry. Karpis may claim his innocence. Mason may crack. Wilson may point the warden in my direction for burning the little book. The possibilities are boundless.

"Alright Field. Nursery time's up." Peters enters the room on the afternoon of the fourth day. My first taste of what lies beyond this room could not be nearer. "Time t'go back t'the real world . . . my world."

I am unsure of the servant's intentions. Despite a cautious mentality, I leave without a fuss, waiting for him to leave me with a departing comment. We are alone. A situation like this is one the captain lives to take advantage of. Let the beast out, captain. He never does, though—the one time I welcome him to say something.

"Did ya get t'the bottom a what happened?" I ask. Anticipation takes control and a question slips out as a result.

He pushes me in the back. The bruises from the self-beating stings. He takes pleasure in this, yet I do not offer him the thrill of witnessing my pain this time. It irritates him until he must open his mouth for a verbal beating.

"Well seein' as you got the shit knocked outta ya I'll tell ya what happened." He indulges his dark side. Finally. "Karpowicz is in isolation. He'll spend the rest a his days without any sorta human contact. No visitation, no yard time n' no detail t'keep him occupied." He pulls the back of my shirt to flip me around. We are facing each other now in the hallway back to the core of the cellhouse. "There's nowhere t'run ya little bastard. There's nowhere t'hide. Karpis may've taken the hit for this but you're caught up in it somehow. We know it."

Another screw turns around the corner. Peters pushes me forward, not wanting to risk word of his free-form dialogue making its way to the warden's office. In his mind, that would ruin his good graces along with the non-existent chance of taking over Madison's position in due time.

"Now shut the hell up n' keep walkin'. I hear one more peep outta you n' you'll get the cell between Karpis n' Wilson."

Wilson—why is Wilson in isolation? It is a question I know

better than to ask and information that Peters knows better than to expose. Perhaps it is a temporary solution while my old neighbor's cell is repaired. Even if that is the case, there are plenty of cells in B-block to serve as temporary quarters. This was not part of the plan, yet it is pleasant news.

Peters tosses me in the dining hall. No further comments from the warden nor interrogation by other screws await me. I am off the hook for now. But why? The warden shared his belief in my involvement while shouting outside of the infirmary. Why let me roam the island like nothing occurred? I should be in the dark now, buried somewhere deep in cell fourteen—my second home.

My tray finds an open spot on a near-empty table. I put my cards in West's hands, so no other allies dwell in this room today. I spot my partner in crime sitting on the opposite end of the dining hall. A guard stands not more than two feet away from him now. Another screw intercepts my stare from the end of the hothead's table. The two guards hover over him like my overprotective mother once did to me. This is a new seating arrangement for my old ally.

West's motions act as if nothing occurred that fateful day. He laughs and continues to recount his many stories to various tablemates, his body language giving the conversation away. He was a loyal partner when in trouble; with Karpis locked away, he is free from my heavy thumb. The mutual threat was neutralized and the hothead murdered a guard to his delight. As if that was not enough of an issue, the con also lacks a conversational filter. The truth could spill out at any moment, promptly sending us both to hell.

"So what really happened in that library?" A bird scoots his tray toward me. A few others also lean over to witness the conversation unfold. I have never seen this man before. I suppose I am the talk of the town after such an eventful afternoon. A guard inches closer in the middle of the dining hall after hearing the curious con's words, hoping to be the screw that causes my downfall. I have grown to spot these spies out of the corner of my eye since my arrival due to the brief advice the expert Lens gave me prior to the incident in the yard.

"Exactly what ya heard," I respond to his disappointment. "It went down the way they're tellin' it."

"T'be honest . . ." a second inmate chimes in from afar. "It don't make no sense how Karpis took down all four a y'all. It don't take a bulldozer t'make any man in here back off . . . even someone his size. Plus he lost his cred with the guards on account a the transfer."

"Like I told you, whatever happened went down the way they're sayin' it did. I dunno anything else. Now can I eat my meatloaf in peace?"

I pick up my spoon with half a cut of meatloaf on it, gnawing into it like a caveman. The two strangers turn away, sensing my rage. Did this earn me some credibility on Alcatraz? My moment in solitude sends Peters' comment circulating through my head. It flies back every time I swat it away. Wilson is in Sunset Strip. Why is he in Sunset Strip? I had shut up the two cons when I needed more intel from them.

"Guys . . ." I catch their attention again with a drop of my spoon on the tray. "I heard Wilson's in isolation too. Is that true?"

"You been outta commission for a while haven't ya?" The bird laughs, turning back toward me. "Wilson freaked when the cap'n told him what went down in his cell. They were questionin' him n' shit t'figure out why Karpis hit his cell with those flames in the first place. The dumbass tried t'grab a guard's poker n' landed a few throws on another turnkey 'fore they chained him up. My guess's he'll spend some good time over there for smackin' a guard."

It worked. Karpis and Wilson are both resolved issues. Wilson has his eyes set on Karpis now; however, a man with his intellect would suspect foul play, so I am sure it will not be long until reason trumps his initial perceptions. He did not have beef with Karpis before the fire. Complete solitude for both Karpis and Wilson takes care of two life-threatening problems for now, though. I can take a deep breath.

West's separation carries on throughout the day, beyond his new location in the dining hall. We are both transferred from garbage detail. Peters leads me back to the Industries Building while West appears to wander over to the kitchen for culinary duty. We could not be any more distant during the day.

"Hey where's Officer Mason these days? D'they still keep him posted in the library?" I sneak a few pressing questions to a nearby inmate as we transfer clothes from washer to dryer. Spreading my inquiries between cons also minimizes the chance of a guard catching onto my persistent curiosity.

The bird ensures the coast is clear before responding, "Rumor has it the warden sent his rat-ass packin' after what happened in the library. He never showed up t'detail the next mornin'. No word from any a the officers or nothin'. They been crackin' the whip 'round here lately. My guess's Hopeful Howard needed an officer t'blame for all that crazy shit n' Mason drew the short straw."

Any and every inmate is eager to discuss the excitement as entertainment is a rarity on this island outside of magazines and books. This is mindless high school gossip on steroids and I remain the focus. This is an unusual change of pace from both my former reality as well as my initial time spent on this island.

Mason did what every guard does in one way or another: protect himself. It is every man for himself at the end of the day—it does not make a difference whether that man is a bird or a screw. Mason flew too close to the sun in that regard, costing him his job. This was an optimal outcome based on the little I knew about the man. He leaves this godforsaken island a free man and does not face repercussions from months of corroborating with birds like Wilson. We did him a favor if nothing more.

Captain Peters shows his face for the second time since my return during dinnertime. He intercepts me as we line up with our empty trays, his hands locked behind his back as he towers over me. He exhales hot air in my face until he is certain of my attention. This is a game to him.

"Warden wants t'see ya now. You can hold your appetite 'til supper."

He yanks the tray from my hands and points toward the core of the cellhouse. Cons from every angle stare at me, curious about what the warden wants this time. I am still centerstage. This is a good observation as it means there are other eyes on me besides the warden and his pet. The warden cannot dispose of me without any consequences.

Peters grips me tight outside Madison's office after our silent trek. His claw digs deep in my shoulder. This is the first time the warden's office door has been closed. It was always open, waiting for me to enter and sit in the chair across from the shiny desk. Peters' tight grasp is a pestering gnat compared to the pain behind the closed door.

Five minutes of silence later and the door flies open. To my surprise, West steps out, escorted by another officer. The big-mouthed hothead looks at the ground as he walks past us, leaving a sour taste in my mouth. Did he tell the warden the truth? My alliance with the man came back to bite me, perhaps in an effort to cover his own ass. He believed I would rat him out for murdering Officer Douglas in cold blood; or maybe this was revenge for leaving him with a baseball-sized welt on the back of his head. Either way, his presence is not a welcoming sight.

"Take a seat," Madison orders. I rotate into West's warm seat. The warden's been busy. "This won't take long." He rises from his desk and approaches me. "How're we feeling today Michael?"

"I'm fine sir. How 'bout yourself?"

I try my best to remember how I acted before my mind was on a single track, wrapped around the logistics of the plan. That successful plan that I cannot seem to leave in the past.

"I could be better." He walks to his personal bar, pouring himself a drink. He pours it three fingers thick. "Listen, I'm quite sure word of Alvin Karpowicz's actions n' consequential punishment has spread t'you vermin by now. It's back t'square one for him. I'm at a loss here Michael." He dips his pinky in the sea of copper liquid to taste it before taking a sip.

"I'm not sure I'm following sir," I mutter, continuing to play dumb. "Sounds like Karpis was punished from what I've been told. Can I return t'the dining hall?"

The fire incinerated the little book, but it was unable to destroy my memory. If it still serves me well, Madison will retire as warden in less than a year. I will no longer have to worry about his wrath if

I can keep his snout at bay for that time. Karpis and Wilson are out of the picture. Even Mason has vanished in the blink of an eye. Yet, the warden remains a tireless threat, committed to taking me down.

"You'll return when I say it's time t'return. Is that clear?" He puts down his glass, two fingers already in his belly. I nod in response. "Now we have another problem on our hands. As you can imagine, word of Officer James Douglas' death made it across the bay. As far as the common folk know it was another scuffle that ensued. The brave officer intervened n' was killed. Now it's time for someone t'take the fall. That person'll once again be Karpowicz." I attempt to count the days until Madison is out of this office the way I fail to count sheep every night. He notices my distracted brain and snaps his fingers in my face. "Are you following Michael?"

"Yes. Yes of course sir. Karpis'll take the fall. Excuse my ignorance here . . . but isn't it only sensible for him t'take the blame for this? After all he was the one who murdered Douglas."

"We both know there was more going on that afternoon than an unprompted outburst," he clears the tension brought on by my avoidance. "We'll deal with that down the road. Right now we needa stay on the same page. That goddamn public defender of his's back in my visitation room as we speak. She's not here on official business so we aren't required t'let her contact Karpowicz. We attempted t'get Allen West t'recount the events in order for her t'back off. Unfortunately the dope is useless. He can't tell his right foot from his left. That's where you come back in the picture. Speak with her Michael. Tell her nothing of significance. You do that again n' we might drop our little internal investigation."

He lies. He knows I am under his thumb, yet attempts to sweeten the deal with empty promises. Hopeful Howard. When Ms. Tillwell leaves, Madison will go right back to focusing on my involvement in Officer Douglas' death. He takes me for a fool while overestimating his own cleverness.

"Why don't you meet with her sir? Wouldn't that be more credible than an unreliable prisoner recountin' his story?"

"She doesn't trust me." He downs the rest of the glass in

annoyance and slams it on the desk, nearly shattering it. "She's not outright said as much, however her actions make that clear. The last thing I need's some op-ed surfacing about what goes on within these walls. Now please follow Captain Peters t'visitation. I won't ask again."

Peters steps into the doorway and Madison motions for my exit. The warden trails behind us until I am out of his office. He is certain this will vanish after my conversation with Ms. Tillwell. If she is coming here out of her own interest, though, this is much bigger than another harmless visit. Madison is not seeing past this second visit and that can be to my benefit.

"N' Michael . . ." he calls down the hall. "Remember what's at stake. Don't let me down."

My fellow inmates have already left the dining hall to resume detail by the time Peters walks me to the visitation window. The cellhouse is empty and the warden's plan can proceed without suspicion. Perfect timing on his part. Ms. Tillwell shines at the end of Broadway behind the fogged glass. She is as radiant as the first time we spoke.

"Make it quick Field." Peters shoves me down at the window.

The woman is draped in a red winter jacket and a matching hat. It is a coordinated outfit like the first one she wore behind the very same window. Her lipstick matches the attire. The outfit exudes power—sophistication. It is almost too much to look at, forcing me to glance down at her notepad to recover my eyes every few seconds. She clutches a pen, writing something down even though our conversation has not yet commenced.

"Good afternoon Michael," the first words soar out of her mouth, tearing through the glass and floating into my ears.

I clear my throat. "Hello again Miss Tillwell."

Nerves bleed through my speech. I worry of the questions she will ask paired with her clever ability to catch me off guard. The mere sight of the woman is distracting, requiring my brain to operate at two hundred percent power.

"I appreciate you taking the time t'chat again." She takes off her black gloves and rests them on the wooden board in front of her.

"Now I wanna be cognizant of your time. Do you mind if I ask you a few more questions about my former client, Alvin Karpowicz?"

"No asking of any questions about rules n' regulations," the moderator interjects.

Ms. Tillwell looks behind her. There was no interference during our previous chat. The warden likely briefed the moderator to ensure the conversation goes in his favor.

"Sir I'm talking about public information covered in every San Francisco-based publication. I have the right t'talk about any of that if I so please."

She flips her hair, with one collection falling on her forehead. She does this a few times and the same lock lands right back in place. "Sorry about that Michael. It appears these men don't have anything better t'do than listen in on innocent conversations. That being said, I'm sure you're very aware of the fatal events that happened within these walls last week. You know what happened don't you?"

"Yeah I know what happened. I wasn't there for it but I know Karpowicz set fire to an inmate's cell. He also got in a scuffle with an officer that led t'the loss a that man's life."

I am unable to hide my truths. She sees through me. "He got in a scuffle with an officer?" She flips through her notepad. "The report claimed he n' another inmate were fighting n' the officer intervened. Are you telling me that's not accurate?"

"That's right . . . sorry," I correct myself. A lack of knowledge of public coverage leaves me in the dark on what the outside world has been told. "I was just talkin' about the fight that resulted in the death. The other one was petty. The other inmate was fine. My mistake."

"D'you know the other inmate's name?"

Peters coughs from behind, letting me know he is once again listening. The conversation mirrors the first time she visited: secrets held behind my side of the glass, a frustrated Ms. Tillwell on the other side and an observant servant behind me. On the other hand, the papers tell a different story than I am aware of this time. This conversation will go south if she continues testing me with these facts. Is this the warden's way of setting me up for the entire event?

"No mentioning of information that's not publicly available," the moderator cuts in again. He saved me from a question that would destroy this delicate work of fiction.

The moderator proceeds to shut down just shy of every question pertaining to Karpis and that afternoon from that point forward. The visit turns into a conversation between him and Ms. Tillwell. This annoys the woman to no end.

"Alright Michael . . ." She tosses down her notepad. "If I can't ask these questions let's change the conversation. You seem like a reasonable man. I've had quite a number of defendants over the years. I can typically tell what type of crime someone's in for by their demeanor alone. You on the other hand are a difficult individual t'assess. If you don't mind me asking, what were you charged with t'get locked away in Alcatraz?"

The moderator does not interject when I need him most. I must handle this on my own. I envision revealing it all, telling her I was imprisoned at the warden's command. This would give her the upper hand over Madison with a hope that she takes the information seriously. Who would consider the concept of an alternate reality? Not the intellectual sitting before me.

"Bank robbery in Dallas." I lean back after a standoff of silence. "Turned ugly n' a teller ended up gettin' stuck at the end of it. Satisfied?"

She analyzes my every movement while jotting in her notebook. "Oh that's quite unfortunate," she responds. "I actually practiced law in Dallas. Small world. Which bank was this robbery located at?" Does she believe I am involved in the murder of Officer Douglas? Is this another test?

"I'll head back t'detail if we're gonna turn this inna a job interview ma'am." I let some impatience slip out. It was a logical response next to fabricating the name of a bank and hoping it sticks. I would like nothing more than to sit and hear her every word, however, the more I say the more I risk slipping; the more I risk drawing Madison's attention.

"Fair enough Michael." She attempts to calm me down with

words alone. "I'll come back t'speak with someone else in that case. It is curious the warden sent you t'meet with me for the second time though. Why send a person who wasn't even present during those events?"

I do not respond. She reaches for her bag and packs her notepad away. Her purse sits on the board in front of her and she places the red hat back on her head. The interrogation is over.

"One last thing . . ." She freezes before rising from the chair, one arm already pushing up against the armrest. "Where'd you get all those cuts? N' those bruises?"

I had put the conversation to bed. She realized as much and took advantage of it. I am unable to craft a lie. I am not in an appropriate position to respond. She realizes this and sits there satisfied.

"These bruises?" I buy myself a few seconds.

She does not break eye contact, aware I am stalling for time. She can put together the general timeframe that I received these bruises if she regularly deals with violent criminal cases. That timeframe aligns with the day West murdered Officer Douglas.

I do my best to leave her with a story anyway, something to chew on during her journey across the bay. "Look around you Miss Tillwell. This's a prison. Shit happens every day n' everywhere. If you don't have a mark on you you're either a fresh catch or the one supplyin' the beatings."

Her stares persist as she rises from the chair. She is disappointed, yet looks prideful of the trap I stepped in. Her interrogation caught me in a lie. She smelled the bullshit a mile away between my hesitancy and inconsistent stories.

"Alright Field! You're needed in the Industries Building," Peters shoves his hand into my shoulder again, yanking me by the muscle like it is the handle of a bag. He sniffed out the awkward final remarks a little too late. "Get your ass up n' march back t'work." The captain sneers at Ms. Tillwell, who is already across the visitation room. They are two predators envisioning their vicious attack. I am caught in the middle of it all.

The unexpected question. The trance she lays upon me. The pressure of Captain Peters. It was too much to bear. One thing is certain: she did not buy the lie about these bruises. I glance down Broadway before turning the corner and spot her standing in the visitation room doorway. She is jotting a few additional notes in her notepad. The final nail in the coffin was her question. She did not receive the information she desired about Karpis, the wrongdoings of Madison nor the flaws in the prison system. Instead, something else caught her attention. I caught her attention.

POETRY IN MOTION

Frank Lee Morris set foot on The Rock in early 1960. I find myself spewing out facts and quotations like that from the forever-lost little book every now and again following a significant event. This particular fact is one I have looked forward to unraveling for over a year.

Morris made it clear he wanted nothing to do with anyone when he arrived. He carried this black cloud around him, sending even the toughest birds scurrying back to their cells like rats caught in daylight. His shadow lingered an extra foot behind him compared to the average man's.

A new era dawned on Alcatraz in 1960. Wilson's crew dissolved without the snake's head. Karpis remained distant—a threat no more. The word around the block is Mason picked up a cheap job at a dinky clothing store in the heart of the city which suits him well. At the same time, the new roadblocks that emerged have lingered for months. The warden keeps a watchful eye over me while Ms. Tillwell's fascination with me keeps the dictator from doing anything drastic. I fuel her interest with useless letters. They are nothing of substance; they could never be as outgoing mail is read by screws before traveling off of the island.

I keep a level head despite the positive and negative changes. This reality requires attentiveness, patience and dedication. I lose my sense of purpose if I fall victim to routine, yet I cannot fight my way to freedom right now. I am slammed between two rocks on the shore of this island while the tide continues to rise. I must be patient so as not to drown.

My sense of purpose soon drifts away as I resume the role of prisoner. I try to remind myself this is temporary, yet days blend into weeks. I find myself going to detail. I eat meals in peace out of habit. I even manage to get some quality sleep—imagine that. I am losing sight of what is important. My mental Walkman has been paused for over a month now. I am waiting for an opportunity to tap the play button again, resuming my role in this strange reality.

"Field!" an officer shouts during yard time. "Field! Here . . . letter for you. Hurry up n' grab it already." He steps past the flock of birds awaiting messages in order to hand-deliver mine. The letter transfers from the officer's hand to my shirt pocket in one motion.

Each individual hopes for a glimmer of life beyond The Rock, a mental boat ride off of this island if only for a fleeting moment. While outgoing mail can be read by prison officials, the same does not apply to mail received. Still, I realize the sole location of sincere secrecy is in my cell. Complete security.

The overhead lights clunk out in unison that night and the letter tears open. My new ritual. The faint light from the guard towers combined with the occasional clear moon provides enough visibility to make out the words on the page. The messages are not as important as the handwriting itself, which is elegant. Each mark is careful. It is the same caution and attention Ms. Tillwell brought to the visitation room.

'Michael,' I silently mouth each word, 'I hope you are well.'

The letter opening ritual is thrilling until initial pleasantries fade into business talk. She is a broken record. Questions about Karpis and news headlines referencing the island tend to follow warm greetings. Part of me wishes I could assist, but any information I provide leads to deeper water with the warden. It is a dangerous game balancing two individuals' conflicting expectations.

My letters responding to Ms. Tillwell are vague. The warden allows these letters to continue as long as he is satisfied with my attempts to describe a picturesque prison. Despite the nickname 'Hopeful Howard,' Madison was not formally investigated or publicly critiqued. The audiotape and little book both supported that fact. This reality cannot be unwound, dissected and put back together as something new. Madison's reputation is solidified in all history books, souvenirs and elsewhere. He is clean in the public eye, so Ms. Tillwell is chasing her tail with the desire to expose hidden evils on The Rock. The letters I write are more so drafted for my own sanity than for her benefit. Letters are a window to the outside world, a perspective on written communication I share with other birds. As much as I loathed society in my former life, this connection allows my brain to exercise the bigger picture of this reality. That, and it keeps Madison from feeding me to his servant. I can sleep knowing Captain Peters will not smother me with one of my cell's rough, straw-filled pillows. What a way that would be to go.

The lawyer keeps me sane while Frank Lee Morris keeps me motivated. He is rather reserved, even for a fish. Robb classifies this as pathetic. Doctor Polk slaps a less-harsh label on it like 'asocial behavior.' To me, Morris is much more than these descriptors. He is a thinker, an over-analyzer. He is a figure who views life in a different lens than others. This is the reason he has not taken well to any attempts at communication despite our similarities. Several brief interactions in the dining hall and yard resulted in him turning the other cheek. He pretends I do not exist. He is cautious—wary of others. The man cannot be fooled like the hothead West or followed blindly like with Wilson's minions. The right motivation is required to light a spark of interest beneath him, and I can respect that.

The little book claimed Morris was the mastermind behind the 1962 escape attempt. The passage stated West never made it out of his cell. It also revealed the two Anglin brothers assisted in gathering supplies. This is useful information at the appropriate time, but there are still missing pieces. The literature and tape focused on the escape itself rather than the origins of the group's alliance. I am at the mercy of Morris—Morris and time.

I am the single variable on this island. My future is locked in place like the rest of the birds, only I do not know what it entails, meaning attention to detail is critical. My bibles cannot guide me at this point. One missed encounter with Morris risks leaving me out of the picture come that legendary night. Morris and the Anglin brothers escape while fate leaves me stranded here. The group distances themselves if I befriend them at the wrong time. I tread on eggshells, careful with each move.

A narrow focus leaves me testing the waters with Morris despite his determination for solitude. I can relate to the man—that leaves me with confidence. The first step is understanding the way this alleged mastermind thinks. There is no more approachable place to do this than during mealtime. Birds are unpredictable in the dining hall, rotating tables and conversing with one another until the final bell sounds. Approaching Morris there feels natural.

"Hey." I sit next to him one afternoon. He eats alone as always. "I'm Michael Field."

I reach out to shake his hand. He goes back to eating after realizing I am trying to speak to him again, the same individual from the other day. He is wise to keep strangers at bay. I would do the same if it was not for the little book and tape—may they rest in peace.

I am living 'Escape from Alcatraz.' I was a fan of Eastwood as a child as the legend seemed like the ultimate rebel. He did what he wanted when he wanted. My viewing of the film was unfortunate due to its portrayal of Morris, though. My mind confuses the film's representation of him with the real-life version. The film makes him out to be the typical tough-guy the actor likes to play on screen. Real-life Morris does not show a single ounce of confidence. He is a lone ranger not to be bothered.

"I'm sorry . . . I don't think we've officially met," I continue despite his non-verbal cues for my exit. "I've heard a lot about you over the years n' thought I'd introduce myself. This place'll eat ya alive n' shit you back out if you're not careful. Just wanted t'give ya a heads up."

He lifts his head from a sunken position, looking forward across the dining hall so as not to look me in the eye during his response. "Appreciate the tip. I'm not lookin' for friends. Go find yourself a queen if you want that."

"I get that," I respond. At least he acknowledged my presence this time. "Again, I only wanted t'reach out t'introduce myself. Word 'round here's you've jumped ship at least five times over the years. That sounds like a man worth knowin'."

The zombie returns his eyes to the tray. "If you're here t'talk

about some plan you're cookin' up then worry about it yourself."
He pauses for a moment to ravel a string of spaghetti up his spoon.
"I'm not the guy you're talkin' about. Not anymore. I have a dime
in here n' I'll be damned if I blow it again."

Morris is brilliant according to the little book. He has an IQ of
over one hundred and thirty. Intelligence of this capacity puts up a
shield to minimize any conversation about jailbreak, especially after
so many years in the clink. Unbeknown to him, I share similar
brainpower. I am not another bird. His destined path is carved into
my mind. He can fool everyone now, but I am aware he is conjuring
up a plan somewhere beneath that blank expression.

"I hear ya man." I sigh, trying to relate. I have a little over a year
on my fake record as of this month. "Enjoy your meal."

He is aware of my existence. It is difficult not to reveal
everything and hope for an optimal reaction, however, my fate is
unknown. Again, eggshells. I cannot jump the gun so quickly.

A year behind bars has skyrocketed past me. An eventful year
also equates to the significant passing of time, though, leading to
decreased fortune-telling. This is not a positive thing. The little
book and tape grant purpose in a formerly meaningless life. They
are religious scriptures revealing a higher power that ceases to exist
when this prison closes in a few years. There is no trail to follow
from that point onward. I am trapped for life in the confines of my
cell without the 1962 escape in my back pocket. My cellmate would
be a collection of forgettable memories. My successful escape is the
rapture if the little book and tape are religious scriptures. My
knowledge of the 1970s prison system is nonexistent, so a transfer
from Alcatraz to another maximum-security prison strips away all
clairvoyance.

A sleepless night recirculates the nightmarish truths in Morris'
words. If he is not the mastermind, that leaves the Anglin brothers
as the geniuses. The more that idea marinates the more absurd it
sounds unless the entirety of the brothers' story was fabricated. The
two are extra bodies in the scheme—forces of power. They are
useful assets with renowned swimming skills and an existing
acquaintance of Morris' from a former incarceration.

Doubt leaves a much more ludicrous idea on the table: what if the inspiration for the escape was planted? These four have no ringleader. There is no mastermind to lead this band of misfits to freedom. No one knows the details of the escape better than me if this is the case. I am a graduate of the little book and tape, the only person with knowledge besides an isolated Wilson.

I dream of the escape during my few hours of sleep. It is stuck in time, moving in an endless cycle without any origin like the little book. The plan is executed. It is told in legends over decades to come. From there, it travels back to the past, beginning again. It is a piece of mail transferred from one post office to the next, never reaching its destination nor returning to its sender.

The dreams crash in the morning, hitting the cold, hard floor the way my feet do upon hearing the wakeup bell. Deep concentration leaves a throbbing headache that clings to my brain. It is a sneeze held in time and again. The shell of the dreams lingers in the morning, desperate to travel into this reality and spread like wildfire. This would be a welcome virus.

My insistent mind goes ignored in the yard as it focuses on what is practical. Is another attempt at speaking with Morris too soon? My headache tries to tell me something as I study the lonely man sitting on the steps. It pushes logic backward. A confident stride toward the strange bird follows the debate that ping-ponged around my head. I am watching my body move from afar.

"Morris!" I yell from the ground. He focuses on a sketchbook by his side, sitting about five steps from the graveled ground. "Morris I'd like t'have a few more words with you if ya don't mind. Can ya at least gimme that?"

He senses my determination. He cannot ignore the shouting as dozens of other birds look wide-eyed at us. The 'genius' weaves through a few cons in his way, slithering down the stairs to avoid making a scene. The blankness in his expression and emptiness in his eyes come into focus as he approaches my position. The determined mute freezes in front of me, his face a mere few inches from mine. Our cold breath wanders from our mouths to form a hazy cloud between us.

"You dunno much about lockup do you?" He looks me in the eyes this time.

"I may not've spent as much time behind bars as you but I know enough t'hold my own," I boast, revealing my newfound confidence. The headache tells me to maintain my position.

"These steps here . . ." He points at the elevated sea of concrete around him. "These steps separate people like me from lowlifes like you. I've earned my spot up there from the time I've served . . . the reputation I've built. You might've been in this clink longer than me. That doesn't mean shit. You're more a danger t'yourself than anyone else. I look at a man like you n' see fear." He leans in closer to whisper, "I know what you've done durin' your stint. I don't want any part of it, or you for that matter."

He refers to Karpis in the yard; he refers to my betrayal of Wilson and his crew; he refers to the murder of Officer Douglas. Praise would replace anger if he knew the importance behind those actions. Unfortunately, I am not willing to reveal as much.

"You can think what you want about me. I'm not here t'bring any trouble. I'm here t'speak man t'man . . . not con t'con."

"You're a cancer. You wanna talk? Talk t'one a the fuckin' screws n' see how they react. Go find another inmate t'bother." He turns back toward the steps.

"Escape." I step toward him with a trailing whisper. A desperate word. He stops to listen, his head continuing to face the stairs. I have his attention. "You know more about escape than anyone on this island. More than any con. More than any officer. What if I could guarantee you vanish from this place without consequence? Freedom. Think about it. Permanent freedom."

He turns to face me. They were impulsive words—words I regret throwing on the table so soon. Yet here he stands in front of me, shoulders squared and interest piqued.

"Escape?" he laughs, repeating my desperate bait. "You have a foolproof plan of escape?" He tilts his head to the cloudy sky, letting out a frustrated grin before looking back at me. "We're a mile from any other land mass. The water's pure ice. There're guard towers pokin' the clouds in every direction. If those aren't enough reasons t'get your fuckin' mind straight then know this: I'm done breakin' outta these chains. I've spent my entire life running away. In ten years I can hit parole n' live out the rest a my days in peace. There's no escapin' Alcatraz. Not for me n' certainly not for someone like you."

The emotion in his response tells me his words are truthful. He is tired—as exhausted as the framed Creepy Karpis. He is done fighting the system and not masking a plan for freedom. Frank Lee Morris does not care about escape, a coward waiting out his time in solitude. The man is not the mastermind. The little book was wrong.

SOMEBODY'S FOOL

The letters of sanity halted in the fall of 1960. It took Ms. Tillwell long enough to realize the conversation ran in circles, which was inevitable. Still, I cherished the pen pal. The slightest distraction keeps a bird's brain healthy in this wretched place.

Counting has been a new form of therapy over these last couple of months. I count the days spent in this uncomfortable little box; I count the number of cracks forever growing longer across the ceiling; I count the steps of the turnkeys at night. Counting sheep is for children.

The last time I heard from Ms. Tillwell woke me from my obsession with her. I was a high school student passing unrequited love letters to a desk mate. Her true intentions came through in that last letter. She is trapped by her own obsession that involves Alcatraz crumbling to the ground. She informed me she collected enough information to toss a warrant in the warden's face. The warrant allowed her to bring a photographer to the island to capture everyone and everything. Fortunately for him, a lengthy notice of the visit provided Madison with time to prepare. The dictator got ready in every way imaginable. Birds were pulled from garbage duty to paint the library. They repaired broken machinery in the Industries Building. They performed any task he requested. There were many late nights of heavy labor that left us incapable of detail the next day. Captain Peters pushed us through the pain anyway.

That next week, the photographer documented a model prison. A masterfully orchestrated cleanup led by Madison and his henchman was obeyed by officers and prisoners without second thought. The photographer documented it all. These photographs will go down in history as the ones that help put Madison's clean reputation on the map. The photographer entered the Industries

Building to snap a few shots of birds doing laundry. He poked his head in the dining hall during mealtime, and wandered up and down each cellblock in an attempt to spot a flaw that did not exist.

History describes Madison as a lenient, compassionate warden. The little book revealed he worked his way up the ranks on Alcatraz, beginning as a correctional officer and working until he reached his destined position as head snake. He knows Newspaper A or Chronicle B devour hero stories like his own. The maestro of criminals sits on his iron throne, letting the press craft his narrative with a wave of his hand.

The fall of 1960 improved some aspects of life. John Anglin—the first of the Anglin brothers—arrived at U.S.P. Alcatraz in October. He is a tough-looking son of a bitch who walks down Broadway every day like he owns the place. Anyone insane enough to pull that act as a new fish is bound to be dangerous. Birds respect the confidence, as do I. That perception of John Anglin soon changed. Frank Lee Morris, a man with few to no alliances on the island, buddied up with the con a few weeks after his arrival. The two are expert actors.

"Morris and the Anglins went way back," the man in my mind once whispered.

The three convicts—John's brother Clarence included—did time within the same four walls at U.S.P. Atlanta. Perhaps John Anglin is open to a more sincere conversation if Morris will not listen to reason, a domino effect that ends with my impactful interaction with Morris.

Similar to West, John Anglin is a bird who does not know much about life outside of crime. He is not the violent type like the hothead, but high-stake thrills still come with a fatal price every so often. John was arrested for bank robbery and shipped off to Alcatraz for frequent escape attempts. John and his brother, Clarence, are quite the magicians. They are an impressive pair when confined in the same sandbox. Alcatraz will learn that the hard way in a little over a year from now.

Why destiny chose the two brothers to partake in the 1962 escape baffles me. There are more deserving birds out there than a pair of troublemaking brothers with a knack for picking locks. Their physical prowess is unmatched, though. John stepped onto the dock looking like he had a direct flight from the last Olympic games. The comparison is not far from reality as the brothers are rather impressive swimmers. The little book claimed they are capable of treading water in even the most frigid temperatures which is more than any physical talent Morris, West or I bring to the table combined. The brothers' exact value will be determined at a later date.

"Field . . ." Officer Bates grabs my shoulder during breakfast. "You're needed in the warden's office. Finish up there so we can get outta here."

"Thanks boss," I respond.

The Madison issue appeared resolved. I now sense another hurdle waiting in his office. Any walk to the warden's lair could be a death march; each time I am summoned, I expect to be capped in the head by Peters or forced to consume some form of poison while Madison observes in delight. I am running out of ways to keep the tyrant satisfied. He and Peters are the only two aware of my mysterious arrival. That idea terrifies me. They know how disposable I am. Another beating from Karpis or Wilson is a welcoming thought compared to what they are capable of getting away with. Anything is better than spinning their wheel of punishment.

"I'll take it from here officer." Peters steps in the doorway of the infamous office.

"Of course cap'n." Bates turns around to return to the dining hall, a servant's servant.

"Well don't stand there like a fuckin' idiot!" Peters yells. "Clock's tickin'. Get inside."

Peters steps aside, resuming his position as the warden's bouncer. The man is desperate for an associate warden position that will never arrive. Captain Peters was not mentioned a single time in the little book nor the tape. This man is destined to have his position flushed down the toilet. He will never amount to anything more. I walk past him into the office while keeping these thoughts front-

and-center.

"It's been quite some time," Madison greets me. It has been three months since my last visit. It feels like yesterday. "Why don't you go ahead n' take a seat."

The routine resumes after an enjoyable hiatus. He circles around his desk to sit down as I sit across from him. He taps a cigarette into an overflowing ashtray.

"Officer Bates said you wanted me in here." I press him to get to the point. The less time I spend in here the better.

"Right. Michael I'm sure you've noticed some rather . . . unwanted folks wandering around my island. You know why that is?"

I shrug, although we both know the answer to his question.

"That woman Tillwell. Your little pen pal. She's informed me there's enough evidence t'start an official investigation with the damn B.O.P. It's more than sending a photographer now. It's much more. She will not quit. Were you aware of any of this?"

The stubborn woman will not stop until someone folds within the Alcatraz administration. The warden will not quit either. This once again leaves me in the middle of a storm as two unstoppable winds clash in the heart of the sea.

"She didn't tell me about that," I reply. "Besides, it's common knowledge outgoing mail gets screened by your men."

He is testing my honesty, dangling my life in front of me until he can dispose of me for good. I am needed right now. I am his personal asset—the only individual on or off of this island who is affiliated with both sides of the coin. He knows this, as does Ms. Tillwell.

"We don't make that a secret. All outgoing mail's subject t'search n' seizure." He lights a new cigarette that dangles between his lips. "However I've not forgotten your rather mysterious involvement in Officer Douglas' death. That dimwit Karpowicz hasn't said anything about it, but I have a feeling he'll break this self-imposed vegetative state sooner rather than later."

"Like I told ya when it happened, we were helpin' Officer Mason clean the library. I'm not sure how you can suspect my involvement in this when I ended up in the infirmary that afternoon all those months ago."

"You certainly sold that story. Every officer I spoke with pitied you n' West. They don't know you like I do Michael. The blood puddling in the library n' fire raging in the other room were clever distractions from the truth. There was no new shipment of books in the library. There was no help needed as Officer Mason claimed. We have the logs t'prove it. The library was tended to earlier that morning before the old man's parole at special request due to the planned arrival of those books. The library was spotless."

Mason was supposed to check the logs, ensuring the date and time were clear to move forward with the plan. Madison hated Mason; everyone hated Mason by the end of his time on Alcatraz. The more the warden speaks of it, the more I am convinced Mason's involvement was suspected from the start. It is all too convenient from the warden's point of view.

"You can think what ya want." I adjust my posture in the chair to meet his eye level. "I'm not the one callin' the shots. I do as told n' I was told t'tend t'the library that day. There was no hidden agenda. The sooner we see past that the sooner this'll all go away."

"That maybe so . . ." He takes a second to craft the appropriate response. I stare at him to pressure his thinking. "N' maybe you are telling God's truth, but you are my black sheep. You've done what I've asked of you. In return I've made sure you continue breathing . . . continue seeing another beautiful sunrise gleaming off the bay."

"I'm not sure I'm followin' sir."

"What I'm getting at is this whole situation with Karpowicz continues t'spiral. It follows me around, a bug that won't leave my side. This will not be the downfall of a career I've worked years t'build. This will not be the end of my reign. I'll step on that bug n' kick its remains inna the bay."

Madison is only warden for a short while longer despite his convincing claims. The little book assured me as much, as did the tape. A man in his position and age can change his mind about ironclad plans. There are plenty of variables to sway his opinion yet he will go to hell and back to maintain his position of power right now.

"N' what's this have t'do with me?" I continue, prying for a crack in his story. Get to the point and slip up in the process. Reveal your intentions of leaving this rock once and for all.

"You'll come forward n' admit your involvement that day." He motions for Peters to stand closer as he anticipates my painful reaction. "You'll admit you provoked Karpowicz, or worse, worked with him t'light that fire. You'll admit you were involved in the murder of Officer Douglas. This whole thing—the public defender, the investigation—all comes back t'you. You're never in the right place at the right time. That's no coincidence."

"I had no role in that! Sir I'm destroyed no matter what if I'm blamed for any a that. You n' I both know that's the case."

Death is a brighter option if Madison pins the plan on me. I sense this dark punishment in his hand. I will wither away, incapable of communicating with Morris and the Anglin brothers, watching the escape unfold without my involvement. The journey ends here.

"Do not raise your voice!" He bangs his fist onto the shiny desk. This spotless desk is a representation of the years he spent climbing his way to the top, yet he treats it like a piece of trash. "If it happens again it'll be your last visit t'my office. No more special attention. In fact no attention at all. I'm giving you a choice Michael. Choose wisely or I'll be forced t'choose for you."

Another roadblock leaves me wracking my brain for a single spark from the little book or tape. Neither resource answers my cries for help. Madison forces a confession no matter how I respond. He hopes I will follow his lead, but I am not calling it quits. He must do all in his power to come out victorious.

"No," I snap. His head tilts in unwelcome surprise. "I'm not settin' myself up t'benefit you. There isn't any tangible evidence for these wild claims t'be taken seriously by anyone except you n' the cap'n."

"Then you will suffer."

Peters stands at my side now. I can feel his breath on my shoulder. The two prepare for my emotional ejection from the seat. I lean forward and Peters presses the baton to my chest like a seatbelt. They are waiting for an excuse to end me, realizing how much is on the line with the other inmates and Ms. Tillwell watching closer than ever. They do not quite have their reasoning yet.

Madison collects himself enough to continue, "You'll suffer like no prisoner suffered before n' then you'll provide that confession once I have you on your knees begging for a few seconds of sunlight. In the meantime we'll see what it takes for your other accomplice t'crack. I have a feeling it won't require many more visits for him. Another daft convict prepared t'trip over his words. That's the beauty of this Michael. It's every man for himself on this island."

The servant obeys his master's non-verbal commands without hesitation. He pulls me back to the cellhouse. I am kicking my way down the hallway and down Broadway. This frustration makes Peters glow with satisfaction. My success was temporary. My actions—the plan—came back to haunt me. We pass other officers who turn a blind eye to the corrupt screw dragging me down Sunset Strip. D-block is my new home. The hole. So much time has passed, yet my memory travels to its first night on the island. Peters dragged me down the hall in similar fashion.

The first isolation cell clanks open. Peters slides me across the slick floor like a bowling ball. I turn around to head toward the doorway and he responds with a smile. The steel door crashes shut.

It is a waiting game. Madison will convince West to speak and will work to break down Karpis if that proves unsuccessful. If both options fail, he will do all in his power to make me talk—to admit my involvement in the murder of Officer Douglas. It is back to square one. Madison made his move and now faces an uphill battle. He underestimates the power of solitude. I have all the time in the world to wander the depths of my mind. There is little else to think about in such an isolated place. I simply must conjure the next move before West speaks.

The race begins.

LITTLE LIES

I'm an addict. Relapse was always around the corner. Everywhere I go—no matter what I do—the memory of Michael haunts me. Turn to the bottle and it draws me in. Turn to family and the bright light at the end of the tunnel sends me making a U-turn.

Family—that awful word. Family's love, comfort and safety. It's that warm feeling difficult to explain yet impossible to ignore. For me, the word reeks of loss, sorrow and betrayal. Loss for the people I called a dad and brother. Sorrow for letting artificial feelings control me all these years. Betrayal from biological parents who tossed me on a stranger's porch like the Sunday paper. Betrayal from my adoptive mom, too.

The time for sorrow has passed. Anger fuels these actions. My fingernails dig into the leather seat of this poor man's cab as a temporary form of stress relief. I'm furious. The torn photo's tucked back in my pocket and I sit with my legs bouncing in frustration. I envision bursting through the front door of that longtime prison. My blood boils with rage toward the one person who buried the past. My adoptive mom—Mrs. Field—knew my origin from the beginning. She held onto those secrets my entire life. She lied about Samantha Eldridge's death. She lied about it all and who's to say there's not more swept under the rug? That selfish woman didn't care about what was best for me.

The front door swings open, slamming against the wall with a thud before boomeranging back to a close. The sound travels through the house. I appreciate what Mr. and Mrs. Field did for me; however, it's time to kill the past. I need to destroy these ties without hesitation. Michael was smart to keep his distance from the Field family. He was their biological son and knew better than to put them first. Family—that disgusting word.

Mrs. Field parked her car in the driveway. She's home. My instincts tell me to shout at her again, but something stops me this time. Brown bags of groceries lay spread across the foyer, a few having fallen over only to send apples rolling across the floor toward the wall like tumbleweeds. There's not a peep in the other room. No hurried feet rushing to pick up the dropped bags nor the sound of food making its way into the cabinets and fridge. Silence stomps on my rage, adding to the fury.

The wooden floor creaks as I head to the dining room, every step becoming more cautious than the next. Did someone break into the house? The bad feeling leaves me wondering what went wrong instead of wanting to teach my mom a lesson about keeping secrets.

"Hello?" I try whispering instead of shouting.

Nothing in return. Typical. I can picture her on the phone upstairs whispering to Meredith again. I lean my body off the dining room wall to peek in the kitchen doorway. I can hear faint sniffling, and my eyes soon lock onto Mrs. Field. She sits at the kitchen table, face deep in her palms. A few more mumbled moans exit the room and reach my ears.

"What's wrong?" I step through the doorway to make my presence known. Still no response.

"What happened? Did Samantha Eldridge call you?"

I walk over to the table and put my hand under her chin to lift it from its sunken position. Tears pour down her cheeks onto my palm. I can tell anger won't make me feel any better right now. She's waiting for me to say something else, so I give in.

"Yes I'm angry. I can't forgive you for keepin' this from me. I'll still always appreciate everything you—"

She leans over and places her head against my hip. The sobbing evolves into hyperventilation, the type of crying that leaves someone sucking for air every time they let out another sigh. She's drowning in her own liquid.

"Robert . . . it's Meredith."

"Meredith? What about Meredith? What'd she say now?"

She shakes her head, not wanting to say more but summoning the courage to do so anyway. "No Robert. Meredith . . . the hospital called. They said it happened so fast. I didn't get the details. She was driving downtown n'—"

She stops to return to rapid breathing, burrowing deeper in my jacket. I'm pulling teeth. The endless stream soaks through my undershirt. I focus on the large puddle she leaves on my clothes rather than pry for more information. How long until this shirt dries? And my jacket? Do tears leave stains? Questions of the least concern fly into frame. I came here to yell at this woman and I've turned into a human tissue. Adrenaline flushed down the toilet. What a waste.

"D'you understand what I'm saying? I dunno what else I can . . . I have no words! Oh lord say something already!"

"No I'm not really following. I can't say you're getting it across very clearly either. Is Meredith injured or somethin'? I mean for the love a God . . . just spit it out!"

The crying. The uncontrollable sobbing is Oscar-worthy. Meredith—it's something with her. It doesn't take a genius to understand what she's getting at. Something bad happened, something Mrs. Field doesn't want to discuss, or rather can't. It's bad, but I'll let avoidance carry me through this.

"Meredith was in a car accident on her way home from work."

She wipes the tears away with a sweater sleeve and sits up in the chair. I sit in the chair next to her, finally free of the waterfall pouring down her face.

"An officer told me she fell asleep at the wheel of the car," she continues. "At least that's what they've gathered. She was working that nightshift n' . . . they didn't say much else. She survived long enough for them t'put her in an ambulance. That's all I know. Robert . . ."

She pauses. I expect her to break down in tears again. Instead, she stands up and pours herself a glass of water. She transitions from heartbroken to mother-like in the blink of an eye as she pours me a glass, too.

I told Meredith those off-shifts at the hospital were a terrible idea. This could've been avoided if she listened to me. She needed to listen to me for once and she didn't. Too proud. Too stubborn.

One late night on the job and the kids' world changes forever. More unwelcome thoughts rush to elbow out a normal reaction. She never listened to me. And now she's gone.

Mrs. Field pats my back. I'm still emotionless. Disbelief and exhaustion have been present for months, squeezing my emotions dry like a wrung-out towel. Michael's missing; there's a woman out there who knows more about me than anyone else; Meredith passed away—the latest addition to my tragic life. Where to begin?

My last conversation with her will stick with me for the rest of my life. It's like that fucking photo I carry in my pocket, except it'll never burn, tear or wilt. It's trapped with me and there's nothing I can do to release it. I do feel some guilt. That conversation didn't kill her, but it didn't improve matters either. Guilt with no emotion makes this impossible to process.

There was hope with Michael; I still manage to find an ounce of hope every day. This news is hopeless. Meredith's gone—forever. I rewind and replay that fact on a loop, a record stuck on repeat despite my slamming it to the floor. The fact is foreign—a beloved cartoon character recast with a new voice actor. The order of the words doesn't make sense.

I want to think I'm brave, maybe even strong. The reality is I'm lost. I'm digging for logic to explain my lack of empathy. This is sensory deprivation in full force. A firing squad drains their ammo on my mind. Each bullet strikes, knocking me in a new direction. I don't have time to absorb the last bullet before a new one plunges inside to rewire my thinking.

Denial gets comfortable as I console Mrs. Field for the rest of the evening. I should need the consoling. I should be on the living room couch wrapped in a blanket, drinking bedtime tea to lullaby myself to sleep. If I can't come to terms with what happened and react like a human, the next best solution's to tend to someone who can accomplish as much. Is this how Michael always felt? Complete emptiness; jealousy of the empathy of those around him; an inability to relate. Comforting this woman's balanced with calls across the country to the nanny. Meredith never came home, so Marybeth moved the kids from a five-bedroom home to a studio apartment.

Brilliant idea. Still, it's relieving to hear they're with a familiar authority figure—if you could even call her such a thing.

The kids won't speak to me. Marybeth calls it trauma when it's really a reaction to their estranged dad reaching out. I'm offering my voice after months of neglect. I force Marybeth to relay messages despite the kids' disinterest. I'm the last person they want to hear from.

"Tell 'em I'm comin' home tomorrow. Tell 'em it'll be alright. They needa get some sleep. Take it one day at a time. I'll be back for them soon."

They're already tucked in bed by the time I remember to relay 'I love you.' That was probably the most important message for them to hear and it's an afterthought for me. A fucking afterthought.

San Fran pulls me back. It yanks me from my grasp on New York like a turbine engine looking to consume an unfortunate bird. Flying back never crossed my mind. Fate tossed a tragedy in the ring to make sure I land on the right side of the fence. Destiny dangled death in front of me to show its threatening might—at least that'd be the case if I believed in destiny. I'm really just unlucky.

What a day. My eyes grow watery throughout the night. I expect the feeling to be a flood of emotions pouring out, yet the reaction's only a result of the clock on the wall reading one in the morning. It's time for bed. Tired eyes, not sad eyes. No much-needed emotional release on the horizon. I suppose there's always tomorrow. Mrs. Field drifts off on the couch while I lean back in the recliner, the real parent in the house.

Meredith. Gone—forever. I repeat it a few more times as a twisted lullaby.

The sun pokes its head out from the night sky. I'm not rested; a night of tossing and turning on the late Mr. Field's go-to recliner was a struggle. It's no longer insomnia if morning arrives, right? The idea of a new day and a chance to start over leaves me with hope. Yesterday was one of the worst days in my life. Little more could go wrong today and that's enough to roll out of the chair.

The kitchen calls my name after a quick trip to the bathroom. I sneak past a snoozing Mrs. Field to cook some breakfast. A surprise breakfast—this is what I do the morning after my ex-wife dies. It's the least I can do knowing neither Mrs. Field nor I have eaten in the last twenty-four hours or so. Again, a task you think the parent would be on top of.

"What're you doing?" She enters the room a few minutes later.

All parents wake at the crack of dawn. I should've expected this yet it gives me a good jump. A cracked egg drops from my hand to the floor.

"Jesus! Breakfast. I'm cookin' breakfast for us."

The gesture's ignored. She walks to the coffee pot and pours herself a cup. Black. Dark. She usually puts cream in it, so I know she's emotional this morning. A change in her morning ritual. How can she hold so much sentiment after all this time? My empathy morphs into jealousy.

"I was saving those eggs for a casserole later this week," she grunts. She grabs some paper towels and wipes the runny mess off the black-and-white checkered tile floor. "Now I have t'buy more eggs."

If anyone has a reason to be snarky it's me. "Last time I checked there wasn't a shortage of eggs in this country. You know I'm trynna do something nice Missus—mom. You'll be gone for a few days anyway. You don't need more eggs right now."

"No . . . I'm not going anywhere." She clutches the cup with two hands now, one covering 'World's Best Mom' written in bold lettering. "I've decided t'stay here. I'm not going back t'California with you. I couldn't . . . I can't bear the grief of losing another right now. Not another so soon. I'll find time t'visit my grandchildren. I just can't—"

"What're you saying?" The spatula flies from my hand to the counter. More egg mess drips down to the floor. "You're not going t'your former daughter-in-law's funeral? For Christ's sake, I booked your fuckin' ticket last night. You were practic'lly best friends with her as a yesterday. I'm jobless as it is. You expect me t'eat that cost too?"

"I know, I know. I'll find a way t'pay you back. It's just that . . . you shouldn't have spoken with her on the phone like that! That's the last memory we'll have a her. She was trynna help you! We were all trynna help you!"

She can't be serious. Sorrow was tossed aside for unwarranted blame in the blink of an eye. This is worse than denial. My blood boils as I lean over the counter. I tried to be civil.

"What're you getting at? Don't tell me what she was trynna do. You don't know her like I do! She left me. She took the house, the kids . . . she took my Porsche!"

"You n' your brother." She shakes her head. She's already moved over to the doorway, checked out from the conversation. "The two a you never had any appreciation for the people in your lives. I spent all night thinking about it . . . wondering how this could've been avoided. Yes Robert. She left you. She took the children n' your home. At the end a the day though none a this woulda happened if you had your priorities straight!"

I'm done. No more peaceful moments. She's not getting another second of this pretend game of mom and son and neither of us are eating these eggs. There's a difference between grief and displacement that I just can't look past. I'm not going to stand here and take this if I don't have to. She did this to herself like how Meredith brought on our argument.

"I'm not standing here taking this . . . not from you!" I stomp across the room. The stove's still on high. No more waving the white flag. "D'you know where I went yesterday? I mean d'ya have any idea at all?"

"I do." This infuriates me to a new level. Say more—I dare her. "You really think Samantha wouldn't call me the moment you left? She told me you visited . . . asking about your past n' all. Asking about that woman who found you. She also told me t'make sure you didn't go chasing after this . . . this Kimble lady."

She knew. She knew I visited Samantha Eldridge and let me comfort her anyway. That's insulting. It was always about her objectives. She's shedding my tears. That's my past she's keeping to herself and she doesn't deserve sorrow nor consolation.

"So you knew about this mystery woman n' didn't think t'ever mention her t'me? I pleaded for answers all day yesterday. This woman knew me from the time I was an infant t'when I ended up in this family. This shithole of a family!"

She dumps the eggs in the trash and points the pan at me. "If that's what you were so bothered about last night then it's no wonder you didn't shed a tear at the loss a your wife." Ex-wife. I scoff at the accusations. She doesn't know the half of it. She continues anyway. "You know I always defended you. She'd say all ya care about is yourself n' my motherly instincts told me t'prove her wrong. She kept in better contact with me as a daughter-in-law than either a my sons. You left me t'rot in this home. You could care less!"

The intermission from sobbing ends. She wipes tears away with the robe she's had for over two decades without a single wash. The son in me should feel bad. At the same time, I know that man can't return. He's gone for good—vanished forever like my ex-wife. I'm too far down the rabbit hole to stick my head out and console Mrs. Field for a second time. My flight's today. I'll be out of here soon enough and she can cry to herself.

"That wasn't my intention." I turn toward the doorway, having switched spots with her over the course of trading fighting words. "I'm sure it wasn't Michael's either. You kept me in the dark for so many years though. You knew telling me the truth was the right thing t'do after all this time yet you pretended like that part a my life didn't exist. Now there's a person out there who can tie it all together n' you don't want me t'see her?"

The kitchen's in the past. The good deed of breakfast is entangled somewhere in the argument. A glance over my shoulder shows the river flowing down her cheek, preparing to topple a decade-old, sturdy dam. I can put forth one last effort to leave on a somewhat civil note. I've done so much already—a little more won't hurt me.

"Listen mom. I appreciate everything you did for me. You gave me a home . . . a permanent life. Right now I have two kids who just lost their own mom n' a woman who can help fill in some missing pieces a my life. I needa do what's best for me now."

The kid in me wants to believe she'll chase after me as I gather my personal items and prepare to head to the airport. She never leaves the kitchen. Life's not a movie with a happy ending—it's just life. No major resolution's in sight. She'll go her way and I'll go mine. Maybe our paths will cross again in a while. I meant every word I told her just now.

'Don't let regret hold you back from doing something in the moment.' Mr. Field's repeated words of wisdom ring as I head out the door. I never understood the meaning behind that advice until now.

Fog City awaits my arrival. Answers do the same. I close the door without looking behind me.

ALL THE WAY

Meredith was the favorite parent and that didn't change after she left me with the kids. It doesn't come as a surprise; she raised them when Marybeth wasn't around. She knew this. I know this. The kids know this and have no shame in making it clear as we sit in silence in the car. I can't blame them. I'd feel hopeless if I spent the rest of my life with myself, too.

People can say what they want about my parenting and about what's right versus wrong. I won't deceive my kids. They're not prospective clients. I won't fill their hopes with bullshit and act like this never happened. False hope won't heal my soul, so it sure as hell won't fix their problems either.

"You guys feel like gettin' some grub?" I speak to the rearview mirror.

The well-dressed boys are draped in black suits. Kids shouldn't have to wear dark outfits like these. Such youthful life deserves happier attire. A shirt with a rocket on it; plaid pajama-pants embroidered with monkeys flinging bananas. I'll blame the nanny for these morbid outfits.

"How 'bout that burger place? In-N-Out? We can get those cool hats. I'll even wear one."

Still nothing. Nothing at all. I can't sell it. The more I speak, the more their faces sink into despair. I came home with toys and food throughout their short lives. I'm the bringer of souvenirs from the land of business trips and the king of fast food that mom refused to buy. That's how I got these kids to smile. They were only fake smiles. I even tricked myself into thinking they loved me—a fantastical magic trick.

"Listen pals . . . I know this isn't easy." I toss my hands in the air in surrender. "It's tough for everyone . . . especially me. I won't sit here n' tell you mommy's coming back. She'll always be with us though. You might not see her now but she still loves you both n' she'll be with you wherever you go. That's for the rest a your life too."

They can read through the clever words. One turns to the other and shakes his head. I'm their dad and they think I'm a joke. I muster every empathic word that comes to mind, yet a five- and three-year-old are not fooled.

The eldest breaks the silence. "Can we stay with Marybeth? She said we can stay with her if we want. Can we stay with her tonight?"

They'd choose the nanny over their surviving parent. It pushes the knife a little deeper into my back.

"What? You know Marybeth only has that small apartment. I'm not sure she'd be able t'have you guys over. You've already stayed there for two nights n' there's barely enough room for her there!"

"We stayed with her when mommy died," the three-year-old chimes in with a verbal gut-punch. "We didn't stay with you. Marybeth told us we can always stay with her. Please dad? Please?"

They both beg in coordinated manipulation. It's the same type of begging you expect from a kid pushing for a sleepover with their best friend. Instead, it's the nanny. The fucking nanny. The old, boring woman.

A good father tells them their daddy will watch over them. He'll take care of them for the rest of their lives. A superhero daddy will make everything better. They don't deserve lies when I'm the villain. I can't argue with the request if they want to stay with Marybeth. I'm too weak to put up a fight.

The air conditioning's our white noise now. I never imagined it'd be this uncomfortable with my own two kids in the backseat, yet here we are. They sat next to Meredith's parents during the funeral this afternoon, which didn't help the tension. The last thing I want's those two pulling away my kids, too. I'll settle for the nanny—at least she's a temporary problem. My former in-laws are a different story. They never liked me, smelling a lack of commitment from a mile away. I was a faithful husband who was by no means a family man. No 'World's Best Dad' mug in my hand. The family requested

I not speak at the funeral. They requested I keep myself contained. I'm sure everyone thought I'd stumble into the coffin, throw up on extended family members or raid the break room for every ounce of liquor. They're wrong. My mind's clear.

"Hey Robert." Marybeth steps outside the gate of her building.

The stocky woman wears the ultimate nanny costume. I can't picture her in anything else. Born to nanny. That wool sweater with the disproportionate horse stitched on the front; baggy, faded jeans covering her shoes. My kids willingly stay with this woman. She bends down to give the kids a tight hug. It's a simple gesture I forget about every time I see them. I can't remember to tell them I love them—how can I remember physical affection? I can't distinguish client interactions from those with family. Leaving my kids with a firm handshake feels more appropriate at this point.

"You two run on in n' put the television on. I taped a few episodes a those PowerCats earlier this morning . . . just for you."

"ThunderCats!" they shout, punching the air with excitement. Fleeting joy distracts from lifelong pain.

They run up the stairwell without thinking twice about the man who dropped them off. I'm the mailman for all they care. They lost a parent, but at least they know what it's like to have both, even if for a short while. That's more than I had growing up. I know they'll be alright in the long run.

"Hey Marybeth." I stop her as she turns toward the stairs. "I hate t'do this t'you. I know we're gettin' inna the weekend n' I said no at the funeral today n'—"

"It's fine Robert." Her eyes pan up and down at the miserable man in front of her gate. "These boys mean the world t'me. If that's what keeps their mind off this awful loss then I'll gladly keep 'em here. They can stay as long as they want."

"Right . . . thanks. Appreciate the help." An awkward silence builds. All I can think to say is, "Let's not let 'em get too comfortable though." The words are packed with worry and jealousy. I don't know where it came from, but it's too late to take it back. She won't take those boys, too.

She nods. Pity drapes her face as she senses paranoia in my

voice. I step backward and leave her with a simple 'Thank you.'

"Robert . . ." she calls from halfway up the stairs. "Pardon my bluntness . . . if you wanna win their affection you needa stop running. You run around. That's what you do. Running's all they know about their father right now."

I toss her a thumbs up. I imagine she doesn't know what the gesture means at her age. I'm not running; I'm chasing something. I've always chased something. A stable career to provide for my family. Answers to Michael's disappearance. Information about my origin. The kids will be old enough to appreciate that one day. They'll understand.

The first destination's where this started. It's time to go home. I was hammered the last time I entered this hunk-of-junk car. I fuddled with the stereo to drown out denial with music. That night's not stopping me from getting anywhere now. Nothing's stopping me.

The house is identical to the day Meredith sent me packing. I stormed out the front door with a backpack and a light suitcase as that's all I needed at the time. Still, a certain unfamiliarity lingers as I explore each room. The silence is haunting. No kids running around, no wife yelling across the house and no nanny cooking in the kitchen. It's overwhelming emptiness that leaves me feeling sick. I don't know why I came home. It felt right—a sensible place to continue this scavenger hunt. Yet an hour into my visit doesn't provide clarity. It's been months since I've stepped on the tile floor or ran my hand along the stairs' finished wooden railing. It doesn't provide direction; it only uncovers more hollowness.

There's a ghost of a former life that creeps a few feet behind me. It persists in the shadows, a ghost of memories that time can't erase. I wanted to let go and look back at life in this house with tired eyes. I didn't expect to feel this way. The self-guided tour changes my path to sadness and regret. It drops me off in the master bedroom and flings me on her side of the bed. She's gone—forever. I close my eyes. Hands run through my hair. Footsteps creak across the wooden floor. She's coming to bed after a nightshift and trying not to wake me. I have to get up in a few hours and she respects that.

She comes home and I leave.

I indulge in the experience. It's another unexpected detour in my journey, yet I find myself wanting more. I imagine wearing those slippers she trotted around the house in or the immense pain she felt when I left. She worked her ass off every hour. My 'thank you' consisted of walking out the door. She sent me walking and I didn't put up a fight. I mumbled 'Okay' and slammed the door.

My heavy head rolls over the pillow. A photo of us stands centered on the nightstand. She continued to wake up to the despicable sight of my face every day despite everything I'd done— despite her claims of letting our relationship float adrift. I stare at the photo for minutes; it's hours for all I know. Every detail's analyzed, burned into my memory like the photo of Michael. My good fight against tears ends. This isn't planned. This isn't part of my path. This is something else.

My face sinks into the pillow. The more I fight the sobbing the further I descend. Every time I think I'm free of the emotional release my nose fills with the scent of her hair. It feels good. I feel relieved. I embrace it, overcome with emotion. The raw moment's a culmination of months of suppressed feelings crashing down at once. I had it all and lost it all. I lost it all again. And again. Meredith continued to think of me despite this slippery slope. She kept this photo on her nightstand, called Mrs. Field every day to ask about me and drove over an hour to bail me out of jail. I returned the favor by lying to her and telling her off on the phone. She's gone— forever. It's my fault.

The evening passes at a snail's pace. Each second's a minute, every minute an eternity. I pace back and forth in front of the liquor cabinet, a shark closing in on motionless prey. Hours of uncontrolled release send me reaching toward the golden liquid. Bottles of power and relief. Each time my hand reaches out, the other slaps it back to my side. Self-restraint can only last so many rounds in the ring. Addiction's imminent with enough time. That barrier's nearly three hours. My hand has had enough of this game, clawing at a bottle only to be dismissed. It wants me to drink the remaining emotion to beyond infinity.

One quickdraw hits a bottle a little too hard. The object stumbles on its surface the way I used to waddle into that motel room every night. I can only stand and watch as five bottles crash to the floor like dominoes.

"Fuck!"

The golden treasures shatter, sending precious liquids puddling on the tile. Glass shards slide across the floor, covering my surroundings. A frustrated hand snags another bottle from the cabinet and slams it against the wall. It's a pitch that sends Steve Young to the minor leagues from my perspective. I bend over, squatting down like a caveman by fire. I reach down to pick up a few larger chunks of glass as something slips out of my jacket pocket, landing in the center of the pungent puddle of booze. The photo. It stalked me from San Fran to New York and back—back to Fog City. It haunts me as Meredith does. It looks like Michael's still here, too. The puddle just about consumed the entire photo, yet I still rescue it from drowning. Black-and-white colors bleed off the print like tie dye. He's still here and I must protect him, so he rests back in my pocket.

What's worse: chasing ghosts or drowning them in luxurious liquid? Two obsessions collide. Michael chooses the former. I'm certain of this. Meredith, if she was forced at gunpoint to decide, chooses the former as well. The bottle was the source of my destruction. If the ridiculous concept of destiny guides me toward one option, it's the ghosts. I'll choose them time and again if it means leaving my destructive self in the shadows.

I stand up from the wet mess. The bleeding photo's in one hand now and the photo of Meredith and me in the other. The ghosts guide me to the kitchen—to the phone. They force me to grab the handset from the wall. If this ends, it's on my own terms. I'll seal what cracked open once and for all.

"Yes hello. I'm trynna reach a Becky Kimble from San Jose. K-I-M-B-L-E. Can you put me through t'that number?"

I wipe my hands of the devil's gold dripping its way onto the handset. The phone balances between my chin and shoulder. One obsession's brushed aside while the other scoots closer, bearhugging me with its might.

"I'm sorry sir. It looks like there isn't anyone by that name in this area. I can—"

"There's nobody by that name? Can ya check the surrounding area or somethin' like that? This's your job isn't it?"

"My apologies sir. I can only assist if you have a sense of the city this person resides in." She's doing her best to stay pleasant, although she wants to reach through the phone and choke me to death. "This is a measure put in place t'prevent solicitors from calling people at random."

"Great. Thanks for nothing."

I slam the phone against the wall. I slam it again and again until the wallpaper peels and grey dust floats through the air. I can't catch a break. The surviving bottles call to me from the other room, begging me to come back to comfort and security. 'We're here for you,' they whisper. 'We'll hear you out.' They're manipulative— cunning. The same motivation from a few minutes ago still holds me back. The other obsession prevails for a second time, metaphorically knocking the rest of the bottles to the ground. They smash and shoot across the floor like shrapnel. I can't throw in the towel after one try. There must be another way to track down Becky Kimble.

My feet shuffle back to the kitchen as my hand reaches for the phone hanging off the wall. I look like a zombie. The obsession dials the operator again. I pray for a different voice across the line this time.

"Yeah. I need a phone number." I spill the words out as fast as I can. The next wave of hopelessness is right around the corner. "Can ya put me through t'the residence of Lucille Park in Napa Valley?"

She must sense the urgency in my tone as she transfers me no more than a second later.

"Hello?" a familiarly frail voice answers. "Who's calling at this hour?"

"Hello!" I respond with relief, maybe even a dash of happiness. "Ma'am my name's Robb . . . Robb Field. I visited you a few weeks ago. I'm not sure if you rememb—"

"Robb?" She's confused. I realize this is hopeless after that one-word question. "I think you have the wrong number Robb. You have a pleasant evening now."

"Wait!" I shout before her deteriorating mind can put the phone down. "Wait wait! Please don't hang up."

I take a step back along with a deep breath. She remains quiet, yet the line doesn't beep. I wrack my brain for any words to continue the conversation, hypnotizing bait to keep her hooked. She shut me down—sent me out the door—when I asked about Mikey Kimble. Her face perked up at the opportunity to chat about their relationship; however, she was quick to put up a wall of silence. The woman doesn't remember me now. I'm a stranger who knows more about her than she knows about herself. She believes her late husband, Jeffrey, follows her around in that shithole of a house. I can use that to my advantage.

"Lucille this's actually Mikey Kimble. D'you remember me?"

"Mikey?" The confusion lingers with a pep in her tone this time. "Mikey you've been gone all this time. How's this possible? Why'd you wait so long t'get in touch? I have Jeffrey here with me. Jeffrey! Get over here! Jeffrey it's Mikey on the telephone."

Poor woman. She won't last much longer if someone doesn't check on her. The act isn't over, though. I'm sorry, Lucille—I'll take advantage of your mental state for a few more minutes. I'll disrespect your unfortunate surroundings a little more. You won't hear from me again after this call.

"Yes! I'm so sorry Lucille. I've been . . . I was waiting for the right time t'speak with you n' Jeffrey. I hope you understand it wasn't easy for me t'get in touch." The salesman's back to work without pay. I roll my eyes at how ridiculous this all sounds.

"Oh of course. We understand, don't we Jeffrey?" There's another pause. I imagine her conversing with her late husband on that plastic-covered couch. "He wants t'know why you're calling Mikey. We both wanna know why you're calling after so long."

"Well it's a bit complicated . . ." I push the speaker to my mouth, searching for the right response. "You see it's Becky. You remember Becky don't you?"

I pray I'm leaving the right breadcrumbs for this woman. If not, I expect a swift clank of the phone on the other end. It's a bold question to drop in the conversation, but I'm confident in this connection. It's no coincidence and that belief's tested right here, right now.

"What's wrong with Becky?" My heart races as she utters the name. "You told us you hadn't spoken t'her in years. Why're you getting in touch with her now dear? Shh quiet Jeffrey. He can do what he wants. He's a grown man."

Her long-term memory remains impressive. Even if she doesn't know where Becky is, it'll leave me with a form of empty satisfaction. My instincts were right for once. Mikey Kimble's associated with the Becky Kimble that Samantha Eldridge spoke of a few days ago. It's perfect. The pieces are falling into place.

I collect my anticipation before responding in what I'm imagining Mikey's voice sounded like the last time they spoke: an old-timey tone like those in black-and-white films. "I needa get in touch with Becky. D'you remember where she lives? My mind's becoming forgetful with each year that passes n'—"

"Becky . . . the last we heard a Becky's whereabouts was through you Mikey. You said you were going your own ways . . . splitting up n' whatnot. You said it was the only way. D'you at least recall that dear?"

Samantha Eldridge claimed Becky didn't want her foster children finding her, especially me. Perhaps Mikey Kimble's one of those foster children—the one kid she adopted out of the litter of puppies. She wanted to turn over a new leaf like how I'm trying to do. Is this the one piece of evidence from her former life she left behind?

"However . . ." she continues after stopping to whisper to her late husband. "Did you call n' see if she's still associated with that darn dock? You know the one with those activities? Jeffrey suggests you check there."

"Dock with activities? Can you explain?"

"Goodness gracious . . . you've become quite forgetful. That dock. You know with the tourists n' that. It's too busy for us over there."

Fisherman's Wharf—it must be Fisherman's Wharf if she's referring to a spot in Fog City. That's the most frequented tourist destination around. Deep-fried desserts, seafood, 'I Heart San Fran' t-shirts and magnets. Fisherman's Wharf was built for tourists.

"You mean Fisherman's Wharf? The one in San Francisco?"

"Yes that's the one." Her frail voice grows quiet as she speaks away from the phone again. "Oh Jeffrey hush. Everyone makes a living somehow. It's in the past now."

"Lucille what'd Jeffrey say?" I fuel the imaginary conversation. The deception appears more immoral the more I think about it, so I remain in the moment rather than thinking about what's really going on. I'll test her fading mind by pushing her to answer for Jeffrey.

"He asked why she had t'go n' work for that dreadful place." She sighs. "Don't mind him he just doesn't believe in that place being treated like a museum. I feel that way too . . . as I'm sure you do. I told him everyone needs a job. He's gone t'take a nap now. Please don't mind him Mikey."

"A museum? What d'you mean? What shouldn't be treated like a museum?"

I won't end it like this. A conversation with these senior citizens is like watching paint dry across an entire house. When one room's done, I'm forced to stare at another for days on end. It's torture. Give me something to work with here.

"Oh sweetie. It's prob'ly a good thing you don't remember much. I envy your forgetfulness." She's fortunate she isn't aware of her own mental state. "They turned that island inna a place for tourists. How disrespectful! You n' Jeffrey spent years in that awful place. They shoulda torn every building down once n' for all after it closed."

This is more complex than simply discovering my origin if the old lady's telling the truth. Becky Kimble's associated with Mikey Kimble and the two stories share a common theme—a common place. The thread's Alcatraz. Out of all the places to work in Fog City, a former caregiver makes a living in the most tourist-ridden location in town. The ghosts in my pocket shoved me in the right direction after all. They're more satisfied than ever. Giving up's behind me. The bottles seep into the cracks of the tile and get comfortable there. Never again will I cash out. I won't convince myself it's over. My origin's a scab I continue to pick, peeling away the same unwanted protrusions. At the end of the day, the only way to get rid of the clotted mess is to let it heal. Months of picking at it will result in a scar that stays with me for life. None of that matters if the answers I've searched for arrive. Jesus—my brain's sounding more like Michael's every day.

Both interactions I've had with Lucille made me happy for the old lady. She sees her husband every day. I can't say the same for Meredith as I don't think we nurtured our love like that. Still, Mrs. Park has fallen off her rocker. Her mental state has deteriorated to oblivion. I do her a favor when we part ways on the phone for the last time, dialing the police. She deserves to spend the rest of her days in reality, no matter how uncomfortable that might be. We all deserve to live in reality. Thanks, Lucille.

HARBOR LIGHTS

The school bully wises up after sniffing out an adult. The bully is cunning, empowered with the false perception of caring for the well-being of classmates and the betterment of the education system. Pull the delightful layer back to find manipulation. An evil human. Of course, this is entirely subjective.

Film positions the prison's bully as a guard or the captain. That is inaccurate. The root of the problem stems from a level above. It stems from the warden's office. The puppeteer. The fear the warden creates spreads like a virus amongst birds. Most officers soil themselves when summoned to the warden's dreaded prison-within-a-prison. Quite simply put, their careers are always on the line. This is Wall Street in their line of work, the cream of the crop for criminal justice. Screws remain silent and obey orders as long as it puts bread on the table for their families. Despite all this, I cannot blame Hopeful Howard. In fact, his dedication's rather impressive. A man like Madison goes years without collapsing his career, protecting it at all costs. It is a commitment I could not dream of in his shoes. Yet I am in the opposite position. I am shoeless. I sit naked in a dreary cell on Sunset Strip.

The door slides open a few times a day. The rapid transition sends a burst of light blasting through the confined area. God envies this type of light. Senses enhance when others are stripped away. Smell and touch surge to inhuman levels if sight and sound are removed; however, those are the last two senses an inmate wants enhanced in Alcatraz. Feces, sweat and mold growing in every dark corner settle in this vacuum-sealed hole. The dungeon had better accommodations.

Captain Peters steps aside to let Madison walk into frame during my second week of the never-ending stint. The light halos around the dictator.

"Looks quite unpleasant in there." Madison smirks. He puffs his pipe and blows the foggy smoke to the furthest corner of the miniature room. Even the scent of warm, exhaled smoke is pleasant. He continues after the smoke clears, "Have you given any thought t'our conversation? D'you need more time t'think it over in that box?"

Nothing sounds more pleasant than leaving this cell and telling the tyrant I have made my decision. Unbeknown to him, I would have a different agenda under these dirty denim sleeves. The truth is I do not have a plan. Two weeks in the hole have only fueled the emptiness. Doctor Polk's silent meditation hinders my thinking process. There is no plan and there very well may never be if this endless roadblock persists.

"I haven't thought it over." My words sound foreign after the stretch of silence as if muffled through the audiotape.

Peters' heavy leather boots trot backward. He shouts across Sunset Strip for the metal door to close. The servant smiles as the door shuts. The irrelevant, forgettable servant is optimistic for no reason. He has no story in the little book.

It is a race between Madison and me. The first one to discover a solution to our mutually troublesome problem wins the world. They win freedom. He shifts any wrongdoing on me while I free myself of the control he wraps around my future—my destiny.

Ideas are flames that are smothered when consumed by constant darkness. There is only sleep left to occupy a blank mind. I am losing motivation. The hole is impacting the way my brain operates and I am bound to have the same fate as Karpis if I do not step back into the light soon. An even worse scenario than that would be having no fate at all.

The same heightened senses kick in a few hours later when a faint knock comes from outside the thick door. The sound tosses my body up from its flat position. I had gone belly-up in this box, prepared to close my eyes for the final time. The narrow flap used to deliver meals creaks open and a beam of light shoots across the dark square, lasering into my eyes.

"Hey Field," a man whispers. "It's Lens."

Most of Wilson's crew separated after their leader's outburst. I suppose raging flames combined with a turnkey altercation is a valid reason for the group's disbandment. The crew dissolved in mere days with Wilson in isolation. Not long after, Lens drew the greatest lottery ticket of all by landing library duty, replacing the now-paroled bird who helped gather our supplies for the plan. Floating under the radar paid off for the four-eyed con.

"What? What d'ya want?"

My voice has nearly vanished compared to the few words I spoke to the warden not long ago. I am wary of the nosey bird as he deals with the blind half-mute on this side of the heavy door. This is not a bargaining position, though. I cannot have it all.

"Listen Field . . . I don't have much time. You know I'm not s'posed t'bring this cart by the hole." He bends down to peer inside the slot, blocking any light from coming into the room again. "Wilson wants t'speak with you. He heard you talkin' t'the king screw the other day n' said it'd be worth your while."

Wilson remains in D-block—Sunset Strip—alongside Creepy Karpis. He has resided there since the outburst toward a screw so many months ago. It figures my old neighbor listened to any conversation he could twist to his advantage. Just because my mind remains a blank slate when it comes to a brilliant plan does not mean I am daft enough to speak with Wilson.

"I'm not an idiot." I align my mouth with the metal flap, a dog waiting for the mailman. Lens is already inching along in fear of a gun gallery guard spotting him and taking action. "There's no way I'm talkin' t'that son of a bitch. You can tell him t'—"

"Dummy up. I don't care what you say. Seems t'me you're in a tight spot in this hole . . . a tighter spot than Wilson for that matter. Think it over. I'll find a way t'roll back this way tomorrow."

He closes the flap. The cart continues down the strip.

What does Wilson want? The more I think about it the more certain I am of malicious intent. Perhaps he spoke with Karpis through paper-thin cell walls. Did the Creep let him know who was behind the fire in his cell? Or worse, did my old neighbor figure out the meaning of the little book? If either is the case, I fear him taking the knowledge to the warden's office.

My brain works away. It takes every ounce of energy not to curl up in another ball and surrender. Meditation is useless. I chisel ideas from raw materials to bring them to life. The ideas are crushed to smithereens when they prove impractical—swept up and tossed in the trash. Dark meals come and go. Guards peek inside the cell to make sure I am breathing. I ignore these distractions and remain focused on Wilson's vague offer.

Peters returns the following morning. I can sense his clunky boots stomping down the strip before the door opens. Madison is running out of time. Ms. Tillwell is as determined as him to bring this place down. She will soon return demanding answers.

"Morning." The servant watches the door open. He sips a steaming cup of coffee. "Any progress since our last chat? Time's tickin' n' looks like we're shorter on it than we thought. Better start thinkin' a that last meal you 'lil twerp."

I push myself off the ground, nearly stumbling over from weeks of useless limbs. Jell-O fights its way to solidity. I inch toward the doorway. The wall guides me with one hand while the other blocks the light burning my eyes. This feels familiar.

"Let's talk," I grunt.

He cuffs me before I take more than two steps outside the cell. He pushes me along in typical fashion as we head to the warden's office. The stumbling stroll down Sunset Strip leaves me time to peer up at the second tier of cells where an elevated Wilson grips the bars, tracking our path.

Peters drops me off in an empty dining hall, a parent dragging their child to school. This is a class I especially despise. Madison sits comfortably at the far end of the room. He requests Peters stand guard at the entrance.

"I was beginning t'think you rather enjoy it in there. I'm sure you're glad t'see some light Michael. T'smell the salty air of the sea. T'hear another human's voice. I don't blame you. The hole breaks even the toughest convicts."

I remain standing, afraid of my noodle-legs losing their balance if I attempt to sit down.

"It's true. I don't wanna spend my life in the shadows. A life there's worse than any perception a hell."

"I knew you were a smart man. I knew you'd make the right decision." The right decision—hearing that from a man as corrupt as him is ironic. "Now here's how things shake out for you . . . for us. Your little friend Rebecca Tillwell requested a private meeting with me in a few days. Lord Almighty knows what she'll try t'accomplish so we'll see if she's open to a different meeting . . . a meeting with you again. We're gonna say you—Michael Field, her long-time pen pal—requested t'speak with her. From there you'll spill it all. You're an open book. You tell her of your involvement in that fire, in the death of Officer Douglas . . . everything. You should have no problem crafting a legitimate story. You're cunning after all."

I nod after the command. "Sounds like a plan sir."

I did not imagine this conversation going in my favor. He believes everything proceeds without a hitch. He no longer need statements from the hothead West or Creepy Karpis to make his tale credible. The light shifts off Ms. Tillwell's focus of Karpis as well. Madison believes she will back off without Karpis at the center of these conversations, but I am betting on that not being the case.

"N' Michael . . . if you decide t'say anything otherwise, that's the last conversation you'll have with anyone on this earth. Catch my drift?"

"I do. So what happens in the meantime?"

I need to know he will not go to Karpis or anyone else for further information. A testimony—a key eyewitness—from those I have wronged during my time on The Rock must be avoided at all costs. It stays between the Warden and me.

"What happens now is everything goes back to normal." He looks from my eyes to Peters' to remind me of his servant's power. He has eyes in every corner of the island, as he has stated on many occasions. "You reintegrate inna the system. Continue detail in the Industries Building. Go t'the dining hall for meals. Do what any other piece a scum would do in my prison. You do not utter a single word a this t'anyone though."

A sort of last supper for my cooperation. I expected nothing less. A dramatic speech to leave me in fear. He would be the one terrified of the future if he knew what I knew. The man has a reputable reputation from the public's perspective that is anything except that within these walls. Warden Madison's time is winding down—there is no avoiding that. After his reign in 1961, Oliver White takes his place. White remains warden until these doors close for good several years later. That is information I will use to my advantage. Madison is not aware of a little book. The tyrant still wears his crown despite the knowledge I possess. He will fall in the end.

Peters follows Madison's orders, working to reintegrate me into prison society. More routine. He ensures I participate in detail each day, keep a full belly and have access to other privileges like the average bird.

Four days until Ms. Tillwell's visit.

The warden's appreciation for my falling on his sword goes farther than expected. He tosses me in my old cell, one-five-four. I even participate in yard time, free to speak to any con. The leash unwinds to its full length. The warden basks in the glory of coming out victorious. This is a temporary victory by a short-sighted man. He believes it is over.

Three days left.

I scoot my tray over to Lens at dinner. The former crew member sits with a few fresh faces. No Sykes. No Wilson for obvious reasons. It must be nice to no longer bend to the beck and call of a self-serving ringleader. He was always the most docile of the crew—the most reasonable.

"Mind if I sit here?"

I take the seat anyway. Morris and Anglin sit at the opposite end of the same table. Many moving pieces of different puzzles. I will deal with them soon enough.

"Field!" Lens nearly chokes on a spoonful of food. "Can't say it's a pleasant surprise . . . it's still sure as hell a surprise. Didn't expect t'see you outside Sunset so soon."

"I didn't either. I did what I had t'do t'get out." The group around him goes about their conversation. It is clear they are not as united as the crew. "I'll cut t'the chase. Is that offer from the other day still on the table? The one with Wilson I mean."

He chuckles. His hand sweeps back his hair in what is a reinvented appearance. For all I know Wilson controlled the look of his crew as well. "I wouldn't go as far as callin' it an offer. The man wanted t'open a line a communication's all. Call it a white flag. He protected me for years on this rock. I owe him the favor of passin' along a simple piece a paper. I don't have a damn clue why he's doin' this. Maybe it's a spiritual awakening or some shit."

It is not a spiritual awakening. Lens is shortsighted despite his much-needed glasses; or perhaps he chooses not to involve himself in the matter. Wilson is using Lens as a middleman. He will use anyone as a mule to get to me, and Lens must realize this by now.

There is no reasonable angle to such a spontaneous request if my old neighbor does not have his loyal followers and did not rat to the warden. These realizations are reassuring, but the decision was already made before speaking with Madison or Lens. A gut decision. I do not know the outcome of this next move on the board; I simply hope it keeps me alive.

"Fine. That's fair enough. I don't expect you t'know what he wants nor get involved with any a this. When can I meet with him?"

He shakes his head and smiles an 'I know more than you' smirk. "Wilson's spendin' the rest a his time on Alcatraz in isolation . . . at least the next few years. I'm no magician Field. You won't be speakin' with the guy at all."

"Then what's this about? You said he wants t'open a line a communication. I told you I'm agreein' t'that. Is he trynna get back at me for—"

I tighten my lips before saying more. I cannot trust Lens if he is speaking with Wilson.

"Easy . . ." He raises his index finger and shoves it halfway across the table. "That temper a yours needs t'cool if I'm helpin' you both. I don't have any personal investment in this. I take books t'Sunset too ya know. Only ones not given reading material are the birds in the hole. That's not Wilson."

Lens tells all. He splices in just enough information so those around us do not bat an eye at the conversation. We are discussing writing letters to loved ones for all they know. He is as logical as I recall. His approach consists of slipping a note inside the cover of a book or magazine each day. He wheels the book cart over to me. He does the same with Wilson the next day. Then it is back to me. A one-way road each day is the best he can do for us.

The single line of communication leaves my stomach feeling uneasy. My tray goes untouched—a child's play food—throughout the entire meal. There is much to think about. Eating is a burden. Each note to Wilson must be concise. It must be pleasant enough to prevent the conversation from ending yet firm enough to benefit me. A difficult circus act indeed.

Ms. Tillwell's imminent arrival paired with this one-man mail system means there is time for a few letters. Around two letters each—even that is a stretch after hearing Lens' cautious process. Fortunately, I am one step ahead. Wilson left a letter for Lens to deliver should I agree to the proposal.

Lights out arrives after a day of waiting. Peters is watching closer than ever, his head poking out from around every corner. I cannot risk him catching me with the letter during the day, meaning the only safe reading space is in the discomfort of my cell.

The anticipation is relieved as the piece of paper floats like a feather onto my mattress. I unravel the small note that is folded over in a cat-shaped origami. Lens informed me this was Wilson's method of ensuring my eyes were the only ones viewing the contents of the letter. Who knew my enemy was capable of such obscure art?

I position the crinkled paper in the air so the reflection through the cell bars makes it legible. This is the same ritual I practiced after receiving a letter from Ms. Tillwell. This is destined to be a much different type of message.

Field—I hope this letter finds you alive.

Let me start by disclosing my plethora of knowledge. If you think I don't know you played a role in that fire then you are more foolish than I thought. It's a wonder you've made it this far. The big Creep lit the match after you coordinated every detail. It was brilliant, I'll give you that.

Fortunately, my memory lasts in a lonely location like this. I never got to the bottom of that book of yours. I read it half a dozen times trying to give it meaning. I never had such luck, even with months in solitude with nothing besides my thoughts and a snoring Karpis to comfort me.

The one fact I'm certain of is the book's accuracy. There are few truths from my many years on this island that I can't confirm in those pages. What's more curious are the details of the events that occurred long before you set foot on Alcatraz. The detail is undeniable.

I don't expect you to reveal its origins . . . we both know it's long gone now. But it still exists in our memories. Fuel my interest of its purpose. Fuel that obsession and I won't run my mouth of what happened that day. I have no interest in divulging that information, but that doesn't mean I won't do so if that's what it comes down to. It's the only weapon I have left. I know you understand that.

The warden's taken an interest in you. I see the way the captain shoves you down the bottom of Sunset. That book must play a role in that interest one way or another.

Humor me this once and maybe we can put this behind us once and for all.

W

My worry turns truth: Wilson associates me with the flames that swallowed his cell. While he makes these claims, he bases them on personal inclinations rather than fact. My sworn enemy spends the rest of his days in this prison until it closes in 1963. He is transferred to another prison and paroled many years after. He does not take part in the 1962 escape. He does not prompt any discussion of a little book—at least any discussion that reaches the public. His path is written in stone, so why is he still a threat?

I pull out a blank sheet of paper from a notebook along with a faded marker. They do not trust us with pens or pencils so this must suffice. A deep breath precedes the writing utensil striking the page.

I write.

I write until my hand hurts.

I write until my mind is empty.

Wilson will receive his much-desired letter without the submissive words he expects to hear.

WALK RIGHT BACK

The cards are on the table. I lie on the ground exposed with Wilson standing above me. I hope the man does not stick me by sharing the letter with the warden. There are two days left until Ms. Tillwell arrives and I have not delivered a single letter to my old neighbor.

Lens rolls the book cart by my cell to retrieve my response in the early afternoon. The piece of paper rests within the middle of a worn-and-torn copy of 'Gone with the Wind.' The novel has touched every cell in this prison at one time or another over the years. I chose the book above other reading material knowing no one will request the familiar title.

A day of detail inches along. I envision Wilson reading the response in his quiet quarters and writing a letter back in frustration. My words were as stubborn as his.

Lens avoids me at dinner. He shakes his head while passing by in line, a sign there is no response yet. My heart races as time crunches. I sit by myself and force down some soup with a piece of bread on the side. My stomach disappeared and has no intention of returning. I am a nervous wreck, as I have been on more occasions than I can count since my arrival.

The long day of worrying is put to rest in the evening as a letter reaches me in the Industries Building. It is the last place I expected to receive a response from Wilson, yet I cannot complain—at least he wrote me back.

"For you," a mysterious bird whispers. He slips the note in my pocket before vanishing amongst the other cons folding, ironing and washing.

I must get a response over to Wilson today if his message warrants one. The timeline is tight. Two letters in a day seems aggressive, however, I must remind myself of these desperate times.

It is a race against Madison and Ms. Tillwell, and I have no intention of losing.

I create an indent within a pile of denim on the table and nestle the note face-up inside, a nest for the delicate piece of paper. My baby bird. A few shirts keep me occupied, providing no more than a minute to read through the single-page letter. My barrier will crumble at any moment. This cannot wait until lights out this time. It is worth the risk of the nearby Peters approaching out of suspicion.

What are you getting at? Wilson removed all pleasantries. The note piqued his interest. *You better start making sense by the next time you write or we'll have a much bigger problem.*

You're right. I do believe the book. I feel foolish admitting that, but it's unlike anything I've ever read. I can't justify it being fiction. It's too detailed to be anything other than the truth.

Now with that said, my offer's changed. The only words that stuck out in your message were 'warden' and 'Sunset Strip.' Seems as if you're promising an escape from this lonesome hell.

Get rid of Madison and we'll put this to rest once and for all. You're the mastermind, planning these elaborate schemes and shit. Think of this as another scheme. One more scheme and it's over.

You said you have a few days . . . if that. Better think fast.

He removed signatures as well. Straight to the point. Madison and Ms. Tillwell tied my hands as Wilson proceeded to lasso my feet. If I could get to Madison I would do so. There would be no desperate outreach to Wilson in the first place if I could bring the tyrant down on my own. Does he not see that?

I believed Wilson reaching out was an indication that if I obliged it would set me free from the warden's grasp. It would be destiny leading me to freedom. This was supposed to be my exit strategy. A smarter man would know Wilson could do as much damage inside a cell as outside.

Matters worsen when Peters begins to linger everywhere. He

stands closer, appearing more attentive than he has been the past few days, or even years. He assures guards and inmates it is routine assessment; however, everyone knows there is another reason for his presence: he wants to keep an eye on my every move. Madison grows more cautious the closer it is to Ms. Tillwell's arrival.

I tuck the letter in my crotch for safe keeping as Peters walks around the room.

"What the hell man?" an inmate whispers across the table. "This's backin' up all the fuckin' orders."

I look back at Peters. He has settled down at a desk across the way after his lap around the room. His feet rest against the side of a laundry machine as he flips through 'Playboy Magazine' while smoking a cigarette. This is the servant's way of simulating the warden's desk that his black slacks will never touch. This is the captain's imaginary office.

"What d'ya mean backin' up orders?" I ask the stranger.

"Orders, guy. Deliveries. You know what I mean . . ." I look at him, still confused. "You some sorta new catch? This whole system's how we get items in n' out." His elbow points to a laundry bin. "You wonder how Peters got his grimy hands on that nudie mag? You don't really think they'd allow that in a shithole like this do ya?"

"So this stuff gets snuck in then . . . that's what you're sayin'?"

He goes back to folding a bedsheet after noticing Peters scanning the room. The bird keeps his head down while responding, "Yeah man. Laundry's our channel t'the other side a that bay. Take it away n' we can kiss the beauties in those magazines goodbye. Same goes for burners . . . no smokes for no one without our system rollin'."

I think back to the crime programs on television that have yet to air in this reality. I had to watch a given episode several times to catch every detail. I thought staying knowledgeable about a television program was a challenge—doing so in real life takes a different level of attentiveness. I was so preoccupied with my many plans that I did not stop to see all that goes on here. Tunnel vision prevented me from discovering how birds obtain banned items within prison walls. I saw nudie magazines and burners floating around for years, yet I never considered asking of their origin. Smuggling these items onto the island makes sense. If nudie magazines can come in—if a bird can enjoy a pack of smokes—can the process be reversed?

I wait for the glaring servant to bury his pencil-thin mustache in the magazine again before responding to the man at the table. "I get it. Yeah. That's how these items get t'the island in the first place. Are you the guy t'talk t'bout that?"

"Would I be spittin' t'a stranger like you if I wasn't? I can sniff out a new client from a mile away." The small talk was a subtle sales pitch. This man has his own plans to pass the time.

"Fair enough. If you can get items onna the island how difficult is it t'get somethin' off? I mean how can I get an item t'the other side a the bay?"

"Why would ya wanna get anything outta here? Nobody out there wants nothin' from our cells. Sure though . . . yeah. You could ship somethin' off this rock if you really wanted." He puts down a denim shirt and looks up at me, leaning a few inches closer across the table. "It'd be a hell of a lot harder t'get somethin' out man. It'll cost ya double what it goes t'get your hands on somethin' from outside. N' with how they been crackin' down 'round here it might just cost ya triple. You know, for the risk n' all."

A sliver of hope shines through the dreary horizon. I need to respond to Wilson. The note must reach him today. The tables will turn if I can accomplish that. A carefully worded letter to Wilson pushes the train into motion.

I craft the entire response in my head during the rest of detail, editing draft after draft without pen and paper. Words are erased and new ones added after every silent rehearsal. Ms. Tillwell arrives in a short while and Peters takes a large step closer each day. Shipping an item off the island requires at least a full day. The timing does not appear promising, yet I proceed with the approach.

A brief break before supper provides fifteen minutes to jot the words down while in the corner of my cell. I sit on the toilet so inmates and screws are not inclined to peer inside the close quarters. The paper is pressed against the sink. I scribble a few words every minute before checking to see if a guard's footsteps are stomping down the block. No time for error. No time for extra words. When it is complete, the letter again finds its way to the front of my pants. It looks like a shave gone awry with the many papercuts I have accrued from carrying the note around for hours on end.

I track down Lens at suppertime, grabbing him as Peters steps outside the dining hall to converse with a fellow screw. The captain leaves the hall at least once during each meal. At the same time, I can always expect him to return to keep an eye on me per the warden's instructions. These observations make his actions—and timing—relatively predictable. Again: routine.

"Lens . . . I need your help. I need ya t'give this note t'Wilson today. Not tomorrow . . . today. Can ya do that?"

"Woah woah . . ." he responds. "Slow your roll. I'm not a miracle worker. I told you this's a careful process. I'm cautious. I can't put my own ass on the line for two nitwits passin' letters like schoolgirls."

I slam my fist on the table, drawing more attention than intended. Peters is already back in the doorway to the hall, conversing with his pal and likely speaking of a promotion that will never arrive. The conversation will not last much longer by my count.

"I need ya t'do this for me. Wilson'll wanna see it today. You respect him don't ya? This note needs t'find its way over t'him today. It's the last thing I'll ask a ya. I promise."

I slide the folded, moist note out from my crotch and onto the table. It rests a few inches in front of Lens' tray. The birds around us stare at the piece of white paper. It is open for the world to see. Lens stares at it. I stare at it. Peters will soon stare at it as well if Lens does not act fast.

The captain and another screw smell the uncomfortable silence at our table. We are the only group not talking amongst the hundreds of cons munching on plates full of pasta. Peters marches toward us for a closer look at the situation. Lens and I hear his heavy leather boots clanking on the concrete as we stare at each other, eyes squinting in a Western-style standoff. I have nothing to lose—he knows this.

"Do this for me Lens. If you won't do it for me do it for Wilson."

The note remains on the table. The footsteps grow louder. Lens senses my commitment. All three of us—Wilson, Lens and I—are screwed if he leaves this letter on the table. He knows this and slides the note in his shirt pocket moments before Peters comes into frame.

"You daisies alright?" The captain hovers above us. His hands are at his side, one gripping his belt and the other fiddling with a dangling baton. "Looked like someone was about t'throw a jab. I'm all for it if that's the case. Let's see you make a move Field."

"It's nothing sir." Lens looks up. "Field got his panties in a bunch 'cause I took his cornbread is all."

"Yeah what the hell was that?" I expected the quick lie from the rational man and had my own on deck. "You think you're some hotshot 'cause ya done more time than me? You don't need that cornbread!"

Peters has no time to assess the validity of Lens' lie as the bell sounds. Perfect timing. I have never been more relieved to have such a short mealtime. The letter delivery was a risk that paid off. Destiny is on my side again. The room full of birds chirps as everyone rises from their seats to line up in a single file.

"You've got balls Field. I'll give ya that." Lens lifts himself off the table.

The line of convicts marches out of the hall. It is back to our cells for lights out after a final count. How Lens plans to deliver the note to Wilson is not my concern. It is out of my hands and the fate of the letter will remain a mystery. My future will soon belong to my enemy.

This could be the last night in this cell—my home for several years. The last night hearing the pitter-patter of guards' shoes on the catwalk. There is no melancholy nor worry as I lie down to sleep. The matter is beyond my control and that fact alone leaves me in peace. No more planning for now. No more thinking of what to do next. A restful mind allows destiny to shape the future.

"Ay Field! Whatcha talkin' t'Wilson's crew for? I keep spottin' ya with Lens durin' mealtime ya know. Eyes like a vulture right 'ere."

I squint my tired eyes outside the cell. It is West's voice, sounding of strange nostalgia. It is nostalgia that carries with it memories from a time when my path was clear—when I knew this place like the back of my bruised hand; back when the little book was not burnt to a crisp and the future was written in stone. Of course, the future remains written in stone, yet it now requires me to attempt to carve out my own path with blind eyes, one line at a time.

West is another issue I will deal with if and when this pressing matter is resolved. His role in the kitchen gave him the opportunity to keep tabs on me since our temporary partnership ended. I do not forgive him for the meaningless murder of Officer Douglas for it haunts me every night. If West is destined to take part in the 1962 escape, I will prevent him from leaving as fate desires. I will keep him behind bars even if it sacrifices my own freedom.

The hothead's taunting whispers do not prevent me from indulging in rest. Sleep is a distant yet welcome concept. I dream of a previous reality at night. Images of Robb and his sad, meaningless life are displayed one after the other, large and in my face like a movie theatre screen. I dream of traveling back to the former reality and telling him of my experiences, impressing him with how much influence I have had over these last few years. This is more than he has accomplished at his precious company.

"On your feet!" Peters shakes me from my slumber with morning count. "Come on . . . another day in paradise!"

We file into the dining hall for the first meal of the day. It is oatmeal again—always oatmeal. That thick, soggy mess is rather unappetizing on a morning like this. My stomach churns with anticipation. Last night differed from this morning. Sleep was a distraction then; anxiety takes the wheel today.

A light tap on the shoulder startles me. Trouble is brewing. Time moves slow as I prepare to see the captain towering over me. I picture him pointing toward the warden's office where swift punishment awaits following the discovery of my letter. One deep breath and I summon the courage to face the servant.

"He says you owe him five packs." Lens stands in the captain's place. "N' you owe me a few too for that matter. We're finished now, you n' me. Let me rot away in peace while you do the same."

The bird walks with his tray, moving past his usual table. He sits on the other side of the room near a random screw. This is his way of showing me he means what he says. He is finished with me and I do not blame him. He knows better than anyone that Wilson and I are magnets to trouble. It is a surprise he stuck around for this long.

Any day now. Any day and the spinning chambers settle without warning. Pulling the trigger either ends my extended cameo in this reality or brings forth freedom. Freedom to further shape events to come on The Rock.

MOVING ON

Ms. Tillwell docked on Alcatraz Island in late November 1961, a trusted freelance photographer at her side. Madison was prepared for this. He once again whipped his birds into shape the day before the duo's arrival. Our job ensured every inch of the island was spotless before they stepped off the boat.

The tireless woman brought a third individual with her as well. Chatter around the cells predicts this new face is a second attorney. The complementary outfits and briefcases showed Ms. Tillwell and her team came prepared. Madison also came prepared. The remainder of the day is anyone's battle to claim victory over.

Yard time was staged upon their entrance despite it being a Tuesday; it is only allowed on weekends. This shift allows Madison to control who is present throughout Ms. Tillwell's unwelcome visit. It eliminates many variables—or rather threats in the warden's mind. This does not stop information from traveling fast in the form of the world's longest game of telephone. The facts are bound to lose credibility after a few deliveries, yet I have no other resources at my disposal today.

Most birds huddle on the yard's steps for the cold San Francisco air only appeals to the icy waters from which it originates. I stand in the middle of the graveled field anticipating a bomb's detonation. Either the captain storms out of the cellhouse doors or Madison waves for me to join them from the doorway. Lens positions himself a few yards away from me despite his intentions to steer clear. I know this is a direct request from Wilson. He hypnotized Lens to once more follow his lead. 'Keep an eye on him,' I imagine my enemy ordering through his solitary cell bars.

The clock above the cellhouse entrance ticks away. The steaming breath of a hundred or more inmates clashes with the cold air. Puffs of white hover above the stairs for a moment before vanishing. This airshow keeps my mind away from the approaching inevitable disaster. Impatience suffocates Lens as well. He steps a few feet closer, hands in his pockets and a knit cap squeezing his eyebrows a bit closer to his hairline.

"You can't stand like that," he complains. "They've got screws in every tower on lookout. They're watchin' you . . . the one numbskull standing in the middle a the goddamn yard."

"Well guess it's a good thing you came over then isn't it?"

He looks around to ensure no one is within hearing distance. "We both know I saw what was in that last letter you forced me t'pass along. He does that origami shit with his papers while yours are folded like pocket trash. All I have t'say's he'd never put himself in a position like that. It's too risky. Save yourself some time with the warden n' go huddle with the rest a the seagulls on the steps."

I expected Lens to follow the correspondence in some capacity, but I did not foresee his sincere interest in the letters' contents. Still, the notes cannot be deciphered in whole to an outsider. He does not have the full picture if he is unwilling to read Wilson's responses as well. Half the truth will not make his theories substantial.

"The guy's spendin' the rest a his time on Sunset." I look at him, away from the clock and the collective fog of breath for the first time in minutes. "I doubt there's a position he wouldn't put himself in t'change that."

Lens does have a point: there is no guarantee Wilson followed through with my request. Any con who puts their trust in another inmate is a fool. His claims force me to second-guess myself, so I bring my attention back to the ticking clock.

We are both disappointed when Officer Bates steps into the yard, the first guard to exit the cellhouse since we came outside. The screw's face, which is usually full of anger, appears carefree as he strolls across the dusty grey gravel. There is no worry in his eyes— no desire to please the warden. It is another day on the job. What does this mean for my future?

"Alright ladies!" he addresses the yard. "Hope ya enjoyed the warm weather! Playtime's over now!"

The officer's playful dialogue mirrors his expression. It does not make sense. I continue to stare at the door, hoping another officer steps out from the shadows to summon me inside. That never happens. Instead, Bates steps in my line of sight and snaps his fingers to move me along. Wilson did not do as I requested; however, I have not spoken with Ms. Tillwell either. Something is off.

We are herded in from the cold at Bates' request and the inside of the cellhouse is as calm as the outside. I choose to hide within the confines of routine while thinking through potential outcomes. The food line to dinner cannot move fast enough. I must speak with Lens again.

"I told ya . . ." Lens leans over the table as I drop my tray across from his. "Wilson isn't dumb enough t'bite that bait. He can smell it from a mile away. Trust me. I wouldn't've partnered with him in the first place if I felt otherwise."

There is a lot Lens does not know. I cannot trust his word with certainty knowing he read one letter, perhaps two. Only a history with Wilson provides his slight clarity.

"Fine. Can ya ask him if—"

"No," he snaps, maintaining his promise of separation. "I'm done playin' middle-man. You pushed me t'the edge yesterday. I don't owe you anything. Everything I did t'help you was outta respect for Wilson. I don't need him outta Sunset t'remember what you did t'Ronnie n' I sure as hell don't need a reminder of the wreck you've caused at this place."

Morris also spoke of the damage I have left in my trail. I decide to lay down my sword and shield with this observation in mind. No more pushing Lens for answers. He did what I asked. My association with the former crew member can end now. If his assessment of Wilson is accurate, though, then Madison moved forward in his plan without my confession to Ms. Tillwell. No confession nor action from Wilson leads to my permanent disappearance, a haunting spirit of Alcatraz stuck in this other world.

"Field!" a grim reaper echoes across the dining hall.

Conversations halt and everyone's eyes, including Lens', lock onto the sound's source: Captain Peters. The servant stands tall like a lighthouse in the doorway. He pats a baton in his palm, preparing for batting formation. I should be worried, yet my memory flashes to the similar motion Robb made growing up. Those fucking baseball games meant for children. I departed that reality in peace; I can do the same here. I am prepared to face what waits beyond this room.

"Yeah . . . I'm here." I stand up as if prepared to deliver a toast. "I'm right here."

"I'm not blind." He points the weapon my way before tucking it back in his belt. "Come with me. Make it quick."

Confidence seeps out of the servant's wide pores when the warden is not present. He is a soft-shelled, emotionless creature who appears impatient at this moment. The stone-cold expression is of a man waiting for unfortunate news. This is not the ruthless captain I have grown to despise.

The room continues in conversation as if nothing happened. Peters and I do not exchange a word while walking out of the dining hall, knowing where destiny guides us. The next move is mine in this rigged game. I will risk my life if this is a delayed opportunity to speak with Ms. Tillwell. Will truth make it off this island or die with me? The potential outcomes are vast and there is not enough time to arm-wrestle with each scenario. This is the end.

Captain Peters knocks on the closed door.

"Yes, enter!" the warden shouts from inside.

Peters opens the door. He walks up to Madison's desk and pulls out a chair from the other side. He slides out a second one and sits in it himself. Peters never sits—he is always on guard, a pawn in the warden's master plan.

Madison stands over his desk, also an unusual sight. He wears his traditional grey suit that—for the first time—has a loosened tie accompanying it. The top button of his white dress shirt is undone and a patch of silver chest hair is finally able to breathe. His head points toward the floor. I cannot read his expression.

"I'll keep it brief." His hands enter his pocket. He makes eye contact with me. "She never did say where it came from. Still, I'll have you know I received some writing for myself Michael. You weren't the only one with a pen pal."

"What're you talkin' about?" I ask. It is the first genuine curiosity I have expressed to the warden in as long as I can recall.

A meeting with Ms. Tillwell must be off the table. Two letters—there should be one letter if Wilson ratted me out. There should be one letter if instead Ms. Tillwell carried it. Never two letters.

His comment about the first letter's unknown source indicates Wilson acted as requested, coordinating my letter's delivery to Ms. Tillwell. This was outgoing mail, the type referenced by my new acquaintance in the Industries Building. There was no way for me to ship that letter while Peters followed me everywhere. He kept a close eye on me from a foot away at any given moment during these last few days and Lens was not a practical mailman after hearing of his dedication to avoiding me. My only solution was to convince Wilson to oversee the outgoing letter's delivery. Two letters must mean he went through with the request in one way or another. Two letters also prompt a degree of concern, so I attempt to comfort myself knowing my enemy did indeed complete his task. Lens was wrong; Wilson moved forward at my request.

"What am I talking about?" Madison responds, waiting for my charade to end.

"The letter ya 'lil shit!" Peters lunges off his chair. He is inches away from ripping my throat out from its sweating neck.

"Calm yourself captain." Madison waves off his pet. "Captain Peters is quite right though. You know what I'm referring to. Let's cut the act of innocence for once. Read it for yourself if you'd like n' then try t'explain your way out of it."

He extends his arm over the desk, handing over an envelope. It is packed full, bursting at the seams with information. There must be another little book's worth of words inside. I reach in the envelope, pulling out the wad of paper. I unfold it and begin reading.

Warden Madison,

Who I am is not of any interest to you. Instead, focus on the man within your grasp. He has always been within your grasp, yet he slips through your distracted fingers.

This man has asked me to send outgoing letters to a Rebecca Tillwell for some time now. He has done so by threatening my life. This man is Frank Lee Morris.

I reread that last sentence: *This man is Frank Lee Morris.* This is a mistake—the wrong letter. I expect the words to morph into others. They do not change. My heart pounds harder the more I stare at the page. This is wrong. The words remain the same. I am unable to move to the next sentence, so Madison snatches back the envelope after noticing my frozen eyes.

That was Wilson's handwriting. Fred Wilson's handwriting was scribbled from one page to the next in that crinkled envelope. I have seen that penmanship too often for there to be any doubt in the matter.

"Are you catching my drift now? I'll be finished here because of this goddamn letter. Months . . . maybe years of a high-profile trial between me n' that bitch. Such madness has put a knife in the back of the beautiful reputation I've crafted for the Federal Bureau of Prisons." He looks down at the floor again and shakes his head. "Someone's paying for this. I'm not sinking with the ship by myself. Peters follows as my second in command, however I will not leave this matter unfinished. I will not float off this island as you smile on the other side of those bars."

That was Wilson's handwriting. This is the sole observation circulating through my head despite Madison's escalating threats. Wilson did not put his name at the end of the letter despite him writing it to the warden. A signature would leave much at risk. Everything could go wrong if he became involved in all of this. There is a reason he did not reveal himself to the warden.

"I don't understand," I reply. The response stems from confusion as to why Morris is called out in the letter rather than from Madison's words. "What's this have t'do with me?"

He shoves the letter in my face again. "D'you see this Michael?

What's it look like? It says Rebecca Tillwell does it not? You, Captain Peters and I are the only ones within these thick walls who know what occurs during the bitch's little visits. You just so happened t'have written her regularly over the past year too. That's no coincidence."

"He went n' ran his mouth," Peters adds. He leans above me as Madison is off to the side. The good-cop, bad-cop routine turns entirely into the latter.

That was Wilson's handwriting—I continue to process the observation over the silence. Madison's rambling goes on as the picture becomes clear. Wilson claims he read the little book. He studied it from front to back as I did. Convincing my enemy to believe in the little book skyrocketed backward and hit me square in the jaw. The letters baited him with the promise of the little book's truths. He saw hope in those truths. He sculpted it to his advantage as the only other person on the island who knows why Frank Lee Morris is important.

In a single turn of events, Wilson knocked Madison off his throne and put me in a headlock by toying with Morris' fate. The only successful attempt to leave this island will be the 1962 escape. Throwing Morris—the documented leader of the escape—under the bus is Wilson's last trick. He believes there is more to his own story, yet does not understand that destiny cannot change.

"Miss Tillwell may very well know who you are but she doesn't know the slightest truth about your accomplice Frank Lee Morris. Mere letters from him, no matter what they said, are just that. She's never met that man like she has you. We'll figure out what t'do with Morris in these next few weeks before my departure. In the meantime it seems fitting we bury you back where this started." He turns to Peters and points at me. "Send this bastard back t'the dungeon where he spent his first night. Let him rot in there for as long as possible. He may die n' that brings a smile t'my face."

He waves his hand across the desk to put his servant into action. Peters grabs the shoulder of my shirt and pulls me up. He tosses a few fists into my gut, sending me to the hard floor. Madison no longer controls his pet. The servant gets one final beating. I struggle to gain my footing as we exit the office, giving one final look back at the warden over my shoulder. The tyrant appears satisfied with his decision.

"Wait a second . . ." he demands. "One more thing for you t'chew on as you perish in that cell. You'll be pleased t'hear I managed t'get your paperwork completed. You're a documented resident of U.S.P. Alcatraz now. Good luck pleading your case of innocence t'the next man who steps inna this office."

He tosses his hand up again in a final farewell. The smug look returns as I turn back to Peters. The two have one final victory in our endless war. Ms. Tillwell received my letter of Madison's wrongdoings, forcing the warden out of the ring. He still manages to come out on top, though. Goodbye, Hopeful Howard.

The prophecy of the little book is fulfilled: Madison retires as a warden with a spotless reputation. I assume that was the deal Ms. Tillwell offered the tyrant and the reason behind him leaving me alive. Captain Peters will follow suit as the servant has as much on the line, bowing out in forgettable fashion. Madison goes down in history books across the country as a fair leader; Peters is left out of any literature, leaving behind a reputation as a simple captain of the guards; and Ms. Tillwell comes out on top for once.

I am tossed into the dungeon as requested. My body tumbles down the concrete steps in the finale of its abuse. The basement is twice the size of cell fourteen—a silver lining in all of this. I do not attempt to crawl up the stairs as Peters is quick to slam the top shut. I am left at the bottom of the stairs with a finger shoved up my nose to stop more blood from leaking out.

This should be a temporary measure. The new warden—Oliver White—will fill the small shoes Madison leaves behind. He will rectify any wrongdoings. If not, he will at least be open to a fresh start for those punished under Madison's dictatorship. This is the vivid picture the little book paints of White and the one I pray is accurate.

A glimmer of the sun shines through the dungeon's imperfections. My old friend, the Sun God. The beast sends beams of light blasting through the room like a laser-based motion detector protecting precious diamonds. I approach the beams using the wall as a guide in a familiar blind state.

Tranquility sets in. I stand in the very spot I stood three long years ago. Three years—has it been that long? I think about my old life—about Robb, my mother and the studio apartment in the heart of New York City; the job I slaved away at for so long with little recognition or personal growth. Much has changed over these last few years compared to my previous decades of existence.

The beam of sunlight fades throughout the intense focus. This is a trance that is unique to me. My meditation. The light creeps along the wall opposite of its entry point. The darkness soon swallows the entire room and I close my eyes to finally process recent discoveries.

Wilson is challenging the little book. He is challenging his and Morris' fates. He sent the letter to Ms. Tillwell revealing the warden's wrongdoings while adding insurance in the process. If Morris is sentenced to solitude, he will not organize—let alone partake in—the 1962 escape. Wilson is determined to change events yet to unfold.

What if the little book is only accurate because of my contributions? I was diligent in ensuring everything engraved in its pages occurred. I am its servant the way Peters was Madison's.

What if Wilson is correct? What if history can change?

STRANGLEHOLD

I can't drag my kids into this; they've been through enough already. The last thing they need to witness is their dad's eccentric behavior. A man who lost his mind. They lost their one parent that day—at least that's the way the nanny sees it. They deserve to be on their own for now. I do, too.

"Hey Marybeth," I whisper into the phone. I'm drunk with confusion. "I know it's late. I know you're prob'ly sleeping n' all. I just need another favor."

"What is it? What's so urgent that couldn't wait 'til morning?"

She's exhausted. I'm sure the boys kept her up with nightmares. Dark dreams of their deceased mom and absent dad. But reality holds the same terrors.

"I'm sorry. I'm sure this could wait 'til morning, I just won't have time t'talk then. Can you watch the boys tomorrow? I know you said there wasn't a rush t'bring 'em home. It's just that I could use—"

"Of course I can watch them. Take the time you need so these kids don't see you in any other light than the one a father should be in." The all-seeing nanny's back with advice I could give a shit about. "They're comfortable around me. I've watched 'em their whole lives. It's really not a problem."

I'm not going to argue with her there. She knows more about my kids than me. Meredith always told me as much. She was right. Deep down I've always known she was right. I've accepted that I made sacrifices for the betterment of their lives—of our lives. Blood, sweat and tears were shed to provide quality living and they'll understand that someday.

I stumble around the larger-than-life house at the crack of dawn. The routine takes me back to pre-sun mornings at the company when I'd be out the door before anyone else woke up. No goodbye kisses, just a dad screeching out the driveway.

The picture on the nightstand joins me as I step out the front door. It's a break from that former routine, a big 'Fuck you' to the man that occupied this body; to the life I barely lived. My ghosts follow me during this journey, Meredith residing in one pocket and Michael crinkling away in the other.

Lucille Park told me the mysterious Becky Kimble landed a job at pier thirty-three, where public Alcatraz Island tours begin. They've done these tours for years without any sort of change, so there's no other place the woman from my past could've worked based on Mrs. Park's description. It's too perfect. If Becky Kimble's still there I'll have the closure I need to start again—a fresh start like she wanted after leaving me with the Field family.

Another cloudy Fog City day leaves the pier vacant. A night's mist is sprinkled over every object in sight. I can count the fanny-packing tourists wandering the streets of Fisherman's Wharf at this time of day. It's rather peaceful without the chaos. Even fewer people stand in line for the day's first ferry. It's early enough to avoid the family that got in late last night from a cross-country road trip, yet there are still some psychos willing to go out in the frigid bay at this hour.

The only employee's the one checking tickets, the same smart-ass teen who's seen my face many times over the last six months. He wears a warning sign on his face, a 'Slippery when wet' stand that's avoided yet harmless.

"Aw man." He shakes his head after recognizing me. "Goddammit. I told you before . . . you can't just linger around here. I thought we already went through this dude."

He puts his hand on his hip as if reaching for a gun that doesn't exist. He's a teen working a part-time job as a ticket taker: his weapon's a walkie-talkie. He takes out the device and brings it to his mouth. It beeps and his chubby cheeks start to flop around as he speaks.

"Wait . . . wait just wait a minute," I plead. He listens after spotting poncho-covered tourists observing the escalating encounter. "I'm here t'ask a few questions. Even better I'd like t'get outta your hair n' speak t'your manager."

"Dude . . . make it quick. I'm s'posed t'report you."

"You must know everyone who works on this dock yeah?" He shrugs in response. "Well I'm lookin' for Becky Kimble. D'ya know where I can find her?"

He shakes his head. "I've worked here every summer since I was fifteen. I can tell ya there's never been anyone by that name working at the pier. Sorry dude. Scram now will ya?"

He glances behind me to see if any of his coworkers are approaching.

"What're ya lookin' at there bud?" I reposition my head to meet his gaze. "You afraid someone's about t'catch ya talkin' t'me? I'll tell ya what . . . if you bring me t'your manager I'll never show my face around you again. How's that sound? Pretty good deal huh? Otherwise I'm prepared t'make one hell of a scene n' make your morning a bitch."

I'm already scaring away the few people in line. He looks at them, then back at me. "Fine, as long as you get off this pier. I'll tell ya again though . . . if you're lookin' for someone with that name you're wasting both our time."

I roll my eyes. "Appreciate the advice kid. Where can I find your supervisor?"

He points to the building on the side of the pier. I should've guessed as much. I give my thanks to the kid, reassuring him this is the last of me. I do hope that's the truth. This pier and that distant island have led to dead-ends every time I return. There's a reason pier thirty-three's my constant. There has to be. Everything leads back to the pier. It can't take me to another roadblock—not this time.

The receptionist stares me down the moment I spin through the rotating entryway. She either has a 'Wanted' sign in front of her with my mugshot or she's dumbfounded by my worn appearance. It wouldn't surprise me if both were the case.

I used to come to this pier to drink the day away. When the library lacked answers, my evenings passed with little recollection.

I drowned the time with a bottle in a brown bag, aimlessly pacing around the pier. Of course, the library always lacked answers, so I found myself here most nights. Loitering's an adorable offense compared to how I spent my time here. I was a plastered man scaring away seagulls—and people for that matter. A much different ballgame. I was escorted away on more than one occasion at the threat of being tossed in jail. This isn't me today.

The receptionist agrees to get in touch with the manager as the look on my face alone tells her I'm not going anywhere. She explains the person coming to get me handles all business relating to Alcatraz tours.

The senile Mrs. Park couldn't conjure up such an elaborate story about Becky Kimble. This is no time to second-guess my decision to search for her. The ghosts in my pockets support me. Somebody in this building will tell me about her before I throw in the towel.

"Mister Field?" A woman pokes her head out from around the corner. "My name's Eve. I understand you're looking t'speak with someone in charge, yes?"

I walk over and shake her hand. Her hair's dyed an unnatural dark brown. She wears bright-red lipstick that clashes with pale, wrinkled skin. Her attire consists of jeans, a button-down shirt and a scarf that doesn't play nice with the rest of the summertime outfit. She's a seventy-year-old woman refusing to accept the passing of time.

"Nice t'meet you Eve. I'm Robb."

She smiles, guiding us past reception and down the narrow hallway from where she came. The hall's decked out with historical photos of the island over the years.

A military fort.

A lighthouse.

A military prison in 1828.

I couldn't begin to count the amount of times I've seen these exact photos. I'll admit it's a fresh perspective, though, when my sight isn't blurred and my mind isn't foggy from half a bottle of liquid therapy.

She walks me into an office. The door's nameplate reads 'Eve

Marttil.' She sits down at her desk, still smiling from the moment she first saw me like her mouth's frozen in that position. I make myself comfortable and sit, too.

The silent stares are rather creepy and too much to handle for another second, so I begin the conversation. "Well I'm sure you know who I am based on how ponytail boy looks at me. Hell even your receptionist seemed t'recognize me. I'm sorry if I caused some discomfort around the pier. It wasn't my intention t'draw so much attention t'myself or impact business in any way. Those were some dark days. I don't remember half a them."

"You don't need t'apologize." She can smell my discomfort, trying to read my emotions the same way Mrs. Field did in the Big Apple. "A man lingering like that has a connection that outweighs the int'rests of one-time tourists. I know you never meant any trouble but you're right . . . this is a business at the end of the day. Those tours are all we have left t'preserve the memory of that infamous island. We can't let people forget about everything that happened there."

I lean back in the chair. These are soothing words, maybe even somewhat therapeutic. Someone finally understands my actions. The woman doesn't perceive me as crazy. She knows I'm here for a reason. I walked into her office expecting to fight for information. Instead, she seems to be on my side.

"It's been a while since you've shown your face around here," she continues. "What brings you back?"

I take a moment to weigh my options. How much can I trust yet another stranger? My mind tells me to proceed with caution while the ghosts nudge me to reveal more. The internal debate's interrupted. With the office door closed, the scent radiating off Eve's clothes fills the room. It's an overpowering fragrance that's predictable on all old women. The scent carries notes of late-summer flowers beginning to wilt. It's a musty smell—a familiar smell. Lucille Park, Samantha Eldridge, Mrs. Field—these senior women proudly owned the same scent. Interrogating this type of person's becoming a habit I don't care to think about.

"I'm sorry . . . have we met before?" The scent prevents me from continuing the conversation. "Like I said I don't remember much a my time on this pier."

She's flattered by the observation. She doesn't need to speak to provide me with an answer. Another whiff of the pungent scent fills my nose. A memory resurfaces from deep within my foggy mind, a picture buried by booze.

"You . . . you gave me that ticket for the ferry all those months ago. It was you wasn't it? You were the one crossing the street that afternoon. You were wearing that over-sized coat. I know that perfume."

"You have quite the memory for someone who claims t'have been in a permanent state of intoxication. Yes I gave you the ticket that afternoon. Like I said . . . I see a certain motivation in a person's eyes like yours n' can't help myself. I needed t'lend a hand. Besides I could make the case that it got you off my pier if anyone were t'question the gesture."

"Well it meant more than you know. Not sure what I'd do if I couldn't get on the island that day. I'd prob'ly be locked up somewhere for punchin' that kid outside."

She laughs at the comment. I reach in my pocket and pull out a photo—one that's not Meredith and not Michael. I grabbed this third companion on my way out of the house this morning. I toss it across the desk. She puts on her reading glasses and studies it.

"You know what that is? It's what used t'be a family. The people I thought were my family." She puts down the photo after hearing the despair in my words. I dig the guilt-knife deeper. "In the last year I've lost a brother n' a wife. I'm about t'lose my kids too. That's why I'm here Eve. I need t'finish what I started."

"I'm very sorry t'hear that." Her eyes water in what looks like empathy but is more likely a result of the room's dry air. "Losing a loved one's never easy. I lost my husband five years ago." She slides the photo back across the desk. "What can I do t'help you Robb?"

"You've already been helpful. What I need's t'find one a your employees now. My search ends there. I'm done then n' at least I'll be at peace with all this."

"N' might I ask which employee that is?"

"Right . . . yeah. It's someone by the name Becky Kimble. I was told she worked here. I'm not sure if that's recently or some time ago. Either way I'm sure you keep records of some kind."

Her smile vanishes as she folds her hands. It takes a minute to find the right response to my request. "I'm sorry Robb. Miss Kimble passed away some time ago."

"She's dead? When . . . or how long ago did she work at the pier?"

I should've figured. No one I spoke with had recently been in touch with her. Years of nothing besides memories and stories. Still, I didn't come all this way for another dead-end. No more dead-ends. There must be something I can use from this woman's knowledge.

"She worked here for a long time . . . more time than anyone I've seen come through over the years. You have adolescents n' college students n' then you had Becky. She had a passion for this place that couldn't be matched. She's the only one that seemed t'like working here. Did you know her?"

At least Eve knew her. She's in a better situation than Mrs. Park or Samantha Eldridge and was the last person to see Kimble out of the three. It's a look on the bright side.

"No . . . I didn't know her. She might've known something about my brother Michael though. Like I said I'm lookin' for closure. Did she ever mention a Mikey Kimble?"

"Hmm . . . Mikey Kimble? I'm afraid that doesn't ring a bell."

I reach in my pocket and throw another photo into the ring. It's the one that went through hell and back. The photo's a dollar bill left in a pair of jeans spinning through a wash cycle. It's useful but rather destroyed from its mint condition.

"Here, maybe this'll jog your memory. You see that guy in the back? That's s'posed t'be Mikey Kimble. Compare him t'the guy in the other photo I showed you." I throw the previous photo back at her, too. She holds the two side-by-side. "See the resemblance? You can understand my frustration if you see that resemblance."

She'll tell me it's a happy coincidence. I'm crazy. Pity will turn into worry—worry for the insane man alone in an office with her.

Mrs. Field's denial was 'everyone has a doppelganger.' 'You're seeing things,' Meredith brushed it off, leaving me to talk to a bottle of whiskey.

Eve lifts the photo of Mikey Kimble. She holds it at different angles to see past the liquor stains, tears and faded ink.

"Ah . . . yes. I can't tell you these individuals are the same. It's awf'ly blurry. I do believe I've seen this man before after a better look at the photograph though. He looks familiar. Again, I can't speak with certainty here. If it's who I'm thinking of then he also passed away. He was close t'Becky."

Two leaps backward turn into a small step forward for once.

"D'ya know if his name was Mikey Kimble?"

"I never met the man so I don't wanna say anything that's not true."

"D'ya know anything specific about him? Did she ever talk about him?"

Another long pause in the conversation. She's disappointed in my follow-up question. "It was all so long ago. I'm not sure what you're getting at here Robb. Are you hoping it's some long-lost family member of yours?"

I lift my hand to call out her ignorance, but a sober mind's quick to dismiss that idea. Why I choose to end the conversation here's a mystery. Maybe it's the possibility of that man being the Michael I had known and lost; or maybe it's not wanting Eve to squander my theories.

"Sorry ma'am. I don't mean t'take up more of your time." I rise from the chair and extend my hand. "I appreciate the information. It means a lot. I think I'm feelin' a little better about all this now."

"It was my pleasure Robb." She accepts my departure with open arms. "There's one other thing before you go." She reaches across the desk and places her hand on mine as I'm about to get up from the chair. "I wanna leave you with as much peace as possible so bear with me as I share some rather silly thoughts." I settle back in the chair, motioning for her to continue. "Near the end of Becky's days she talked some crazy talk. She talked about a previously life left behind . . . like she hadn't been herself in many years. Call it getting old or call it something else. Do whatever you want with this information. Take it cautiously though."

Is she satisfying a man desperate for closure? If so, it's working. She must be referencing Kimble's former life as a caregiver—the life she left behind to 'turn over a new leaf.'

"I might be telling it wrong. I can only say it was something along those lines." She chuckles at her own words. "I viewed it as lingering on the past. Who am I t'dismiss her claims? Take care of yourself Robb."

I nod to her and crack a grin of my own in appreciation, the only gratitude I can express while processing the intriguing information. She put Samantha Eldridge, Lucille Park and the entire library to shame with a fifteen-minute visit. I didn't meet the legendary Becky Kimble, but I did collect enough information to put this matter to bed. A life-consuming obsession. It satisfies the ghosts in my pocket. I'm satisfied, too.

I leave the building with my head held high. I feel relieved for the first time in half a year. A deep breath of Bay Area air fills my lungs. It's crisp, cool and heavy. It's the first deep breath I can remember taking in months. I give the ponytailed teenager a nod of appreciation as I pass by. He shakes his head. I look around the pier one final time and head to the street. I'm satisfied.

A few steps on the sidewalk and my muscles freeze like a miming street performer in the heart of Fog City. I half expect someone to walk by and toss a quarter at me. A force I can't explain draws me back to the dock. Natural instincts wrestle my recovering mind. I'm at peace and at the same time find myself unable to leave this place. The pier begs me to stay. It's my body's desire for this high to stick around for as long as possible.

I turn around. My back faces my future while I continue facing the past. I start toward the building—toward Eve's office.

HOME SWEET HOME

A knock on the door leads to a startled screech on the other side.

"Oh my . . . yes please come in!" the voice shouts. I enter the room and Eve sits in the exact spot I left her in. "Robb! I didn't expect t'see you so soon. Did you leave something behind?"

"I need a ticket t'the island." I keep the request brief to ensure my mind doesn't pull away from the high, sending me back toward the car. "I don't mean t'keep bothering you. I really don't. I'll be eternally grateful if you can help me this one last time."

She raises a brow, studying me before reaching for the phone. "Not a bother at all. There should be a ferry leaving in twenty minutes or so. Gimme a moment."

The woman dials the phone and puts it up to her ear. A faint ringing echoes down the hall from another room. "Yes. Morgan. I need a favor. Can you please register one extra ticket for the nine o'clock ferry?" She waits for a response. "Right. I know it's at capacity. Please make an extra ticket. My visitor'll grab it on his way out."

She hangs up and gives me a wink.

"Thank you," I respond. "I won't be barging in here again . . . or lingering around the dock. I owe you that much for your help."

"It's no issue at all. It was a pleasure seeing you again."

Twenty minutes later and I'm standing at the front of the ferry as it pushes off the dock. The mental high flows as strongly as the water crashing on and off the bay. The large craft inches toward the spec of a foggy island in the distance. One last visit to Alcatraz is my finale. My epilogue.

The gentle ride provides an opportunity to digest the conversation I had with Eve. She confirmed the two Kimble individuals were connected. Becky had a tie to the island and these mysterious tales suggest there's much more at play. Tell me as much a year ago and the practical man would've laughed in Eve's face. I can see clearly with my life stripped away. No distractions.

The boat glides up against the dock and another group of clueless tourists pile onto the island. Their cameras are at the ready like cops locked-and-loaded to raid a cartel base. I'm one of the last people to step on land, taking the time to soak everything in. Is this where Michael spent years of his life? I laugh each time the idea comes to mind yet refuse to dismiss its validity. Anything's plausible.

The one-man visit's filled with a comprehensive tour of the island. There's a new appreciation for every wall and pile of bird shit on the broken ground. I put myself in a prisoner's shoes—in Michael's shoes. I toy with the idea of stepping where he did at one point long ago.

The guided audio tour puts the harsh reality of the former prison into perspective. No longer am I reaching into a bag to fiddle with sales reports. I'm not distracted with leading a bullshit meeting to the benefit of a group of self-centered assholes. I'm living in the moment, walking in Michael's shoes.

The trip wraps with a visit to the museum—the tiny gallery above the sally port. This is where I first discovered the familiar photo of the man folding laundry in the Industries Building, the same photo that's tucked in my pocket. Mikey Kimble. I save the room with the original photo for the end of the tour like a closing ceremony. This photo's untouched unlike the destroyed copy in my pocket. It's as clear as my mind. This is the photo that started the journey, shattering my life and forcing me to gather the scattered pieces.

The photo isn't the only object my sober mind spots this time. I was so distracted—so drunk—that I didn't see the full display during my previous visits. A small stand with a metal plate sits beside the photo. The metal sign's engraved with a brief description of the Industries Building. I missed this. What hammered individual could read such blurry words anyway? This is my excuse for the oversight.

"Several prisoners assigned t'the Industries Building for laundry detail fold clean clothes," I read aloud. "Donated by Vincent P. Nolan."

My heart races as another door opens. The ghosts push me along despite my satisfaction. Closure isn't enough. The constant urge forces me to pursue the origins of the photo. The end looked near. Unfortunately, I'm no stranger to relapse. No dead-end this time, though. No steep cliff to dangle from only to fall off.

"Excuse me . . ." I bother a tour guide on his lunch break outside the gallery. The rotund man has half a sandwich in his mouth. "I'm wondering if you can point me in the right direction."

He places the rest of the sandwich next to him. He looks up at me, annoyed at the request. "Yeah sure. What is it?"

"Well I noticed this old photo in the museum . . . that gallery building or whatever you call it. D'you have any information on the stuff in there?"

"Those artifacts don't preserve themselves. We have a few individuals here who specialize in preserving this place's treasures. Your best bet's t'speak with Bill Mason. They call him Doc. He's about the only person we know who can take an indistinguishable object n' breathe new life inna it."

The man wants to get back to his sandwich, so he tells me Doc's scheduled to give a presentation soon. "It's basically a live Q n' A," he says. Another sign from my pockets that I landed back on the island at the right time. Doc must know about the photographer I'm looking for.

The preservation presentation takes place in the dining hall ten minutes later. About a dozen people show up, a sad sight knowing how much work likely goes into the job. Yet the presenter, Doc, still proudly rolls a cart full of various objects into the empty room. He takes simple objects—clothing, photos, plates—and crafts magnificent stories. He's a magician with his words. The man's worked on the island since it opened to the public. "There's rich history on this island." He holds a plate above his head like a priest preparing communion. "We can't let time take that away from us. That's where I come in." His personal connection to every object assures me he knows the origins of that photo from the gallery. He can point me in the direction of Vincent Nolan.

The room clears out at the end of the session and Doc spends a few minutes returning the objects to their glass cases. I catch his attention when a lingering tourist finally leaves the dining hall. We're alone now.

"Doc? Mind if I keep ya for a minute?"

"Yessir . . . did ya have a question?" he responds while continuing to pack the cart.

"Yeah I have a few questions actually. I won't take too much a your time as I'm sure you're a busy man." I pull the ghost of Michael—Mikey Kimble—out of my pocket. It sits on top of his cart. "You see this photo? I wanna know where it came from. Can ya help me with that?"

He stops packing to look at the photo. "This photo?" I nod in response. His eyes grow wide. He looks nervous, like I said something to threaten him. "I do know about this photo." He shakes his head and pushes the cart forward. "Come with me. Let's go t'my workshop."

I follow him out of the dining hall. He pushes the creaking cart through the cellhouse as I trail behind. We make our way over to a long hallway with various offices. He pushes his cart into an open doorway, entering a dark room. The open door touts his name—Bill 'Doc' Mason. He flips a light switch on and the pitch-black room reveals itself, a cluttered mess of metal, wood and other materials. He treats his workspace like shit for such a renowned conservator, or whatever people in this line of work are called.

"Ya know there was a Doc Barker on this island some fifty-plus years back?" He leans against a workbench to catch his breath from the short walk, supporting the other half of his body with a cane.

"Capone, Birdman n' other infamous criminals get all the attention," he continues. "They get the fame when it was really the no-names that ran this place. There's a lot more history in this one room than whatever's included in those over-priced books from the giftshop."

"I know a good amount about this place too," I challenge him. "I've studied just about every newspaper article, book n' photo in the Bay Area. Doc . . . did ya pick that nickname because a Barker?"

He's already working to unpack the cart. He looks at me and shakes his head. "Of course not. It's a nickname I've developed over the years. A mere coincidence is all. People think this job requires a fancy PhD. All it takes's someone passionate about the work." He stops moving around and grabs the photo from the top of the cart. "Now let's talk about this old thing. There's plen'y a history behind this single photo."

"I think there's someone I know in that photo. It caught my attention one a the first times I visited Alcatraz. What can you tell me about it?"

He continues to stare at the photo. The conservator transforms into someone else for a moment, closing his eyes in thought. "I was an officer on this island in a former life. I'm pushin' seventy believe it or not."

My jaw hits the floor. He was an officer.

"Don't worry . . . that's no secret here," he chuckles. "It's actually the only reason they gave me this job in the first place. Like all U.S.P. Alcatraz officers we weren't the ones who went down in history. We never did . . . even today's prison guards don't."

"You were an Alcatraz guard?" I need confirmation. If this is true, it's the closest I'll ever be to Mikey. A personal perspective.

"You heard me right. I spent over a year working under Warden Howard Madison. I wasn't suited for that line a work in the end. Learned that the hard way."

"So you're in direct contact with anyone who donates artifacts, is that right?" I try to get him back on track. I came to this workshop for a reason despite the appeal of his personal history.

"Indeed." He shakes his head, swatting away pesky memories. "I know who donated this photo. Why're ya botherin' yourself with this? You said ya recognize someone?"

"The guy in it . . . I know it's difficult t'see. I'm hoping you know the photo based on the rough composition. I've been chasin' this guy for half a year now. I was wonderin' if you could point me in the direction of the photographer, Vincent Nolan."

"It always comes back one way or another." He grabs a

handkerchief from his pocket and wipes his sweaty face. The cane guides him to a nearby barstool where he sits down. "The man upstairs won't let me live this one down. I was a kid. I was a stupid kid doin' what I believed necessary t'protect myself."

"What're you talkin' about? Did you know the photographer?"

"No." His stare stabs my eyes. I take his spot over by the workbench as he gets comfortable on the stool. "I didn't know the photographer. I met the guy once when he came over with a batch a photos a few years back. This photo though . . . I knew the guy in this photo."

He hands the photo to me as if it was too much to look at. His reaction assures me I was sent here for a reason. There's more to learn than what Eve revealed. The past isn't done with me. If Doc knew the man in this photo—if he knew Michael—there's one question left to ask.

"Is his last name Field? Is it Michael Field?"

He squints. His face crunches again as if in pain from the sound of the name. It hits close to home. The words don't sit well with him. He opens his mouth after a heavy gulp.

"How d'you know that name?"

"I'm not a cop, reporter or anyone else you needa worry about." I don't know how he knows this name, but it's somehow pushing him to the edge. The last thing I need's this guy keeling over in front of me. "I don't care what you did in your past. It's behind you now. Everyone deserves a chance t'start over. I just want answers. I needa hear it . . . the answer t'my question. I've been through hell n' back these past—"

"Alright. Like I told you, I'm payin' whatever debt I owe this island. Yes that man's who you say he is. He was a prisoner on this very island some thirty years ago."

He rises from the seat and paces around the room, his cane clunking around all sorts of garbage on the ground. He's rattling his brain as if waiting for the next memory to pop up from the toaster. Ding.

"He's the reason I got sent on a ferry back t'the city. He's the primary reason I didn't step foot on Alcatraz again 'til I got this gig.

He's what keeps me here year after year despite my age n' my declining physical state."

A confirmation—the words I've waited to hear. I wish I could act more surprised; he only confirmed my beliefs. I didn't need his word to back me up. I was at peace with the information Eve provided on the pier. This takes things to new heights now.

"Why's that? What'd he have t'do with you leaving your position as a guard?"

He's overwhelmed with emotions and the more he speaks the more he's relieved. He's releasing years of bottled-up emotion like I did not long ago. "He exposed me for who I was. I was an ignorant punk. I screwed up his life. I let the prison get the best a him. I did that 'til it came back t'bite me in the ass. He woke me up . . . ya know, t'see the man in the mirror n' all that jazz. I saw a monster instead."

"N' what was he in there for?"

"Lord knows. I was low in the ranks . . . even lower than some cons if ya asked around at the time. All I know's he had it bad. The warden, the inmates . . . hell even me."

A knock at the door startles us. It also provides him with an easy escape from the conversation. Another employee enters and Doc's moment of clarity suggests he's revealing more than he desires. This is about much more than a single photo now.

"Yes excuse me . . ." a woman interrupts, inching her way into the room. Only her arm and head stick out the doorway. "I hate t'interrupt sir. It's just that you have that session at noon. People are already gathering in the dining hall."

"Right . . ." He waves her off. "You tell 'em I'll be right there then. Just needa collect a few new items."

She rolls her eyes at me and exits the room, leaving us alone in the cluttered office again. Not so fast, Doc—you don't get off that easy.

"I have t'go now Robb. I hope you find whatever you're lookin' for. As much as I'd love t'stay n' chat I believe my stories'll only leave ya with more questions. Seems you have what ya came here for."

He shuffles to the door. The snail's pace allows me to rest my hand on the doorknob before he can do the same. "Listen, I get it man. You have a bad history here. That sucks. There's some bad blood with this place that you're hopin' t'rectify by locking yourself in a cell of your own. But if there's anything else you can share that'll help me out you know I'll appreciate it. Right whatever wrongs you had with the man in this photo n' lemme know about this Nolan character."

"Vincent Nolan," he mumbles. He's digging through the vault of dusty memories again. "Vincent Nolan. He donated several more photos almost a year ago. That's the last I heard a him. He had his own storefront. Nolan Studio over in Sausalito. If he's still kickin' I'm sure you can find him there." He pushes my hand away. "I needa go now kid. I trust you'll find your way out without any trouble."

Bill 'Doc' Mason vanishes, a ghost forever trapped in the one place he hoped to never step foot in again. It's ironic—a fitting end for him based on what he told me. Am I bound for the same destiny? I suppose I've got to believe in destiny first.

'You're satisfied,' I tell myself again on the path back down to the dock.

I'm satisfied, yet I press on. The ghosts aren't finished and neither am I.

DIRTY WATER

Oliver White came to power less than a month after I landed in the dungeon. It was the longest stint in the dungeon's history as far as any bird can recall. I even overheard a few turnkeys talking about my unfortunate accomplishment. Most would perish in such harsh conditions. I am unlike most, especially after what I went through these last few years.

White's transition was seamless from what I heard. One corrupt, power-hungry warden says farewell to this cage and a different man rolls in. It was like nothing changed. Like Madison, White came prepared to be molded by history like a chunk of wet clay. He, too, is destined to be written about as one of the island's four wardens.

The man believed in new beginnings upon his arrival. A fresh start allowed us zoo animals a clean slate. He was a warden sent from heaven as far as both birds and screws were concerned. To be fair, any individual was bound to be better than Hopeful Howard. Call White's forgiving nature a sign of weakness or brand it as an incentive for birds to behave. At the end of the day, all I cared about was the opportunity to reintegrate myself into routine.

"He's still got beef with you ya know?" Clarence Anglin bumps me in the shoulder. Red pasta sauce drips from his mouth and splashes onto the tray with several droplets getting on his clothes as well.

Despite lingering fears of a fluid future—altered by a single action—Clarence made his appearance right on cue. The arrival assured me all is right with the timeline—for now, at least. He stepped foot on the island some short months after his brother, John. Why the Federal Bureau of Prisons decided it was a good idea to put these two together again will forever astound me. The cherry on top was White assigning them as cell neighbors. It was a laughable decision.

"I know. A course I know he's got beef with me," I respond. "What happened has nothin' t'do with me. I dunno how many times I have t'tell him that."

Madison punished Frank Lee Morris for his non-existent involvement in providing Ms. Tillwell letters of the tyrant's wrongdoings, a concluding move in our game of chess. The real man coordinating the delivery of the letters was Wilson. My old neighbor shifted the blame to Morris in his own notes to the warden, a complicated exchange of written words. I give him unspoken credit for the elaborate scheme.

Wilson used his knowledge of the little book as a weapon. He knows Morris plays a central role in the 1962 escape and he will not let up until destiny is challenged. This maneuver led to Morris receiving an extra ten years in prison. Ten more fucking years. He was also sent to the hole before White gave him a fresh start.

Morris is livid. He has not spoken with anyone in months. The Anglin brothers remain aloof and the hothead West remains distant. The team is not assembled. What makes matters worse is the audiotape suggesting this escape will take an entire year to piece together. The escape will not occur if Morris does not join the team soon. Wilson emerges victorious without the assembly of the team.

It was not difficult to befriend the brothers. Both have a history of non-violent crimes, so approaching them was not a concern. I suppose armed robbery is not a victimless crime, yet it is more humane than other offenses. Any victimless crime is not a crime, after all. Their mild history is one of the many reasons I have them at my side. The core reason to stay close to them, though, is so I can reach Morris. They are my allies—my version of Wilson's crew.

Clarence called me out in the dining hall after catching me in another trance. This is a common occurrence as of late. I stared at a lonesome Morris eating his lunch at a table not far away. The leader is supposed to be allies with the Anglin brothers. He is supposed to link up with West and put this plan into motion. Instead, Wilson's calculated actions leave Morris shriveled further inside the shell he arrived in.

"You guys talk t'him yet?" I ask the brothers.

They shrug.

"Not since he got another dime," John adds.

"Yeah he don't want nothin' t'do with anyone that's for sure," Clarence echoes. "I wouldn't neither at this point. The guy was gettin' straight . . . doin' the time he owes n' startin' all new n' shit on the outside. Don't imagine he has much t'look forward t'now."

Madison used convenient connections to ensure the request for the extended sentence went through. He did not tell me this, but I can only imagine it is not a more difficult task than fabricating my prison record. Morris looked at twenty years in Alcatraz within a week after Madison's discovery of the letters. He fought it and wrote his own letters. The warden ensured not a single envelope made it off the island. It did not take Morris long after that to throw in the towel. That is an additional reason I am unsure of the future's stability. He is one of the most prominent individuals in every Alcatraz or general prison-related history book; every article; every television show or low-budget movie. It is bothersome that this sentence extension goes unmentioned in historical records. Another ten years stacked onto an existing dime. I cannot imagine what is flying around his head now considering he was unhappy before.

Morris can wait a little longer. I have two other issues to deal with at the moment: Wilson, the man who ratted to the warden, and West, the fourth man involved in this quest for freedom. I cannot juggle both situations at once. West is the easiest to reach—that pursuit will keep me occupied for the foreseeable future.

Peters and Madison suspected an alliance between West and me during Karpis' framing and they were alone in their beliefs. Both men are out of the picture somewhere far across the bay. This is my chance to reconnect with a former partner in crime. The hothead. The murderer.

"What the fuck ya think you're doin'?" West gives me an icy shoulder after I approach his group in the yard. He boxes me out from the other birds.

We have not had a civil conversation in a year. Captain Peters' primary mission—besides earning the warden's respect—was keeping West and me separated. No overlap in detail. Opposite sides of the dining hall during meals. He even moved West to a different cell. West's worried response is somewhat rational.

"Wait . . . stop." I grab his shoulder. He turns around and raises a fist. I know he will not touch me with so many officers around. "Woah . . . listen. Hopeful Howard's gone. Peters's gone. No other screws were concerned with what we might or might not've done. If White's lettin' the Anglin brothers be neighbors he won't have a problem with us talkin' either."

The flock around him turns a blind eye. They know any affiliation between the two of us is for deaf ears. They fear the hothead's violence.

West rips my hand from his shoulder. "I dun give a shit. I'm not tellin' ya t'screw off 'cause I'm 'fraid a what the big man'll do. I'm tellin' ya t'take a hike 'cause you're trynna leave this rock while keepin' me in the dark."

He has been a phantom to me, a foreign memory from a peculiar time when we operated side-by-side. The Allen West I saw over the last year was an ant in the distance, a speck of dust floating all the way across the room. How is he aware of my plan to leave the island? I have not spoken to him nor hinted as much to the Anglin brothers yet.

"Yeah that's right . . ." He steps closer, getting in my face. My mouth is wide open yet empty for words. "I sure know you're organizin' some escape. I also know you didn't plan on includin' me. So scram 'fore I get one a my guys t'stick ya like a pig."

"What're you talkin' about?" Is he fishing in the dead of night or did I let something slip without realizing it? "We're all lookin' t'skip this island one way or another."

"He was right about ya. You're a sly son of a bitch . . . manipulatin' people like that. If there's one bird who deserves t'escape it's me. I killed a man t'protect your sorry ass. I've not said a fuckin' word 'bout what happened that day neither. This's how you repay me?"

He does not need to utter the name for me to know who he is referring to: Wilson. Two problems merge, clashing in a way I never imagined possible. They form something greater. I was in isolation for weeks before White arrived, providing Wilson with an opportunity to progress his scheme. My eyes were locked on a stray Morris the moment I stepped down Broadway. I prioritized winning the trust of the Anglin brothers. These distractions left me vulnerable to Wilson's puppeteering. He is the manipulator, not me.

I cannot summon a single word before West kicks gravel across the yard with his allies. He chooses to remain at an exceptional distance in protest. Another asset in the 1962 escape plucked away from my hand like a feather. He floats away in the cold wind toward the other side of the yard. Destiny calls for West's involvement if even in the slightest form. We are seven months out; the wheels should be spinning ten-times faster at this point.

The lights thud off on cue later that night. Silence echoes through the cellhouse. I sit up in bed to avoid drifting off—I must think. Wilson will not quit. I strip the sheets from the mattress. I toss my single pillow next to the toilet. No plan of attack means no sleep. Obliviousness is not rewarded with rest. This is punishment.

My tired eyes pace around the room, staring at various cracks that seem to have grown over the course of my time here. I stare at bubbles of worn paint prepared to burst off the wall like zits. New perspectives allow my brain to reset, yet each observation leaves me spinning my wheels. I do this for three hours until I am holding my eyelids open with two fingers.

My eyes shift to the back of the cell, moving from the toilet to the sink, from the sink to the single shelf on the wall; the shelf to the grate in the corner. The green grate is a dog door designed for a creature no larger than a chihuahua. Somehow this hole in the wall plays a crucial role in the 1962 escape. The world's greatest magic trick.

The little book provides exceptional storytelling without outlining the details of the escape, but the man from my mind guides me from room to room on the audio tour. He stops me at various signs and notable locations throughout my journey. He leaves me in an empty dining hall. He drops me off at Morris' cell. He even dedicates a paragraph's worth of dialogue in front of West's cell.

This is knowledge Wilson does not possess as he never held the tape. This perspective can put me a step ahead of my enemy. He does not know about the grates.

I catch the brothers in the library the next morning.

"We needa talk guys. Right now."

Clarence's face is buried in 'The Complete Poems of Robert Frost.' John flips through a copy of 'Popular Mechanics,' skipping past the pages that do not have pictures. He is a bored child in the doctor's waiting room. They place the reading material down to see what is so pressing.

"You see a ghost or somethin' Field?" Clarence laughs. "Of all places t'want a private conversation ya choose the library. You could hear a mouse fart on the other side a the room for Christ's sakes."

"It's the only place turnkeys slack-off." I lay my fists on the table so they quit joking around. "In all my time here the library's been the most docile place."

They do not need to know about the time we roped-up Officer Mason in the closet. Or when I bashed West over the head with a bloody baton. Or how I grabbed that same baton and cracked it on my skull. This information dies with me.

I lean over the table. "Escape. Let that word simmer. I think I found a way t'ditch this rock." They crack a smile again, expecting a punchline that never arrives. "This's no joke. I trust you two. Ya bring experience t'the table n' I can't do this unless I have you both on board. What d'ya say?"

"You're serious?" Clarence raises an eyebrow. "Look at his face Johnny. I think the bastard's serious."

"Shh . . ." I lower their tone before any heads turn. "Keep it down. Yeah it's serious. It'll take work though. More work than you've put inna any previous attempt. It'll take work . . . work n' time."

If Morris refuses to take charge of this band of misfits then it is my job. It is not the Anglin brothers' role and not the hothead's responsibility. Wilson is determined to test the timeline and it is my duty to protect it. History books do not need to know I am the man behind the curtain.

Getting the Anglin brothers on board is basic recruitment. John and Clarence make up half of the four escapees. A step further in that June night makes them two of the three birds that make it off this island. John and Clarence are instrumental, acting as worker bees while I focus on recruiting Morris. Once that is complete, it is time to make amends with West.

Each evening I am uncertain of the next day and each sleepless night staring at the grate reminds me of what I know. Wilson is bluffing, hoping he made the right decision by befriending West. The grate is my secret.

John is tasked with collecting hair from the barbershop throughout the week. He is not provided with any context. He is asked to trust me. I keep this task hidden from Clarence, who collects rain jackets from the dock, grabbing one extra jacket on a given rainy day. Similar secrecy is asked of him. These tasks take weeks to accomplish.

My own challenge is Morris. 'No' is not an option this time. The ideal opportunity to approach the leader is during mealtime as he cannot move his tray from one table to another. He must hear me out whether he pretends to listen or not. I gather that courage paired with a convincing speech four days into the plan's execution. The brothers are moving fast and I must do the same.

Every bird files into the dining hall for breakfast after morning count. John, Clarence and I grab our trays of oversaturated oatmeal and soon meet at our usual location. My eyes flash between their heads to the spot where Morris always sits by himself. There is no one in that seat this morning, a blank wall staring back at me behind the empty pocket of air. I have observed Morris for months now without a degree of change in his routine.

"Morris isn't here today," I whisper. "He never misses a meal. After everything that happened not once has he missed a goddamn meal. Not once has he sat in another seat in this room."

"There ya go again with Frank," John laughs. Clarence does the same. "If I didn't know better I'd say you were int'rested in the man. Ya won't find him with the queens if that's what you're goin' on about."

"No." I silence their laughter. "I have t'speak to Morris. We'll need him t'get our plan t'work." They look at me, confused. Their expressions reveal doubt. They are contemplating the sincerity of the plan and the legitimacy of their mindless tasks. "He's broken outta just about every prison I can rattle off. That's someone we want on our side isn't it?"

"Four of us?" Clarence looks at his brother. They share the concern. "Don't that seem like too many birds flyin' for one jailbreak?"

"Not the way I'm plannin' it," I respond. This is misplaced confidence on my part.

They still look hesitant, which is expected of two cons notorious for escaping prisons on their own. They do not take kindly to orders of this nature. I force them to listen anyway.

"Ya have t'trust me."

"Alright . . . we'll trust ya," Clarence answers.

They possess physical strength yet lack the mental prowess of Morris or me. They need a leader here and will follow one without question when all is said and done. Leadership is my role until Morris comes into play. A substitute teacher of sorts.

"Anyway . . . I saw Morris gettin' friendly with Allen West," he continues. "They were spittin' when they lined for detail n' all." He pauses to take a spoonful of runny oatmeal to the mouth. It spills down his chin like baby vomit. "I haven't seen them two chat before. Guess everyone likes t'talk to a new face every now n' then. He just doesn't want that t'be you Field."

West. The hothead. That son of a bitch. Wilson kept his mouth shut for a year about the new reading material. A transfer to Sunset stirred the pot, settling to form his plan to sabotage the escape. He did not intend to keep Morris from escaping; he bought himself time. He is trying to leave The Rock on that fateful night as well.

There are two routes the escape can go down with this new theory: either I am the mastermind or Wilson is. The brothers are in my corner of the ring, which is reassuring as they both escape. However, Morris also breaks free and he is a crucial asset that

Wilson attempts to poach. To make matters worse, my old neighbor has already hypnotized West.

Morris is in the Industries Building with me. This convenient position lets me keep a close eye on him throughout the next week. I try to sniff out changes in his demeanor and unusual conversations amongst other inmates. I even go as far as assessing the way he folds each denim shirt. His tough shell prevails over my detective work. He acts the same.

Three days pass before I identify an opportunity to approach him. I spent so much time looking for an opening that I forgot my lengthy dialogue. My persuasive speech or, as West called it, my manipulation. Anxiety takes control and the first words on my tongue trickle into the salty air without second thought.

"Don't trust West," I whisper over roaring dryers.

Morris looks at me with the same solemn eyes he has carried for months now. He steps backward. "I don't trust any a you creatures. Lemme get on with this before I get you thrown in the hole . . . or the infirmary."

His reaction appears truthful, although I have not seen him in any other light. Wilson's attempts to break Morris have failed if he is telling the truth right now. He is on a one-man team, a variable on the fence between Wilson and me. He is destined to fall over one way or the other. I will be damned if he lands on my enemy's side.

CHAIN GANG

The questions pour in after the brothers' tasks are complete. They see their assignments as pranks—jokes I am playing on them to buy time as I escape on my own. Human hair and rain jackets. Everything they collected is vital to the escape's success—they simply do not realize it yet.

"We need Morris," I remind them in the yard. "He still locks himself away from everyone. If there're any criminals on this island who can break him it's the two a you. You have history with the man. He'll listen t'reason from you before he'll let me anywhere near him again."

Pieces of the little book continue to be useful. Morris can be swayed by a few old acquaintances if he will not speak with me nor anyone else for that matter. The brothers' valid worries of betrayal will disappear once Morris is on board. The additional partnership comforts all parties. They have a new task with specific instructions. I cannot afford them to scare away their soon-to-be leader nor feed Wilson any information by mistake.

"We tried talkin' t'him plen'y a times," John assures me. "He's not budgin'. We've known Frank for a good time now n' we haven't ever seen him like this."

"I know a way t'break him," I reveal. Their curiosity piques as they stop tossing around a plastic ball. "I just need you t'be the ones t'speak t'him."

I glance around the yard to make sure no screws are locked onto the proceeding actions. The coast is clear. I slip a note into Clarence's pants pocket.

"Don't read it. It's for Morris' eyes. No need t'convince him yourselves . . . that's what this's for. Read it n' ya might as well cozy up in those cells 'til you have grey hair pokin' out your nose and skin resemblin' a worn leather couch."

They visualize the colorful scenario and leave as instructed. I cannot trust a word out of their mouths, so I instead leave them to think over the vivid image. They play mailmen while I am the sender and Morris is the recipient. The four of us have a chance at making it across the bay if none of those roles get mixed up.

The gravel crushes louder behind me while the same sound fades from the brothers in front of me. Worry intensifies as I envision a guard approaching to inquire about the drop-off. I turn around and West stands proud, his arms folded in obvious curiosity.

"Looks like you n' the Anglin duo are hittin' it off real nice." His voice resembles nails on a chalkboard. "We both know those clowns are useful as a box a rocks." He pulls out a piece of paper from his pocket and cups it in his palm as if offering Communion. "You're not the only bird that knows how t'write."

He puts the paper in my shirt pocket and leaves me with a wink, carefree as to whether anyone saw the delivery. Another fucking note. The hothead struts away without uttering another word as origami edges stab my chest. This contains Wilson's handwriting. I know better than to read it in the open, so it remains safe-guarded an inch above my crotch until the evening.

A guard stomps by like clockwork minutes after lights out. I reposition myself in bed, shifting around so the letter falls just right into the night's light. The endless sky is somehow brighter than the blackness inside the cellhouse. The absence of nighttime sight is one of Alcatraz's many menacing qualities. A blackhole.

I unravel the Rubik's cube of a letter with care so as not to destroy its contents. Wilson is my sworn enemy, yet I still manage to feel guilty about ruining a simple piece of art. A craft like this is rare in such a dull place.

The thin beam of light shines on the fully opened page.

Michael—

It's been far too long my friend. I've rather missed our regular notes. I'm glad to see you're out of that abysmal hole Howard threw you in. I hope you understand that needed to be done.

If you've made it this far without crumpling this note and tossing it in the toilet, then I know you'll read until the end. We're both intelligent men—you're book smart and I'm street smart. At the end of the day, we know what it takes to survive. We do what it takes to survive without fear, hesitation or regret clouding our judgment.

I want to propose a truce—an opportunity to work together. Let's leave our many differences aside. Let's be the six who escape from hell. I'm aware you don't belong in this plot either, so from my perspective we don't have anything to lose.

You have John and Clarence Anglin. I have Allen West. We're only missing one participant if we combine forces: Mr. Morris himself. Time's running out. This is the only way the elaborate strategy will work.

If you don't agree to cooperate, none of us will make it off this boulder. I wrote a letter to the warden once—don't think I won't do it again. Think it over before moving along.

W

Another double-edged sword. He is concerned that West will not be able to sway Morris into their camp. At the same time, he shares a dangerous point: who knows what will happen if he reveals all to Warden White? A fair, strict king screw means there is no doubt a man of his stature takes the note at face value. Any word from Wilson becomes a serious threat. The escape is on the line.

This was Wilson's failsafe. He continues to wipe the board clean while I work to maintain the timeline. We cannot go back to square one. The past—even the future—tells me not to leave course correction to time itself. I was sent here for a purpose and this is it.

Clarence approaches me in line at breakfast the next morning. He fails to act subtle. "He wants t'talk t'ya on detail later today."

Good news is tossed on my doorstep. This is the first time Morris has agreed to speak with me. My letter worked. These are desperate times as the words that bled onto every inch of that single sheet of paper revealed.

No one on this island is aware of the knowledge I possess besides Wilson through his stealing of the little book. There are facts about a dozen current birds and screws that cannot be ignored. Any man would kill to get his hands on such rich information, no matter the peculiar source. I chose to dangle a few drops of that information in front of Morris. Again, desperate times. It appears even the stubborn leader did not have the strength to resist such tempting truths.

Morris' eyes look less droopy than usual. There is a pep in his step and he lacks the usual hopeless appearance that followed his sentence extension. These are my initial observations from afar as we arrive at the Industries Building. These also provide me with confidence leading up to our much-anticipated conversation.

He approaches the station where I am posted thirty minutes into work. Sweat beads from his pores due to the flaming dryers around us.

"You've got one minute t'tell me how the fuck you know that or I get the first turnkey I see on your ass."

Morris has never expressed this level of aggression before—at least in front of me. The reaction is both satisfying and terrifying. I anticipated more time to prepare my verbal pitch on joining forces. I need to think on my feet to secure his loyalty.

"Watch the volume," I whisper, gambling with his willingness to speak. "If you wanna make a scene n' send us both t'the hole then that's your choice. If not let's leave the threats aside. Let's speak man-to-man, not con-to-con."

I call the empty bluff as his face transitions into desperation. He is at a loss for fighting words. He scoots across the concrete floor in a slight shuffle while shoving denim into a dryer.

"Fine . . . you win. Let's talk then. I'm here n' I'm listening. How'd you get your hands on that stuff?"

"Sure Frank." My memory flips back to the pages of the little book. "I know you're Frank Lee Morris. You were born September 1 1926 in Gallinger Hospital. You worked as a shoe repairman in the only legal job you ever had next t'a brief role as a mechanical draftsman. You're five feet seven inches tall n' have an IQ of a hundred thirty-three. I know your life story. That story goes beyond what prison records say too."

I put the shirt down in front of me and turn my head, risking any nearby guards observing our conversation. This is worth the building suspense.

"More importantly I know things about your life that haven't happened."

He stops feeding the machine with the ocean of blue fabric. He is frozen in place, wondering if these words are complete lies or not. He is defined by his lack of trust and realizes this.

"You've got my attention," he admits. His lips move as his body is motionless in disbelief. "Now I'm askin' the next words out your mouth make some damn sense for once. None a this science fiction garbage."

Honesty is a funny concept after living in a new reality constructed with bricks of fiction. Where do I begin when the truth does not make sense to me? These are repressed words—even thoughts. My mind has held them in for years as they carry a spell that sends the universe collapsing upon itself; or worse, forces me to spend the rest of my life within prison walls. I test the stability of the timeline. Morris must lead this plan to success from here on out as documented.

"You've never heard my name nor my sentence," I begin to close my speech. The reveal has taken an hour with frequent pauses to scan for spies. "Don't ya find that fact alone rather odd?" He shrugs, still in disbelief. "Frank . . . you're one a the most infamous prisoners in the system. If I'm locked in the same maximum-security prison as you then you'd've heard a me once or twice. Name another con in here you don't know a single fuckin' thing about n' I'll shut right up."

"What're you gettin' at?" His voice grows with irritability. He sticks out his neck of solitude for the first time, wondering if it is worth it. A turtle exiting its shell while fearful of predators.

"I'm gettin' at I don't belong here in the first place. I came here on a tour a the island. That tour's thirty years ahead. How can I make this up? Why try so hard t'chase you down if I was just playin' some prank?"

I surrender myself to Morris. I dropped the cards face-up. He is as knowledgeable as Wilson and me after this comprehensive reveal. There is a third variable in this mess of a reality now. The words were all over, my best attempt at focusing on the crucial details while appearing sane at the same time. A complex monologue.

"That's the most fucked story I've heard." He turns back to the machine and tosses in another handful of fabric from the endless basket of blue. "Not heard a more ridiculous tale in my life. Honestly . . . I dunno how you expect anyone t'react t'that."

"So you believe me then?"

"I never said I believed you. I have no reason t'believe a single word that comes outta your lyin' mouth. I have an extra dime tacked onna my original sentence thanks t'you. Madison told me that before he left . . . rubbing it in my face n' all."

He tries to maintain his composure only to cave into sadness. He is not angry at the extra dime; he is upset—defeated despite his efforts to maintain a trouble-free sentence.

"Alright . . ." I inch closer to get my point across. "You don't have t'believe me. You can think I'm a scumbag out t'get ya. If I'm a liar though . . . well you said it yourself you're lookin' at another nineteen years behind bars. What's the point?"

I am not below making the man question the worthiness of his life within reason. The prophecy of time is bound to protect him at any cost. He is a genius. Suicide is not an answer for him. I am confident he will fold. It will be my responsibility to protect him if time will not do so.

Officer Bates strolls past us in his first round since the start of the shift.

"Is that how your momma taught ya t'fill a dryer Morris?" The officer grabs a handful of clothes from the machine and tosses the pile to the ground. He brushes past Morris' sunken shoulder. "Start over."

After Bates is out of hearing range, Morris lifts his head while picking up the pile on the ground. "Alright Michael. I'll play along with your little jailbreak. If you're so certain we'll come outta here without a bullet t'the dome then that's a feat I'd like t'witness firsthand."

The vision of Bates tossing his sufficient work to the ground for another nineteen years was enough to send him over the edge. Nineteen years of hell, avoiding conflicts with screws and birds, and eating the same pile of oatmeal every morning. The visions alone paralyze the body.

"Mark my words though . . . I'll make sure you spend the rest a your days behind bars if this costs me more time. Like I said before, I know what you're capable of n' I'm not gonna be another puppet takin' the fall. Not like Wilson n' not like West n' certainly not like Alvin Karpowicz."

I extend a hand down to the crouching man. He looks at it for a split second before looking back at the pile of laundry in the machine. He looks back at my hand, reaches out and shakes it. The connection lasts a second yet it is long enough to move forward. Another piece of the puzzle resurfaces from the trash. All three confirmed escapees are lined up in front of me. The day looks noticeably brighter.

The victory does not leave me in a more restful place that night, though. I prop my head on the pillow to stare at the grate across the room. It calls to me again. The right cons are at my side, but there are two loose ends to tie up for good. They need to be double-tied this time to ensure neither man can cause more damage.

Wilson's signature origami letter revealed his intention to remain a distant threat. My partnership with the escapees is temporary, destined to go south at this rate. Wilson will foil my entire plan if I do not act as he requests. There is no opportunity nor time to pull a Karpis-level plan on my old neighbor; any attempt to do so results in months in the hole courtesy of the ever-attentive White.

Oliver White is a firm but fair warden, which I can use to my advantage. He makes Warden Madison's time look like a bird ran a prison rampant. White cares about the well-being of his prisoners, dedicating most of his time to developing personal relationships with each inmate. He is not afraid to destroy those relationships with swift punishment, though. Any plan that risks catching the warden's attention must be avoided for the escape is risky enough.

My eyes lock onto the grate for the third time tonight, again entranced by the object. This crucial yet simple element of the escape is a motivational poster, inspirational quote from a film and everything else required to force an idea out of a tired mind. It is a reminder that there is hope for me as long as Morris and the Anglin brothers are here. There is hope to create a new life—one of my own choosing.

I will no longer linger on the contents of a little book or tape. Instead, I will work with time to define my path. I was tricked into thinking I have a normal, stable family from the time I could first analyze the world. I can leave that all behind if I can drift off this island. I was fooled into accepting family. They promised a cookie-cutter life packed to the brim with an education and a career. I did not want any of that. If I was groomed into adapting to these societal norms, then a group of prisoners obsessed with escape can be manipulated all the same.

The solution to my Wilson and West problems becomes clearer. The cliché of two birds with one stone is more relevant than ever. Time is of the essence. The West problem is a much simpler obstacle than my old neighbor. West plays a prominent role in the escape. It is crucial he be at the center of the plan leading up to that final night even though he is not destined to venture into the bay's cold waters.

The audiotape revealed Morris and West are cell neighbors leading up to that night. The Anglin brothers are also neighbors at that time. These are two crucial facts. One neighbor must scan for screws while the other digs around the green grate. White's strict practices trickle down in the form of well-behaving, straight-edge screws. Any blind attempt to dig at the grate results in failure. The plan is foiled, as is destiny, if the proper precautions are not taken.

A group of five was never going to work; an even number is necessary. Wilson has a purpose in this after all. I do not need an audiotape or little book to tell me where the road leads from here. Wilson is my spotter—my neighbor.

It will be a group of six.

NOWHERE TO RUN

A brief letter to Wilson turns the tables. He is positioned as an ally—one of my own crew members. The same goes for West after the information trickles from Sunset to Broadway. A rivalry is arm-wrestled into a short-term partnership. Wilson and West are no longer threats.

"You really think six of us can break at the same time?" Morris asks. "I mean I thought four was a stretch when you brought me on. I told ya that. I don't see six of us goin' a few feet before stirrin' up trouble."

I widen the conversation to the entire team. "If any a you don't wanna take part in this then speak up now. I'll be happy to help ya out there. Just trust me. If everyone trusts me you can bet your asses all six of us make it out alive. Wilson too."

The hothead is also at the table. I welcome his violent reputation; it allows us to control half the table without others listening in. Of course, West cannot simply absorb the conversation. He is here for another reason—another role. He is a mouth for my isolated enemy.

"When's Wilson come inna this? In case you have'n noticed he's still cooped up next t'Karpis. Don't seem like he's goin' anywhere soon does it?"

Part of me hoped West forgot about Wilson's involvement. The selfish man cares for no one except himself. Wilson must have sweetened the deal. I ought to thank the hothead for his persistence. He reminds me Wilson is a crucial element of the escape—my escape. He is my spotter while carving around the stubborn concrete hole.

"Leave Wilson t'me. You all focus on your assignments. The paint, the clay, the vent . . . everything we discussed in the yard. You know your tasks right?"

"Yep, sure do," Clarence confirms. "They're clear as day."

"I'm on the diggin' tools," Morris adds. "Everyone else worry about gathering the rest a the supplies. I'll hook you up with the right equipment when the time's right." The man lifts a half-bent spoon from his tray and waves it in the center of the table to ensure everyone is listening. "I spoke with Field n' mentioned these spoons aren't gonna get the job done even if we can carve them down t'the level of a sticker. I'm workin' on something better . . . something automatic that does the job for us."

The escape is recreated the way history documents it. That story revolves around Morris. He receives the most credit as the mastermind behind the jailbreak. The leader. I met with him before looping in the rest of the group on next steps. Morris is referring to creating custom drills for digging. Like this idea, many others were planted in his head. He is credited as the genius while I remain behind the curtain. The Wizard of Alcatraz.

There are many times nerves or forgetfulness get the best of him. This is when I take matters into my own hands. 'Morris said . . .' and 'Morris had the idea . . .' precede most of my statements these days. He is wise like me yet requires a slight push to gain momentum.

My primary concern—my new assignment—is communicating with Wilson. I keep the man happy from afar. Lens proves a little more useful despite his previous statements of disassociation. It turned out he was the one passing letters between Wilson and West. The forever-loyal crew member was also the individual who slipped Wilson's anonymous letter to Madison. He claimed he was finished playing the role of errand-boy for Wilson, yet the leader managed to keep him locked under his thumb. Lens owned up to the deceitful actions and as a result was more inclined to follow my requests.

He has no one else, Wilson wrote in one of his letters. *He's seen what I'm capable of and won't cross me. If I tell him to run letters, he runs the fucking letters.*

I nudge the former four-eyed crew member while filing out of the dining hall. He rolls his eyes, holding out his hand and grabbing the sealed letter.

"You two love birds again huh?" He lets out a chuckle steeped in fear.

Deep down he is worried about my growing affiliation with the man who controls him. I do not respond to the mailman—I never do. It is in my best interest to use Lens for his singular role. He is nothing more than a deliveryman wishing to keep the peace for his own benefit. That is not to say Wilson and I are allies. Neither Lens nor I confuse my old neighbor's desperation to leave Sunset Strip with friendship. There is a mutual agreement of civility until it is no longer necessary. Our differences are temporarily locked away.

A day of detail ends downstairs in the showers. The cold, exposed room full of bare men avoiding eye contact is the last place any bird desires to be, yet it is the second-least guarded location on the island next to the library. After all, who wants to spend their time staring at a bunch of ass-naked criminals?

I approach one of the officers before undressing my sweat-drenched denims. The same action without clothes results in a visit to the infirmary, which I have seen firsthand more times than I can count. I prefer not to be added to that long list.

"Hey! Get the hell back over there!" the officer yells after spotting me. He yanks out his baton and grips it like a hand holds onto a cliff's edge. He is a half-second away from crashing the object on my face.

"Woah woah!" I back up, holding my hands in the air as if in a stickup. "Just wait a second. I'm not tryin' anything. I wanna speak with the warden."

He pulls me aside to avoid making a scene. "N' why would I do that?" He spots a few other birds staring in our direction. "What're ya buncha queers lookin' at?"

"You'll do that 'cause I'm requestin' t'speak with him." The baton remains elevated as I continue to address him. "You wanna risk him findin' out one a his inmates asked t'meet n' was denied that privilege? Doesn't sound like the type a thing he'd be happy about. Maybe Madison . . . but not White sir."

He signals another officer who proceeds to step toward us. The two screws turn away to exchange a few words before the first officer addresses me again. "Alright . . . fair enough. Officer Arnold'll take ya to his office. That's your last time tryin' t'blackmail an officer though runt. You better make this worth the man's time."

The officer grabs me by the arm and pushes me out of the room, up the stairs and into the middle of a cellblock. The last time I entered the warden's office was courtesy of Captain Peters—the servant. That same fear caused by uncertainty resurfaces during this walk. Instead of fear of death, this worry originates from challenging time itself. The timeline does not say anything about this part of the plan, yet here I am attempting to guide it.

"Mister Field." White greets me at his door. "I don't believe we've spoken as of late. I appreciate you taking the time t'set up a meeting with me. I don't have much of it t'spare as I hope you can appreciate." The officer does not enter the room. Instead, White nods his head in contentment and closes the door behind us. We are alone. This is unlike Madison's approach, who usually let his servant watch from afar. "Now what is it I can do for you?"

This is my first formal meeting with the man. Looking at him feels strange as his eyes bounce off my own. I know so much about this older man as his headshot stared me down for months in the little book and is engraved in my memory. It is odd seeing his face move from the static image I am familiar with—the same was true with Madison. White has a look in his eyes, though, a sort of sincerity that captures attention and encourages openness. That sounds welcoming to most, but in reality, it is more of a threat than Madison's impulsive actions. It is a subliminal tactic designed to capture and control his prey.

"It's nice t'see ya too sir," I respond, hoping to appeal to his therapeutic nature. "I didn't wanna discuss anything too significant. It's just I'm lookin' t'resolve an issue that's troubled me over the last year. Ya see I've gotta work on conflict resolution in order t'better myself within these walls."

He writes away in a small notebook. He is calm and collected, displaying mannerisms like those of Doctor Polk. I would never see this sort of sincere listening from Madison. It is baffling to think the man sat in the same chair not more than half a year ago.

"That's good t'hear." He smiles, putting his pen down to study me. "Acknowledging your wrongs n' facing them with confidence is the most fruitful way t'grow as a human. N' how can I play a small role in that process?"

The long shot was rehearsed numerous times over the last day. It is time for another performance. Hand me my top hat and cane as I take centerstage.

"Well it's actually a conflict with another prisoner. The inmate's Fred Wilson. I'm sure you know a good deal about this man sir. The two of us go way back. We were even cell neighbors at one point n' rather pleasant with each other."

"So what occurred between you n' Mister Wilson?"

He is intrigued. He opens a drawer to sift through files, looking for an incident report. There is nothing to find for Madison did not document half the crooked events during his reign. I would be on trial for framing Karpis if there was any written evidence outlining the conflict. West would get sentenced for murdering Officer Douglas. The plan would not have been successful.

"We had a minor confrontation in '58. That was years back now so I think I needa come full circle t'put myself on track. Quite honestly it's holdin' me back from tranquility n' permanent personal development."

He is still digging for any sort of file. "I couldn't've put it better myself Mister Field." He closes the drawer, retiring the search. "Sounds like you're already on the right path. I can organize a meeting with Mister Wilson so the two of you can discuss your differences n' make amends. How's that sound?"

It sounds like I will not be next to Wilson. No digging spotter for me. A meeting will not suffice. If anything, it will frustrate my old neighbor even more. White's solution wastes precious time that is already slim.

"I appreciate your understanding . . . but I really believe a simple meeting won't provide a permanent resolution. What allows for personal growth is replicating the exact scenario we were in during the conflict. I mean bein' neighbors again . . . one cell door t'the next. It's a chance t'start over. It's a chance t'see how far we've come since our last encounter. I've thought about it time n' again. I'm confident this's the only solution that'll lead t'accepting the past n' growin' in the future."

I sound poetic after years of listening to therapists' attempts at dissecting my brain.

White scribbles a few more lines in his notebook. The diary entry precedes another search through a nearby file cabinet. The man is organized, the type that manages to wrangle an entire room full of files into order. I imagine Robb prioritized similar structure in my former reality.

"Ah . . . here it is!" he exclaims. He slides a folder out from the drawer. He flips through the file, licking his finger before each turn of the page. "Yes, Fred Wilson. Let's see . . . looks like Mister Wilson assaulted an officer a little over a year ago."

"Sir, I assure you that had nothin' t'do with our relationship," I defend my lie.

He steps past me with the file in hand and heads toward the door, opening it to reveal the attentive officer on the other side.

"Officer Arnold, you've been here quite some time now. D'you recall the circumstances leading t'Mister Wilson's placement in solitary? A lifetime in isolation seems like no way t'help an inmate improve himself."

"Yes sir," the officer replies. He stands stiff as a plank, another servant hoping to take the warden's role one day. Of course, White is the fourth and final warden of Alcatraz. "I believe Fred Wilson was sent t'isolation following a violent outburst. The inmate's cell was burnt t'a crisp. As far as I'm aware he took it out on the guards."

"The outburst didn't have anything t'do with me," I repeat. The warden lets the words from the officer settle as he walks back to his desk in contemplation. I continue, "If I remember correctly it had somethin' t'do with Alvin Karpowicz. That's why Warden Madison put 'em both in D-block."

Officer Arnold is quick to agree. Every screw is aware of White's lack of authoritative positioning—no hierarchy ranking one servant to the next. They realize this and continue to impress the warden with their attentiveness, hoping it leads to the natural development of a tiered ranking of every turnkey.

White leans back in his creaky desk chair and looks off into the corner of the room. I track his gaze and spot some chipping paint, perhaps from recent plumbing issues or a lingering piece of Madison's former office. The man stares at the spot for what feels like minutes. This imperfection clouds his mind.

He finally responds, "Well I suppose if Officer Arnold concurs that Mister Wilson's placement in isolation originated from an altercation with Mister Karpowicz then it doesn't make sense t'keep them near one another." He takes his eyes off the crusty corner to address me. "Howard Madison wasn't the best at conditioning his prisoners. He couldn't care less about their development. I can't carry down that tradition Mister Field. I believe this place'll help those in need if the individual has an appetite for such change. It appears you are a shining example of this dedication. I will grant your request."

It worked. He is easier to influence than Doctor Polk, a therapist in a grey suit inside a dinky office on a miniature island. My mother forced professional treatment on me for more than a decade. This form of treatment tricks the weak-minded into hopelessness. It does not help them, instead forcing individuals to reach deeper into their pockets to spend a pretty penny on prescription A or meditation B. Simply because the warden granted my wish does not mean I will fall victim to the familiar methods of persuasion he practices. The man appears harmless; however, that is a quality I often find in the most dangerous men.

"Understood sir. Thank you for taking the time t'meet n' hearin' me out. I look forward t'moving further down the right path . . . a better path."

These are words of blind hope and optimism. These sentences are the bane of my existence. The words are empty, meaningless remarks to build trust in an individual I will never trust. These were words I uttered to Doctor Polk and the rest of the nutjobs who wished to force ideas into my thick skull. They tried and failed.

"Expect the transfer t'move forward within the next few days," he adds. His eyes break from the corner again to view the rest of the room he has ignored. He looks at my reaction, Officer Arnold's attentiveness and the rest of his renovated office. He is content. "If that's all please return t'the cellhouse with Officer Arnold."

Wilson's temporary role is solidified. My digging spotter will soon arrive, and the entire team will assemble for the first time. The Anglin brothers remain neighbors and destiny makes my life easier as Morris and West are randomly relocated as well.

Six men prepare for months of meticulous work while Wilson and I continue our unspoken battle—a rivalry for the ages. My enemy challenges time while I continue to preserve it.

MIDNIGHT HOUR

Days blend into weeks as we carve the concrete like crouching cavemen. Weeks blur into months. Lights out allows for variance in our respective routines. Reading, writing, painting and other hobbies are discarded with our complete focus on the small holes in each cell. The work replaces simple pleasantries, stripping back the last remnants of temporary freedom for a form with more permanence. Each day is a photocopy of the previous.

Turnkeys never trust convicts with much more than a roll of toilet paper and a few magazines in their cells, making proper silverware nonexistent. A fork was a convenient innovation for eating in my former reality. On Alcatraz, the object is considered a lethal weapon, which is why we eat meatloaf with a spoon. We slice chicken Kiev with one side of the utensil and scoop up the buttery bits with the other end. Every meal is a challenge.

The lack of forks and knives leaves the six of us chiseling away with dull spoons. We are lucky if an ounce worth of concrete is knocked off the wall in a given night. We sharpen each utensil after smuggling it out of the dining hall, but it does not take long to revert the spoon to its former smooth surface. The work is an odd form of self-imposed torture.

Morris had a brilliant idea that revolved around a single musical instrument. The team laughed at his peculiar request, claiming he was more focused on mastering music than escaping The Rock.

"You can grab an instrument when you're a free man," I told him in front of the team one afternoon.

The leader was quick to close our mouths and share his true intentions. He had received approval to play an instrument in his cell, an innocent request in the eyes of a warden dedicated to developing his prisoners. Of course, this was no ordinary instrument. No violin, no harmonica and no acoustic guitar. Instead, he kept an accordion on his bed during the day. During the evening, he cursed the cellblock with hours of deafening practice. This was intentional. The inconsistent noise from the odd instrument masked the sound of aggressive digging, a genius idea the little book failed to mention. I tip my hat to Morris for a precaution that was not planted in his mind.

The accordion did not improve our rate of digging, however, so I knew something had to be done. The tape revealed that Morris fashioned a drill from a broken vacuum cleaner. Vacuums are used in every section of the island, including the Industries Building. Lint and dirt puff out from the dryer onto the floor when a load is finished.

Each evening after detail, a single inmate is assigned to clean the day's mess. The assignment consists of sweeping and vacuuming the concrete floor. A light push in the right direction sent Morris on a quest for the broken vacuum cleaner while I stood guard from afar during detail. He removed the motor before rolling the dysfunctional machine over to Officer Bates. The annoyed officer sent Morris looking for a functional replacement. The final step from there was smuggling the old yet secretly reliable motor into a laundry bin. The motor was ours.

A motor makes far more noise than a scraping spoon, though. Fortunately, it does not take a genius to create a house for the machine. I fed this information to Morris during one of our one-on-one connections, handing him a copy of a recent 'Popular Mechanics' magazine outlining several do-it-yourself projects. He proceeded to tell the group to imagine the house as a makeshift sound-absorber. This type of encasement contains the machine's inevitable vibrations. Slip the house on the motor and it may as well be a silencer capped over the mouth of a pistol.

A second drill chiseled my grate for over a month before the invention of Morris' drill. None of the other five escapees know this. My carving is weeks ahead of the team's progress, a precaution to ensure I am one step ahead of everyone at all times.

The little book remains a trusted resource. I learned to flow with time by claiming simple instances like the creation of the custom drill as my own. Natural course correction can reveal itself as needed while I take it upon myself to guide time along until it informs me otherwise. I protect time by working with it. The same concept applies to actions by the foolish West. He stumbles on an open ventilator shaft while working on a project outside his usual kitchen detail, claiming the discovery as his own with immense pride even though I sent him looking for the opening after encouraging him to volunteer to help paint the ceiling above the catwalk. I smirk at the ignorance of future historians across the country who will never know what went on within these walls. I am crafting their works of fiction.

"I'm itchin' t'get outta here!" John slams his fist on the table during dinner. "How much diggin's left? We've been at it for months now! Christ . . . I dunno I'll have the strength t'crawl outta here after all this labor."

"Shut your mouth Johnny-boy," Wilson snaps. He flicks some rice pudding at the Anglin brother. "You wanna ditch this bitch? You listen t'us. We're the ones with the plan not you."

My enemy and I remain on two distant wavelengths. He works to refute his fate as a lifelong detainee despite reading as much in the little book. His frustration is misplaced. At the core of his anger is him knowing the material is written in stone. He is nervous, so challenges destiny with blind hope and aggression.

"It'll take as much time as we need," I chime in, easing the tension. "We've got a few weeks left. That's plen'y a time t'get the job done. Keep your head down n' dig."

"I've been meanin' t'ask ya Field . . ." Wilson pauses. "Why're you so set on the eleventh?"

I shake my head in annoyance. He knows why that date is important—we both do.

"We need a firm date," I respond. "We'll never be successful if we fly by the seat of our pants. June eleventh's reasonable. The bay's water'll be at its warmest. The tide's on our side. This means our skulls won't crush against the rocky shores a the island like dropped watermelons. If that's not enough t'chew on then you should already know we're not finished diggin' yet."

"I'm done diggin'," he reveals. The team drops their spoons in unison. "Hell I dunno what's takin' the rest a you pansies so long. If you want me t'come over for a slumber party just lemme know n' I'll dig for ya. Put some muscle on kids."

"What d'ya mean you're done?" I ask my enemy. This is a glaring obstacle. Wilson was the last to know about the drill yet claims his digging is complete. He is as ahead of schedule as I am.

"Done. Finished. No more." He chuckles with confidence while worry creeps across the rest of the team's faces. "However you wanna put it. I'm done with that bullshit."

This is a path I hoped time would course correct on its own. Let Wilson's digging not be sufficient. Let him sleep through the plan. Have him transfer cells at the last minute. It appears as though I am not lucky enough for such convenient scenarios. This is yet another challenge requiring my interference.

Wilson nicknames the team 'The Shoveling Six' to put his accomplishment on a pedestal. The team takes his words to heart despite my insisting there is plenty of time left to dig, leading to evenings of late-night drilling. Clarence claims he and his brother stayed awake for a full night once, digging through sunrise and only stopping when the overhead lights thudded on.

Despite creating the drill in the eyes of the 'Shoveling Six,' Morris was the last to get the job done. "It needs t'be perfect," he argued. The little book chose him as a worthy escapee and the leader of the plan. I should not judge his timing. He is cautious. His attention to detail and patience make up for the slow progress around the grate.

He eventually informed me the reason for the delay was due to the creation of paper-mâché grates. The wise man created stunning replicas out of simple objects like old newspapers so we no longer need to return the actual metal grate to its hole each night as we have been doing. He acquired the same mossy-green paint color as the original grate by convincing White that he wished to try his hand at visual art. Needless to say, the replicas look spot-on and rest perfectly over the holes.

The fake grates were Morris' brilliant idea while I claim dummy heads as my own. The tape mentioned these creations, informing me of their existence as well as their general composure—another fact that floats from one reality to another without a point of origin. I am nonetheless appreciative of this knowledge as I would otherwise not have the slightest idea of how to construct these crafts.

The hair on each dummy head is real, pulled by John Anglin during various visits to the barbershop. He was relieved to hear his strange task was not useless after all. Meanwhile, West sourced flesh-colored paint while repainting the catwalk's faded ceiling. Old newspapers and rolls of toilet paper soaked in warm water in our sinks once all items were gathered. The stew-like concoction brewed for a full night. It took another evening to apply the paint and hair.

All the stars align after months of focused preparation. The openings around the grates are ready for use after Morris completed his digging. The dummy heads hide under our beds at night and behind the fake grates during the day. The 'Shoveling Six' are in optimal health as judgment day approaches. These many accomplishments assure me it is time to tie a bow on a few loose ends.

The first bow consists of a final letter. It is the most complex letter I have written or received in these last years. Every word must deliver the impact of a thousand pages of substantial writing. Sheets of paper find their way into the toilet as I start from scratch time and again. I write through the night. I consider myself practical— cautious—in nearly every instance other than this one-time exception. My freedom will be at risk should this escape attempt end with failure. This last letter is worth it, for the time and care I spend on each page will not go unnoticed.

Wilson's stubbornness vanishes as an ally. My enemy is no longer a rock set on his desires or way of thinking. He needs me now just as I relied on him to spot my digging. I use this to my advantage in the form of a favor: organizing another secret letter delivery. Of course, I have a failsafe if our alliance is not enough to sway him into coordinating an off-island shipment. The con's life before prison was irrelevant. He weaseled his way to dominance as a jailbird, but he was not always this way. Wilson was once a family man, and he still has children waiting for him on the other side of the country.

"If you're lookin' t'see 'em again you need a safe spot t'meet." I use the little book's information to strike fear in my enemy. "First place the F.B.I.'s headed's t'our homes. Give your family a heads up before we leave. You're riskin' everything if ya don't."

Manipulation does not come without its share of guilt. He will not see his children for many years to come no matter his intention of escape—time will ensure as much. This is what destiny requests, though. I must see through what has always been bound to occur. My enemy will see his family once more in the very, very distant future.

He agrees a letter to his family is a sensible caution. The suggestion leaves him with pen and paper while also opening the door for my own well-composed script to make it off the island. I envision the envelopes soaring across the bay like silent seagulls until landing in the proper hands.

Wilson realizes I am in the Industries Building with his primary contact for the task, the postman. My enemy brings the three of us together in the yard one afternoon to ensure both our letters see it off Alcatraz. The self-made postman earns six packs of smokes for the deed as the sealed envelopes travel to freedom buried within piles of old laundry—shirts with blood on them, sheets with fecal matter and ripped denim sleeves. These are items no industrial laundry machine can breathe new life into and are therefore useless on the island.

The second loose end requires a much timelier solution. It cannot be resolved during yard time, detail or following a meal like the former challenge. The window is narrow and grows thinner by the second. Destiny informs me it must seal itself tonight—the night before the infamous escape. I cannot shake these whispers, so I embrace them.

The cellhouse is consumed by darkness. Ticking footsteps echo as screws walk down the block like the swinging hand on a grandfather clock: slow and steady. This is their accepted nightly routine and one that is Warden White's ultimate downfall. A guard marches down the block every fifteen minutes, which is not enough time to accomplish this detailed task. Fortunately, the dummy heads are finished, providing a little more time when moved from beneath the bed to the pillow. The heads are destined to work once—why can they not serve a purpose for a second night as well? Consider it a test-and-learn before final execution tomorrow.

The dummy head rests on my pillow, ready for its motionless slumber. Blackness guides me to the hole in the wall seconds after footsteps echo past my cell. This evening is especially dark; no beams of light shine into the cell. I squeeze through the microscopic opening and a crouching Morris greets me on the other side of the grate inside the storage closet. He stands barefoot to limit the sound of shuffling and only wears shorts. Like me, he is taking all precautions to avoid getting discovered.

"You're sure about this?" he whispers. His face is already covered in beading sweat. "If they catch those fakes in our bed then tomorrow's escape's already ruined. It'd all be for nothin'."

I grab a pail of water and scoot it between us, easing his mind with thought-provoking words. "You're the one person who knows just as much as I do. Everything's already ruined if we don't do this tonight . . . if we don't do it right. I've brought us this far. Step a little further n' let fate determine the rest. We're doin' all we can t'guide it along."

Morris was immersed in my crowded headspace two days ago. He heard every tale from the moment I arrived in this reality, much more detail than he received during our initial conversation. He heard about Karpis. He heard about Madison. He heard every documented detail of the approaching escape. Morris now shares my intellect, a parallel understanding of the world that no one else can access. I knew I had his complete trust the moment he agreed to take part in the escape. The leader would have fled in the opposite direction that day in the Industries Building if he did not believe the unbelievable words leaving my mouth.

The escape has consisted of too many moving parts to operate as a lone bird, requiring another timekeeper in order for events to unfold the way they were designed to. The plunge of shared information became inevitable the moment I offered Morris a taste of the truth. He did not pry for more information nor did he threaten me with revealing the new knowledge. He simply accepted the details without question, therefore also agreeing to his role in this reality alongside my own.

I have not been the only individual revealing truths over these last two days. One of Morris' more peculiar hobbies was collecting seashells while on dock detail some time ago. Let any other con touch one of those shells and it results in a bullet to the head courtesy of a tower's watchman. Morris was not any other con. His solitude and calm demeanor made him trusted by most screws. The serial escapee maintained his model inmate status for an unspoken reason: he had an escape of his own in the works.

"I didn't have it figured out. I just knew I needed those seashells," he revealed. "Seashells were gonna be a key part a the plan one way or another."

I asked him why these curious collectibles were so important. Why did he bring this up out of the blue? He responded by quoting, word-for-word, an article from a magazine he had read.

"A substitute for concrete is available to anyone near the sea. This perceived complex substance is not difficult to create. In fact, the average person can create homemade concrete using only a few simple ingredients."

The quick development of this unspoken bond, solidified with these shared truths, leads us to the storage closet behind our cells the night before the eleventh of June. It is the very storage closet we will climb through tomorrow night; however, we are crouching on the floor with another purpose right now.

Morris steers the ship tonight. He pulls out a bag from the back of his pants and its contents clink. He opens it and seashells spill into a small clay pot designed by him in the prison's workshop. A simple, homemade pot. How could a bird use this innocent object as anything other than cell décor?

A match lights a fire beneath the clay cylinder. We stand with our backs to the nearby grates, playing cavemen again. We act as human shields to the growing heat and fumes despite the warmth beginning to burn our skin. We cannot raise suspicion. Fifteen minutes pass and the footsteps from outside the cell return. Another ten minutes pass. The shells crackle like popcorn kernels in the microwave.

We transfer the contents of the pot into another clay bowl from Morris' innocent collection. The icy pail of water streams into the same pot, sending the shells cracking some more as the waves crash onto the jagged objects. Some elbow grease is all it takes to complete our peculiar concoction. What is left is a sort of thick, gooey substance—an unappetizing soft-serve flavor.

It is time to take care of the Wilson and West problems. Our mission is clear as timekeepers. The little book and tape make the cons' fates our responsibility. Everything must move forward according to plan. Wilson rots in here until he is saved, paroled in the far future when he is nothing more than a dry sack of bones. I receive my payback on the hothead West as well. Officer Douglas' murderer will not roam the streets of San Francisco looking for another victim. The wrong remains contained by the right. There is a reason West stays behind bars until his death. Maintaining balance is not my own desire but rather what time demands. Balance is inevitable.

We crawl over to Wilson's grate. Ten more minutes pass. The man snores on the other side, confident of his fate tomorrow yet too foolish to suspect any form of betrayal. Repairing the damage done to the wall surrounding his grate is tricky for the little book and tape did not mention his involvement in the escape. His role cannot reach ears beyond the six of us.

The real grates remain hidden in the storage closet behind each cell. We carefully maneuver the piece of metal back into the front of his cell in a game of 'Operation.' Morris holds the object in place while I pack it tight with our grey soft-serve substance. White cannot know of Wilson's involvement. My enemy can claim what he wants, but I am confident no one will believe him.

We inch over to West's grate next. Another five minutes tick past. Footsteps approach and fade, right on cue. West's involvement in the escape will be public knowledge. The hothead will spill all to authorities and even attempt to position himself as the leader of the plan to the public. The work on his grate is much simpler than the elaborate repair in Wilson's cell. All it takes is some light padding of the large hole carved into the concrete. We reverse six months of work in mere minutes so the short, stockier man can no longer slide through the hole.

West will unsuccessfully attempt to crawl through the opening. He will moan and cry in frustration as his torso gets stuck. Wilson will realize what happened. He will understand what had to be done as the only other reader of the little book. Destiny got the better of him. He will be forced to accept his long-avoided path of imprisonment when he sees the grate repaired to its original state. He will know it was me.

All components are put into motion. Morris and I return to our cramped cells. For the first time in years, sleep settles in the uncomfortable bed the way a newborn baby goes down. I dream of a distant life in New York. The few who knew my name celebrate my return, yet I inform them it is a fleeting moment. We share our goodbyes and I leave their reality with the fading sun. A new path has opened. This is my distant reality.

Morning arrives and I welcome it with wide eyes and a smile. My head is clear. My path is open. My mind is empty of the burden of knowledge. Today, I am any man within these walls or on this planet. I do not know what the future holds. Although these walls keep me trapped, I am free in a much more important sense. I can taste freedom for the first time in my life.

Time is a solid stream. Many variables shape its path without disruption. I'm one with these variables. Any days to come are packed to the brim with uncertainty. Those who surrender control to time are rewarded. Time foresees my path as I step forward into darkness.

SUNDOWN

Logic comforts the practical businessman, but that's not me anymore. A new force drives me forward with every drop of a former self lost along the way. I move without purpose, looking for answers to please a hungry mind. I have no family to disappoint, job to lose or fortune to burn this time. There's no room for regret when everything's already gone.

Sausalito's less than half an hour's drive from the pier. The quaint town resides on the other side of the Golden Gate Bridge, yet it's labeled a foreign place by me. It's a tourist trap filled with repetitive souvenirs, day-old crab sandwiches and a sea of strollers. I've never stepped foot in this town until today.

A sore thumb rests in the middle of stores displaying 'I Love San Fran' t-shirts in their windows. Nolan Studios—the only storefront for miles without a neon sign frying my eyeballs with advertising. It's a dark building in daylight—an old place on the decline.

The inside doesn't look much better. Simple décor designed for a minimalist instead tastes like arrogance. The irony of the studio's attempt to stand out from the rest of the town is its lack of foot traffic. It's empty—even the life-size portraits on the wall refuse to speak to me. Dozens wander past the storefront window in a matter of minutes while not a single individual turns to look inside.

"Hello?" I ding a bell at the counter. The ring bounces off each of the eggshell-white walls. "I'm looking for a Vincent Nolan."

"Yeah yeah . . ." a man responds from behind a door. "I'm comin'. Hold your damn horses will ya? You're gonna break my bell."

It's no wonder this place isn't thriving. The annoyed response makes me want to tear every print down from the wall and piss all over them. I was sent here for a reason, so I'll pry the answers out of this guy's stubborn head if I have to. He'll give me what I came here for.

A middle-aged man steps out from the shadows of the doorway. The well-dressed individual's outfit complements the studio's pretentious appearance. He walks to the front counter, placing his hand over the bell so that he doesn't have to hear it ring a fourth time. His eyes pan from my shoes to my head. He twitches his mustache.

"You're Robert, yes?" he asks. His bothered tone disappears.

Did Doc Mason phone this man before my arrival? He seemed paranoid after my spontaneous visit. Samantha Eldridge did the same with Mrs. Field, so it wouldn't be a surprise. Betrayal takes its time punching me in the heart and mind while tossing up new roadblocks.

"Yeah . . . that's me." I know better than to ask irrelevant questions. It's all bullshit small talk with these strangers. I sink my teeth into his greeting. "If ya know who I am I'm assuming you know why I came all this way."

He reaches behind the counter. "Know why you're here? D'you even know why you're here?"

"I'm not certain. I think—"

"It's nothing against ya . . ." He continues to blindly feel around behind the counter. "I can assure you ya don't know a damn thing though. Don't come in here actin' like you have answers. There's nothing either of us can hold over the other's head."

A drawer behind the desk clicks open. He proceeds to pull out a metal box from the other side like a lame magic trick. He rests it on the counter and stands motionless across from me. Does he expect an applause?

"What's this?" I raise an eyebrow.

He grabs the box and walks past the counter, unimpressed by my lack of insight. He makes the unnecessary effort of flipping the studio's sign to 'Closed' and locks the deadbolt. He walks over to a bench beneath a minivan-sized print of the Golden Gate Bridge during sunset and sits with the box at his side.

"Join me."

The strange action nearly sends me diving out the glass window with my arms waving for help. The ghosts convince me otherwise. There's nothing to lose. No regrets. I walk over and sit on the same bench. The box sits between us, providing a comfortable gap like that between two middle schoolers at a dance.

"Okay . . . I have t'be honest with you. I'm not here t'buy your photos. I'm sorry if you had an appointment with another Robert. I need t'clear the air before this gets any weirder."

"You'll wanna buy some a these when we're done." He laughs and pets the box like it's a lapdog. "I've been hangin' onna these for quite some time. It's a relief they'll finally make it inna the right hands."

He rustles through his suit pocket and pulls out another key. It enters the front of the rusted box and sends the lid creaking open. A pile of items crushes down inside. It's the type of box a psychotic ex-girlfriend locks away, maybe the same girl that sits a few feet from her date at the school dance, too scared to actually talk to the guy she's obsessed with.

"I was the first person she contacted that morning. Bet you didn't know that." He digs inside the box, using the lid to block my view to maintain suspense. "I was the only other person on this planet who had an inkling of what happened right then n' there." He extends a hand my way as the other continues to bury itself in the box. "Vincent Nolan. I own the place . . . but you already knew that."

I shake his hand. "Robb Field. What's all that? I'm not in the mood for guessing games. It's been a hell of a day as I'm sure you can tell."

"Let's go one step at a time then. Sound good?"

He flips his hand up from the box like a successful angler and drops a photo on my lap. The photo's black and white. It's focused on a rather tall woman. I bring it closer to my face, trying to find a hidden message. Nothing. The young lady dons a stern look, the type all women from past decades decided to wear in any and every photo. She carries a briefcase and is draped in a dark suit. She means business.

"This's Becky Kimble. Pretty good lookin' eh?" He nudges my shoulder.

"What's she wearing?" I contain my reaction to focus on getting answers. This is already more insight than I promised myself. It's bonus information from what Eve—the woman at the pier—told me. "I was told she used t'be a caregiver . . . and an employee at Fisherman's Wharf at one point."

"Doesn't look like the attire for either of those roles does it?" he responds with another question. He wants me to work for answers.

"Alright then . . ." I submit to his delight. "Well she looks serious. I know business when I see it. Is she some sorta government official?"

He grabs another photo and tosses it on my lap. I study this one, too. A younger Vincent Nolan—the man next to me—strikes his fingers on a typewriter in part of the photo. A smiling Becky Kimble stands with her arms crossed in the other half of the frame.

"I worked with her for a few years. She paid my bills. I was a kid runnin' around with a camera so I'd do just about anything for a gig back then. Anyway Becky helped me afford this place many many years ago." He takes out a third photo, unable to pause in his little game. "There was one caveat t'the funding. That caveat demanded I keep these belongings hidden . . . this pile a memories. She demanded documents be destroyed. She demanded conversations be erased from my mind. How could I do that after everything we'd gone through?"

"What's so important about this junk? Looks like someone's personal possessions you managed t'get your hands on."

He places the third photo on my lap with great care, an egg on the verge of cracking open. I don't stare at this photo the same way I did with the previous two. Instead, I focus on him looking at me. He places his hand on my shoulder. I flip the photo over. It's a woman—it's Becky Kimble again. Next to her stands another man. A closer look reveals the bearded man isn't Vincent this time. She's with someone else.

I put the photo up to my face; it doesn't make it any clearer. A magnifying glass wouldn't make a difference with this crappy resolution. I hope it leaps off the print and speaks to me. Vincent lets me process the photo until something deep inside me takes control, bringing my hand to cover the man's beard in the photo. The upper half of his face is one I've seen many times.

"Is this Michael?" I vocalize what was intended to be internal dialogue. "The man in this photo . . . is his name Michael Field?" He remains silent while studying the photo himself. I already know the answer from Doc Mason yet crave a second opinion. There are no coincidences. "You took the picture didn't you?" I throw it back on his lap. Frustration gets the better of me as it has many times. "D'you know who it is or not?"

"Yes, I know who the man is," he responds following a long sigh. He stands up from the bench, leaving the open box next to me. "Mikey, Michael . . . whatever name you wanna throw out there. That's him. Hell I've only met the man a handful a times. I haven't got a damn clue what his real name is." He comes back to the bench after taking a walk to the counter. He points to the photo. "N' that woman . . . that woman's not some mysterious Becky Kimble. I knew her as Rebecca Tillwell."

"Rebecca Tillwell?" My question echoes through the vacant room. "Why would she change her name? Why would they both change their names?"

The frustration escalates, the same rage that sent me punching the wall at Mrs. Field's house. I have to stand up from the bench, too. I was satisfied with the closure from the pier. I'm satisfied. It's time to leave once and for all. I have to separate myself from this.

"I'm tired of runnin' in circles Vincent." I break down. A single tear flows from my eye to my cheek before I swat it away like a bug meeting windshield wipers. "I always believed I had everything needed t'move forward. Yet someone sends me on another fuckin' treasure hunt t'find some ancient person. I'm done with this shit. I'm sorry. It's over."

"I'm not here t'run you in circles Robert." He places his hand on my shoulder again as we stand in the center of the gallery. "You came here t'stop running. You can stop chasin' the past for once if you just stay a bit longer."

He guides me back to the bench. We sit in the same spots and he reaches back inside the open box—his treasure chest.

"They changed their names for protection. We can argue Rebecca had a choice while there was little say in the matter for Michael." The photo of Vincent and Rebecca ends up on my lap again. "I worked for Rebecca as a freelance photographer. She was a lawyer n' a damn good one at that. We went everywhere together. If she asked me t'be somewhere I asked 'What time?' Of course that changed in the early '60s."

He rambles for some time the same way the other strangers have done these past six months. I sit in silence, absorbing every word from this man without a response. Rebecca—the woman of many professions and names—and Vincent investigated Alcatraz Island back when the prison was operational. He didn't know much about what they did there. After all, he was a photographer looking to make an extra buck. "Just point n' shoot," Rebecca told him. "I'll take care of the rest." He said Rebecca was in touch with someone from the inside—a prisoner—during that time; his name was Michael Field. Michael Field. This isn't a coincidence, yet I continue to process the information, suspicious of Vincent's claims. The name rings like a bell on the stroke of midnight on New Year's Day, expected and a surprise at the same time.

Rebecca was fascinated by Michael. The fascination was a secret she couldn't keep from Vincent. "I loved her in my own way," he tells me at his most vulnerable moment. "There were countless letters from that prison. One day I came inna her office n' opened one of 'em."

The discovery led to Rebecca cutting ties with Vincent. It was a betrayal of trust for her while Vincent felt a different form of betrayal. His heart shattered. It wasn't more than half a year after the two parted that Vincent received an unexpected visit from Rebecca. She greeted him in a hurry. "I offered her coffee and she responded by rushing me along." Within moments of her arrival, she was yelling at him to destroy countless photos and documents. These are photos he planned on putting on his short resume. Rebecca removed the knife only to insert it back into Vincent's chest.

His love for Rebecca prevailed that day as he destroyed the photos without question. She returned the favor by writing a check for the building of his studio. What the gesture really did was prevent him from ever mentioning the visit. Call it hush money.

"I was devastated," he rests his head in his hands. "If she asked me t'jump off the Golden Gate Bridge my funeral would be a few days later. I knew that visit somehow involved Michael. She realized I knew that too. She'd get in touch every few years from then on. She said it was t'make sure I was doin' OK. She was really just makin' sure I kept my mouth shut about that strange visit."

Rebecca skipped town with Michael in the summer of '62. The couple returned to San Francisco not more than two months later. Who moves away for two months?

"The funny thing is the whole country's busy lookin' for those other three crooks. Lord knows why Michael wasn't reported missing. It didn't take long for him n' Rebecca t'realize authorities didn't give a shit about his whereabouts. Of course they kept their new names anyway. You can never be too cautious right?"

"Hold up . . ." I freeze. I try to find the right words after half an hour of Vincent fueling the conversation by himself. "You said three other crooks? You suggested Michael escaped, not three other prisoners."

"Who am I t'confirm anything? I figured they were connected. You think four criminals fled a high-security prison at diff'rent times in the same year? I don't needa be a detective t'put that together n' tell you the answer's 'no.'"

"Fair enough," I agree with the argument. "Tell me this then . . . why're you here with these photos if you were told t'destroy everything? Why hold onna these for so many years if you cared for Rebecca so much?"

He smiles, his damp cheeks still recovering from tears of the past. "Like I said, this box was diff'rent. I was t'keep it safely locked away until she said otherwise. I burned the rest a those photos as instructed. I destroyed documents n' everything else the day she ordered me t'do so. She told me she expected you soon when she dropped by this mornin' . . . n' here ya are."

This morning? Eve stated Becky—Rebecca—passed away years ago. It doesn't make sense. Either Vincent's trapped in denial or someone's lying. Neither sounds ideal for me. Another dead-end awaits.

I snag the box from Vincent's hands. He scoots toward the edge of the bench, watching my frantic movements. He knows there's no logic in these actions. The remaining contents in the box are tossed all over the floor. I bend down and shuffle through the disorganized pile of prints. Countless photos of Rebecca and Michael turn up. None answer my lingering questions; they don't fuel the inescapable hunger. What was Rebecca's true fate?

The couple ages as I dig deeper into the mess. Hand-printed dates on the back of the photos range from the '60s to early '70s. A decade of photos and not a single one provides me with closure. One photo from the '70s reveals a small bump beneath Rebecca's flowery shirt.

"A baby?" I ask myself, yet it reaches Vincent's ears. He continues to stare at my discoveries in silence.

Rebecca's arms carry the baby a few photos later. These are family photos. My hand digs for more answers, feeling along the solid ground and always coming up short. I'm greeted with ground and more ground until my hand lands on a final photo. I flip it over to find a single headshot. It's an in-color headshot standing out from the remaining crinkled, black-and-white photos. Color. This was recently taken.

"I know this older lady." I turn toward Vincent, holding the photo to his face. The familiarity is numbing. "She's the one from the pier earlier today. That pier at Fisherman's Wharf." She gave me the ferry ticket to the island all those months ago. She gave me another trip on the same ferry this morning. "Her name's Eve."

"She didn't want there t'be any chance of you runnin' inna her. Not sure how she managed t'go about unnoticed all these years. I'm still digestin' the news myself. She told me she wanted t'turn a new leaf after quite an eventful life. She was exhausted."

"She's alive!" I hop off the ground.

I've heard 'turn a new leaf' several times lately. No coincidences. The tone in Vincent's voice was sincere. Rebecca's alive. Eve is Rebecca. They're the same person and I can speak with her about everything. She knew Michael and kept it from me this morning.

The bell on the counter dings as I motion to unlock the door. I turn back and Vincent stands across the room with a subtle smile. He holds an envelope in his hand.

"I opened a letter back then . . . but this one's still sealed. Check it out for yourself."

I accept the envelope and head to the car. I'd stay to question the photographer if I didn't need to speak with Rebecca today. There's still time to reach her before the pier closes.

The car flies over the bridge. It weaves in and out of traffic as the clock ticks. I zoom up and down every side street of Fog City in the middle of rush hour. The pier closes at five o'clock. It's four forty-five. She's the manager, though. She's got to be there until close. I provide myself with empty promises.

The car screeches to a halt in the middle of the crosswalk. Five minutes left before the pier closes. Humility sets in as my car sits at the same crosswalk where Rebecca handed me the ticket so long ago. She was right in front of me—a mystery woman, Becky and Eve. I was just too preoccupied with Michael's disappearance to see it.

The same teen working the ticket line's still at the dock. He's off his ass for once collecting the line's rope before heading out for the night. I'm sure the arcade awaits him. He's startled as I sprint toward the empty line, so he reaches for his walkie-talkie.

"Hey! It's me again . . . the guy from this morning. I spoke with you . . . I spoke with you n' Rebe—Eve, remember?"

"Woah slow down man." He drops the rope and holds the walkie talkie to his chest. "The dock's closed. Take your drunk ass somewhere else."

"Listen . . . Luke, is it?" I look at his nametag. "I don't wanna bother ya anymore. Can you just tell me if Eve's still here?"

"She's not here. If that's why you keep comin' here you better find a new place to go, psycho. It doesn't look like she's comin' back anytime soon either." He continues winding the rope.

"What? What d'ya mean not comin' back?" I grab his shoulders in desperation.

"Like I said dude . . . she's gone. She resigned today. It was her last day. All her shit's gone. Go ahead n' check if ya want. I dunno how else t'say it."

"You're serious?"

"You bet. You're looking at the new temporary manager. You can also bet this loitering you're doin' isn't gonna be tolerated come tomorrow morning."

I bolt to the pier's building. The revolving door swirls open like a tornado.

"Sir you can't go back there!" the receptionist yells as I run past her down the hallway.

Rebecca's office is empty. The desk's cleared out with the décor and other knickknacks removed. The only item remaining is the nameplate on the door, 'Eve Marttil.' She's gone and that wasn't even her real name. An alias for an alias. What'd she hide?

No contact information's left with the receptionist; even she's baffled by that fact as she fumbles through files, hoping it'll get me to leave. Rebecca's staff photo on the bulletin board's stripped away. The background of each image reveals the missing photo was the one I dug up in the rusted box at Vincent's studio.

She built this new life for herself all these years. My presence alone sent her running for the hills. Why would my sudden appearance make her leave everything behind? My mind pulls out one last resource that might provide an answer in its most desperate moment.

I sprint off the pier and hop back in the car. Cars honk as my hazards continue flashing in the middle of the crosswalk. Nothing matters except the envelope sitting on my lap. A thick stationery envelope. It's yellowed with many stains on it. It's been through hell and back, and it's addressed to me. I tear it open to reveal a date: November 18, 1985.

Robb,

I hope this letter finds you well—or finds you at all. The last time we spoke, you were flipping through a pile of work. You were doing so while walking through a place with more history than you could ever imagine. If only then you knew what I'm about to tell you. You know more than I need write in this letter if this lands in your hands at the right time. However, I will do my best to fill any remaining gaps.

How I got here does not matter. Why I was brought here does not matter. What matters is that I was brought here for a purpose. Discovering that purpose required years of confusion. I was imprisoned in U.S.P. Alcatraz during those years. That was the most difficult time in my life, but it was also the most meaningful. I discovered who I was—who I was meant to be—because of my time on The Rock.

You also know by now that I was able to leave that island. I desired an adventure of my own. That, and I realized there was a different calling—a woman named Rebecca Tillwell. I wrote Ms. Tillwell over the years. At the end, I wrote her one final time from prison. Sending that letter would either make her run to the authorities or welcome me with open arms. It was a leap of faith. She met me on that final night—the night of the 1962 escape.

The events unfolded as destined over the night. Frank Lee Morris, John Anglin, Clarence Anglin and I broke out of our cells. We climbed the roof, made our way to shore and swam into the freezing waters of the bay. We swam a quarter mile in that water. We swam until Ms. Tillwell pulled up at the exact coordinates I mentioned in my last letter.

How was I able to remain free while drifting around San Francisco for so many years? I was a ghost. There was no legitimate criminal record of a Michael Field beyond what Warden Madison forged upon my arrival in 1958. In fact, there was no record of a Michael Field with my description on the face of the earth. I was conjured out of thin air.

The decision to leave me out of the papers—out of the investigation—remains a mystery. I can only theorize around government interference as it's easier to let go of a ghost than chase one for years without any luck. After all, they already had a target on their back after three known felons escaped. Admitting anything additional would have led to more embarrassment.

This brings me to life beyond a cell. When I escaped, Ms. Tillwell and I fled to Napa Valley. Thankfully, a former inmate paroled years back resided there. The man gave us a place to stay until we believed it was clear to move forward. That did not take long.

Life beyond a cell is where you come into frame. My experience on Alcatraz was only the start of my journey. Rebecca and I moved back to San Francisco under new identities. She was pregnant. We knew a cautious life on the run was no way to raise a child.

Then, the baby entered the world on November 18, 1965. It was five days before the child's due date. The little one was familiar—sky-blue eyes and a face I saw many times before. I knew this face. The same urge that sent me protecting the timeline on Alcatraz pushed me to protect a new timeline: yours.

After I'm gone, your future will be protected by Rebecca, your mother. She will ensure you end up where you belong. I have asked her to watch over you from afar with no interference. I have asked her to give you this letter unopened when the time is right—if the time is right. You must discover it on your own. Your mother knows this and will respect my final wish.

If this letter reaches you, your mother is free from the burden of protecting the timeline. She is no longer tied to that awful place that I owe so much to. She can start anew—for real this time. I asked her to leave the decision of locating her up to you. You must make that choice for yourself. If you wish to start over, you have no obligations to anyone, anything or anywhere. This life is yours alone.

At the end of this letter, you may ask yourself 'What now?' That's a question I asked time and again growing up on that island and continue to ask myself. Your path is written, but that doesn't mean you can't influence it. Shape it into what you want it to be—into the person you want to be.

Michael

The earth is stripped of oxygen. My eyelids slam shut without effort. I expect to be in a dream or another intoxicated state. Every time my eyes open, the pages are still in front of me, the same words refusing to change.

Denial fades into raw emotion. No more denial. Tears seep out my eyes and roll down my cheeks. These aren't tears of sorrow, grief, hatred or love—these are tears of relief; tears of opportunity. Tears that I never expected to feel pour down my face and onto the letter on my lap. Ink drips down the yellowed page, blending words together.

For once in my life, I don't need another person or photo to guide me to a new destination. I don't need money, success or a bottle of liquid gold to solve my problems. My hand jumps on the wheel as the other turns the ignition. A brief drive across the city takes the car to Marybeth's shitty apartment building. My finger punches the buzzer until a voice comes over the speaker.

"Yes? Who's this n' why can't you stop buzzing that darn thing?"

"It's Robb . . ." I respond, letting stubborn tears linger on my cheeks for a few more seconds before wiping them away. "It's Robert. Bring me my kids Marybeth. Tell 'em it's time t'leave. Tell them whatever you need t'get them down here . . . just make sure they get down here."

My boys are piling their stuff in the backseat a few minutes later. They're confused, but so am I. We are in this together now. The ghosts remain in my pocket after a day—after half a year—of haunting me. We pull out of the driveway together. Jackson leans forward in the front seat, rubbing his tired eyes.

"Where're we going daddy?"

I glance at him in the rearview mirror.

"Home.

ABOUT THE AUTHOR

Nick is a Chicago-native storyteller. He's been writing since his youth, from crafting homemade greeting cards to devoting too much time on TV-related forums spilling theories on Sci-Fi show A or B. This passion pointed to a life destined for the written word, so he set out to professionally pursue that path.

He's a firm believer that the pursuit of one's aspirations doesn't have to come at the cost of abandoning the familiar. His first project took over two years of researching, outlining, writing, editing and more editing (that last part with the help of friends, family and a few professionals) before it was complete. At the same time, he's balanced a full-time marketing job as well as life as a dog-daddy, the latter of which is alongside his supportive fiancée.

Get in touch online at njanicki.com or Facebook.com/NickGJanicki and see what's coming next.

Made in the USA
Monee, IL
10 December 2019

18302600R00229